Thank Sophia
for Sam

R.D. Power

Written 2010-2012

Edited by Michael Garrett
Cover design by Peter Ratcliffe
Formatted by Polgarus Studio

ISBN 978-0-9917983-6-0

Dedicated to:

My son, Bret

PROLOGUE

July 2012

Then something wonderful happened: she got hit by a bus.

CHAPTER ONE

War – April, 2008

Dust.

Dust in his eyes and nose. Dust in his mouth. Dust between his molars when he chewed. Dust on his hair. Dust on his clothes and on his boots. Dust on the helicopter. Dust hurricanes when the helicopter came and went. Dust on the coffins.

Dust in Afghanistan was inescapable. It suffocated everything.

This was Specialist Daniel Beaton's first lesson upon debarking at Jalalabad Airfield on April 1, 2008. He closed his eyes and held his breath waiting for the dust to settle, but just when it was becoming bearable, an aircraft or gust of wind would stir it up again.

He picked up his heavy duffle bags and scanned JAF and Forward Operating Base Fenty, which it encompassed. Not much here for the size of it, he thought. The base was protected by razor wire, barriers of earth, and guard posts.

American and Afghan National Army soldiers patrolled the perimeter. The tarmac was lined with Apaches and Kiowa Warrior attack helicopters, Chinook troop transports, and UH-60L Black Hawks. In a built-up area were rows of trailer-like plywood "bee-huts," tents, some brick and mortar structures, and shipping containers everywhere, all surrounded by concrete barriers. Wooden walkways connected the living and working areas, constructed over dirt and millions of small rocks.

Daniel quavered. Bad enough it was his first day on the job; few jobs were more treacherous, and the place was among the most dangerous on the planet. An Apache helicopter lifted off to his right and rocketed ten feet off the ground toward the mountains in the distance. He was so startled, he dived to the ground. When he realized it was no threat to him, he stood quickly and looked around in embarrassment. A couple of privates were snickering. Dusting himself off, he picked up his bags again and made his way across the flight line past three Black Hawk helicopters with red crosses toward the tactical operations center of 1st Platoon, C Company, 6-101 Aviation Regiment to meet Captain Fowler.

Arriving there, he asked for the officer. Captain Fowler came out, and Daniel saluted. "Welcome to FOB Fenty, Specialist. Leave those here for now," he said, gesturing to his bags. Daniel put them down next to a desk.

The captain proceeded, "Flight medics are the key to our operations here. Everything we do is aimed at getting you to the casualty as soon as humanly possible, so you can keep him alive until we get him back here to our fancy new medical center. Let me get the bureaucratese out of the way. Our primary mission is to provide continuous medical evacuation support for Nuristan, Nangahar, Konar, and Laghman. We always have two ships ready to go. We have forty-eight-hour shifts. The first twenty-four is 'second-up,' which means the backup ship that responds to a call after 'first-up' has been called out, and the next twenty-four first-up, and unless you're stupid, you know what that means. We have three Black Hawks, and we fly to the various FOBs and outposts to pick up American troops, Afghan troops, and even enemy fighters. We also pick up people injured by IEDs in the middle of nowhere, accident victims in the cities, towns, and villages, farmers who've been attacked by animals, you name it."

The captain walked to a special section of the center with Daniel following. "Here is where our evac calls come in. We call this the 'nine line,' our coded alert system. I'm sure you know what each line refers to." Daniel nodded. He'd learned all this during medevac training. The captain handed him a walkie-talkie. "This is a part of you from now on. It'll screech 'Medevac' three times when you're up. Our missions are ranked as urgent, priority, or routine. For the urgent calls, you better not even blink before you run your ass off here to get the information you need. For priority, you get to blink once. If you take too long, you'll learn I'm not as nice as you think I am now."

The captain told a corporal to take Daniel to his quarters. Picking up his bags, he walked with Corporal Denham toward the plywood shacks he'd seen earlier. Daniel asked how many people were on the base. Corporal Denham didn't know precisely, but guessed at 1500 to 2000, including American soldiers, Afghan soldiers, locals, and private contractors. He pointed to a wooden cabin on the flight line and said, "That's hooch, where you'll spend most of your time when you're not in your room. The porch is called Club Medic. It has the insignia of every medevac crew that has rotated through here." Daniel noted three men sitting in boxy wooden chairs smoking cigars, feet propped up on a boxy wooden table.

As they approached one of the bee-huts, he heard an engine nearby that sounded like a snowmobile; he turned quickly. It was a small aircraft. "Predator drone," said the corporal. "They take off every hour or so to spy on the enemy and launch a Hellfire missile or two."

They walked up to one of the shacks, and Corporal Denham knocked. "These shitholes are so great, you have to share," he explained. No one answered, so the corporal opened the door. "Welcome to the asshole of the universe," he said as he dropped the key into Daniel's hand and walked back to the center.

Daniel dropped his bags and looked around at his spartan quarters. Two double beds. A couple of wooden shelves. Two tiny night tables. Not much else.

With nothing to do in his room, he went to the hooch. The men who'd been smoking appeared to be snoozing now. Daniel was walking past them when one opened his eyes and said, "You Beaton?"

"Yes, sir," answered Daniel as he saluted the lieutenant.

"You're on my crew. I'm Craig Ng."

"Pleased to meet you, sir."

"Never mind the saluting and sirs with me," said Craig. "We're in the middle of the war here. My crew puts up with enough real shit, so I don't worry about that Fobbit shit here."

"Fobbit?" said Daniel.

"Soldiers on Forward Operating Bases—FOBs," explained Lieutenant Ng. "Bureaucratic assholes who've never seen combat. Petty tyrants who bug you about wrinkles in your uniform and dirty boots. In civilian life they were failed security guards, but they make it big in the army. They take the humiliation they suffered in life before the army out on anyone under them in the army. Bagram is loaded with them."

"Glad I'm here, then."

"That makes you the first, then. You'll change your mind soon enough." Craig snickered and said, "Let's walk." The two walked along the tarmac. "So tell me about yourself."

"Uh, okay. I'm from Halifax."

"Yet you joined the American Army?"

"Well, it's a long story."

"Do I look like I'm busy? Our biggest enemy here, besides the Taliban, is boredom."

"If boredom is your problem, my story won't help."

"Just the highlights, then."

"Haven't had any. My Canadian parents went down to Tennessee, where my deadbeat dad went to law school, and I was born there, but they returned home when I was three, so I'm a dual citizen, but pretty much Canadian."

"Okay, skip to the part that brought you here."

"I was a paramedic in Halifax, and I liked the work, but the money was shit and the women I met tended to be screaming in pain and not very open to sex. Seeing all the asshole, ugly doctors driving BMWs with a pretty woman in the passenger seat, I decided I wanted to be a doctor. But I was too lazy to dedicate ten years to studying and training, so I looked for shortcuts and discovered the Australians had five-year medical programs that accept students right out of high school. So, I went to Monash University medical school in Melbourne."

"But something went wrong?"

"I ran out of money during my fourth year there. I managed to finish fourth year by working part-time and borrowing every available cent my mom had. But I had nothing for fifth year."

"Couldn't you get a loan?"

"My student line of credit maxed out at a hundred and fifty grand. With that huge debt and no collateral whatsoever, no other bank would lend me a cent. And what do you suppose my cheap-shit lawyer father, who abandoned me and my mom when I was eleven and never paid a cent in support, said when I begged him for a loan?"

"Piss off?"

"You know him."

"I know lawyers."

"In desperation, I went to the Canadian Forces recruiting office looking for a short-term contract. Monash had told me I could take up to two years off between years without losing credit. But the Canadians had nothing short-term to offer me. I'd given up on the idea when I read a report that the U.S. Army was beefing up its medevac units in Afghanistan, and they were in particular need of flight medics. So I went to the army recruiting station in Boston."

"Which landed you here."

"After drawn-out arguments trying to convince the army to give me a two-year contract in return for paying for my final year at Monash. They kept saying flight medics need at least five years of experience working in critical care. That four years in medicine is light-years beyond the training that a typical medic or flight medic has, seemed to make little impression on them. But finally, they did me the huge favor of accepting my proposition with the shitty rank of specialist at a whopping nineteen hundred bucks a month. After basic training and a couple of weeks in the flight medic course, which I got out of early because you needed someone right away, here I am."

Craig said, "So I got myself an almost doctor. Glad to hear it."

"What happened to your last flight medic?"

"He kind of went nuts, but he was an uptight type to begin with. Don't worry; we spent a year in Iraq before this, so we have a lot of experience. That's the good news. Now for the bad. I don't want to scare you, but I have to prepare you. Iraq was child's play compared to this—not much shooting at us, not many American casualties by the time we got there, no mountains, not much bad weather. Dealing with the sand and dust when landing was the biggest problem. We thought we were hot shit veterans after a year there.

"Then we got sent here, and we realized that was nothing. There were a lot of chopper crashes here because we weren't prepared. Our company's choppers have crashed into pretty well all the mountains here. We replaced a crew that flew into a valley wall. The survivors have gotten better, but we need to learn a lot more, so we spend a lot of time training. And we get shot at a lot. The Black Hawks have plenty of protection, so it's not as grim as you might think, but taking flak is never fun. You look ready to shit yourself."

"I was ready when you said I replaced a medic who went nuts. I let go when you told me we replaced a splattered crew. I haven't heard a word since."

Craig patted him on the back. "We have the best pilots and crew chief in the business, and my guess is you'll be the best flight medic, too. We're second up tomorrow. I'll get our crew chief to show you our chopper, and you can get set. Welcome aboard, Dan."

Returning to hooch, Daniel walked into the small sparse room that served as a lounge where "All American DUSTOFF" company soldiers and Apache pilots relaxed between missions. In the room were an old couch, a decrepit table, a couple of ratty chairs, a flat screen TV, and a few other things, such as magazines and soldiers. The TV news was showing the foundation of an old country church razed by a tornado Sunday in Oklahoma claiming forty-seven worshippers in the process.

"That'll teach the bastards," commented a woman sitting in one of the chairs. He couldn't see her face as she watched the TV. Curious was he. "Sunday certainly isn't a day of rest for God. He's as busy as ever massacring helpless people," she went on. Daniel chuckled.

She stood and turned around. Five and a half feet tall, slim figure perfectly proportioned, and, despite a crew cut, cuter than any girl who ever lived next door to him. He did a poor job of hiding his attraction to her, betrayed when his chin bounced off the floor; she made fun of him by parodying his expression. Before he could say anything, she jabbed his chest with her forefinger and said, "I'll say this once. I'm here to do a job. Period. I'm not interested in anything else. So keep your hands, eyes, and thoughts away from me! Got it?"

This seemed like a rude and unpromising greeting, so he came back, "I think I get what you're hinting at, but just in case, could you repeat that?" She flashed him a frigid smile and walked away. "If you think I can't keep my eyes off you, don't flatter yourself," he called after her. "The only thing appealing about you is you don't have a dick."

"That's the only thing appealing about you, too," she closed without breaking her stride. Laughter filled the plywood lounge, so he smirked and exited.

Daniel went back to his assigned quarters and met his roommate. The roommate held out his hand and said, "Talon Okeeweehow."

Daniel stood confused for a moment, then clued in. "Your name is Talon Okeeweehow?" The man nodded. "Lord Thundering Jesus. That's the best name I ever heard."

"Thanks, dude. I think so, too."

"Native American?"

"Father Cree, mother Ukrainian."

"There must be a joke there somewhere, but I can't think of one. I'm Dan Beaton."

"Oh, your call sign has to be Beat Off."

"No, don't do that to me, sarge. It brings up shitty memories from grade six on."

"I'll consider it. So, you're our new flight medic. I'm the crew chief."

"So I can legitimately call you chief?"

"Sure."

"What about blood-thirsty half-breed savage?" Daniel waited for a reaction with some trepidation. Maybe he'd gone too far with someone he just met. This six-foot-two, 200-plus-pound man could inflict a generous dose of pain, Daniel knew.

Talon merely said, "I'd prefer Chief." Daniel relaxed and laughed. He liked this man already. He had friendly eyes and a sense of humor. Talon proceeded, "Our last flight medic went out of his mind, and they had to ship him home. Welcome to JAF."

"Sad to be here. I met our lieutenant. He seems great."

"We lucked out. He's real easy-going and even competent. I can't tell you how rare that is for officers in the army."

"So who else is on our crew?"

"Chief Warrant Officer 2 Samantha Hawkins is our co-pilot. She's one of only two women in our little medevac and Apache group, and the only female pilot in Jbad DUSTOFF."

"Foxy feral female about yey high, makes a guy feel as welcome as locusts on a farm, a frown that unmans every man in its path?"

"That's her."

"It's uncanny how she could tell from subtle, nonverbal cues like my tongue dragging on the ground that I wanted to go spelunking with her."

"You and the rest of the camp. She's one of the only good looking women here, so she has to come across mean to fend off constant harassment. She does her best to blend in with the men by acting like one. She plays sports hard, curses a lot, contributes her share of perverted jokes, and keeps her emotions to herself. I'm not sure if she has no femininity, or just hides it real well. She never shaves her legs or arm pits, wears no makeup, and gets a buzz cut every month."

"With those big gorgeous eyes, pouty lips, high cheeks, and long neck, she's not hiding that she's a fine woman."

"Don't come on to her or she'll make you pay."

"I don't plan to go that far until at least our second date."

"Seriously, dude, treat her with respect. We're all protective of her and Barbara, who's a crew chief on another crew. A specialist can't date a warrant officer anyway."

Seeing how serious Talon was, Daniel nodded and proceeded to unpack and settle in.

*

Meanwhile, Samantha had gone to her room and picked up her laptop to write an email message to her sister. Samantha phoned Terry every week, and communicated most days via Microsoft Messenger or email.

From: Samantha Hawkins
Date: Tuesday, April 1, 2008
To: Terry Hawkins
Subject: New medic

Our new flight medic, our very own April fool, started today. His name is Dan Beaton, and the Apache pilots immediately christened him Beatoff. Shitty call sign to be saddled with.

From what I've heard he was a med student at some no-name Aussie school, but had to drop out because he ran out of money. I don't believe that. Med students are future gold, so I can't imagine he couldn't get some sort of loan. He probably flunked out. He's cute and he was a med student, so he probably had a bunch of women after him in Australia, and he thinks it'll be the same with the women here. Before he even said hello he had undressed me with his eyes. I had to put him in his place. Then he insulted me, and I insulted him right back. Talk about lack of respect. It really pissed me off. Anyway, I can't imagine some mollycoddled med student lasting a month here. He'll end up in the loony bin like our previous medic.

Study hard for finals. Almost halfway through college. Wow. I'm proud of you. Love, Sam

*

Talon took Daniel to the defac, the army's dining facility on the base. From the outside, it was like most structures on the base, a long, plain, single-floor unit, surrounded by concrete barriers. Inside, it looked like a high school cafeteria, with the food on display along one wall where people lined up to choose the dishes they wanted, and brown, rectangular tables, each with four padded, brown chairs. On the table were napkin holders and salt and pepper shakers. Flat-screen TVs hung near the ceiling in each corner of the main dining room. Pictures, plaques, banners, and flags adorned the cream-colored walls. There were no windows, but dozens of fluorescent lights lined the ceiling, making the room bright. And the food, surprisingly, wasn't bad. They had roast beef sandwiches for lunch.

Talon next showed him the shops, the PX, the gyms, the laundry facility, the coffee shop, the fire department, the latrines and showers, the living quarters—which ranged from old tents sprayed on the outside with insulation to much fancier single unit apartments for the officers—and the MWR recreation facility, where they shot a game of pool. He also took him into the new medical facility and introduced him to the medical team.

On the way back to their room, Daniel said, "Does it always smell like a steaming pile of shit in a reeking garbage dump here?"

"On a good day."

"What else is there to do here?"

"Have you run for your life to the shelter during a missile attack yet?"

"Not yet."

"Once you've done that, you've done all the fun things to do here."

"What about Jbad? Anything to do in town?"

"Nothing fun, unless you like exploding. You have to find hobbies. Have any?"

"Despoiling virgins," said Daniel as an Apache swooped in for a landing.

"I'm afraid we're fresh out of those."

"What about Sam?"

"She's twenty-two. For her sake, I hope she's not still a virgin."

"Maybe not, but I can pretend. She's pretty, eh?"

"I think the world of her, but physically she's too skinny for me. I like a lot of meat on my woman."

"To each his own, Chief. She is too skinny now, but I see her body as a hedge against inflation."

The two got to their room. Daniel sat on his bed and asked Talon, "How'd Sam get in as a pilot, anyway? She's much younger than any pilot I've seen, and apparently she's been one for about four years already. A couple of the Apache guys said she blew or screwed some colonel."

"Watch out about spreading that rumor; I don't believe she would do that, but if she did, that's her business, not anyone else's. You need to know something about her. Three weeks ago someone tried to rape her."

"Shit. What happened?"

"We were new here, and no one warned her that rape is a real problem at JAF; on all the bases here. The army deals with them quietly, when it deals with them at all. It was dark, and Sam was returning from the shower when some bastard attacked her. She screamed for help. Tommy and I happened to be walking back from the gym then and heard her scream. By the time we reached her, he had ripped her housecoat off and had her pinned down while lowering his pants. She got her licks in. His face was scratched and bloody, but he was too strong for her. Tommy and I kicked the shit out of the fucker and held him until the MPs got there. Son of a bitch was charged and jailed. But that hasn't stopped the rapes. We all watch out for her and for Barb."

"I will, too."

"Good. Keep in mind what it's like for her here. She's surrounded by sex-starved men, all of them a potential threat to her. She's scared of them, and no one blames her after what she went through. Sam was really rattled, and she stays away from men as much as she can. Respect her and protect her."

Daniel nodded.

*

On the morning of April 2, 2008, Daniel awoke to his first morning on duty. He put on his tan tee-shirt, tan camouflage pants and flight tunic, and pulled on tan boots. He holstered his sidearm and checked the various pouches that festooned his uniform. Sunglasses completed the picture of the professional soldier as he left his room and strolled across the tarmac to the washroom under a bright, blue sky for an overdue pee.

As Daniel approached the bathroom, "Medevac, medevac, medevac," squawked out of the walkie-talkie clipped to his pocket. His heart stopped, then zoomed as he darted to the platoon's tactical operations center to get information on the nature of the nine line medevac request. All he could ascertain was a U.S. soldier had been poisoned. "With what?" he asked. No one knew.

He met up with his lieutenant, who was in the operations center to determine the grid coordinates and plot the best route to the pickup zone, and they jogged to their helicopter. Samantha was running through her checklist, and Talon was conducting his checks when Craig and Daniel arrived to strap on Kevlar body armor and don flight helmets, before strapping themselves in. While Craig programmed the GPS and got permission to take off, Samantha rolled up the twin 1,600 hp engines to a thunderous roar. Craig nodded, and Samantha eased the 20,000-pound craft into the air.

Daniel looked up and saw the rotors sparking. He pointed it out to Talon, who said, "Dust." He surveyed the flying emergency room he was in charge of, crammed with life-saving supplies such as blood packs, drugs and oxygen tanks, and life-saving equipment like chest and intubation tubes, pressure infusers, splints and defibrillator, and shuddered at the awesome responsibility he had. What would he face out there? Never mind the potential for bullets and bombs, or crashing. He looked down at the unforgiving terrain as they reached the mountains. If they crashed here, he knew it would be over. What injuries would he have to deal with, and was he up to it? He'd been a paramedic and a med student, but he'd never dealt with bodies shattered by bullets or bombs. How would he react? Would he mess up and cost a life? Would he panic? He was so nervous, he felt nauseated.

The helicopter was suddenly thrown toward the earth by a convection cell. Daniel gasped and gawked at his crewmates, who seemed unconcerned. Must be normal, he concluded as he worked to slow his racing heart.

He stared out the window. They were flying fast, maybe 180 miles per hour, and low, maybe 500 feet. He'd learned in training that this was normal, fast and low to avoid missiles. Below, he saw a valley with a river winding through it, an irregular patchwork of farmers' fields and an occasional pre-historic village perched on a rocky hillside. Ahead, the jagged, snow-covered peaks of the Hindu Kush blazed in the bright sunshine. Hard to believe it's so dangerous down there, he thought.

The helicopter's ear-splitting roar was deadened by his flight helmet, but nothing could subdue the stink of jet fuel churning through the helicopter and churning his stomach. With the aircraft's altitude increasing in concert with the rising mountains, the thinning oxygen made him light-headed. Daniel grabbed an air sickness bag and vomited. "You get used to it," said Talon.

"Muzzle flashes," cried Craig. Samantha took evasive manoeuvres, turning the helicopter first on its left side, then its right. The escort Apache spun down and poured fire into the hillside where the fire was originating.

Talon noticed his flight medic on the point of panic, so he said, "Don't worry. The Apache will take care of the problem. Those guys get all the fun. We just curse and run away."

Daniel's heart slowed to a thousand beats a minute with that news, but then his head began aching. And did he ever have to pee! He tried to occupy his mind by going over the ABC's of paramedics—airway, breathing, circulation. *The basics are simple*, he told himself. *Make sure the casualty can breathe by clearing the airway. If he's bleeding, stop it. Replace fluids if necessary, reduce pain as much as possible, keep him alive until you hand him off to the surgeons. That's all; nothing fancy. You can do it, Dan. Cripes, I have to pee so bad.*

After about ten minutes of bouncing through the air, he was ready to face whatever they could throw at him on the ground as long as he could get out of the helicopter and relieve himself. The helicopter hurtled through the serpentine, narrow gorges that led into the Korengal Valley. It banked sharply, plunging in a tight spiral. Daniel's eyes grew large as the ground loomed large, but just when was about to scream,

Samantha pulled back on the control, flared, and landed safely at the KOP helipad.

They were in the Korengal Outpost, "the KOP" as it was known, a Forward Operating Base in the Korengal Valley, about fifty kilometers north of Jalalabad. Talon hopped out of the side window, carrying his M-4 rifle. Daniel grabbed his medical rucksack and ran behind Talon through the dust storm created by the helicopter to a small, dusty tent where the outpost's medic team was gathered around a private on a cot lying on his side in a fetal position, dressed only in yellow gym shorts. He looked like a boy. A lieutenant was sitting on the next cot talking to him; the platoon medic stood next to him. Daniel said, "All I know was he was apparently poisoned?"

"He took something. We don't know what."

"Did you ask him?"

"Of course. He won't tell us."

He sat and whispered to the officer, "So, he's trying to kill himself?"

The lieutenant nodded.

Daniel slipped on rubber gloves and squatted next to the patient. The man's face was flushed, his pupils dilated. He was tense and confused, and he was twitching. He was complaining of a headache. Putting his stethoscope against his patient's chest, Daniel heard a rapid heartbeat. There was vomit on the ground next to the cot. The smell turned Daniel's queasy stomach, and he had to work to keep from supplementing it.

"Does anyone in this camp have antidepressants?"

"Why?" said the lieutenant.

"He has the classic tricyclic antidepressant overdose symptoms. Did he use them, or might he have gotten someone else's?"

The platoon medic said, "Christ, a third of the men here take antidepressants."

"Like protriptyline or amitriptyline?"

"Uh, Prozac, Elavil."

"Okay, we need to get an IV going, maybe try some activated charcoal, and get him back to Jalalabad right away." Talon got the litter set, and he and Daniel tried to put the man on it, but he pushed them away. With the help of the field medic, they secured him to the litter and ran him to the helicopter.

Daniel, by now clutching his crotch in pain, asked where he could piss. They pointed to a pipe sticking out of the ground. He ran over and cursed as he struggled to get his armor out of the way, bobbing this way and that until he finally pulled it out and unleashed a torrent that would have drilled down to the earth's core if he had had a few more ounces, along with a loud, "Ahhhh!" that conveyed a relief bordering on ecstasy. A private passing by laughed.

When Daniel returned to the chopper, Craig said, "From now on you hold it till we get home." Craig nodded at Samantha, and the Black Hawk rose out of the plume of dust it kicked up and quickly gathered speed. Get up and out fast, before a missile could take them down, Daniel recalled from training. He hooked up the heart rate monitor to his patient to monitor vitals.

Ten minutes into the flight, while he and Talon were conversing about having a relatively easy case to deal with his first time out, the monitor started blaring. Daniel turned to look at it and saw the patient standing; he had pulled off the leads and taken out the IV needle. He had a small knife in his hand, with which he had cut the straps holding him down. As Talon and Daniel got to their feet, the man leapt sideways to the door, pulled it open, and jumped. It all happened in about three seconds, leaving the crew no time to react and gasping in horror. Talon and Daniel hurried to the door and looked down. There was no sign of the private.

"What the hell just happened?" asked Lieutenant Ng.

"He jumped. He just got up and jumped out," said Talon. Daniel was speechless, still gaping down through the open door.

"Sam," was all Craig had to say to his co-pilot.

She warned, "Hang on back there," and executed a sharp turnabout.

"Go down to fifty feet," ordered the officer. She obeyed. "All eyes on the ground." As the chopper flew back and forth over the mountain, the lieutenant asked, "Wasn't he strapped down?"

"Yes, sir," answered Talon. Daniel remained too astonished to speak. "He cut through the straps with a knife."

"No one thought to check a suicidal man for a knife?"

Talon answered, "He had only shorts on. It was a really small knife. He must've had it clutched in his hand."

"God dammit, if you two were trying to screw up, I give you an A plus."

The crew searched in vain for forty minutes, but it was an impossible task finding the body in the thick pine forest. With fuel running low, they gave up and flew back to base.

Daniel stayed in his seat long after the aircraft touched down. His negligence had cost a life, he told himself, first day on the job. He was so devastated, he couldn't move. Finally, Lieutenant Ng called him out and said, "I shouldn't have put this on you; it wasn't your fault."

"Yes it was. He was my patient, and I blew it. He's dead because of me."

"He's dead because he killed himself. That was his second try in two hours. If he didn't die of the overdose, he would've succeeded the next time or the time after." Daniel's head hung down.

His crew commander put his arm around his shoulder and went on, "Don't do this to yourself. You won't last two weeks here if you do. Learn from it and put it behind you. Resolve to do the best you can every time out, and you'll do more good here in a year than an average man does in a lifetime. I promise you, once you're on your hundredth mission and you've saved over ninety-five percent of the people you've reached alive, you'll put this in proper perspective as a casualty of war. Once you've seen your hundredth corpse, you'll put the death of a single individual into perspective. There's too much pain here already. Don't add to it by beating yourself up. You'll hurt not only yourself, but your entire crew. Understood?"

"Yes, sir."

Talon gave Daniel more or less the same speech, and it did make him feel better. Instead of giving in to despair, he resolved to do his utmost to save every life he could. That, he hoped, would enable him to forgive himself for this avoidable tragedy.

The next day, Craig sent Daniel to talk to Sergeant Andrew Ward, the most senior flight medic at FOB Fenty. Daniel dropped by his room and couldn't help but notice what looked like an amateur shrine. The shrine included dozens of pictures of the same woman hung around his bunk and a crude altar with a place to kneel and a few unlit candles.

"Hi, sarge, I'm Dan Beaton, Craig's new medic." They shook hands. "What the hell you got here?"

"Isn't it obvious? It's my altar to my goddess."

"She's some actor, isn't she?"

"Some actor? Some actor! Blasphemer! This is the most spectacular creature on the planet, my goddess, Sophia Bush."

"My apologies."

"Don't apologize to me. Get on your knees and ask her forgiveness."

Daniel smirked and said to the pictures, "I meant no offense, Goddess Bush." He turned to Andrew and said, "Tell me, are you a frigging nutcase?"

"Absolutely. I'm also a man who has a six-foot-four roommate who happens to be gay. This is my way of proclaiming my heterosexuality. I sleep with my ass to the wall. How would you like to worry every minute you'll wake up with your ass full of Tommy?"

"Not interested in your ugly ass," mentioned the dozing Staff Sergeant Tom Kinman. "But your friend's not bad at all."

"Nice of you to say, Staff Sergeant, but I pray to the heavenly Bush," said Daniel.

"Welcome, my convert," said Andrew. "You're my first apostle."

"That bottle of cream and box of Kleenex to help with your devotion?"

"Get your own, apostle. You may borrow one picture at a time, so you can worship her in your own room."

"Does she grant prayers?"

"Well, she could actually grant my main one if she were here and if I used my gun to persuade her."

"If he believes in the real God, does he have to give Him up?" asked Tom.

"Holy Bush will tolerate no fooling around with other gods, so yes, he has to give Him up, but remember, our goddess has two major advantages over your god: she's a she, and she exists."

"Prophet, I came to ask for any advice you can give me about being a flight medic in Afghanistan."

"Prophet; I like that. I heard about your first medevac. Tough one; not your fault. If it took the Chief by surprise, no one in the world would have caught it. So first lesson: expect the unexpected here." Daniel nodded. "You were a paramedic back home?" Another nod. "So I'll assume you know what you're doing medically. The main difference, you may note, is that all too often someone is trying to kill you while you're trying to save a shrieking marine who's lost both legs. The other difference is battlefield injuries tend to be much more, uh, horrendous than your typical case as a paramedic at home. Bullets and bombs do incredible damage to the human body.

"My advice: don't think; just do. Get it done fast without thinking about anything other than how to keep your patient alive until you get him back here. Don't think about anything on the way there, don't think about anything other than helping your patient on the ground and on the way back, and never, ever think about any of it after you get back. Focus on the help you're giving to the person in pain, not the person in pain. Without your help, he'll likely die. That gets you through it. Other than that, I'd advise you to pray often to the sacred Bush. It'll keep you relaxed. Now take this picture and fuck off, my apostle."

CHAPTER TWO

On-the-job Training – May, 2008

Samantha was correct in assuming that Daniel had been popular with the ladies in Australia. They tended to gravitate to him and want to stay in orbit permanently. A girl could do worse than a good-looking doctor with a pleasant demeanor. Neither did Samantha's conjecture that he expected more of the same at FOB Fenty miss the mark. If he had such an easy time attracting female med students, why not army women? Surely the former were a higher class of woman. He knew the army was overwhelmingly male, and its females tended to have more testosterone than the typical male civilian, but there had to be a few desirable ones, and surely they would be attracted to him. His only problem would be keeping the woman from getting too serious.

During his first month on base, he'd seen but a handful of pretty women, most of whom were married or engaged. From what he could determine, there were only three available pretty women, one of them being Samantha. She'd made it clear she wasn't interested, but the other two were enough for him. He wasn't greedy. To his surprise, however, they reacted much the same as Samantha to his overtures.

Confused, Daniel took the case to Talon. "I just asked Nurse Sweetland to watch a DVD with me at the MWR."

"And she said no."

"She never actually said no; I just inferred it from the way she was bent over laughing. Chief, how come women in the army hate me? They can't all be lesbians."

"First of all, an officer can't date an enlisted man. And even if the army allowed it, a female officer would never date a subordinate. Remember how girls in high school would never consider dating a boy in a lower grade? They considered it social suicide. Same thing for a woman in the army to date someone she outranks."

"But, shit, Chief, if the G D army wasn't so stupid, I'd be a lieutenant with my education and experience."

"But the army is stupid, so you're a specialist."

"But it's not only my shitty rank. Corporal Cox looked at me like I was a cockroach on her tit when I suggested pizza together."

"Put yourself in her place. You're a woman on a base with over a thousand young, single men. Unless you're an absolute scag, you can have your pick. So, who are you going to pick?"

"Me. I'm everything I ever wanted."

"And you can have you. But she'll choose a doctor, a pilot, or an officer."

"But she can't date an officer either."

"But, like you, she can try, and there are so many possibilities here for her. The penalty is severe for the officer involved, but if one wants to take the chance for a pretty woman ..."

"Yeah, men will risk anything for a pretty girl. Glad I'm not a woman or a gaylord. I'd hate to be attracted to something as pathetic as a man."

"Don't worry, dude. There'll be more women than you can handle when you're a doctor."

"But what do I do in the meantime?"

"Get on the Internet, find some pictures, and, you know."

"Back to high school. Great."

Daniel gave up for the time being on dating but didn't want to give up the company of women. He hoped Samantha would be open to spending time with him, with no personal relationship implied. To her room he went in search of accompaniment to the store. The countryside blew in with the wind when Samantha answered the knock on her door. "Hey, Sam," said Daniel. "Want to come with me up to the fancy shopping mall? I need to buy a laptop. And we can take our time strolling along the boardwalks getting to know each other."

"No," she said as she tried to close the door.

He put his hand out and said, "Wait! Not a date or anything. Just crewmates."

"No."

"How can you say no to Mohammed's General Store or Haji Guljan Carpet Palace?"

She pushed his hand away and shut the door.

He yelled, "Qasim Hand *Make* Knives, for God's sake. Who wouldn't want to see that? The new gym? It's got all the newest equipment. The PX? I'll buy you Pop-tarts. Need

Kotex? My treat. Or we can do laundry together. That's not too romantic for you, is it? Sam? Shit."

He went by himself to pick out a computer at the PX.

A few days later, Samantha, returning from the shower, stopped at her door and gawked at Daniel, who was sitting on her bed. "What the hell are you doing in my room?"

"Well, I definitely wasn't rooting through your panties." She clicked her tongue and went to the drawer holding her underwear and checked. Daniel said, "You might find that some of them stick together now."

"Oh, gross! Get off my bed, perv." He stood. "How did you get in here?"

"Barbara was just leaving when I got here. She let me stay because she said you'd be right back."

"Get out of my room."

"Don't you want to know why I'm here?"

"No! Get out!" she insisted as she pushed him out and slammed the door.

"You need to chill out in the Warrior Resiliency Room, Sam," he said through the door. He left with his left hand in his pocket clutching her frilly black panties; better than a thousand Internet pictures.

*

At 1003 over her radio came the voice of her lieutenant. "Sam? It's 1003. Where are you?"

"I'm in my room. Why?" she said.

"Training mission at 1000. Didn't Dan tell you?"

"Uh, no. I'll be right there," she said while she grabbed what she needed and dashed out to the flight line. When she got there, she glared at Daniel, who smirked in return.

Craig yapped, "Next time I ask you to do something, Specialist, do it! Now let's go."

Soon they were underway. Craig told them, "Chief, you'll practice lowering and raising Dan on the hoist while Sam ensures we avoid ground effect so that Dan doesn't spin out of control in downwash. Questions?"

"Can we not?" said Daniel.

"Get set back there; we're a go in four mikes." Four minutes later, Craig pointed to a narrow gulley and said to Samantha, "There. How high should we hover and why?"

Hovering the aircraft, Samantha answered, "Between fifty and a hundred feet with our configuration to avoid settling into rotor downwash and possible loss of control."

"And loss of our flight medic," added the lieutenant. "Hover at sixty-five. Dan, are you ready?"

"I guess."

"Chief, you're on." While Talon commenced lowering Daniel to the jagged, rocky terrain below, Craig asked Samantha, "Your main job now?"

"Keep us steady."

"And listen to Dan and Talon for guidance."

"We're drifting a bit to the right," observed Talon, who was sitting operating the remote control with his legs hanging out of the open door.

"That's the effect of the wind," concluded the lieutenant. "Sam, keep that in mind." She moved left slowly so as not to throw her medic into the canyon wall. "Good speed on the winch, Chief."

"I'm on the ground," said Daniel.

"Okay, reel him back up," commanded Craig. As soon as Daniel left the ground, a huge gust of wind threw the helicopter to the right.

"Watch it!" warned Craig.

"Oh, shit!" said Samantha while struggling to steady the aircraft. She did so, but not before Daniel bounced off some sharp rocks on the side of the hill. He yelped.

"You okay down there, Dan?" asked Craig.

"That depends. Is my ballsack supposed to be hanging off my chin?"

"Did I hurt you, Dan?" Samantha said as Talon upped the speed on the hoist.

"Did you not hear the question I just asked?"

"You'll just have to tell people you have a really ugly beard," she said. "Tell me if I hurt you."

"I have a scraped leg. Is that good enough to get me sent home, Craig?"

"Afraid not, Dan," he answered as Talon pulled him inside. "Okay, let's go home," he told Samantha.

"I blew it; I'm sorry," said Samantha.

"In my mind you did a good job maintaining control in that wind, Sam. I only had time to begin wondering when you were going to react when you reacted, so you might have been a second faster, but good job for someone with your experience."

Climbing out of the canyon, Samantha glanced back at Daniel. He was examining a nasty scrape on his right leg. His pants were shredded, and his leg was bleeding. She winced and turned forward, and they flew back to base.

Feeling bad about hurting him, Samantha decided to be nice to him when they got back. At defac that afternoon, she was civil with him for the first time.

Lined up to get food, Daniel stood there trying to decide which potato dish to get. He said to the man at the counter, "Hey, buddy, all three of these are called potatoes."

"That's because they're all potatoes, or a reasonable facsimile."

"But these are mashed, these are scalloped, and these are fried."

"We just call them all potatoes."

The wise ass said, "Then I'll take the potatoes," without indicating which type.

The wiser ass returned, "Bad choice. They're reconstituted from some flaky shit."

"Okay, then give me the potatoes," said Daniel.

"They're burnt."

"All right, I'll settle for the potatoes."

"What am I, a fucking mind reader? What kind?"

Samantha, standing next to Daniel throughout this exchange, laughed, and Daniel joined her. He said, "Screw it, I'll take a burger." Samantha made the same choice.

Daniel set his tray on the table and sat across from Talon. "You see that planet over there?" opened Samantha as she placed her tray on the table and sat next to Talon. Talon nodded. "Private contractor, no doubt. She told me to go around her while she decided which fifteen dishes to have. By the time I orbited her, my hamburger was cold." Daniel chortled.

"She does have an ass of biblical proportions," agreed Talon. "I wonder what the Afghans think when they see her. She must eat enough to feed a small city here."

"Good idea. Let's donate her to a small city for supper," suggested Samantha.

"You see the new nurse, Chief?" said Daniel. "She's your type."

"His type?" asked Samantha.

"Type double D cup. I talked to her. She's a ditz. Sophia was chintzy in supplying her with brains, but was positively munificent with tits."

"I'll look for them," said Talon.

"Who's Sophia?" said Samantha.

"Sophia Bush."

"The actress that Andy has pasted all over his room?"

"Actress and goddess."

"So, Sophia is your god, too?" said Talon.

"That's right." Talon shrugged. He seemed to be copacetic with pretty much anything. Daniel went on, "What about you, Chief? What do the Cree believe?"

"The Cree learned a long time ago not to talk much about that because the whites tend to snicker. In fact, my white half snickers at my red half because its ancestors believed that anything alive, and a lot that was never alive, has spirits."

"What is the nature of a dung beetle spirit, or for that matter, a dung spirit, Chief?"

"See? Snickering. I should add that my red half snickers at my white half because its ancestors were stupid enough not to question how either Cane or Able had to be a mother fucker."

"Many Christians are still too stupid to question that." Turning to Samantha, Daniel said, "You've actually been nice today. What's the matter? You sick?"

"I know I haven't been friendly with you, but I have my reasons."

Talon said, "I told him. He needed to know."

She said to Daniel, "I don't know the ratio of men to women on this base, but it wouldn't surprise me if it's ten or fifteen to one. Fifteen young, horny men with no outlet for their powerful urges. There have been four rapes that I know of on this base since I got here. The men somehow get a hold of alcohol or drugs, and they abuse it to drown out their stress and sorrows, and they go wild. We're not even safe on base. It's really scary. I'm still freaked out about that bastard who tried for me. Our only defense is to shut down any male advances immediately."

"Your nasty wit is enough to scare most men off. We'll help protect you from the rest."

"My nasty wit hasn't worked to scare you off."

"It wouldn't, no. I love it."

"So if I get boring around you, will you leave me alone?"

"Impossible. You could never bore me. You're the most fascinating woman I've ever met."

That was the nicest compliment a man had ever paid to her, and she almost smiled, but caught herself in time. She said in jest, "Chief, protect me from this man."

The two were friendly for a couple of days, but then she overheard a conversation he had with Talon.

Sitting in the hooch gazing at her, Daniel said, "You know, Chief, there are glories galore in our universe, but nothing comes close to a gorgeous set of eyes in a pretty girl's face." The objects of his veneration noticed their admirer and forthwith crossed, thereby casting off his eyes.

"Personally I'd give the honors to a big pair of tits," countered Talon.

"Big tits gross me out. I like them small."

"Why?" said Talon.

"I just think they look nicer. And there are benefits to small tits."

"Name one," challenged Talon.

"Uh, well, they don't sag. And if we lose power, we can always wash our laundry on Sam's chest."

"I heard that, asshole," said Samantha while peeling a banana.

Daniel blushed, lowered his eyes, and said, "I swear, that woman could hear a butterfly fart." After a few moments, he returned his eyes to her. "God help me, look at her, Chief." Talon glanced up and chortled at his young friend gazing at Samantha putting the fruit into her mouth. Daniel went on, "Yes, do that, woman. I could watch her eating bananas all day." She looked up, frowned, and turned her back to him.

"You're a sick man, dude," opined Talon.

Concluding Daniel had taken her affability the wrong way, Samantha went back to her standoffish attitude with him. She was forbidden from fraternizing with enlisted men, and she took the rule seriously.

From: Samantha Hawkins
Date: Sunday, May 4, 2008
To: Terry Hawkins
Subject: Becoming a better pilot

We spend a lot of time training; thank God, or we'd have died of boredom, and incompetence, long ago. Yesterday I practiced flying from the right side of the cockpit (I'm usually on the left), then practiced flying over and between the mountains in heavy winds so I can hone my mountain flying skills. The chopper gets thrown around pretty hard. I had to use a puke bag for the first time in months. Beaton threw up three times, which made me feel better.

Today I tried some complicated hovering techniques. I lost control while doing something called hovering out of ground effect—imagine dying due to "ring vortex state" after dodging bullets and missiles—but the lieutenant recovered us. Then he made me do it again and again. So instead of coming back to base in failure and embarrassment, or not coming back at all, I came back having learned how to manage landing under difficult conditions and much more sure of myself. He's such a great teacher. I finally feel confident with all this heavy responsibility, though I'm sure I can still improve.

Glad to hear of your summer job at the hospital. And no, I won't stop depositing part of my paycheck into your account. I don't need it here, and you might need it. Put some away for a rainy day if you can.
Love, Sam

Eating breakfast, Samantha said, "Mmm mmm powdered eggs and coffee recycled from the toilets, just part of what makes this place great."

"Medevac, medevac, medevac, second up," squealed her radio. Leaving behind her breakfast without regret, she sprinted to the Black Hawk. Her gear was ready on the chopper to hasten preparation for takeoff. Crawling on top of the aircraft underneath the rotors, she carried out a quick external check, then jumped down, put on her flight helmet, armor, and personal equipment, and sat in the co-pilot seat to rapidly run through her checklist before starting the engines. Craig and Daniel arrived with the rotors already whirling, and shortly thereafter the helicopter lifted off.

"This is going to be fun," Daniel remarked.

"What you got, Beaton?" asked Samantha.

"Marine's leg's caught under an upturned Humvee, and there's a live IED a few inches away."

"Can't you wait until they disarm it?"

"Explosive ordnance disposal team is apparently twenty-five minutes out. He might die before then," he answered.

They flew for eight minutes east of Jalalabad. A red plume rose from a smoke grenade, marking the patrol's location, and Samantha took her aircraft down seventy meters to the west.

*

Daniel grabbed his medical bag and ran through heavy dust unsettled by the chopper to the stricken marine. Talon followed. Marines had set up a perimeter to protect the man.

The corpsman had stabilized him, but there was no budging the vehicle on him, and no one dared try with an IED maybe a foot away from the soldier's head. He had to lean over the bomb to get at his patient.

"Having fun?" said Daniel while setting up for the operation.

"The guessing is that, as long as we don't touch it, we might survive this," answered the corpsman.

"How comforting." *This isn't real,* he told himself. *It's just a nightmare. I'm asleep in Melbourne. Big exam tomorrow. Worried about bombing it, I guess.* "What have you done so far?" Daniel asked the corpsman.

"I slowed the bleeding and gave him a shot of morphine."

Daniel nodded and gave the patient a midazolam injection for sedation. He looked at the leg. It disappeared under the Humvee just below the knee. The corpsman had cut away the uniform to expose the upper leg. "His lower leg has to come off," concluded Daniel.

The corpsman concurred, "I'm sure it's crushed anyhow."

"Shit. You've earned your pay already today; my turn."

The corpsman nodded and said, "I'll make sure he doesn't trip the IED."

Daniel extracted the saw and placed the blade against the leg. Leaning over the bomb, he started the saw and cut through the soldier's skin and muscle. When he reached the bone, the patient began screaming and flailing. "Jesus Christ!" Daniel said. "Don't let him hit the bomb!"

His partner intercepted the man's right arm as it came down toward the bomb and held it fast.

"Fuck, man, I thought the combination of morphine and midazolam was enough to knock down a horse."

"Get me out of here!" shrieked the injured marine as he continued to thrash. The man's left arm came down, landing an inch from the trigger.

"Grab that arm!" yelled Daniel.

"I'm trying," answered the corpsman. "He's unbelievably strong."

Again the marine lifted his left arm, and as it plunged toward the trigger once more, with both medics looking on in terror, Talon lunged in to intercept it.

After a few seconds to calm down, Daniel said, "Thanks, Chief." He gave the marine another dose of midazolam, and he settled down.

"Don't leave me here," the man said.

"We won't," said Daniel.

"Am I going to die?"

"No. You'll be home soon, I promise."

He fell asleep, and the medics got back to work. The saw went through the leg in less than a minute. Daniel then applied a vacuum-sealed sterile pressure bandage. Stepping across the bomb, the two medics gingerly lifted him and put him on a litter. Four infantry men hustled the soldier to the waiting chopper where Daniel secured him. He shook the medic's hand, closed the door, and Samantha lifted off.

"You okay?" Samantha asked, glancing back.

"Yeah," he replied as he attempted to put an IV in the soldier's arm with the aircraft bouncing around. "Right now I'm still high on adrenaline, but I think the horror of it will hit me later, and often. The bomb was inches below my ball bag as I was working on him."

"Shit. Better you than me," said the lieutenant.

"All I can say is, if Sophia takes my bag, she better take me. I can face anything with my faithful sack swaying beneath me. Without it, I'd be, I don't know—Sam."

"You do look a lot alike," contributed Talon, "except I think she does have a bag."

"Watch out, Okeeweehow, or I'll give you fucking smallpox," said Samantha, which got Daniel laughing.

"And I'll harvest your scalp," returned Talon, which got Daniel laughing more. And he needed to laugh after what he'd just gone through.

From: Samantha Hawkins
Date: Sunday, June 15, 2008
To: Terry Hawkins
Subject: Sick humor of war

Not much happening here, as usual. So, mostly it's dealing with boredom and keeping up with my studies. I just started my sixth online course.

Beaton is funny sometimes. Whenever I can, I'll jot down the funny things he says so I can pass them along to you. I figured you'd enjoy some of them.

Last week we went to pick up an Afghan farmer injured by a butterfly mine. On the way there I asked Beaton what we had, and he answered, "Some guy seems to have misplaced his leg." Sounds heartless, I know, but it helps him, all of us, cope with the madness here. If we took it as seriously as the situation would seem to demand, we'd all go crazy in no time.

On the way back from another mission, Talon was saying that the Taliban insurgent had been "redistributed." I asked how, and Beaton answered, "Rule number one when arming an IED: don't fucking sneeze."

One poor Afghan last month crashed a helicopter due to pilot error. Dan said, "He convinced himself he could fly the chopper, but he couldn't convince the chopper." And just after that, a woman got hurt in a car crash and Daniel concluded, "She thought she could negotiate the curve, but the curve wasn't budging."

And this morning, which is what gave me the idea of writing this to you today, we were discussing in the debrief an ordnance disposal expert who'd lost an arm in an explosion, and Dan said, "Unfortunately, before he could disarm the bomb, the bomb disarmed him." That got him into trouble with the CO. He's so inappropriate, but you can't help but laugh. I think it's our way of defying death or horrible injury; laugh at it.

Write soon. Your letters are one of the few things I look forward to here.

Love, Sam

CHAPTER THREE

Sexual Fantasies – Summer 2008

Walking along a narrow dirt road in the Pech Valley, a platoon of G.I.s made their way back to camp just after midnight. It was a miserable, rainy, hot night, and the men were soaked. They walked a few meters apart; groups present targets and too many get hurt if a roadside bomb explodes as they walk past. Corporal Ben Lanning, the platoon medic, was third in line. Exhausted after a long day of marching up and down steep hills, he tried to forget his fatigue by transporting his mind to his girlfriend back home in Oklahoma. It had been so long, so many horrible months since he'd seen her, he was having difficulty picturing her face. "What I'd give to be holding her."

Suddenly there was a huge explosion.

Ben had no idea what was happening to him; he seemed to be hurtling, but then there was a thud. He felt nothing. His ears were ringing. He blacked out for a few moments. When he opened his eyes again, the world was spinning. He was down on the ground. Where? "Where the hell am I?" He looked around and saw a few men scurrying by in the dust tossed up by the explosion. He was beside a dirt road.

Someone nearby cried, "Ahhh! I'm hit. Oh, fuck, I'm hit! Doc, I need help!"

Ben tried to collect his thoughts and move, but he couldn't for the moment. His sergeant ran to him and shouted, "Doc's down, too." Ben looked down at his left leg; it was sore. He couldn't move it. His heart fell through his stomach as it revved up.

The lieutenant ran up and, seeing his men down, got on the radio to call in the medevac chopper.

"Help Marazzo," the sergeant called to a private as he knelt beside his medic. "I'll cut away the pant leg so we can see what's what," he said.

Coming to his senses, Ben nodded. With the cloth cut away, he could see his femur sticking out through the skin. The pain started in earnest. "Fuck!"

"Marazzo's bleeding bad!" said the private.

"Oh, Jesus, I don't want to die! Stop the bleeding!" exclaimed Marazzo.

"Where's he bleeding from?" said Ben.

"Arm."

"Use the tourniquet in your kit to stop the bleeding, Jeff. I'll be right there." He turned to his sergeant and said, "Help me get to him."

"You sure?"

Ben nodded. The sergeant helped him to his feet. Ben put his left arm over the sergeant's shoulder and limped to Marazzo. Ben's head ached fiercely. "Okay," he said to let the private know he would take over. "I need some light, sarge." The sergeant shined his flashlight on Marazzo, who was grimacing in pain. He looked pale; he'd lost a lot of blood already. There was a gaping wound on his upper arm about eight inches long and three inches wide, exposing the muscle beneath.

"I'm dead," concluded Marazzo.

"You'll make it. Medevac should be here soon."

"They aren't flying in this shit. We're both fucked," Marazzo opined while looking at Ben's leg.

"They'll come; they always do." He turned to his sergeant. "Anybody else hurt?"

"Sheppard's gone. Goddamn IED blew him apart."

Ben felt faint. Digging into his medic's bag, he got out a tourniquet to put on his own leg, though the bleeding was light. The lieutenant saw his distress. "How can we help, doc? If you black out, you can't help your patient or yourself."

The sergeant put the tourniquet on for Ben. He asked his lieutenant for an ETA for the medevac.

"A good fifteen minutes."

The sergeant shook his head as Ben took some ibuprofen and gave some to his patient. Ben continued to work on Marazzo until he began to black out eleven minutes later. Marazzo was in and out of consciousness.

"Where the hell is the medevac?" screamed the lieutenant.

Just then they heard the thump of a chopper, and his radio blurted, "DUSTOFF inbound. Give us some light."

"Digby, swing your chemlight," ordered the lieutenant.

Ben lost consciousness.

*

The light helped guide the co-pilot in to a landing spot twenty-five yards away from the injured men. Out hurdled the crew chief and flight medic, each carrying a litter. They sprinted to the injured men. Daniel quickly assessed the obvious wounds. "Your medic do this work?" he asked the lieutenant.

"Yeah. That's him there. Doc worked on George with a bone sticking out of his leg."

"Good man. He saved his life." Daniel turned to Talon and said, "This man will need blood, hypertonic saline, and oxygen right away, Chief. Can you get him to the chopper and set him up with an IV while I work on the medic?"

Talon nodded and said to the officer, "I'll need help getting him on the litter and carrying him to the chopper." The officer barked out a command, and Talon had all the help he needed.

Daniel checked Ben and saw the leg was stabilized, but he was concerned because his breathing was labored. "I don't see much blood loss from this wound on the leg. Did he pass out, or did he take something to knock him out?" he asked the lieutenant.

The officer answered, "Just some ibuprofen; he wanted to stay alert to work on George."

"Then why did he black out? I need more light," said Daniel as he took off his NVGs. The sergeant pointed his flashlight on the subject. Daniel saw the telltale signs of approaching death in the eyes and face, almost as if the patient was blurring. He took Ben's blood pressure. "110 over 100. He must be bleeding." He turned Ben over, and the three men looking on gasped at the large pool of blood underneath the field medic. "Shit!" said Daniel. He radioed to Talon. "Chief, I need saline and the EZ IO on the double!" Looking at the sergeant, he said, "Help me off with his armor, sarge." They took off his vest; his shirt was soaked with blood. Daniel extracted his scissors to cut his patient's shirt open. There was a chunk of shrapnel sticking out of the base of his neck.

Talon arrived with the intraosseus drill and saline. Daniel turned Ben on his side, swabbed Ben's right leg, and drilled into the tibia marrow in a matter of three seconds. He removed the sheath and said, "Get that going right away, Chief, wide open and squeeze it. I need to stop this bleeding." Daniel removed a scalpel from his rucksack to prepare for extraction of the shrapnel. While Daniel removed the projectile, Talon got the saline flowing.

Surrounded by the platoon, Daniel worked feverishly to stop the bleeding and close the wound. "Okay, let's get him … Shit!" Ben had stopped breathing. Daniel flipped him over onto his back. He took off his helmet and put his ear to the man's chest. He pulled back and screeched, "Defibrillator, Chief! Hurry!" As Talon sprinted to the chopper, Daniel pounded Ben's chest, then administered mouth-to-mouth resuscitation. His buddies held their breath.

Talon was back in seconds. Daniel attached two pads with wires to Ben's left side and upper right chest. He pushed the ANALYZE button, and the screen read "SHOCK ADVISED! Charging to 300J." Then the screen changed to, "Stand clear push shock button." Daniel called, "Clear!" and pushed the SHOCK button. Daniel checked for a pulse and began CPR, pushing hard and fast. He counted thirty chest compressions, then gave him mouth-to-mouth ventilation. Once again he checked vital signs and nodded. Talon placed a breathing bag over the man's mouth and commenced squeezing as Daniel packaged Ben for evac.

As they ran Ben to the helicopter, the distraught officer asked Daniel, "Will my men live?"

"I hope so, sir. We'll do our best."

"Thanks, doc."

Daniel nodded while sliding the door closed. The lieutenant backed away, and Samantha took off, heading full-speed for Jalalabad. Talon attached Daniel to straps to preclude his being thrown around as he stood inside the moving helicopter while attending to both patients during the fifteen-minute flight. He worked with night goggles on to see in the dark, infusing packed red blood cells and plasma, affixing oxygen masks, and connecting heart rate monitors. He handed over both patients to the medical facility alive.

*

Sitting on a homemade chair in Club Medic trying to study a medical text with hard rock blaring from the hooch, Daniel was accosted by Samantha. "Okay, Beaton, where is it?"

"Where is what?"

"Don't play coy with me, you bastard."

"I believe the sobriquet normally attached to my person is asshole," answered Daniel.

"Have it your way, asshole. I got your pictures and ransom note. You're my only suspect."

Craig asked for the pictures and laughed to see Samantha's ragged, white housecoat posed on a fence with its arms up. A man with his back to the camera was pointing an M-4 rifle at it. The other picture was of the housecoat splayed on the runway in front of a taxiing Predator drone. Craig passed the photos to Talon who also laughed. "What's the note say?" asked Talon.

Samantha read, "You'll never see this horrid bunch of threads in one piece again if you don't deposit a kiss on the lips of one flight medic with the initials D.B. before noon on Independence Day. Do not contact MPs, or the housecoat is toast. Enclosed is a thread from the arm. That should convince you I mean business." Craig and Talon sniggered. Samantha had laughed heartily upon opening the envelope and examining its contents, but was now hiding her mirth. She didn't want to encourage him.

Daniel said, "It wasn't me."

"That's what I thought you'd say," she said as she tossed him another picture. He looked at it and burst out laughing. It was his flight helmet being water-boarded. "Even trade," she said while ambling away. He handed the picture to his crewmates, who also chortled. After one more night of sleeping with her housecoat, he traded it for his flight helmet. Samantha washed it right away.

From: Samantha Hawkins
Date: Saturday, July 19, 2008
To: Terry Hawkins
Subject: Obama and crying
    Guess what? I shook hands today with the man who might be the next President! Mr.

Obama didn't notice me, I'm sure, as he shook dozens of hands, but it was pretty exciting for me.

To answer your question, regardless of what we see in the movies, of course soldiers cry when they get hurt here. I hear some, but our medic hears much more. I asked him to answer your question, and since he will do anything for me, he wrote me a couple of paragraphs, which follow.

A medic in wartime hears a lot of crying. Most of it is soldiers in excruciating pain. The bravest among them sobs like toddler who's burned his hand; all semblance of bravado evaporates in the face of terrible agony. As an act of basic humanity, I'd like to relieve their pain before I deal with the cause of it, but morphine is sometimes out until a bleeding wound is stabilized, or their blood pressure can drop enough to kill them. And until I can deal with their pain, they cry and screech. Yesterday we were sent to help a man who had broken his back. This six-foot-five marine was shrieking, howling and writhing in utter agony. The company medic had been killed, and this marine had been in this misery for at least twenty minutes with his helpless fellow soldiers standing by forlornly. I administered a generous dose of morphine, which settled him down to a quiet sob.

A lot of the crying is done by other manly soldiers standing by their fallen comrade who is dead, dying, or writhing in pain. They do their best to hide their tears, but the abject sorrow overcomes

```
them. I can't do much to relieve their
pain. And some crying is done by the medic
himself. He sees so much pain, so much
catastrophe, so much hopelessness, so much
upcoming sorrow for the soldier and his
family. Crying in this case is one
necessary way of relieving the pain and
staying sane, and I do that sometimes when
I'm alone. But don't tell anyone.
Love, Sam
```

By midsummer, Daniel was beginning to fall for Samantha. Sitting in Club Medic reading medical notes on the mouth and throat, he said to Talon, "I want to bop Sam's uvula."

"Her what?"

"That punching bag thingie that hangs at the back of the mouth." He showed Talon the drawing in his notes.

"I won't even ask what you want to bop it with."

"She has a flawless mouth, you know. I'm speaking as a medical professional. Plump, pouty, pink lips, picture perfect teeth, healthy pink tongue; but I really do need to bop her uvula to make sure it's healthy, too."

"Considerate of you."

"Isn't it?" He lowered his notes and proceeded, "She's so different from any woman I've ever met. She's beautiful, and she doesn't know it. That alone sets her apart, but she's smart and funny, too. Maybe a lot of women hide a wicked wit from men because it routs them and scares them off, but I gotta tell you, Chief, I never came across a woman who can make me laugh like she can. Being with a person like that makes life so much more fun, don't you think? And I can't imagine a more courageous, skilled pilot."

"So, your interest in her now goes beyond sex," said Talon.

"Way beyond sex, and that's saying something when every single one of my billion sperms is pining over a picture of her egg and would give its life to take a long swim up a heavenly canal for a one in a billion chance to mate with it."

"Truly heroic of you to make that sacrifice. Sounds like love to me."

"Before you cut me off with biting sarcasm, I was about to say that Sam is the most intriguing woman I've ever met. In my dreams I see a white picket fence, and Sam sitting on the porch. Naked."

"Careful, Dan, the army doesn't allow romantic relationships between officers and enlisted men. You'd both get in deep shit, her especially."

"I know, but I can't help myself. Oh, here she comes." Samantha and Craig arrived. Daniel said to her, "Stop there, Samantha." She stopped. "I love the way you silhouette the moon as a Warrior takes off in the background to unleash bloody havoc. It's all so poetic." She cast her eyes upward and walked onto the porch. "I'm sure you've heard a thousand times that you're the finest conglomeration of atoms and subatomic particles in the universe." Again her eyes went north. "Come on, Sam. Romance is in the air." Craig sat next to Daniel.

"That's dust," she responded.

"Dust, flies, the moon, Kiowa Warriors, and romance."

"Specialist, there is no romance, and that's an order."

"You can order my body, but not my heart," he said.

That unleashed a groan among the men sitting on the porch as Samantha replied, "Then I'll skewer your heart."

"You already have, heavenly maiden; with Cupid's arrow."

Another group groan.

Samantha said, "Cut out the sweet stuff, Beaton, before you give me diabetes."

Craig, like Talon, warned his medic that fraternization is not permitted. Daniel nodded, but he didn't listen. He couldn't.

July 30, 2008. It was 121 degrees at Jalalabad at 1416, and the tarmac appeared to be boiling off in waves to the sky. "Fuck, it's hot," observed Daniel. "I'm frying like jeezly bacon on high." As Andrew applied ChapStick to his lips, Daniel said, "Give me some of that lip balm, Prophet Andy. My asshole's chapped. Come on, I'll give it right back."

"Gross, Beaton," stated Samantha as Andrew shrugged and tossed it to Daniel. He started to lower his pants, but Samantha said, "Cut the shit, Beaton!"

Daniel desisted and smiled. He looked at the product and pretended to read, "Side effects include exploding spleen and sweaty balls."

"I was wondering why my balls were sweaty," responded Andrew. "Keep it, apostle."

"Medevac, medevac, first up!" squawked all the radios in the cabin.

Craig and his team dashed to their respective posts to get ready for the mission.

"Priority evac of marine suffering from heat stroke," Daniel informed his lieutenant as they ran to the aircraft. Samantha had the ship ready to take off as Craig and Daniel assumed their seats. Craig programmed the GPS and asked the tower for permission to take off. He said to his co-pilot, "I feel like flying today." She nodded and sat back. Craig lifted off and headed west.

Just west of Khayrow Khel, Samantha pointed at the red smoke and Craig banked his Black Hawk left, then abruptly turned right and circled, with the chopper leaning steeply over to enable him to identify a good spot to land. He made his decision and set his aircraft down gently, though that didn't stop the dust from oppressing them. Marines rushed the debilitated man to the chopper. Craig lifted off after less than a minute on the ground.

Daniel noted the temperature on his patient's forehead written by the corpsman: 107.2. The man's shirt already open, Daniel poured cool water onto his chest. He set up an infusion of dextrose fifty percent in water solution and put an oxygen mask on the man. Daniel took his vitals, noted the temperature of 106.6, cursed, and poured more cool water on the man. The man lost consciousness. Cursing again, Daniel removed the oxygen mask and got more aggressive with his treatment. He removed the soldier's shirt and pants and took ice packs and put them between his legs and under his arms.

"Chief, we need to blow this man," said Daniel. "So, hand me the fan, or I'll leave you two alone if you want to do it."

"Gross, Beaton," noted Samantha as Talon handed him the fan.

"Our patient's been busy hosting sand flies. Lots of lesions and it looks like he's developing leishmaniasis. Infection's spreading up his leg. Pentostam injections in store for him; poor bastard. Gotta love Afghanistan!"

The patient regained consciousness and began shivering. He was agitated. Daniel administered benzodiazepine as the helicopter touched down at Jalalabad. He wrote this information on the man's chest, right above his INFIDEL tattoo. The marine's temperature had fallen to 105.6. As an ambulance pulled up, Daniel doused the man with water once more and continued blowing air across his body with the fan. He accompanied the patient to the Forward Surgical Team. The marine's temperature had fallen to 104.8. Daniel, soaked through with sweat, retired to the shower.

*

In mid August, the temperature was 120 degrees in the shade. Soldiers were warned not to sleep too long or they risked getting dehydrated. The crew spent as much time as they could in air conditioning, but it wasn't possible much of the time.

Sitting in the hooch, Daniel watched Samantha walk by and commented to Talon, "There she goes, Miss America, traipsing by sexy as a hairy biker, smelling like she fell out of a tumbling outhouse, ass crack etched in sweat on her horrible baggy shorts that reveal only her knobby knees and disgustingly hairy calves, nauseating hairy armpits partly exposed by her loose, frumpy drab green shirt so drenched in sweat she could wring it out and start a new ocean, crew cut so short her head looks like a thumb with a dirty nail, natural mud mask made of dirt and sweat that lends her complexion a turdian quality. All she needs to complete the picture is that snot bubble that grew out of her nose when she was crying last month. So, tell me, Chief, explain this to me. Why the hell is that woman the most entrancing creature I have ever met?"

"You admire her for what she is."

"True, but I admire her for what she looks like, too. But she looks like a vagrant who just climbed out of the sewer."

"Well, she's not exactly at her best. Who could be in this cesspool? Look at you; you're a disgusting, sweaty, shitty mess yourself."

"But she's a pretty woman. Everyone knows pretty women don't sweat or stink or shit, or if they do, it smells like perfume. So, what's with her?" As Daniel dropped a few M&M's into his mouth, he gazed at Samantha and said, "I know her bum is perfect, but I wonder about her labia. I bet they're tight and tidy, not those icky mishmashes that look like a pouch of mangled tongues."

Because the comment was so outrageous and so unexpected, Talon burst out laughing. Samantha came over and said to Talon, "What did I miss?" And the thought of conveying what was just said about her made Talon laugh harder. Turning to Daniel, she said, "What did you say?" He just sat there looking guilty. "It was about me, wasn't it?" She turned back to Talon. "Chief?"

Talon was by this time out of breath and red, but managed to say, "Tell her, Dan."

Daniel taking the fifth, she gave him a deprecating stare. He said, "Your scorn and I are old pals, Sam. You'll not loosen my lips, no matter how tight yours are."

And with this, Talon fell out of his chair, the firestorm of laughter refueled.

"What did you say about me?" she demanded.

"Uh, I just sort of said you have a nice shitter and stuff."

She stood and looked at him for a moment as if he were a skunk raising its tail. Then she remarked, "Shakespeare said,

'What's in a name? That which we call a rose/By any other name would smell as sweet,' but Beaton says, 'Nice shitter and stuff.' You're so pathetic," she said as she stomped away.

"Good thing she didn't know that 'nice shitter' was much more romantic than what you actually said," noted Talon, still chuckling.

From: Samantha Hawkins
Date: Wednesday, August 27, 2008
To: Terry Hawkins
Subject: A mission

You asked what it's really like here, by which I assume you want me to tell you how dangerous it really is. I have to tell you, Terry, all of us here withhold those kinds of details from our loved ones, so we don't needlessly worry them. After all, what could you do about it?

The truth is, it can get very dangerous, mostly for our guys who have to leave the chopper and rescue the injured. For pilots, believe it or not, the greatest enemy is ourselves. We do get shot at all the time, but we're well protected in here, and it would be next to impossible to take down the Black Hawk with bullets. A missile could ruin our day, but fortunately the bad guys don't have many effective ones. The Black Hawk automatically drops magnesium flares when it detects incoming flak. What kills most chopper crews is when a pilot messes up. The terrain here is treacherous. The mountains have strong, unpredictable winds, and the weather can get bad fast.

Flying with night vision goggles on in the mountains is hard because the goggles rob you of depth perception, and we have to fly because otherwise people on the ground will die. But we're trained well, and as I've told you before, our lieutenant is terrific and very particular that I do everything just so.

We practice all the time so we can handle whatever might face us, and Craig is in the seat right next to me to help out whenever necessary. I've gotten so good at this that I surprise myself. Even after thirteen months flying in Iraq, I was so terrified when I first started here, I was sure I was going to kill myself and my crew on some godforsaken mountainside. Now I fly through valleys and over mountains at night in the wind and rain and don't give it a second thought. The guys have complete trust in me, and I will not let them down. All of which is to say that if I was going to kill us through inexperience or incompetence, I would have already.

Things are seldom typical here, but today's first call was not unusual. A small boy had fallen down a steep hill. We were called to rescue him (a lot of our calls are to help the locals). Whenever we arrive at the pickup zone, I have to circle to identify potential landing spots. It was a bit dicey there today with the steep, rocky terrain. At first I concluded we should use the hoist, where Talon lowers Dan down to the ground, but it's always preferable to land because the hoist can be dangerous for our medic and for us. In the off chance someone had a rocket down there, we'd be sitting ducks hovering at that altitude. I thought we had a big enough area to land on the side of a terrace, and Craig, as usual, told me to do what I thought best. He had probably identified it right away and waited for me to come to the same conclusion. I managed it without incident.

Dan hopped out and went down the hillside. Talon stood at the top of the hill with his rifle ready to defend Dan if necessary. Several Afghan villagers were standing there with Talon. Two more were down the hill with the little boy and Dan. You never know which might be insurgents, so Talon is always on his guard. Dan radioed that the boy had a broken back. I could hear the poor boy scream in pain. That part of my job has become no easier. While Dan did what he could to comfort his patient, Talon ran down a stretcher. We were going to have to hoist him up, so Talon climbed the hill and got on board to ready the hoist while I lifted us into the air. My job at that point was to hold steady while Dan attached the litter to the hoist and Talon raised him up and into the chopper. Hovering over mountain crags has its own unique challenges, but after endless training and dozens of live extractions, I'm really good at it now. I don't mean to brag, but I want to reassure you I'm not in great peril here. We landed again to pick up Dan and returned to base.

I don't know what will become of the poor child. We rarely find out what's become of our patients, and it's probably better that way. Mental anguish is our biggest enemy here.

Sick humor by Dan this week. We were sent to pick up a bomb disposal expert who got blown up, but he died before we could get to him. The expert was renowned for bragging there was no bomb he couldn't defuse. Our lieutenant asked what happened and Dan answered, "He told the bomb he never met a bomb he couldn't defuse, and the bomb replied, 'BOOM!'"

Love, Sam

*

Bored as usual, Daniel sat next to Andrew on the porch for a meaningless conversation. "Prophet Andy," he opened, "I'm having a crisis of faith."

"Confess, my apostate."

"Well, I saw a movie last night with Rachel McAdams in it, and I think, maybe, she's prettier than the sacred Bush."

"Did you pray to this false goddess?"

"Last night. My pillow was her."

"Our first and only commandment, my Judas, is Thou shalt not two-time Sophia."

"I ask your forgiveness, Prophet."

"Say three Hail Sophias and give me all your pictures of McAdams."

"I don't know Hail Sophia."

"That's three more Hail Sophias."

Laughing, Daniel said, "But, the words?"

"Oh, uh, Hail Sophia, uh, you … thou art perfection; thou giveth me an erection. Amen. Oh, shit, the colonel. Look sharp." He reached around into the hooch and knocked on the open door to let the soldiers know something was up.

Andrew and Daniel stood and saluted. The colonel returned the salute and said, "Just a friendly visit to check on my medevac crews." He walked inside and said, "I want to first congratulate you all on our record; a 97.3% survival rate point of injury to the theater here if we reach a casualty alive. That's one of the best records in the army!" The women and men clapped. "And given the nature of the cases we typically deal with, as opposed to those namby-pamby ass bangers at Bagram, I'd argue we're number one." The assembled laughed and cheered. "Keep up the good work. Oh, and I wanted to crow about becoming a grandfather for the first time."

The soldiers clapped again and said, "Congratulations, sir."

"Isn't she beautiful?" said the proud grandfather, holding up a photo of what looked to be a hairless monkey. The soldiers decided to treat the query as rhetorical, but he pressed and asked again.

Samantha stepped in with, "Sir, she looks a lot like you." That masterful political stroke satisfied everyone.

Later, she remarked to Talon and Daniel how amazing it is how a bit of DNA in common can blind a person to such overwhelming homeliness. Then she went on wondering aloud how anyone can think for a minute that other people would care what your granddaughter looks like. "When I'm a grandmother, I'm not bothering anyone with pictures of my grandkids."

"Sure you will," put in Talon. "And you'll be telling your grandchildren how you met their grandfather."

"That's understandable. They're family." She turned to Daniel and joked, "I can just see you sitting with little Irma on your knee telling her you first saw her grandmother dancing at a club. You noticed how pretty she was when she threw her g-string at you."

As Daniel laughed, he thought he could tell his future granddaughter he knew he loved her grandmother when she told the one about meeting at the strip club.

Later that day, Talon walked into his room and asked his roommate, "Everything okay? Sam said you looked like you were in pain."

Daniel said, "Good. She didn't know."

"Didn't know what?"

"I'm a scientist, Chief. I like to run experiments, so today I tried one on myself. My hypothesis was that by merely staring into the most spellbinding eyes in the universe for a sufficient period I could, uh, cream my drawers."

"Uhg."

"That's the first time I've heard you use your native tongue. I'd been planning this for some time, but I had to wait till the perfect place and time; some privacy, a chance to look at her eyes for long enough before she saw me staring and yelled or crossed her eyes. Today I got it.

"I was on the porch alone reading medical crap, and she was just inside the hooch on the phone to her sister. She started laughing at whatever they were talking about, and I looked up. She was looking beyond me into the sunset, and her eyes were so magnificent half the blood in my body rushed to my nether region. So I held my book in front of my lap and did nothing other than gaze into her eyes and think of us together, and no more than forty-five seconds later I had confirmed my hypothesis. Trouble was, just as I, um, confirmed, she shifted her attention to me, probably something to do with my panting. Have you ever tried to pretend nothing was happening while you were in the midst of an intense climax, Chief? I imagine it's something like trying to act dignified with your hair on fire. Sam at first scowled at me for staring and panting, then looked confused as I tried to hide what was only then peaking. I was shaking and breathing hard, so I tried to steady my body and hold my breath, which was impossible, so the next pant came out through pursed lips as kind of a mouth fart. I was grimacing by this point. I can well imagine my face had that strained look like I was trying to push out a stubborn turd.

"She said, 'What's wrong? You're all red,' and I was concentrating so hard on trying to look normal that I forgot about the textbook I was holding, which, of course, fell onto my lap. Did you know that your sexual organs are particularly sensitive when in operation and that dropping a heavy book on them is unadvisable?"

Talon laughed.

"It hurt so much I jumped up, but then I realized she might see the evidence, so I immediately bent over and covered up. She asked, 'Are you sick?' I was so flustered I couldn't answer. I knelt down, picked up my book, placed it in front of my lap, stood up, and shuffled to the shower."

Still laughing, Talon said, "So I'll just explain to Sam what really happened?"

"Just leave out the part about all of it."

Samantha strolled up at that point and asked Talon, "Is he okay?"

"He's fine."

She jutted her head into the room and said, "I know what happened." Daniel and Talon looked at each other, Daniel's eyes communicating *Yikes!* Sticking out a hairy leg and lifting her arms to show off her hairy, sweaty armpits, Samantha proceeded, "You were so taken with my beauty, you were overcome and collapsed to your knees."

"Remarkably close," said Talon chortling.

*

"Medevac, medevac, second up," squawked Samantha's walkie-talkie hanging on the hook on her pants pocket. "Shit," said Samantha as she bounded out of the shower and quickly donned her clothes without drying herself. Still buttoning her shirt, with laces undone on her boots, pants unlatched, and hair dripping, she sprinted to her Black Hawk to prepare for takeoff.

"Bad one," noted Lieutenant Ng as he put on his gear and assumed the right seat in the cockpit and Specialist Beaton did likewise in the back. "Mass casualty evacuation. Looks like one KIA and four or five casualties in the Chowkay Valley. And the landing zone is hot."

Samantha lifted the Black Hawk into the air behind first-up medevac and two Apache escorts. After flying northeast for seventeen minutes, the four helicopters banked toward red smoke from a smoke grenade and black smoke from a fire. The gunships opened fire on muzzle flashes coming from both sides of the valley. "Looks unhealthy down there," noted Samantha. Craig nodded.

After the gunfire ceased, the first-up chopper circled in search of a landing spot, but found nothing promising. As the Black Hawk hovered at fifty feet, flight medic Sergeant Andrew Ward hooked himself to the hoist and swung out through the open door. Crew Chief Staff Sergeant Tom Kinman lowered him to the ground as Andrew kept the pilots apprised of his positioning. On the ground, Andrew unclipped himself from the line and ran to the stricken soldiers. Samantha cycled in after the first medevac helicopter moved out. Talon lowered Daniel on the winch. Daniel ran to help Andrew triage the wounded men while Samantha withdrew her aircraft to a safe distance.

*

One American soldier was dead. Daniel glanced and winced to see his hand yet holding a picture of a young child. Two more Americans were wounded, as was a Taliban insurgent. The Taliban man had the most serious wounds. Both his legs had been blown off, along with a chunk out of the left side of his torso. "Fuck me," Daniel said as he beheld the extent of injury to the man's body. "How the hell are you still alive?" Since he was at great risk of dying, the medics naturally focused on him first, until the American lieutenant demanded they see to the wounded Americans first.

The medics obeyed the officer and moved to help the Americans. One, the platoon's medic, had a bullet wound to his stomach. His armor had stopped the first three bullets, but not the fourth, and he was in considerable pain. The other had had a piece of his triceps blown off. With the medics working to stabilize their patients, the gunfire resumed. The medics moved their patients out of the line of fire while the Apaches went back to work, pumping thirty mm rounds into the hillsides. While Daniel worked on the stomach wound, Andrew finished bandaging the injured arm and went to pull the Taliban man out of the line of fire, but the American lieutenant howled, "No! If those fuckers want to shoot their own man, let them. I don't want you at risk pulling him behind cover."

"But, sir, he'll die if we don't help him right away," protested Andrew. Before the officer could reply, another American took a bullet to the thigh as the assault continued from the hillsides. Andrew dashed to him and got to work staunching the bleeding.

The Apaches managed to put a stop to the shooting. Daniel finished stabilizing his patient and ran out to check on the Taliban. Shaking his head, he gave the man morphine to ease his last few moments on earth.

Meanwhile, Andrew radioed for his chopper to cycle in to hoist up the most seriously wounded soldier. A few minutes later, Daniel looked up from his patient as he heard over his radio the lieutenant asking Andrew, "What about this man?" He was pointing to the soldier with the injured arm.

"Sir, he'll be fine," Andrew replied. "Every second counts for your other man; we need to get going. Our other chopper will take him." The officer nodded. "You get that, Dan?" asked Andrew.

"Got it," answered Daniel, watching Andrew being hoisted into his helicopter. As soon as Andrew swung into the chopper it departed for Jalalabad, along with the chase Apache.

Back on the ground, the shooting had recommenced, supplemented with RPGs, and an Afghan soldier took a large piece of shrapnel to the upper chest. Daniel asked an uninjured soldier to prepare the litter for packaging the soldier with the thigh wound. Then he sprinted through gunfire to the Afghan soldier who was gasping for air.

"Sweet Jesus!" said Daniel as bullets slammed into the ground inches from his feet. He pulled the wretched man behind a surviving wall of a demolished house. The man was suffocating. Coughing and choking on the dust and acrid smoke, Daniel applied an Asherman Chest Shield to the wound, then worked to restore fluids and reduce the pain. He wrote "Ringers, 20 mg morphine, 1351 hrs" on the man's chest in black Magic Marker. The soldier started to breathe again, though it was still a struggle, as the lung gradually re-inflated.

Daniel was inhaling hard to get enough oxygen at 7000 feet.

*

After thirty-five minutes of circling, Craig radioed down to Daniel that they were getting low on fuel and had to pick up his patients right away. Daniel told him that he had just finished strapping the casualties to Skedco extraction litters, and they were ready for pickup. As Samantha hovered the bird fifty feet above, Talon hoisted the wounded men up at top speed. The weather had deteriorated, making it difficult for Samantha to judge where the aircraft was in relation to the ground. "Keep it level with that outcropping there, Sam," suggested Craig.

After Talon pulled the second casualty in, Samantha, exhausted holding the craft in place, handed control over to her lieutenant.

Sporadic gunfire strafed the area. "Hurry the hell up, Chief!" urged Daniel as the third wounded soldier was on his way up.

Samantha looked down at Daniel and saw dust kick up where bullets were hitting the ground in his vicinity. In reaching up to grab the winch line, Daniel got walloped with a bullet in his armored chest plate, which laid him flat.

Talon screamed, "Dan's hit!"

At the same time, Samantha yelped, "Oh! Dan? Are you all right?"

"Ow, my Obliquus externus abdominis," Daniel said in a whiny voice while struggling to his feet. "Got me in the side of my stomach. Hurts like hell and hard to breathe, but I'll live."

The Apache loosed Hellfire missiles on the persistent Taliban, halting fire from the areas hit, but the shooting continued from elsewhere. Daniel attached himself to the line, and Talon began to wind him up. Craig handed control of the helicopter back to his co-pilot. But then the Black Hawk took machine gun fire. "Dushka," said the Apache pilot. The medevac crew heard the distinctive "thunk" of bullets hitting their ship. "I'm out of ammunition," continued the Apache pilot. "Get the hell out now."

"Sam, go now!" ordered Craig.

"But, Dan isn't—"

"Now! We're taking fire."

Samantha obeyed the command. Knowing Daniel was dangling below, she was careful to clear the canyon wall vertically before moving forward. As they climbed above the ridge and left the gunfire behind, Samantha radioed, "Dan? Are you still with us?"

"Hell, yeah!" he said. "This is great, and much safer than down there. Cold, though, and my stomach stings. Sam, I need a hug."

"Chief, hug Beaton when he gets in," said Samantha as she recovered her composure.

She glanced back as Daniel was pulled in by Talon. After rubbing his hands together and blowing into his fists, he provided treatment to his patients on the way back to JAF.

*

After they transferred the patients to the hospital, Talon and Daniel stood by watching as the fire department hosed the blood out of the helicopter.

They then went to Club Medic. Samantha walked out of the hooch and joined them.

"Good work out there today, Beaton," said she. He smiled. "Lucky you weren't hurt or killed."

"Sophia protected me."

"And how does she protect you?" Talon asked.

"I pray to her."

"How do you figure she hears you?" challenged Samantha.

"I just focus on her picture and revere her." He moved his fist up and down over his crotch. Samantha smirked. "That's our holy sign," he added. He'd just thought of that and made a mental note to tell Andrew. "And just like with your god, whenever things turn out swell, you credit it to her, and when they don't, you blame something else, like Satan. If that's proof enough God listens to prayers, it's proof enough Sophia does."

CHAPTER FOUR

Autumn 2008

Dripping wet and shivering, Specialist Beaton peeked around the corner to see if the coast was clear. Seeing no one, he dashed to the next building and again peeked around the corner. A pair of soldiers was strolling by, so he ducked back behind the wall until they passed. Another peep proved the way free of meddlesome eyes, so he darted to the next building. Jutting his head out, he looked at the wide expanse to the cover of the next structure. Seeing no one, he took a deep breath and sprinted.

When he passed the halfway point, twelve soldiers from his regiment stepped out from behind two bee-huts, laughing at the naked man and clapping. Daniel, whose clothes and towel had been pilfered as he showered, stopped, his hands cupping his privates to keep them that way. He gawked at his audience, Samantha among them, and wondered what his next move should be. Run away? No, too pathetic. Rage at them? No, not cool. Uncover himself and walk by as if he couldn't care less?

No, not with Samantha there and with the cool evening rendering him unimpressive. He decided to turn away from them and bow. A great cheer arose from the crowd. He turned, hands still covering up the bit of modesty he had left, and calmly sauntered to his room. "Nice butt, Beaton," said Samantha with a grin as he passed.

A smile invaded his red face. He got to his room and reached for his keys in his pock—"Oh, shit!"

His roommate rescued him, opening the door and frowning at the sight of him. "Forget your keys?" said Talon.

As Daniel pulled on his underwear, Samantha knocked and delivered his clothes. "I didn't take them," she was quick to claim to preclude any reprisal, "but I enjoyed your em*bareass*ment." He smirked and took his clothes.

*

"They've fired several RPGs already, and there's significant gunfire," said Lieutenant Ng as his medevac approached the landing zone where a convoy had been ambushed. Along for the ride this day was Flight Surgeon Captain Paul Telfer, because one of the casualties was a colonel, and another had a life-threatening chest wound. Samantha had already glanced back several times at the handsome man.

"In and out in ten seconds, Sam. Get ready, boys," said Craig. Apparently thinking twice about addressing a captain as boy, he added, "and sir."

With no time for niceties, Samantha took her aircraft down with a jolt and was revving up to take it back up when Paul, Talon, and Daniel jumped out. Unable to see through the dust, Talon stumbled over a rock, and Daniel went head over heels over him and Paul fell on top of Daniel. They cursed, got up, and rushed toward an upside-down Humvee in a ditch beside the dirt road.

By the time they ran the fifty meters, Samantha was at two hundred feet and climbing rapidly. The helicopter started dropping flares. Talon and Daniel looked up to see a missile rocketing toward their chopper. Samantha turned sharply to the left, and the missile shot past the helicopter and exploded in the distance. "Jesus, that was close," said Talon. Daniel nodded as his heart pounded.

There had been two casualties, but one had died before the medevac could reach him. Talon carried a body bag. The other casualty had a broken arm, which had Daniel shaking his head. "The only reason we're risking our lives for a broken arm is that the arm happens to be attached to a Christly colonel," he mentioned to Talon as they approached said colonel. Talon shrugged. The colonel already had his arm in a sling and had been given a shot of morphine. Paul checked him and confirmed there was nothing further to do until he could set the arm at the base. Talon radioed Craig and told him they were ready.

*

Craig decided that his greater experience was critical in this hazardous situation, and he took control for the landing. While they circled, another blast rocked the convoy, upending a second Humvee. Samantha screamed, "Shit! Chief? Beaton? Captain Telfer? Are you still with us?" An AC-130 gunship arrived overhead and commenced pounding enemy positions as Apaches and Kiowa Warriors blasted targets surrounding the convoy. Craig pulled his aircraft up as Samantha attempted to establish communication with her crewmates. "Dan? Talon? Please answer!" Samantha started trembling.

*

Neither man could hear Samantha's radio calls over the clamor on the ground. They scampered to the smoking vehicle and stood by as some marines pulled two injured comrades out. "Watch his neck!" said Paul, pointing to a man who was obviously in bad shape. He had a head injury, and his breathing was labored.

The marines put their colleague down carefully while Paul supported his neck with his hands. His jaw was blasted apart, and his tongue was hanging limp and clogging the airway. Daniel took out a safety pin to clip the man's tongue to his upper lip. "What the fuck are you doing?" said the colonel.

"Sir, one of the tricks of the trade to keep the airway open. He's out; he can't feel it."

The colonel maintained his scowl.

"You take care of him, Specialist," said Paul, gesticulating to the other injured marine. As Paul worked on the more serious case trying to plug the bleeding, the man stopped breathing. "Fuck!" said Paul, as he began chest compressions. Mouth-to-mouth resuscitation was out; the man had no more mouth. Paul removed his flight helmet, took out his noise-canceling earplug, put his ear to the marine's chest, cursed again, pounded his chest hard and resumed chest compressions. He turned to Talon and said, "We need the portable defibrillator. Where's our goddamn medevac?" The crew looked up but couldn't see their helicopter. "Take over here for a minute, Chief. This is exhausting work."

While Talon continued the compressions, frantically bellowing, "Come on, come on, kid. Come on back to us. Come on!" Paul radioed the chopper and asked where they were. The insurgents stopped shooting.

"Oh, thank God," said Samantha when she heard Paul. "Are the Chief and Dan all right?"

"Yeah. We need the paddles right away."

As Craig executed a tight spiral descent and approached the LZ in a steep trajectory, Paul stepped in to resume work on the patient. He put all his weight into his pushes right above the soldier's heart.

While Paul and Talon were working on the stricken marine, Daniel and the corpsman had been working on the other injured marine. There were no penetrating wounds, but he'd been cut and burned on his head and upper body and had been in significant pain. They had administered morphine, sterilized his cuts, and bandaged his head. Daniel looked in the marine's mouth and saw it was filled with blood. His eyes were also blackened.

By the time a marine arrived with the defibrillator, Paul shook his head. The young soldier's eyes had sunken in, his face was pale as snow, his temples hollow; the telltales signs of death were undeniable. Paul pounded the ground with his open hand and yelled, "Fuck!"

As he packaged the marine, Daniel said, "Corporal, can you see?" The man shook his head. Daniel turned to the corpsman and said, "Let's get him to the chopper right away."

With the crew and all casualties on board, Craig launched his ship and sped back to JAF. The colonel and two dead soldiers occupied three positions on the carousel. Paul and Daniel worked on the other soldier all the way back to base, suctioning the blood from his mouth, setting up a saline drip, administering pain killer, and cleaning out his eyes. By the time they landed, the marine reported that he could see light.

"Now that you have a sec, doc," said the colonel to Paul, "could you see your way to giving me a bit more morphine? This hurts like hell."

Paul looked at the colonel, whom he'd apparently forgotten. "Oh, shit, sir, I'm sorry."

"No need to apologize, doc. You were working your ass off to save my soldiers. I'm putting you in for a commendation."

Daniel gawked at the colonel. He'd done this job for seven months, saving hundreds of lives, and did as much this day as Paul, yet all he'd ever got was thanks from some of the soldiers he'd helped. But then he shook it off. The marine whose eyesight was returning was squeezing his hand in gratification, and that was worth a thousand commendations. Paul gave the colonel ten mg more of morphine.

From: Samantha Hawkins
Date: Sunday, November 2, 2008
To: Terry Hawkins
Subject: New Guy in Town
    I was surprised at your question about Beaton. Yes, he's cute and funny, and I

know I often write about the things he says, but I can't have a relationship with an enlisted man. He's my crewmate, that's all. But, there's this other guy who just got posted here, Captain Paul Telfer. I met him yesterday when he went on a mission with us. He's a flight surgeon, and he's smart, caring, funny, and so handsome. To me he looks something like a young George Clooney. He's great at his job. He's getting a commendation for his work on his very first medevac!

Paul looked at me with an inviting smile after we got back, and I almost jumped his bones. I wouldn't have a chance for a guy like him anywhere else, so I'll try for him here. I'll keep you posted.

Sick humor last week. An Afghan soldier got his middle finger shot off. Talon said, "Dude just lost half his sign language." In Bagram we saw a man on a stretcher being taken to our hospital in Germany. He was in a full body cast, and his head was wrapped in bandages; all we could see were his eyes. I said, "Off goes Tutankhamen to another exhibit." And Beaton said, "When he gets home, his wife is going to say, 'Wait. There's something different about you.'"

We were all laughing, which was unfortunate because some Fobbit captain was lurking. Beaton and Talon were taking their time moving an ANA soldier from our chopper to the ambulance, and the Fobbit screamed at them for their "lackadaisical attitude," and asked them what possible excuse they had for not helping this

patient "with the utmost expeditiousness."
Beaton answered, "Hurrying won't help,
sir. He's past his expiry date." The man
was dead when we brought him on board.
While the Fobbit bitched at him for
another five minutes for joking about a
soldier's death, Beaton stood there
smirking, making no attempt to disguise
his contempt. Insolent SOB. I swear, he
catches a case of Down's Syndrome every
time we visit Bagram.
Love, Sam

*

In the early fall, Daniel had started escorting Samantha to
the gym, where she jogged on a treadmill and lifted weights on
her days off. Daniel would go in to watch Samantha, until she
told him he wasn't welcome if all he was going to do was
goggle. So, he had to start using the equipment as well. While
he spotted for her, she teased him. "Okay, your turn, girly-
man. See if you can bench press a hundred pounds." That was
what she was bench-pressing.

"I can easily do double that," he boasted.

"No way. What are you? A hundred and sixty-five pounds?"

"Thereabouts."

"And you're trying to tell me you can bench-press two
hundred?" He nodded. "Do it." He added a hundred pounds.
"Maybe I should get another spotter."

"Relax," he said as he lay underneath the bar, put his hands
on it, and easily pushed his arms straight up.

Her eyebrows rose. He sat up, added another thirty pounds, but she said, "Don't push it." Not answering, he lay back down and positioned himself underneath the bar. "Andy," said Samantha, "help me spot for Dan, please." Andrew came over to watch Daniel struggle to raise the two-hundred-thirty pounds, but he did it. "You don't even lift weights. How can you be this strong?" said Samantha.

"Genes. Came from my maternal grandfather apparently. My mother bragged he once picked up a big man and threw him over the fence when he insulted his wife. If anyone insults you, Sam, I'll do the same for you."

"Then you better throw yourself over the fence. No one besides you ever insults me."

"Just playful banter," he said as Samantha went over to a treadmill and began running. Daniel and Andrew joined her.

"My prophet, I have a question related to our faith," said Daniel, trotting in place.

"Shoot, my disciple," returned Andrew, keeping pace.

"All gods grow old, except gods that don't exist, which is all of them except Sophia. When Sophia grows old, do we get to ditch her for a goddess who still has her beauty?"

"Good question, heathen. It is written that—"

"It is written?" interrupted Daniel. "Do we have a holy book?"

"It's on my to do list. I've heard this young lady here is a good writer. Perhaps she would pen our holy book."

"I already have the opening verse," said Samantha. "In the beginning, two losers who had no prayer for a real woman resorted to humiliating themselves in front of doctored pictures of a little-known actress. It may have been original at first, though nowhere near as clever as they thought, but they have beaten a dead horse, and parts of their own anatomy, ad nauseam."

"Excellent opening. Bring me a first draft next week," responded Andrew.

"Welcome to the fold, Samantha," said Daniel. "Unlike all the other religions, ours is not a patriarchy; we acknowledge that women are equal to men in every way that matters, except in beauty, where they're much superior. You may show your devotion to Sophia whenever you please. All we ask is that you let us watch."

"Okay, but I show my devotion by skinning alive a sexual deviant."

"Oh, you're looking for Catholicism, then. They have a bunch of priests sorely needing your devotion." Addressing Andrew, Daniel repeated his original question.

Andrew replied, "Any goddess who earns her worshippers through her beauty must expect to lose said worshippers when she becomes a dried out old hag. Then we transfer our allegiance to a fresh new goddess with big tits." Turning back to Samantha, he said, "Did you get that, scribe?"

Samantha frowned and continued her running.

*

With December's arrival, Craig, Samantha, and Talon began their tenth month in the Afghan war. The army was anxious about replacing helicopter crews at JAF because in the previous two rotations, new crews flew into mountains on a weekly basis during the first couple of months. Also, the military was adding troops to the war effort and more medevac crews would be needed. The army was pondering ordering the current crews to stay another year at JAF, but decided first to ask the medevac and Apache crews whether they would consider staying for another year, adding a financial incentive of a thousand dollars a month each, with one exception: Specialist Beaton's contract assumed he would be posted in Afghanistan or Iraq and was generous enough already, concluded some Fobbit. All but one Apache crew and one flight medic said yes. Despite the danger, they knew the good they were doing here and knew nothing else they could do in the army would be as meaningful.

Talon had to break the news to his wife, who had apparently been counting the days until he was to leave Afghanistan. He opened with the news he was to be promoted to staff sergeant, which his wife received warmly, but the phone call went downhill from there. He lowered the phone and asked Samantha for help. "The wife is pissed, and I'm trying to calm her down. What should I say to her?"

"God, Chief, I don't know. I guess reassure her you love her."

He said into the phone, "I love you. I did this so our future together will be brighter."

"Together!" his wife said with such volume that Samantha and Daniel heard her through Talon's head. They both snickered. Talon moved the phone away from his ringing ear, then resumed the discussion.

A minute later, Talon again lowered the phone and said to Samantha, "She asked, 'Do you know what I gave up when I married you?' What should I say?"

"Besides sex?" joked Samantha. Daniel laughed, and Talon followed her suggestion, with Samantha saying, "No, Chief, I was only joking."

Talon next said, "She hung up." Daniel hooted at that as Samantha apologized and advised him to let her cool down and try again in a little while.

"You should be a couples counselor, Sam," teased Daniel.

Talon decided to stay the matter until Christmas leave, which was coming up in three and a half weeks.

From: Samantha Hawkins
Date: Monday, December 8, 2008
To: Terry Hawkins
Subject: Bitch

Just a quick note before I leave on another training mission. Apparently I have some serious competition for Paul. When I dropped by the little hospital on base hoping to see him, I saw this pretty nurse with boobs about twice the size of mine practically slavering over him. She's a lieutenant and a nurse, which gives her two advantages over me (four if you count her tits). She works in the same building, which I seldom have a good reason to visit, and she's an officer, not just a warrant officer. Paul saw me, smiled, and said hi, and the look she gave me could have sunk a thousand ships. She leaned against him, pressing her boobs right into him, to tell him something and wiggled away. The way she touched him, I swear they're doing it already, and she can't have known him for much longer than a month. Floozy. I talked with Paul for a

```
few minutes and disappeared, which wasn't
hard since I felt invisible anyway after
seeing that bitch. I won't give up on him
yet. I'll try to find a way to spend more
time with him, but it doesn't look good.
Shit.
Love, Sam
```

*

Eight days before Christmas, Daniel joined Samantha and Talon for dinner. She had just tasted the meatloaf and dropped her fork in disgust. As a private contractor who worked in the kitchen strolled by, she said, "Tell the cook, next time don't bother. I'll just shit on my own plate." The contractor nodded vacantly.

Daniel chortled at her remark. She smiled back. He'd noticed she was making an effort to be more feminine, growing her hair and wearing nicer clothes when they weren't on duty. He was hopeful she was finally coming around.

"I need to get going on fixing my helicopter that you fucked up," Talon said to Samantha as he got up. The Black Hawk had stopped several bullets that morning.

Turning to Daniel, Samantha hesitated, but eventually remarked, "I have a hard time showing my feelings." His laughter betrayed his absolute rejection of the notion.

"I *mean,*" she explained, "when I have, you know, feelings for someone."

Intriguing news this. "Who is the poor bugger?" he jested.

"Someone you know. He's smart and funny and good-looking. He's got a great future. And he saves so many lives, he makes such a wonderful difference here. I admire him so much, but he hasn't got a clue that I really like him."

Daniel blushed and smiled. He suggested, "Just come out with it. Let him know you're attracted to him. I'm sure he'll be thrilled."

"It's dicey. Different ranks in the army and all."

"I can keep our secret."

"So I can count on you?"

Beaming at her, he said, "Of course."

He was leaning over to take her hand under the table when she said, "How are you going to get me together with him?"

Confusion. There was some sort of misunderstanding afoot. "Him?"

"Captain Telfer. I think he's gorgeous."

"Oh."

"What's the matter?"

"Uh, just a sneeze coming," he lied; he turned around and deposited a faux sneeze into his hands. Recovering slightly, he turned back to her and posted a hollow smile.

"So, how are you going to get us together?"

Daniel replied with a slight tremor, "Uh, I can invite him to play poker," as he got to his feet and grabbed his tray.

"Great idea. Tonight?"

He nodded and shuffled away. He desperately wanted to extirpate her from his heart, but he couldn't. *When, Sophia? When will you be through toying with me?*

Daniel asked Craig to invite Paul to their game, "officer to officer," as he put it. Craig asked why and saw Daniel's face grow longer in explanation. Commiserating, he said okay, but warned, "I can see you're falling for her, Dan. She's not permitted to date an enlisted man. If she did, it could well end her career."

"Can a warrant officer date an officer?"

"Warrant officers are considered officers where fraternization rules go, and dating between officers isn't strictly speaking forbidden, unless it compromises the chain of command or can adversely affect discipline or morale. I'll keep my eye on the situation."

Paul agreed to come that night for a game of Texas Hold'em. He and Craig's crew sat around the plastic table in the hooch. Daniel was there even though he hated playing cards and had never joined them before. Paul, Craig, and Talon were smoking cigars. Samantha skipped the cigar, worried about what Paul might think, Daniel surmised. Chips were disbursed and a card dealt to each player to select the first dealer. Talon got the high card. "Okay, Craig, small blind," said Talon while shuffling the cards.

Daniel furrowed his forehead, wondering what the hell a small blind was. To him, poker was handing out five cards, dropping the worst ones and getting replacements. Craig threw in a ten-cent chip. "Big time players, we are," joked Daniel, having no idea what the chip implied. Daniel was next in line and put in two twenty-five-cent chips.

"What are you doing?" said Samantha.

"Even on my salary, I can afford fifty cents," he answered.

"Don't tell me you haven't played Texas Hold'em before," said Paul.

"Okay."

"You have to place the big blind, which is usually around double the small blind," said Paul, shaking his head.

"Of course!" Daniel said, withdrawing the chips and replacing them with two ten-cent chips.

Craig explained, "The blinds dictate the stakes of the game. We buy in for a hundred times the size of the big blind."

"So the stakes are twenty bucks?" asked Daniel.

"To start with."

Daniel's expression turned to "Shit." He couldn't afford this.

Talon dealt two cards to each player. Daniel looked at him, wondering where the other three were. Paul, sitting next to Daniel, looked at his cards and threw in two ten-cent chips. "Paul raises," said Talon. Samantha did the same. "Sam calls," said Talon. Craig threw his cards in. "Craig folds." Daniel had no idea what a four of spades and queen of diamonds meant, but if he dropped out now, he'd probably drop out all night. "Dan calls." Talon then dealt the top card in the deck face-down on the table and put three cards face-up. "Seven, six, king on the flop. Okay, Dan?" said Talon.

"Okay what?"

"You start the post-flop betting round. You can check or bet."

"Uh, check," Daniel said, hoping that meant he didn't have to put in more money. Paul bet, and Samantha called. Daniel then had to call to stay in.

Talon then dealt one card face-down followed by a single card face-up and said, "Queen on the turn. Dan?"

Daniel stood, took out his wallet, tossed it on the table, and said, "Fuck it, just take my money."

Paul took eighty dollars out of Daniel's wallet and tossed it back to him. Daniel withdrew to sit behind the table and watch the proceedings. He fixed his eyes on Samantha, who had fixed her eyes on Paul.

Paul kept the table entertained with a series of one-liners that had everyone guffawing, especially Samantha. As much as Daniel hated to admit it, Paul was funny, and even though he was in no mood to laugh, he had to a few times. This man was superior to him, he had to admit. But then Daniel recognized one of his jokes. It was a Jimmy Carr one-liner. Daniel had battled boredom in country by spending a lot of time on the Internet. Watching standup comedy clips was one of his favorite pastimes.

With the warm reception he'd gotten to the plagiarized one-liner, Paul proceeded to steal more Carr: "I'm Catholic. The thing that annoys me about church is all the standing up and sitting down and kneeling. I wish the priest could just pick a position and fuck me." This had Samantha crying with glee. Paul went on to thieve from other comedians.

Daniel guessed Paul was born with everything but a sense of humor, so he borrowed one whenever he wanted to seduce a woman. He admired the chutzpah and the way Paul worked the purloined jokes into the conversation so naturally that they seemed to be his own, but he hated the deception because Samantha was his object. He decided to burst his bubble.

"Now do the dead parrot routine," he suggested. Paul shot him a glare that conveyed such wrath and scorn, Daniel thought he must have stolen it off Satan; the one the evil one used when he first saw the Care Bears.

Samantha saw the scowl and said to Paul, "You won't notice him after a while. He fades into the background like a chirping cricket."

After the game, Samantha took eighty dollars from her winnings and offered it to Daniel. He thanked her, but refused it. "Wasn't Paul great?" she asked.

Daniel couldn't believe she asked him this question. *She really has no idea what I feel for her*, he mused. He answered, "He has a simian flair for pitching shit."

"What?"

"Never mind."

"Didn't you find him hilarious?"

"The only time I laughed all night was when he said he hated to brag."

"Come on, Beaton. I saw you laughing. He's funnier than you."

"That's because he has all the best comedians writing for him."

"What's that supposed to mean?"

"Let me show you." Opening the Internet, he went to YouTube and found a Jimmy Carr routine. Samantha sat and watched the hilarious video. Four of the jokes Paul told were on that video. Samantha sat there cogitating for a minute, then turned to Daniel and said, "Is that ever sweet of him?"

"What?" he said, which was short for "What the hell?"

"It's obvious he was trying to impress me."

"His sneaky theft of someone else's jokes is impressive?"

"No, his need to resort to this to impress me is impressive. It's not much different from your claim that you're six feet."

Daniel was five-ten and three quarters, which he naturally rounded up to five-eleven, and since any man who's five-eleven rounds his height up to six feet, he reasoned, he might as well claim to be six feet. He responded, "It's much different. I rounded up a bit; he pinched his entire comedy routine to make it seem like he's something he's not. He's obviously not funny."

"Everyone laughed at him all night. Uh!" she warned to preclude his next objection. "Someone else wrote his material, which is probably the case for a lot of comedians, and he did a great job delivering it."

"He even stole the deadpan delivery!"

"Don't be jealous, Beaton."

"I'm not," he lied.

"Uh-huh," she said as she left for bed.

Although Samantha didn't appear to consider Paul's behavior untoward, Daniel felt it marked Paul as a phony. Misrepresenting one's self was a major character flaw in his opinion. Daniel hoped this would prove to be Paul's undoing with Samantha. It gave him hope.

*

The next morning in the hooch, Samantha was writing to her sister again, about Paul. Daniel stood behind her until she shooed him away. From across the small room he helped her with a suggestion: "Last night I hit it off with flight surgeon and anal sex enthusiast, Captain Paul Telfer."

"Take your tedium elsewhere, yokel."

She continued to write, so he continued, "Handsome, smart, funny, likable; these were some of the many attractive qualities he lacked."

That unleashed a chuckle before she could constrain it, which was unfortunate for her because it gave him the incentive to plow forward with more unwelcome comments.

"His rheumy eyes were pretty, but they were a little too much to either side of his head. I don't care much for him, but I imagine lady pickerels are always throwing themselves at him."

"Go out and collect dust, Beaton."

"What's in it for me?"

"I don't give you a concussion."

She resumed writing, so he resumed, "Some might call him ugly, but that would only be because they were fond of the truth."

She turned to address him. "Everything you've said about him is precisely what I think about you. And you are definitely not Paul."

"True, I'm not Paul, but that's not a fair criticism. I'm not Bill or Ron either. I'm not a lot of people. And Paul isn't as many people as I'm not."

"You know what bothers me most about you? You're breathing."

"What bothers me most about you is that every day I discover something new that bothers me most about you." She continued to write, so he went on, "Rumors abound over his affinity for livestock."

"I'm not getting through your thick skull," she said as she turned and hurled her empty coffee cup at him. His inclination to duck struck him right after the cup. He fell to the floor. "Oh, shit! I'm really sorry, Dan," said his assailant; she came to his side and knelt. "Are you all right?"

"I guess you were serious about that concussion business," he answered as he rubbed his head. Looking at his hand and seeing blood, he added, "You got through my skull, all right."

"Here, sit up. Are you dizzy at all?" He got to his feet and swayed. "Careful," Samantha cautioned while holding his elbow. He yanked his arm away from hers. "You're bleeding a little. Maybe you should see a doctor," she suggested. Saying nothing, he walked out. "I'm really sorry," she repeated.

From: Samantha Hawkins
Date: Thursday, December 18, 2008
To: Terry Hawkins
Subject: Paul

Yesterday I played cards with Paul. He's so handsome I couldn't keep my eyes off of him, and he caught me staring a few times. He simply smiled. And he was so funny, my sides were aching. Afterward, we talked alone. I actually got up the nerve to ask if he's seeing anyone, and he said "kind of," but that she'd be rotating out of here at the end of February! So Nurse Sweetland has a little over two months to hook him, and if not he's …

I just threw my coffee cup at Beaton. It bounced off his head and knocked him to the floor. Neither of us moved for a second; we were both too shocked. Then I knelt down to help him up and to apologize. He was bleeding from his forehead. He said something, I don't remember what, and left. Another man might have hit me or laid assault charges, but he seems to have just let it go. He was bugging hell out of me over Paul and wouldn't let up. Why do I let him get to me like that? I just don't know how to relate to him.

It's been a problem since day one with him. Before he even introduced himself he stood there drooling over me. To say the least, it was inappropriate for him to act like that with a superior. So I put him in his place. Trouble was, he liked how I dealt with him, so he continued his inappropriate behavior. Every time I put him in his place, he laughs and considers it an invitation for a kind of verbal jousting. I try ignoring him, but then he says something funny, and I laugh, which gears him up for more.

I think the main problem now is he really likes me. At first I thought it was just because I'm a woman, and he wanted what every man wants, but now I know that it goes deeper for him. He admires me. I know he wants to take it further, but that is out of the question. A warrant officer is strictly forbidden to have a romantic relationship with an enlisted man. Now with my interest in Paul, Beaton's continual hints that he wants me have become more than inappropriate; they're aggravating. Out of jealousy he's started badmouthing Paul. That's what he was doing today, and he wouldn't let up even after I told him again and again to stop. Despite his obvious regard for me, he still doesn't respect me enough to listen when I tell him to stop.

So, how do I deal with this man? I could make it an order to leave me alone, but it

```
isn't that simple, even in the army. Crews
go   through   so   much   together   they   get
really   close,   so   it's   hard   to   pull   rank.
It's   not   easy   to   act   the   part   of   superior
with   a   guy   who   is   older   than   I   am,   who's
smarter,   and   who   will   be   a   doctor   two
years   from   now.   And   I   still   enjoy   his
company.   He   keeps   us   all   laughing,   and
that   is   so   important   in   this   place.
Whatever   I   do,   I'll   have   to   come   up   with
something better than coffee cups.
Love, Sam
```

When Daniel got to his room, Talon looked up from his computer and said, "What the hell happened to you?"

"She was distant with me."

"Sam?" He nodded. "Temperamental, isn't she? What did she do?"

"Threw her coffee cup at me."

"She cracked you with a cup?" He laughed.

"Glad it entertains you, but I'd have sooner missed it myself."

"Did you deserve it?"

"Debatable, but only one woman out of a thousand would have done it. Damn minx."

"What did you do?"

"I collapsed and bled. I was quite pathetic. Chief, I know you'll be brutally straight with me. Is Sam out of my league?"

"I don't think so, and I don't think she does either, but she can't date you anyway."

"I know. Warrant officers can't date enlisted men."

"You got it. What are you worried about? Once you get back to civilian life and finish your degree, the women will be throwing themselves at you, not cups."

CHAPTER FIVE

The Holidays – 2008

"Medevac, medevac, medevac. First up," crackled the radio hanging on Talon's pants pocket over a chair in his room. Getting up to pull on his clothes, he looked at his watch. 11:52 PM, Dec 22.

"Come on, Dan, hurry, the call is urgent," said Talon.

"Let me sleep until it's grave."

"Now, Dan. Move it."

Daniel rolled out of bed and protested, "We got back not twenty minutes ago. What'd we get, five minutes' sleep? People should be more considerate about when they get blown up." He quickly dressed and dashed to operations while Talon trotted to their helicopter.

Craig and Daniel boarded the Black Hawk. Craig told his co-pilot, "Platoon ambushed on their way back to base. At least three urgent casualties, so second up is going with us. There's still enemy activity, so we have two Apaches to escort us. We only have rough grid coordinates, but we know it's a high, rocky ridgeline, so we'll be doing hoist recoveries. Hold here for a minute to let one of the Apaches get a head start and check the area out before we go in."

Samantha nodded as the Apache left and headed north. A minute later, she pulled her night vision goggles on, lifted her aircraft into the air, and flew northeast.

The soldiers on the ground directed the helicopters to a narrow trail at the base of one steep ridgeline and topping another steep declivity. Craig said, "This is good, Sam. Hold it here. Talon, ready the hoist. Dan, get down there and assess what we've got, and put together a recovery plan."

With Daniel on the ground, Samantha took the helicopter away from the danger area to circle with second up. The Apaches circled above them.

A few minutes later, Daniel reported, "Sir, there's zero illumination down here, so it's hard to do a proper assessment, even with the goggles and infrared searchlight. So far, we have one KIA and four wounded down here, but there are two others missing. One of the wounded is approximately seventy-five feet down a steep hill; I can't get to him. We'll have to use the hoist. He's alert enough to swing his chemlight. The other three are with me. Two were stabilized by the medic, but the other is in shock and in bad shape with head, arm, and leg wounds. Poor bugger got his arteries smacked on his left arm and left leg. We have tourniquets on both, but he's lost too much blood and I can't find a vein for the IV, and he's still bleeding from his head. You need to get Andy down here with the EZ IO and saline now, or this man will be dead within ten minutes."

"Copy that," responded CW3 Jim Herrera, the pilot in charge of second up medevac. The co-pilot hovered his ship over the stricken men while Daniel packed the leg wound with Kerlix. Daniel told Craig, "We'll need to get this man out of here the minute we stabilize him. What? Just a minute … Sir, the platoon sergeant just located another of his men on the hill. He's about twenty-five feet down and won't respond to our calls. Looks in bad shape. I think I can get to him, but we still have to stabilize and package my first patient here."

Andrew arrived with the intraosseus drill, saline, and supplies, and proceeded to assist Daniel with the gravely injured man. His helicopter left the potential line of fire. While Andrew went to work on the head wound, Daniel cleaned off the skin just below his patient's right knee, then drilled through the bone with the EZ IO. He then pulled off the sheath, thereby establishing a direct line to the bone marrow. He started the IV flowing.

"Sir," a private said to his lieutenant. He was standing next to a bloody piece of flesh that looked like part of a shoulder. "RPG blew Saunders to hell. Fuck."

As senior medical officer at the scene, Andrew was in charge. When they got the patient stabilized, he suggested, "Dan, while I package him, see if you can get to the man down there and check him."

At this point, a fireball lit up the ridgeline above the troops, followed immediately by a deafening roar. Rocks and dust came cascading down the hill. "Cover them!" said Andrew to the medic and another GI attending the wounded as he knelt over his patient. "Appreciate the cover, Gunmetal, but remember gravity," said Andrew while checking his patients in the wake of the mini avalanche.

"Sorry," said the pilot. "Two enemy were approaching."

Daniel descended the precipice as carefully as he could with night vision goggles and rucksack, but that didn't stop his slipping down several feet and scraping his legs and buttocks. "Shit!" he hollered.

"What happened, Dan?" asked Craig.

"I just left half my arse deposited on the side of this Sophia-forsaken mountain; unpleasant sensation."

Andrew's chopper cycled in once more to pick up the critically injured soldier.

Meanwhile, Daniel got to the injured man and reported, "He's alive, but unresponsive. Fragment shattered his hip bone, and it looks like he smashed his head hard in falling down here. Also some burns on his face. I can't possibly work on him on this grade, but I think we can move him without further damage."

"Does he need to get back to base right away, Dan?" asked Craig.

"I'd say so, yes."

"So, our situation is we have two critically injured soldiers that we need to immediately get back to the hospital; we have three other wounded soldiers, one of whom is fifty feet below Dan on the mountain; and we're still missing a soldier. Do I have that right?"

"We just found a piece of our last soldier," said Lieutenant Moss, who was in charge of the beleaguered platoon on the ground. "Two KIAs. No one is missing."

"Sorry to hear that," replied Craig. "Just to make this more interesting, fuel is becoming an issue now. We have to be on our way within fifteen minutes. Okay, Dan, Sam will come in and take you and your patient to level ground. In the interest of fuel, we'll do this while Jimbo picks up the other critical case. Jimbo, if your crew can then pick up the casualty with Dan now and leave for home, we'll get Dan down to the other soldier to see what's what, then we'll have some decisions to make."

As the second up ship hoisted Andrew's patient, Samantha maneuvered her aircraft above Daniel's position to hoist him and his patient to the flat ground above. The two aircraft were hovering so close together, Samantha had to deal with rotor downwash from the higher ship. But she managed it well and got Daniel and his patient to flat ground. Andrew hurried over to take over that case while Daniel was lowered to the other soldier seventy-five feet down the rocky hill.

While second up medevac collected its patient and medic and returned to base with its chase Apache, the first up aircraft circled, waiting for a report from their medic. It wasn't good. "Sir, he took a fragment to the foot. I'm working on that, but the bigger problem is I'm pretty sure his neck is at least cracked. And his right arm is broken. We definitely can't move him until I carefully secure his neck or we might paralyze him."

"Shit," returned Craig. "I'm afraid we're going to need to go to our FARP."

"Your what?"

"Forward aiming and refuelling point. That'll take us a good twenty minutes. Will your patient be okay, Dan?"

"I'm worried about shock, but I can use the heating chemicals from an MRE to keep him warm and, with luck, prevent shock."

Craig informed Lieutenant Moss that he would be back for the other injured soldiers in twenty minutes, but when the remaining Apache informed him he, too, had to leave for refuelling, the lieutenant asserted, "No! You're not leaving me and my men exposed on this shitty trail without cover. If we stay here, we're dead, but we can't leave with two of my men unable to walk."

"What do you suggest?" said Craig.

"I suggest you winch my wounded men into your bird and get them the hell out of here."

Craig looked at the fuel gauge and said, "We have a window of five minutes to get them up. Sam, bring us in quick. Dan, can they be picked up without packaging?"

"Should be okay. Chief, check their bandages when you get them inside. If they're soaked through with blood, let me know."

"No problem."

"Uh, sir," said Daniel as he pulled a neck brace from his rucksack, "your plan has but one flaw. You're leaving me behind on the side of a mountain in the most dangerous valley on earth. I don't like to complain, but it's cold, uncomfortable, dark, and scary, and I'm tired and my arse hurts, but how can I sleep when the neighbors are making noise with A.K.s and RPGs?"

"Hold tight, Dan. Stay in the dark; they can't see you. We'll be back ASAP."

As his helicopter approached the trail, Daniel noticed a flash in the distance. He watched in horror from below as an RPG closed in on the ship, holding his breath while the helicopter practically inverted as it pitched over, then rolled back. The RPG barely missed the copter and exploded on a rocky outcrop below them.

"I swear it missed you guys by a cunt hair," said Daniel. "Great flying, Sam."

Over the radio, Daniel heard Craig say, "Christ, Sam, that was quick. We owe you our lives on that one."

While the Apache disintegrated the area from which the RPG was launched, Samantha returned to the mountain trail and hovered over it for four and a half minutes while Talon winched the injured soldiers on board. Then she left for the FARP, leaving Daniel and the last injured man waiting for rescue. The rest of the platoon headed toward its base, trusting the medevac crew to protect its man on the hill.

About twelve minutes after his helicopter departed, Daniel looked up from his patient when he heard something. On the trail above he saw two men. He instinctively lowered himself, but realized they couldn't see him without NVGs. Another two men joined the first two. They were looking down the slope. They must know the helicopter left him here, concluded Daniel. He saw one man point an RPG down and held his breath, but another of the insurgents pushed the weapon down. Too valuable to waste unless they know where the enemy is, thought Daniel. He glanced at his watch and figured they had at least another eight minutes before the Apache and Black Hawk would return. One enemy soldier pointed a flashlight down the hill. Its beam was weak, but if it happened to point directly at him or his patient, they were dead.

Daniel's patient complained of chest pain. "Shh!" Daniel whispered. "Taliban up there." His patient's pulse was rapid but weak, his skin clammy, his breathing shallow. His patient was now in the early stages of shock. *Not satisfied that things aren't as bad as they can get yet, Sophia?* Daniel mused as he took off his coat and put it over the soldier. He shivered; the temperature was around freezing, and snow flurries commenced. "I need to get your legs elevated," he told the soldier. Daniel supported the man's neck as best he could while turning him so his head was down slope and his legs up slope. "This should help restore your blood pressure," Daniel explained.

In moving the injured man, Daniel kicked a couple of rocks, and they noisily bounced down the hill. He looked up and saw that the noise had caught the attention of the enemy. The insurgents pointed the flashlight in their direction and began shooting down the hill. "Fuck!" Daniel whispered; he covered his patient. Bullets hit just below where they were lying. Daniel picked up a rock and threw it about thirty feet to his left, but the enemy didn't hear it over their guns. One of the bullets hit close enough to kick debris up into his patient's left eye, and he cried out. Daniel covered his mouth, but he feared this had doomed them. The bullets got closer.

The flashlight stopped on him. Daniel's heart raced. He saw the Taliban point the RPG. But then the Taliban disappeared in a bright flash, which was followed directly by the roar of an explosion. Covering his patient again to protect him from some sliding rocks, he heard the Apache whirl above. Over his radio he heard Craig saying, "Dan, please tell me you're still with us."

"It's about damn time," he answered as he worked to clear his patient's eye of dirt. Samantha brought in the Black Hawk and hovered over them as Talon lowered a litter. Daniel secured the hapless soldier, and Talon winched him into the Black Hawk. Daniel, by this time nearly frozen, followed and continued work on his patient until they landed and handed him off to the hospital.

Daniel stood in a hot shower for twenty minutes to shake the shivers.

*

The crew had to work on Christmas Day, but was given nine days leave starting the next day. The medevac and Apache crews drew names for Christmas gifts and had a small party with alcohol-free beer.

Craig went home to his wife and daughter in Atlanta. Samantha found a half price Mediterranean cruise and invited Terry. Daniel invited himself along, but Samantha uninvited him. She felt guilty about it, but knew he would perceive going on a cruise with her as the ultimate green light to his driving ambitions for her. Impossible! He had a nerve even attempting to woo her. Was he trying to ruin her career?

*

Talon, apparently feeling bad because Daniel had no one to see and nowhere to go, invited him to his home for Christmas, but Daniel didn't want to bother them because Talon got so little time with his wife, who was already displeased with her husband. They agreed to meet for the last weekend in Athens for drunken revelry. With so little money to spare, Daniel had no choice but to stay at JAF for the first few days before flying to Athens on Thursday.

On Saturday afternoon he met Talon, and they started drinking. They drank for eleven hours, ending up at a strip bar. Daniel went to the back room with a pretty blonde. Talon went for a buxom brunette.

Daniel emerged with a smile on his face, over a year of sexual frustration taken out on and under the blonde. "Holy Sophia, Chief, she was wild. Too bad I'm too liquored up to remember tomorrow."

"Even if you were sober, I don't think you'd remember tomorrow," responded Talon.

"How was your babe? I bet you had to gather up her huge ass with both arms spread. And I imagine her frontage is just as roomy. Must've been like fucking a garage."

"Didn't bone her."

"Y'know, I don't expect much from my prostitute. She doesn't have to cook or clean; no need to shop; no rearing my bastardly little kids. But she does have to fuck, or at the very least get fucked. If she doesn't, she's a disgrace to her profession."

"I'm married, dude, and I'm not cheating on my wife. So, I just played with her mammoth mammaries for a while."

"Pretty sure a wife would frown on that, too."

Their tenure at the strip club closed when Daniel grimaced, then casually asked Talon, "Chief, is a fart supposed to have bubbles?" Talon's plastered mind must have construed this into the most hilarious whiff of scatology mankind had ever expressed, for it directed him to elicit a colossal guffaw, which kindled a thunderous belch, which his stomach used as the opening it required to rid itself of the poisons it had harbored for too long just as a bouncer arrived to deal with the commotion. Evidently disenchanted over the new coating on his expensive shoes, the bouncer summoned his cohorts and the two souses were regurgitated from the establishment. Under the starry Athenian sky, the bouncer cleaned his shoes on the two prone drunks with an assertive kicking motion.

They tottered back to Daniel's hotel room where they continued drinking, but were ejected from there at 6:50 in the morning and more or less at random got on the bus to the airport, where their flight was scheduled to depart at nine AM.

When the flight was called, both were snoring loudly on uncomfortable chairs, and they would have missed it had airport authorities not been anxious to get rid of the pair who were reeking of Talon's stomach.

On the plane, Talon once more had a laughing spell that ended with another loud burp, which was dry this time, but not terribly fragrant. They were seated in the emergency exit aisle, Talon next to the window and Daniel beside him. The steward asked them if they knew what to do in an emergency, and Daniel answered, "Well, I can't imagine that if we slam into the ground at 500 miles an hour I'll have to worry about it. At best the recovery squad would find my shitty arse still safely belted in my chair, and maybe my left ear floating on an oily puddle a mile away. But if by some miracle I survive, I'll be out of here so frigging fast all my buddy here will see is the bottom of my shoes as I scurry over him in my panic to get the fuck out." That earned Daniel a rebuke for foul language and Talon one for disturbing the other passengers as he howled and belched. Later, as the two snoozed, the steward sprayed them with Glade. Daniel opened his eyes, coughed, and went back to sleep.

The soldiers found themselves back at JAF late that afternoon and had no idea how they got there. Talon went straight to bed, but Daniel went to defac to try to get something in his stomach besides vomit. Samantha showed up while he was walking back to his room to sleep for a decade or so. She asked him, "Hey, how was—"

"Not so loud! And tell those moths to keep it down. A million tiny woodpeckers are hammering at my brain stem."

"How was Greece?" she whispered.

"Can't tell you much. I remember some big guy seemed to take issue with being puked on. And I remember a blonde ... uh, mind if I throw up?" He turned away, bent over and vomited.

"A blonde?" she said when he stood back up.

"A blonde?" he said, wiping his mouth on his sleeve.

"You were with a blonde?"

"How did you know?"

"Never mind. Where's the Chief?"

"He's in bed hung over. Do you wish to view the remains?"

"I'll see you guys tomorrow."

*

With the new year and some crew rotations, Samantha got a new roommate. Chief Warrant Officer 2 Susan Humphrey was five-foot-ten and built like a tank. She wore an ugly face, featuring drab eyes, a pug nose, and a lunar complexion, and it became her: she had a surly temperament. Unlike Samantha, she didn't have to act the part of a male; it came naturally to her. She was an Apache co-pilot and loved her job.

From day one, she saw Samantha as a weak female in need of her protection and treated her like a little sister.

Because Daniel was pursuing Samantha, Susan took an immediate dislike to him, considering his overtures disrespectful to a superior. She urged Samantha to discipline him, but Samantha told her she worried about what that would mean for crew morale. Susan then made various suggestions to get rid of male pests. Samantha tried one.

Afterward, Samantha asked her roommate, "You remember suggesting yesterday that a surefire way to get a lovesick man off your back is to play the brother card; you know, I love you like a brother?" Susan nodded. "Well, I used a variant of it, because I didn't want to use the L word with him, so I told him I feel a strong sisterly attachment to him. You'll never guess what he said: How do you feel about incest?"

Susan said, "You didn't laugh, did you?"

"You led me to believe he'd take it hard and I'd have to soothe his feelings, so what he said was so unexpected, a kind of involuntary laugh popped out."

"Every time you laugh at him, you just encourage him."

"I know, but the shit head is funny."

"No, he's not. He's merely disrespectful, and I think you should put your foot down."

Samantha thanked her roommate for her opinion, but said she would handle Beaton.

*

In early January a new major at Bagram visited FOB Fenty to meet the medevac crews and make his mark. There had been a case in late December where a G.I. had been declared dead by medics only to wake up screaming at Bagram hours later. The major, a flight surgeon with no front-line experience, decided to make an example of this case and toured the FOBs to admonish medevac crews to do a better job. He had a file in his hand, which, unfortunately for his purposes, concerned one of Daniel's cases. The major said, "Which one of you is Specialist Beaton?"

"Me, sir."

The major eyed him. "Do you remember picking up one Private Peter Egan on December 16 in the Pech Valley? He was supposedly dead at the scene."

"Yes, sir."

"I chose this file as an example of how *not* to run our business."

Daniel opened his mouth to respond, but shut it upon receiving a punt to the ankle from Samantha.

"I see in this run sheet no indication whatsoever that you bothered to take any life sign readings; no BP, no temperature, no pulse, no information about airway, breathing, or circulation. No information whatsoever. You just wrote KIA in the narrative section. It appears you determined he was dead without checking him at all. So, Specialist, tell us, how did you determine he was dead?"

"I just looked at him."

"What medical procedures did you use to confirm death?"

"None."

"None? Was he breathing?"

"I don't think so."

"You don't *think* so. You didn't check?"

"No."

"Did you check his pulse?"

"No."

"This is what I'm talking about, people. This type of carelessness or laziness is inexcusable. Were his pupils dilated?"

"Couldn't tell."

"Why the hell not?"

"Couldn't find his head."

The gale of laughter almost blew down the hooch.

"You think this is funny?" said the major to the assembled. The laughter subsided. "You think a dead American soldier is a joking matter, Specialist?"

"No, sir," Daniel answered.

"Yet you stand there joking about it."

"Sir, all I did was answer your questions. I made no joke about a dead G.I."

"You obviously made a joke about it. Why else would everyone laugh?"

"If people were laughing, it's because my answers made it clear how stupid the questions were."

Craig cast his eyes up. Talon elbowed him. Samantha booted his ankle again. Daniel winced.

"You have some goddamn nerve, Specialist!" exclaimed the abashed major. "Why was the detail that the private was missing his head not in the file?"

"Sir, the run sheet has no category for beheaded. I didn't write on his chest that his head was missing, if that's what you mean. It seemed self-evident." More laughter.

"Enough!" said the major. "You're still making light of this."

"It's so easy for people to sit in Bagram looking at a sheet of paper and second-guess what we do in the field dealing with mangled bodies. Our job is horrific. What we see every day will scar us for the rest of our lives. We never laugh at the misery we see; we laugh despite the misery to preserve what sanity we can. So, thank you, sir, for helping to keep us sane."

That outburst earned him a hundred pushups, which he had to complete in two minutes or spend the next week in the stockade. Samantha grimaced, apparently thinking he didn't have a prayer. Daniel didn't begin struggling until about seventy-five, and he had about forty seconds left. The medevac and Apache crews cheered him on, but the major shut them up. He was counting on Daniel's doing jail time.

With about twenty seconds left, Daniel got to ninety, and Craig began cheering for him again. Talon and Samantha joined in, and when the major again shouted for them to stop, they started clapping, and when he told them to stop that, they stomped their feet. The other crews joined in. Daniel got to 99 and seemed to have nothing left, until Samantha said, "Come on, Dan!" He shuddered as he lifted himself one more time and collapsed onto the floor with two seconds to spare. The air crews gave a raucous cheer, and the red-faced major departed in a pique, his mission a failure.

*

Daniel later said to Talon, "That's the army for you. Spend day and night for months on end risking your life and saving other lives under the worst conditions imaginable for shit pay, and no one up the hierarchy says a Christly thing. But tell one of those morons he's a windbag, and *that* goes on your record. Anyway, who gives a shit? Once my stint is up, I'll be gone so fast."

CHAPTER SIX

A Day in the Life, Winter 2009

Beaton's Journal – February 2, 2009
0610 Sam suggested I pick a day and record everything noteworthy that happened, so someday I could look back and remember exactly what it was like here. Why I would want to is anyone's guess, but I want to keep Sam happy. Anyway, today is the day.
0923 The winter wind is driving us all bonkers. What else is new?
2150 I'm going to bed.

Beaton's Journal – February 3, 2009
0614 Sam read my journal from yesterday and accused me of not taking her idea seriously. I objected that I recorded everything that happened yesterday, but she suggested I try it again.
0700 Weather's worse than yesterday's. It's snowing and the ceiling's in the basement. Second up today, but no flying unless all hell breaks loose.

0728 Checked our bird to make sure supplies are ready. Not sure if there is enough of anything, because I couldn't stop checking out Sam's bum as she checked the bird for whatever the hell pilots look for.

0830 Sam's at her computer studying for another exam in the university courses she takes online. She worries about it, yet she always aces them. She keeps yelling at me for bugging her because I keep bugging her. Shit, she just went to her lair. I'm bored.

0935 Just sitting looking out at flight line. Snow stopped, but can't see more than a hundred feet. Bored as hell.

0948 Saw rat. Hope cooks don't see it.

1012 Went to room to pray to Sophia, but thought of Sam's bum.

1100 Ceiling up to ground level. Thick cloud deck hanging at my feet. I'm hungry and really bored.

1155 Watched Pat Condell shitting on religion on YouTube. If Sophia wasn't so much better looking, he might be my god.

1227 Ate with Talon and Craig. Tasted like rat.

1310 I'm goddamn bored. This Samlessness is trying.

1328 There are forty-seven knots in the plywood here.

1331 Amazing coincidence, but every woman I'm crazy about in the world just walked into this one small room at the exact same time, as follows: Sam.

1345 Sam's writing to her sister again. She has a perfect profile when she writes, or when she doesn't. She just told me to stop staring. I told her it's more interesting counting her than plywood knots, but she didn't appear to consider that a compliment.

1400 Her eyes. So perfect they make me wonder if there is a God. Better stop staring before she blinks me off again.

1446 Threw a football with Chief and Andy. Told Andy to stick to proselytizing. His response used 'fuck' as a noun, verb, adjective, and adverb, something like, "Fuck you, you fucking fuckly fuck." I pointed out that he can't use the adverb 'fuckly' to modify the noun 'fuck,' and he replied, "Eat shit, you shitty shit."

1700 Read medical stuff for last two hours. Discovered that doing something boring doesn't alleviate boredom.

1730 Update: I'm bored. And hungry. Went to my room to pray to Sophia. I think I might out-pray Andy. He considers it a hobby whereas for me it's a fetish. Sam keeps me primed.

1805 Invited Sam to Pizza Hut trailer, but she said no. Went by my lonesome. They still don't have ham and pineapple, and I'm pretty sure they use goat cheese. Douchebags.

2022 Chief and a few of the others are smoking cigars again. Even Sam has one sticking out of her mouth, though she isn't inhaling. I frown my disapproval, and she flashes her repertoire of sign language at me. I long to invite her to stick something healthier in her mouth, but I'm sure she would bite it off. I'm considering if it would be worth it.

2100 Sam just asked to read my journal, but that is out of the question, what with Sam's bum and thing-in-her-mouth business. Now she doesn't believe I took it seriously again, so I have to do this crap again tomorrow.

Beaton's Journal – February 4, 2009
0548 Awoke. Awaiting developments.
0700 Checked bird. Maintenance crew were frigging around in there, looking for morphine, no doubt. New private could be a problem. The boy's dealing with sparse grey matter.
1055 Just back from medevac mission. Nine-line call for an urgent medical evacuation of American soldier injured by IED in Pech Valley. Sam and Craig and chase pilots did a great job flying through the clouds along the foggy mountains. Conditions were bad enough, the pilots discussed turning back, but felt that would doom the soldier, so we flew on slowly. When we landed, there was enemy activity in the area, as the army puts it when jeezly fuckers are shooting at us, so Chief and I had to run our arses off to get to the poor bastard, whose legs were destroyed. The field medic had done a good job with the limited supplies he had, but the man needed blood immediately. Bullets were zinging over our heads as we prepared the young soldier for evacuation. Gunmetal blasted the bejesus out of the ridge where the enemy were. The shooting stopped, and we ran the patient to the chopper. Sam took off right away as I got some blood going. He was writhing, and his shrieks raised our hackles. Chief restrained him while I checked his BP and upped the morphine. His screaming stopped, but the poor bugger started puking from the morphine, so I gave

him some promethazine. As if this guy didn't have enough problems, IV pump kept screwing up: piece of shit. Worked around it. He started losing consciousness. I was worried if he blacked out he'd never wake up, so I knuckled his sternum. He grimaced and cursed at me, but stayed awake. Got him back to JAF alive, but he'll likely need to go to Bagram soon.

1147 Craig just volunteered us to fly through the cloudy mountains again to get our patient to Bagram, I guess because he thinks saving his life is more important than my peace of mind. We leave in five minutes.

1306 Made it to Bagram with soldier still hanging in there. Was happy to hand him over to ground ambulance. Flight was hairy. Visibility was so bad, Craig had to use the river at one point to help him navigate while Sam flew and I shat my pants. They really are fine pilots. We're stuck here until the fog lifts.

1620 Saw a couple of cute nurses, but one on arm of square-jawed pilot and other attached to hunky flight surgeon. Both sported fancy engagement rings. A pretty woman here can have her choice of all the doctors, pilots, career officers; anyone she wants. Makes me wonder if the marriages made under the desperate conditions of a male to female ratio of fifteen to one will last. Flight medics also have women after them, but her name is Bertha the Hutt.

1750 Looks like we'll be here overnight. More to do here than at JAF. Going to dinner

```
with Craig, Chief, and Sam at TGI Friday's,
then to a movie.
```

Daniel shared this day's journal with Samantha. At the movie that evening, he sat next to her, and he opened the discussion, "Doctors are a dime a dozen here. Toss a dart in this theater and you're bound to hear one whining, 'Oh, shit, my eye!' but I'm the only medical student, unspoiled by adoration, money, and success."

"Because you have none of those."

"Not yet."

"And do you suppose if you had them, I'd be all over you? Do you think I'm that shallow?"

"No, I—"

"And if I was and, God help me, we should get married, do you suppose it could possibly last? I mean, after all, you were so desperate here you had to settle for me."

"That's not what I meant."

"I know what you meant. You couldn't have been more clear if you shouted into my ear, 'You're not good enough for Paul. He'll use you, then dispose of you as soon as he finds someone worthwhile.' Am I right?"

"I, uh, I mean …"

"Don't bother lying, Beaton." She got up and moved to the other side of Talon, while Daniel cursed inwardly.

After they left the movie, a woman called to them, "Hey, you four, stop."

"Ah shit, a Fobbit officer and his lackey," muttered Talon.

"Lieutenant, these your men?" said the officious major. A master sergeant glowered at Daniel, who was the most unkempt.

"Yes, ma'am."

"If Sam's a man, I've turned gay," noted Daniel.

"Was the major addressing you, Specialist?" bellered the master sergeant. He was under the impression screaming would make up for his small stature.

"No, but Sam is a woman."

"Shut up, Specialist! Tuck in your shirt." Daniel looked at his lieutenant, who nodded. "Why the hell you need your lieutenant's approval to execute my order, Specialist?"

"I guess I couldn't believe anyone could worry about my shirt tails. Must be a big day for trifles."

"What? Are you questioning the orders of a superior?" bellowed the major.

"Dan, listen to the major," said Craig.

"I don't need your help, Lieutenant," said the major. Daniel tucked in his shirt. "You're this close to a written reprimand on your record."

The master sergeant next looked down at Daniel's boots and his eyes widened. "Your boots are a disgrace. They're filthy."

"That's blood."

"What the hell is blood doing on your boots?"

"Curdling, I suppose, if it's listening to this."

"Dan, don't," Samantha advised. Apparently, she could see the sarcasm boiling up in his eyes.

He didn't listen, continuing, "I told the soldier who lost his legs to bleed somewhere else, but all the little christer was worried about was his lost legs. You should've heard the sooky baby whining, 'My legs, oh, shit my legs are gone!' as if the world revolved around them. I told him he'd better get his priorities straight and start worrying about my boots because, as anyone devoted to irrelevance knows, clean boots are what will win this war, but he didn't care. He just kept bleeding on my boots to spite me. That son of a bitch even got his boots blown up, just to spite you. He also said you were an up and comer in the inner circle of morons at Bagram. I can tell you his name if you want to arrest him."

"Dan! Shut the fuck up," hollered Craig as Samantha and Talon chuckled.

Daniel, who respected his lieutenant, shut his mouth.

"What the hell are you laughing at?" barked the master sergeant at Talon.

Turning to the master sergeant, Craig said, "Tell me, have you seen action?"

"I've been in Iraq and Afghanistan."

"Have you been in combat? Have you exchanged live fire with the enemy?"

"What's your point?" asked the major.

"My point? My fucking point?" screamed the now exercised lieutenant.

"Easy, Lieutenant," admonished the major.

"My point is my crew risked their lives today to save another man's life. My crew chief and flight medic were getting shot at while they sweated to save a man in dire need of help. My medic was covered in blood and mud from head to toe; that's what happens in real war. Maybe not where you sit, but where we go every goddamn day. My co-pilot flew through pea soup to rescue him and bring him here. So, I'm sorry, Major, but I don't need to hear this fucking paper pusher reprimand my crew."

"Get out of my sight, the four of you, before I lose my temper," ordered the major as they walked away in a huff.

"Thanks, Lieutenant," said Daniel.

"Oh, shut up," yowled Craig. "Christ, that mouth of yours, Beaton. I'm ordering you to bunk down for the night and keep your mouth shut until we lift off tomorrow."

Daniel nodded and intended to say nothing further, but then a captain walked by and roared at Daniel, "Salute me, Specialist!" Daniel sighed and saluted. "I want to see a proper salute." Daniel tried again. "I don't believe my eyes. Look at your fucking boots!"

Daniel blurted out, "Oh, Anti Christ! I swear they drafted the officers here straight out of the Special Olympics."

And he spent the night in the stockade.

*

In late February, after four days of doing nothing, Samantha sat on the porch and whined, "God, I'm so bored."

"I can think of something to keep both of us occupied," mentioned Daniel.

"Beaton, you're as predictable as the sunrise, which makes you a large part of the monotony."

"Think how I feel. I have to be with me all the time."

"I can't think of anything worse. Thanks. I feel better. But I'm still bored."

"At least that means none of our guys are getting hurt," began Talon before the walkie-talkies clipped to their pockets screeched, "Medevac, medevac, medevac!"

The crew dashed to make their varied preparations and assembled at the helicopter nine minutes later. "What do we have?" said Samantha as she spun up the aircraft for launch, which enveloped the crew in dust.

"Avalanche in the Hindu Kush," answered Craig as he programmed the GPS. "Apparently hundreds are buried under the snow and God knows how many more are trapped in a tunnel. We have cars and at least one bus swept into the gorge; not much we can do for them, I'm sure.

"We're going to be doing some shoveling, Chief," said Daniel, reaching for his heavy coat. "No shitty little army poncho for me."

Samantha took off and headed northwest.

As the helicopter approached the scene of the disaster and the pilots looked around for a safe spot to land, the crew surveyed the panorama of calamity in the snowfield below. They could make out parts of cars, trucks, and buses buried in the snow. Hundreds of people were milling about, some right at the precipice and seemingly in a stupor. "God, where do we even start? It must go on for at least two miles," observed Samantha. Other army helicopters were circling the area making their own assessments.

"Let's take a quick pass over the gorge to check for any sign of survivors," ordered the lieutenant. Samantha veered over the defile and nosed down before Craig said, "Never mind, Sam. No one could survive that plunge. Put us down over there."

Samantha looked at the small space between an overturned bus and a sheer cliff rising above the buried highway and commented with a slight tremor in her voice, "Room enough for the rotors plus a toothpick." It was also windy. This would be tricky.

"Want me to take it?" asked Craig.

"No, sir," she replied while flaring for the landing.

"Take us in fast before the snow kicks up and blinds you," advised the lieutenant.

Samantha nodded and landed with a muffled thud. Talon and Daniel sprang out and got to work. "Let's see what we can do to help," said Craig as he left the aircraft. Samantha followed. When the rotors came to a stop, she gawped wide-eyed at the two-foot gap between the main rotor and the mountainside. "Cut it a bit close," the lieutenant observed with a smile. "I notice you're always a bit off to the starboard. Take that into account in the future." She nodded and looked around for Talon and Daniel. Daniel was giving mouth-to-mouth to a young woman. He stopped, shook his head, and looked around for someone he could help. Talon was heading back to the helicopter with three shivering children in tow.

"We need to focus on the seriously injured," said Craig.

"They can't find their parents," said Talon. "They were standing on the edge of the cliff freezing."

"Sam, get them on board and watch them."

Samantha's expression queried, *Why? Because I'm a woman?*

The lieutenant said, "You rather dig people out of the snow?"

"Babysitting it is," she said as she led the children to the chopper.

Looking for help and warmth, dozens of shivering people approached the helicopter. "Shit," said Craig. He called his flight medic over and said, "What's it look like, Dan?"

"Just in this little area, there are three corpses, a few minor injuries, and a lot of people standing around freezing. And we'll need to check all the buried cars."

"Let's get the injured out first. Do whatever you can for them quickly and get them on board." The lieutenant turned to the assembling crowd and said, "Anyone understand English?"

One man answered, "I am learning people the English in Kabul."

"Good. Ask these people, 'Who is hurt?'"

"Who is hurt?" the man called out in English.

"Sophia dealt buddy here a winning hand in the imbecility stakes," noted Daniel to Talon.

"In their language," rejoined Craig.

The man complied. Nearly everyone indicated they were hurt. They must have known it meant getting off the mountain sooner.

"Shit," repeated Craig. "Dan, get some kind of triage going, will you?"

*

With the help of the translator, Daniel sorted out the injured from the cold. He gave out some Tylenol for the pain, and a few minutes later the helicopter lifted off with fourteen civilians heading for Parwan Hospital in nearby Charikar, leaving Talon and Daniel with a few dozen grumbling people.

Wind and rain suddenly picked up, setting off another avalanche sixty meters up the highway. Talon and Daniel watched in horror as five people were swept off the cliff screaming. "Jesus Christ!" said both men in unison. They ran up the road to render any assistance they could, but there was no one left to help. They looked down the cliff, but saw only haze and mist. Turning to look at each other, they saw reflected dismay. As they walked back to the crowd of onlookers in silence, trying to repress yet another horrific memory, they glanced from time to time above them. Any more avalanches in store?

Talon asked the translator to ask for help digging out some cars they could see buried. A few people stepped forward, but most huddled together shivering with a wary eye above for further avalanches. Together they dug enough snow off six cars to check for survivors. In four cars they found at least one survivor. Daniel was treating them when another army helicopter arrived. The crowd loped across the deep snow to clamber on board before it was safe to do so. One man had the top half of his head taken off, which reduced his wife and many of the other civilians to hysteria. The crew chief jumped out and waved people away as the flight medic checked on the man. There was nothing she could do for him.

The CW3 in charge of the helicopter called Talon and Daniel over to get their perspective on the beheading, which they provided. That helicopter left several minutes later with the dead man, his wife, and thirteen other civilians.

The remainder of the day and much of the night were spent getting people off the mountain. They attempted to get the injured, those at most serious risk of exposure and children off first, but it wasn't always possible with the rush of hapless victims every time a helicopter landed.

*

A few days afterward, Daniel and Talon were called in to help with the investigation into the death of the man partially decapitated by the helicopter rotor. Both testified it was circumstance only and no fault of the crew. Talon said it appeared the man had actually leaped up, perhaps in a panic. Daniel corroborated this. Asked for any recommendations he could make to avoid such a mishap in the future, Daniel said, "If you're ever going to confuse ducking with jumping, make sure you're not underneath a helicopter."

That earned him a verbal reprimand. His superiors apparently did not understand his absolute need to wall off his emotions and make light of everything to preserve his sanity. But Samantha laughed hard after Talon communicated Daniel's quip, which cheered up the flight medic. Her primary defense against the pervasive insanity was also her sense of humor.

*

From: Samantha Hawkins
Date: Friday, February 27, 2009
To: Terry Hawkins
Subject: Paul
Paul came on a medevac with us yesterday
and afterward asked if I'd like to see a
DVD with him some time! I wanted to jump

for joy, but I just smiled and said yes sweetly. Yippee! It was awkward, but I had to ask if he intended to keep up a long distance relationship with his girlfriend, and he said she wants to (I'll bet she does) but he doesn't. Poor Nurse Sweetland ran out of time before she could corral him. But I have ten months to build an inescapable corral.

We'll be doing without our flight medic for our second-up shift tomorrow (Andy will fill in), because Beaton is in the stockade for the second time this month. A captain, recently stationed here, handed him a sentence of two days in jail for insubordination. We were just back from an awful mission with three critically wounded marines. While Beaton was walking to the shower exhausted and soaked with blood, this Fobbit gave him shit for not saluting, so the cheeky bastard saluted him with his middle finger. After screaming at Beaton for a few minutes, Captain Fobbit demanded an apology. As Beaton later put it, "I intended to say I'm sorry, but somehow it came out, 'Lick my hairy crack.'"

Love, Sam

CHAPTER SEVEN

Going to the Dogs, Late Winter 2009

As Talon and Samantha sat on the porch smoking cigars and Craig sat strumming the Beatles' tune *In My Life* on his guitar, they heard from within the hooch a smack and a thump.

Craig sang in phlegmatic tone, "In my life, I heard a thud."

"Did it sound like a Beaton thud?" said Samantha hopefully.

Talon leaned over to look inside and reported, "Two of the Apache dudes horsing around."

Daniel walked out and took a vacant seat.

"I was hoping you were involved in the brawl, Beaton," said Samantha.

"I was for a minute. Chang made the mistake of shoving Stedman into me, and I fell against the wall."

"It was a Beaton thud," Samantha returned with a grin.

"They'll be fishing my boot out of Chang's colon after they finish pounding each other." Addressing Craig, he said, "That's a nice tune you're slaughtering." Turning back to Samantha, he said, "A woman shouldn't smoke those things. If you want something—"

"Else to puff on, blah, blah, blah," finished Samantha. "You're a goddamn broken record."

Undaunted, he continued, "Weird coincidence, two Americans meeting here so far from home." She cast her eyes up. "You know, Sam, the memories we're making here will haunt us forever. Let's you and me make a great one together to see us through the dark days ahead."

"Okay, but the next time you open your eyes you'll be in the back of an ambulance."

"My kinda girl!" he said, laughing.

She got to her feet and announced, "I'm going to the operating theater."

"I'd go with you, except it's all clogged up with Telfer," said Daniel, who tried to cover his disconsolation.

"If he doesn't bore me to death, he'll be a step up from you," she said as she put her cigar next to Daniel's crotch, pretended to rip it away, dropped it on the floor, and snuffed it out with her boot with gleeful zeal. She smiled wickedly and walked away.

"That's enough to put a damper on your dick," observed Talon.

Daniel nodded and said, "But it was kind of exhilarating, wasn't it?"

"One of us has to keep an eye on her until she gets there," said Craig.

"I'll do it," said Daniel, who could at least gaze at her butt while she went to see another man.

Approaching the theater, their radios squawked, "Medevac, medevac, medevac."

Cursing, she turned and darted to the helicopter. Once he made sure Samantha was close enough to Talon, Daniel sprinted to operations to learn about the mission.

Seven minutes later, as he and Lieutenant Ng climbed into the Black Hawk, Daniel resumed the conversation he'd been having with his lieutenant. "I still say it's bullshit. I mean, putting our lives on the line for this? It's beyond any man's logic."

"What is?" said Samantha as she completed her checklist.

"And how many thousands will this cost?" continued Daniel.

"Will what cost?" asked Samantha.

"It costs a whole bunch to train these dogs," said Craig as he programmed the GPS.

"Dogs?" said Samantha.

"Yes, a damn canine; that's our mission. A goddamn dog got himself shot and tangled in C-wire. And we're risking our lives to pick it up."

"The dog is a marine," said Craig.

"You mean he works for marines," said Samantha.

"No, I mean he *is* a marine, with a rank and everything, probably higher than yours, Beaton."

"Oh, it wouldn't surprise me. He probably makes better money, too."

"We're really flying to pick up a dog?" she said.

Craig nodded. Receiving clearance to take off, he turned to Samantha and said, "Let's go." Samantha pulled pitch and lifted the aircraft into the air.

Talon turned to Daniel and asked, "What's wrong with dogs?"

"Doesn't matter what's wrong with them; the mission is bullshit."

"But what's wrong with them?" persisted Talon.

"A dog is just a walking gullet."

"You're just a walking fuckstick," held Talon.

"Not yet I'm not, but that's my goal. You want to know what's wrong with dogs? If you had a ten-pound steak and gave a dog nine and a half pounds, it would gulp it all down in two minutes, then stare at you salivating over the bit you were eating. If it thought it could get away with it, it would bowl you over and get the rest of the meat."

"It's just their nature," argued Talon.

"Lazy, greedy animals, worse than any welfare bum. That's what we're risking our lives for. It's bullshit!"

"It probably sniffs out explosives and Taliban assholes, so it's probably helped save a lot of marines' lives," said Talon. "That's why it outranks you," he supposed, chortling. "Probably gets laid more often, too."

"By the marines," put in Samantha to everyone's laughter.

"And what do they expect me to do for a dog? What if it needs blood? And I'm not exactly up on dog anatomy."

"You know your own. Close enough," commented Samantha. He barked at her.

The helicopter arrived near the border with Pakistan in the Konar Valley, and Samantha flew toward the pink smoke rising in the distance. Banking left, she descended quickly and flared for landing. "Debarking," quipped Talon as he and Daniel hopped out the window and trotted through the dust sucked up by the rotors to a group of soldiers standing around the wounded dog. It was lying down and softly whining. The marines had managed to free the animal from the concertina wire. One man was petting its head.

"It's about fucking time you got here," greeted the sergeant in charge of the dog.

"We had to see about an Afghan Hound in Asadabad," snapped Daniel.

The sergeant grabbed Daniel's collar and growled, "Take this seriously."

Daniel brought his arms up between the sergeant's arms and thrust them outwards, forcing him to release his grip. The sergeant appeared surprised by Daniel's strength.

"Careful, Specialist," said the lieutenant.

"Sir, if he attacks me, I'll defend myself."

A black man in civvies covered by a flak jacket stepped forward to calm things down. "How about letting this man get to his work," he suggested. Daniel looked at him and figured him for Special Forces. He saw them a lot at JAF.

Daniel went to the German Sheppard to make an assessment. The bullet was still lodged in the dog's hind quarters, and the concertina wire had cut the animal in several places. The corpsman had done what he could, but the dog looked in bad shape. "He needs blood," said Daniel. The corpsman concurred. "I'm sorry, Sergeant, but we aren't equipped with canine blood. The best I can do is an IV to restore some fluids until we can get him proper help."

"Can you get the bullet out?"

"I can, but he'll bleed more. Best plan is to preserve as much blood as we can and get him to a vet as soon as possible."

"He's not going to make it, is he?" said the distressed sergeant.

"He's in bad shape, but we'll do our best." As Daniel put in the IV needle, the dog yapped and bit his crotch. Daniel yelped in turn and withdrew. His body armor protected his privates, but a tooth scratched his inner thigh. "Maybe he's in better shape than we thought," he said, rubbing his thigh.

"He's trained to go for the groin to incapacitate as quickly as possible," explained the sergeant. "Lucky for you he's weak now and just gave you a playful little nip."

"When he gets better, I'll give him a playful little kick in his balls."

With the sergeant petting the dog, Daniel applied a bandage and gave the dog a fentanyl lollipop. The sergeant carried Sergeant Paws to the helicopter. Samantha glanced back at Daniel as he strapped the injured dog to the stretcher. She saw it mouthing the lollipop and laughed as she took the craft airborne.

"There have been a few firsts today," noted Daniel while putting on his seat belt. "For instance, this is the first patient who was licking his balls when I got to him. It seemed to soothe him. Maybe I'll suggest it to my future patients."

"This marine is *Sergeant* Paws," announced Talon with a grin at Daniel.

Craig laughed and said, "It does outrank you, Dan. Did you salute him?"

"With my foot. Fucking thing bit me."

"In the groin," said Talon.

"You need to lick your balls, Beaton," remarked Samantha with a titter.

"I can't reach. I've tried. Can you do it for me, Sam?"

"I walked into that one. I was just thinking how improved you'd be if the dog took them right off. Not so perverted with your thoughts or provoking with your mouth or pesky with your eyes."

"Ha! Little do you know I have one ball left, and let me tell you, Sam, it's a real turn-on for me when you talk about my balls," retorted Daniel.

"I'll just shut up now," said Samantha.

"Do I get a purple heart for this, sir?"

"Maybe a purple sack," answered Craig.

Three minutes later, they got a medevac call directing them to return to the same pickup zone. There had been a firefight, and a man was down. The Apache escort spun around and headed back. Craig whirled his forefinger in the air to direct Samantha to turn around. She banked at a ninety degree angle and followed the Apache.

When Daniel arrived, he saw the Special Forces operator was in trouble. A bullet had clipped his neck and cut a carotid artery. "Move!" he said to two soldiers by his side as he knelt beside him, and asked the corpsman what he'd done so far. Blood had been spurting out of his neck. The corpsman had pinched off the carotid, but could make no further progress with what he had and what he knew. No army medic had the training to deal with this, except for one who had four years in medical school and who happened to be here. The injured man was conscious and responsive.

"How long have you been applying pressure?" asked Daniel.

"I'm not sure," answered the corpsman.

"Five minutes," said the injured man. He held out his hand to Daniel and said, "Jason Carter."

Daniel shook his hand and said, "Dan Beaton. Glad you're lucid; it's a good sign. The corporal here's done a good job containing the bleeding, but we can't constrict a carotid for too long, so we have to work fast." He examined the artery. "Good; it's not completely severed."

"If it was?"

"I'd have to cut your neck, find both ends, and hope one of these Medieval Mullahs around here is a vascular surgeon on the side, but I wouldn't need to go beyond step one." Jason chuckled. Daniel marveled at his sangfroid. "The artery needs to be sutured. You'll need a surgeon to do a proper job, but I can patch you up well enough to get you back alive." While he took out his suture kit and got to work, he asked Talon to take Jason's blood pressure.

"How is it?" asked Jason.

"A little low, but that's to be expected," replied Talon.

Daniel handed Talon packed red blood cells and plasma and said, "Get these going."

"I hear, maybe, a Maritimes lilt?" said Jason.

"Halifax."

"I'm from Mississauga."

"Great. What the hell you doing here? Most Canadians are at Kandahar." Jason simply smiled. "Oh," concluded Daniel. "JTF2 business." Daniel explained to Talon, "Joint Task Force 2, Canada's spec ops. This man can kill us with a blink if he wants." He turned to Jason and said, "Well, I was considering letting you die, but I can't let that happen to a fellow Canadian."

The Canadians continued speaking for the first few minutes of the suturing. "Say something in Bluenose," said Jason.

"I'll say something in Cape Bretoner. My mudder was from New Waterford, and my fadder was from Louisburg, which makes me a Caper tru and tru, and if you don't friggin' like it, I'll puck you in the mout, by."

Smiling, but by this time dozy, Jason interpreted: "I'll punch you in the mouth, boy?"

His face falling, Daniel said, "Oh, uh, I didn't mean any disrespect with, you know, uh, 'boy.' That's just what—"

"Relax," said Jason, "no offense …" He lost consciousness.

Daniel looked at the corpsman and said, "Let go." The corpsman took pressure off. The bleeding resumed. Talon took the man's blood pressure again. Speaking to the corpsman, Daniel said, "Pinch it off for another minute or so while I get one more suture in there, and squeeze that plasma bag."

Four minutes later, with Jason stabilized, Daniel and Talon put him on a litter, and the GIs jogged him to the waiting chopper. Samantha pushed the engines to reach top speed back to base. On the way back to Jalalabad, Daniel communicated with Captain Telfer. The Captain, evidently satisfied the patient was stable, directed the helicopter to Bagram's Level III hospital because Jason needed a vascular surgeon.

The crew was given permission to stay and eat at Bagram, where the food was decent. A pretty nurse walked by with a tray of food, and Daniel picked up his tray and sat beside her. Twenty seconds after that, he was back. Samantha laughed and said, "I'll have to ask her what she said to get rid of you so fast."

"Two simple words."

"Fuck off?" supposed Talon.

"That was the subtext. She said, 'I'm married.' I don't think it would've worked out anyway. Right from the beginning of our relationship there were trust issues between us. She called me a liar right to my face. It was really insulting she didn't believe I was a top neurosurgeon."

"Oh, look at her, would you?" said Talon, who liked hefty women. "Those pants must've been drawn on her."

"I think the artist went outside the lines," said Samantha.

A medevac crew from Bagram walked in and, recognizing Craig's crew, sat and started some friendly teasing by calling the JAF crew minor leaguers.

"Shit, you Fobbits don't even know what real war is, flying tail to tail," replied Craig. "You just transfer the wounded from a safe base where the professionals brought them to your safe base here. Glorified ambulance drivers."

"Oh, we get our share of harrowing operations," replied the Bagram pilot. "Last week we had to deal with a marine who had fallen out of a chopper at 2000 feet."

"So it was a mop-up operation," quipped Daniel. The flight medic, who had had to manage the mess, jumped on Daniel, then punched him. Daniel, much stronger, stood, picked him up, and threw him over the table. The crew chief tried to grab Daniel, but Daniel shoved him back and he, too, fell over a table. Craig interceded, and being the only officer among the eight, ordered the other crew to leave.

"Keep your ignorant fucking trap shut around us, Specialist," warned the pilot as he led his crew out of the mess hall.

Lieutenant Ng turned to his young medic and said, "I guess I don't need to tell you after being attacked that not everyone shares your sense of humor. Joking with our crew and the other crews at JAF is one thing. We know it's how you blow off steam, and we know how good you are at your job, how you put your life on the line every day to save our guys, so we cut you a lot of slack, even when the joke is in poor taste, but as your commanding officer, I ask you to use your head before opening your big mouth in front of anyone else."

In marched a major who walked up to the table and said, "Which one of you assholes is joking about dead marines?"

Daniel, knowing he was in trouble anyway, looked at him and said, "Waiter, it's about time. We've been ready for our after dinner digestifs for quite some time. I'll be damned if I'm tipping you. And where's the dessert menu? The chef hasn't punished us enough yet."

Samantha couldn't help but expel a large guffaw as the major worked himself into a majestic frenzy. Craig said, "Sir, my flight medic has sustained a blow to his head. You can see the bruise. He doesn't know what he's saying."

"Nice try, Lieutenant," said the major. "You're under arrest, Specialist. And CW2, what is your name?"

"Sir, Chief Warrant Officer 2 Samantha Hawkins."

"You will receive a written reprimand."

"Sir, she meant no disrespect. It was my fault," said Daniel.

"Keep your big mouth shut, Specialist!" said the major.

"Sir, may I speak to you outside?" appealed Craig.

"No, you may not."

"Sir! If *you* cared about marines dying, then you wouldn't be arresting my flight medic, who saves marines for a living, because he made a stupid joke!" screamed Craig.

"Do I need to reprimand you, too, Lieutenant?"

"Oh, for Christ's sake!" cried the exasperated lieutenant. He walked outside, pulled out his phone, and called the colonel in command at JAF.

Two minutes later, as MPs were arriving to arrest Daniel, Craig handed the major the phone. The crew watched as the major turned red listening to the shouting coming out of the earpiece. They heard bits of the tirade: "Fobbit dipshit ... on duty ... to save lives, you bumfuck ... back behind your fucking desk whacking off ... leave my crew ... deal with him."

An incensed major gave the phone back to Craig with a scowl and said the colonel wanted to talk to him. He dismissed the MPs and waited for Craig to hang up. When he did, the major said, "I'll remember this, Ng."

"Good," Craig said. "Maybe next time you'll get the pole out of your ass and laugh it off when someone is being facetious." He turned to his crew and said, "Come on, we're leaving."

When they got outside, he warned his medic that there will be consequences; the colonel was furious. Craig, too, was infuriated and let Daniel know it all the way back to JAF.

Two days went by, and Daniel, having heard nothing from the commander, was starting to hope it had all blown over, but then Samantha arrived at his room to inform him the camp commander had summoned him, adding, "I was anxious to tell you, so you'd be miserable that much sooner."

"You don't have to look so happy about it."

"I think you're in for a critique," said Samantha with a grin.

He went to see the base commander. After a few minutes of screaming and dire warnings, the Colonel concluded, "So shut the fuck up, and keep shutting the fuck up for the rest of your time here, Specialist. Now get the hell out of my sight!"

"How'd it go?" said Talon when he got back to Club Medic.

"Was he irritated?" said Samantha at the same time.

"I guess, if you think a rabid badger with a thorn in its arse is irritated, and, if you ask me, he wasn't very tactful, the way he called me an immature fuckup."

"Did he really call you that?" asked Craig.

"Yup."

"Any punishment?"

"I forfeit seven days' pay, which I think is about a buck fifty. What pissed me off most was the presumption of guilt despite my insistent lies to the contrary. He told me to stop trying to joke, but, dammit, Craig, that's my safety valve. If I can't blow off steam that way, it's going to come out some other way that'll probably be much worse. Either that or I'll go the way of your last medic. They don't know, they don't fucking know what this job is like."

"Then joke with your crew, and maybe sometimes with the other crews here, but zip it at Bagram or with any other officers."

From: Samantha Hawkins
Date: Wednesday March 11, 2009
To: Terry Hawkins
Subject: Paul and stuff

I went to that movie with Paul. We held hands, and he tried an open-mouthed kiss at the end of the date, but I pulled back. Not on the first date, I told him, so he immediately asked me out for Friday. He wants to see me again before he goes away for two weeks starting this coming Sunday. The army is sending him on some course for the newest in combat surgery. So, it'll be late March until I can see him again. Shit! He's so wonderful!

Winter here means not much fighting and not much flying, so I've been spending most of my time on my correspondence courses. But I'm bored with that right now, so I decided to write to my favorite sister. You've said you enjoy the accounts of our missions and the sick humor, so I'll cover both.

Three days ago, on our last medevac, we picked up this marine who got shot in the knee. He'd been screeching so loud I could hear it over the engines as we took off. Now, ten minutes later, he was silent. I was curious how he was doing. Craig was flying, so I looked back at him. The man was lying on a litter with his head propped up. He was sucking a medicated lollipop. There was an IV drip in his arm and a slight smile on his face; he was listening to his iPod and moving his head to the beat. This is medical evacuation in the iPod age.

Beaton saw me looking back and asked what's up. I answered that I noticed an unusual silence back there. He said, "Not sure what you expected to hear, but tell me what you want to hear and I'll make it come true."

So I answered, "I want to hear a rush of wind, followed by a loud Beaton scream that steadily wanes until it suddenly stops with a distant splat." Instead of jumping, he just laughed.

Sick humor last week. Soldier lost his arm to a roadside bomb. Beaton worked his ass off to save the guy's life and got him on board unconscious, but in no danger for his life. He sat down and said, "Poor guy can only swim in circles now." I started to say, "On the other hand," but Beaton cut in, saying that was mean. Ignoring him, I continued, "Anything he accomplishes from now on, he can brag he did it singlehandedly." Then Talon said, "He'll have to throw away his clapper." I was chuckling a bit, but then I turned around to see Beaton pretending to clap feverishly with one hand, hitting only air, with this manic, retarded face, and I laughed so hard I had to hand over control to Craig while I settled down.

To show you how thin the line of emotions is, though, the next day a crew was down from Bagram to pick up this marine, and the man was sobbing. He couldn't have been any older than nineteen. I felt so bad thinking of the hardships he'll face for the rest of his life because of his disability that I began crying, too.

Love, Sam

CHAPTER EIGHT

Crash, Spring 2009

In late March, Samantha and Paul started seeing each other regularly. Daniel watched in frustration and sorrow as Samantha actively pursued Paul and swept him aside at every turn. He couldn't give up on her, however; he had fallen in love. If he could somehow keep them apart, and if he could get her to love him, maybe after he left the army they could get engaged and he could finish medicine and maybe even join the army again to be with her. That many ifs and maybes equaled a hopeless cause, he knew at some level, but he couldn't let it dissuade him; he had fallen in love.

Daniel took every opportunity he could to interact with her, trying his utmost to impress her. On the anniversary of his arrival at JAF, he dropped by her room to remind her of a promise she never made to have dinner with him. Her door was open to air the room. Stepping up to the door, he overheard Samantha telling her roommate, "I just couldn't help but think he was disappointed. I guess maybe I looked like shit last night after flying for … What the hell are you loitering there for, Beaton?"

He stepped into their room and said, "You *guess* you look like shit? Remove the guesswork and look in the mirror. Unless it perjures itself as it does with so many, it'll tell you the sad truth."

"Get lost, Beaton," returned Samantha, "or a month from now all you'll be is a lingering stench we can't get out of our room."

Daniel chuckled and said, "Okay," but his tone implied something left unsaid.

"Wait. Another training mission?"

"No. Just wanted to remind you about our dinner date tonight for my first anniv—"

"Do me one favor, Beaton, and I promise I'll never ask you for another thing. Drop dead."

"Don't worry; eventually I'll either die of boredom or of intersection with a mountain. One way or the other, you'll be responsible."

Samantha pulled out her gun and said, "There's always a faster way for me to end your unfortunate habit of not dying."

"Go on, Sam, shoot the little bastard," urged Susan.

Samantha put the gun away and shook her head.

Daniel said, "What's bothering you, Sammie?" She looked squarely at him, but said nothing. He went on, "Come on, get it off your chest before it flattens you more. Sam? No rejoinder? Any flatter and you'd be Saskatchewan. Sam? You're certainly cold enough. Sam? No witticism? Sam? Sam!"

"Go away!"

He stood still, so Susan got involved. "A superior has given you an order, Beatoff. Obey it, no questions asked."

"What's the matter, She-man?" He called her by her call sign whenever he saw her because she hated it; likewise for her. "You seem disgruntled. Haven't exploded a village for a while?"

"She might take your lip, Beatoff, but I won't. I'm writing a reprimand."

"Sophia Christ, She-man, I face bullets, bombs, missiles, and fire. I see pieces of human beings strewn everywhere, some of which you likely strew. Do you actually think I'd worry about a reprimand? Write a hundred for all I care."

"Sue, I'll handle him, I promise. Can you leave us for a minute?"

Susan walked out glowering at Daniel. He smiled. After she closed the door, Daniel said, "Every time I see her I just want to kick her clit up through her nose."

"I wouldn't. She's as big as you. She boxes men and often wins."

"She's a girl, sort of; she can't beat me up."

"She's an Amazon, and her husband is twice her size."

"She's married? You mean, in a moment of blind insanity someone actually thought of her as a woman?"

"Never mind her. I want to talk to you alone. I was going to discuss this with my roommate before I came to you about it, but since you're here, I might as well say it. Dan, I realized last night that I don't love Paul. I mean, he's handsome and brave and funny and smart and so on, but he's not the man I thought he was. And now that I'm seeing clearly, I've noticed someone so much better."

She took both his hands in hers, lowered her eyelids a tad, and beamed him a salacious gaze. Staggered by the sweet explosion of eroticism discharged by her striking eyes, his mouth fell open and he gasped. What caustic words had failed to achieve over months, a naughty glance accomplished in a heartbeat; disarmed him utterly and dumfounded him. Maintaining her sultry gape, she extended her neck, puckered her lips, and brought them within one micron of his. With his lips pursed and quivering, she backed away, let go of his hands, and broke out laughing. "God, Beaton, you're so easy to bullshit. Get the hell out of my room." He left with Samantha still snickering.

The incident embarrassed and angered Daniel. He said nothing, but it primed him for hostility the next time they clashed. After another gruesome mission in the Korengal valley in mid-April, Daniel went to the hooch, seeking comfort from Samantha. She was understanding, but when he tried to hug her, she stopped him. Hurt at still another rejection when he was in particular need of her, an angry glare supplanted the smile on his face, and he said, "You think you're too goddamn special for a little hug?"

Apparently displeased with his tone, she growled, "I'm more than a little tired of your disrespect."

He yawped, "And I'm long past tired of your condescension." The volume and ire of his voice startled not only Samantha, but Craig and Talon. "A specialist is beneath your notice, but take us out of the army and your attitude that I'm beneath you is laughable."

"We *are* in the army."

"Not one hour ago I was washing brains off my arms. I don't need to be reminded I'm in the jeezly army. And you know damn well I should actually be an officer with my credentials; it's only American arrogance and ignorance—and whatever you did to get in as pilot—that have you outranking me in the army."

Hands on her hips, she said, "And what do you suppose I did to get in as pilot?"

Ignoring that, he continued, "If I were a lieutenant, which I should be with my education alone, you wouldn't dream of treating me the way you do. I only put up with your abuse because you amuse me, but I have my limit."

"I amuse you? Oh, how patronizing is that? Would you dare say that to Talon or Craig? This is what I mean about disrespect."

"All I meant was I like trading jibes with you. You're the only woman I ever met who can give as good as she gets. It doesn't mean I disrespect you."

"What this is really about is you want me, and you're pissed because I want someone else."

"You want him because he's a captain, a flight surgeon—"

"Who the hell are you to tell me why I want someone?" she screamed. Craig and Talon continued to look on as the argument escalated. "He's better than you in every way in or out of the army. Any woman would choose him over you."

"Who the hell are you to speak for all women? Maybe they're not as blind and gullible as you."

"Do you hear this?" she said in exasperation to Craig and Talon. They smirked and looked away to communicate, *Leave me out of this.* Turning back to Daniel, she yelled, "You're implying that he's leading me on, and I'm too stupid to see it?"

"To him, you're just a nicely decorated hole."

Before he could blink, she slapped him hard and thundered, "Asshole!"

"Whoa," said Craig as he moved to intervene.

"Calm down, you two," advised Talon as Daniel rubbed his cheek.

Ignoring them, Samantha continued, "You find it impossible to believe he wants me because you think I'm not worth loving."

"How can you think—"

"Shut up! It's you who looks down on me, not him. Would someone who really respected and cared for me expect me to throw away my career to have a fling?"

"A fling?" he said while she proceeded to her next point.

"You think I'm incapable of judging him for myself. What gives you such keen insight into his mind? Have you ever once spoken to him about me?"

"No, but—"

"So you know nothing about the way he feels about me."

"He gives off bad vibes."

"Is that your four-fifths doctor's opinion? You've taken a class or two in psychiatry and you're such an expert you can sense vibes?"

"He smiles with his mouth, but not his eyes. He talks with the same enthusiasm no matter if the topic is saving a life or boiling an egg. He steals jokes from others. He's a phony. Don't trust him."

"Get this through your thick skull," she said, jabbing her finger into his chest. "Even if the army didn't forbid it, I wouldn't date you. I am *not* interested in you and never will be. Stay out of my business, Specialist!" she said, stomping out of the hooch.

Shattered by that declaration, he struggled to conceal a sorrow so intense, he had to hold his breath and clench his teeth to keep from breaking down. To hide his anguish and hurt her back, he shouted a parting notion when she reached the door. "Grab him now if you possibly can, Chief Warrant Officer, ma'am. Take you out of a place where the men don't outnumber desirable women a hundred to one, and you disappear!" She saluted the remark with her middle finger over her shoulder.

Craig nudged Talon, presumably to suggest he take Daniel out to settle him down. Talon took Daniel by the elbow, and said, "Come on, Dan. Let's walk and talk."

As they stepped outside, Talon said, "I gotta tell you, Dan, if you said what you said to Sam to any other superior, you'd be cooling your heels in jail."

"Much better than baking my balls here. Bring it on."

"Easy, roommate. Transport your mind to your happy place."

"My happy place is nestled between the legs of the most irritating woman in the universe."

"You don't like the decoration?" he asked with a smile.

Daniel chuckled and acknowledged, "That did go a bit too far."

"I don't suppose any woman would like being referred to as a decorated hole."

"They do get touchy." He rubbed his cheek again.

"Listen, dude, you two are going to have to apologize to each other. We have to work together in close quarters."

"I don't want anything to do with her for a while. Lord jeez, she pisses me off with her snooty attitude. She thinks she's so much better than me, but she's not. Is she?"

"No, and I'm sure she doesn't think so, but you know she can't even consider dating an enlisted man."

"There's life after the army, which is only months away for me, but she just said she wouldn't consider me anyway. Ever." He hung his head.

Talon patted his friend on the back. "She was mad at you, and she seems to love him. You attack her endlessly over him, so you have to expect her to come down hard on you."

"He's such a fake dipshit."

"Probably, but she loves him, and you really do have to respect her feelings on this. If you actually believe she'll disappear after she leaves here, it shouldn't matter to you anyway."

"Shit, Chief, I was just mad. She'll shine wherever she goes."

"Don't tell me, tell her. Give her some time to calm down, then go apologize."

Daniel nodded and went for a walk on his own.

*

Meanwhile, Craig had gone to see Samantha. When he knocked on the door, she immediately launched into a tirade. "Do you believe the nerve of that bastard? Who the hell does he think he is talking to a superior like that? It really pisses me off that he shows me absolutely no respect. I mean, he would never say anything nearly that insulting to you or Talon. I'm so tempted to press charges."

"Then he'll press charges for striking him."

"He deserved it. He called me a decorated hole, for God's sake! He's lucky to get away with a little slap."

"I heard it above the roar of a Kiowa Warrior taking off."

"Do you blame me? Did you hear how he spoke to me?"

"Yes, and Talon's talking to him about it right now. And I'm here to talk to you, not to listen to you. He was disrespectful, yes, and we'll deal with him, but you were, too, Sam."

"He—"

"Uh! Listen. As the superior, you need to show better leadership judgment. You say he wouldn't dare treat me like he treated you, but let me ask you this: would you dare treat me as you just treated him?"

"Of course not."

"When that's your answer for everyone you serve with, not just your superiors, then you're showing leadership." She looked down in embarrassment. "I want you to apologize."

"No, Craig, please don't make me do that."

"Tell me, Sam, do you think Dan's a good medic?"

"Yes."

"I think you know he's the best here, maybe the best the army has. You also know how well he's fit into our team. I for one like working with him."

"I do, too, but he has such a big mouth."

"That big mouth helps keep us all sane. If that weren't the case I'd have shut it a year ago. Apologize!" he finished as he walked away.

Later that day, she went to Daniel's room and said, "Craig told me to apologize, so I'm doing this because I respect my superiors. I'm sorry."

"I was also told to apologize, and I'm doing this because Talon and Craig know how to treat people they outrank with respect. I'm sorry."

"I know you don't respect me."

"I—"

"Answer me this. Do you expect me to sacrifice my career to have an affair with you?"

"No, not an affair."

"Whatever you want to call it, it would end my career. I'm going to get personal here because I need you to understand what the army means to me. At the end of twelfth grade, my mother took her own life. She'd never recovered from my father's death in a car crash a year to the day earlier. That left me and my sister with nothing and no one; our only living relative, Uncle Trevor, was living in his truck and couldn't or wouldn't help us. We were one day away from living in the streets when the army took me in. They stretched the rules and let me claim my sister as a dependent. The army saved our lives, so don't be surprised that I'm completely dedicated to it, and don't be surprised that I resent anyone who would put my career in the army in jeopardy, and that's just what a relationship with you would do. That's why every time you make a pass at me, you show me disrespect. And your outburst today just confirmed that you don't think much of me."

"No, Sam, that's just wrong."

"Oh, and what were you implying when you said I did something to get in as a pilot?"

"Nothing."

"Uh huh. I hope maybe knowing what I overcame to get where I am, you'll start to take me more seriously as a person. You can't imagine anything worse than the police showing up on a Thursday afternoon and telling you your father has died in a car crash, and what it takes to bounce back from that."

"I can think of something worse."

"Don't you dare joke about my father's death."

"This is no joke. Worse than hearing your father is dead is when your dad disappears and hearing nothing. For weeks. Every minute is torture, thinking he must be dead, but not knowing, and crying for days on end and watching your mother cry. Helpless. Then at long last you hear he's alive and well, but he's not coming back. You don't believe it at first. He's my father. He loves me, doesn't he? Maybe someone kidnapped him and brainwashed him or something. But eventually you come to accept the awful truth; he's abandoned you. So you suffer through months of anger and grief. You wish he was dead. He's gone anyway, and it's better than being thrown away. Then time and necessity assert themselves and somehow you pick up the pieces and go on, though your mother is never the same."

"I know that story. It ends badly."

"I know. I'm not trying to say I had it worse than you did. My mother went on, but with her self-confidence shattered, she threw herself at some lowlife who beat her and eventually ground her down to nothing until she died at age forty-nine. I just want you to remember that your father and mother loved you, and you always have that consolation. You'll never hear your rich father telling you he can't loan you any money because he has his own kids to educate." Daniel stopped for a minute to ward off tears. Then he continued, "We've both overcome a lot to get here. It just convinces me more that we make a perfect match, but you can't see beyond the issue of rank."

"And you can't accept that the issue of rank is so serious it could end my career, and you can't accept that I want another man. Until you do, we'll be at each other's throats. If you do, I think we can be good friends. We can be nothing more. I'm sorry."

From: Samantha Hawkins
Date: Friday, April 17, 2009
To: Terry Hawkins
Subject: Beaton

Beaton and I had it out yesterday, yelling at each other, again over his refusal to accept I've chosen Paul and not him. I ended up slapping him. Craig was angry with both of us, and we had to apologize to each other. We had a good talk, and he was serious for once in his life. I hope we've put it behind us because we have to work together for another eight months. He's a nice guy, and I feel sorry for him that I can't return his feelings.

Sick humor this past week is a bit grisly. We were called out to help a man who had been attacked by his neighbor with an ax, believe it or not. The man died before we got there, so we turned around. Anyway, Beaton said, "I bet you I know what his last words were: what's with the ax?" Then Talon said, "I think it was, hey you ugly pig fucker, give me my ax back." Then I said, "What do I look like, a fucking tree?" And Dan, "I get the impression you're pissed." And Talon, "Your wife has sexy ankles." And Craig, "Ouch." That seemed to be the last word on the matter, but then Talon started it again by asking, "What do you think the ax murderer said?" And I answered, "I'm going to cut you a new ax hole." And Craig said, "Timber!" Then I said, "Rashid, think fast!" And Talon: "Hold still, there's a spider on your face." And the kicker by Dan: "Why the hell does this tree keep crying out? Bathsheba, where the fuck are my glasses?"

Love, Sam

*

On the way to medevac an Afghan man who had been injured by an IED in early May, Craig's Black Hawk began deploying flares, onboard computers having detected a threat. "Muzzle flashes everywhere!" exclaimed Craig.

"It's an ambush," concluded the Apache pilot. "Get the hell out of here. We'll cover you."

Craig turned to Samantha and said, "Let me take this." She nodded as Craig pitched the chopper down and into a steep port bank. "Radio our situation to command," ordered Craig. Samantha complied.

The Apache escort returned fire as it, too, spit out flares. As Craig brought his Black Hawk out of its turn, his crew saw an intense flash in the sky. "Jade and Pimp!" screamed Samantha, referring to the call signs of the two pilots in the Apache. Before they had time to radio to confirm what they all knew, their Black Hawk nosily dropped more flares. The pilots saw a stinger anti-aircraft missile streaking toward them. Craig banked hard to the right. "Another one!" Samantha screeched, pointing to her left, and Craig once more turned hard.

The crew held their collective breath as the chopper maneuvered violently to escape the missiles. The first missile passed them by, but the second exploded on a ridge just to the right of the chopper, sending debris and shrapnel rocketing through the chopper.

With the helicopter rapidly closing in on a mountainside, Samantha, wondering why the lieutenant wasn't climbing or turning, looked to her right and noticed Craig's head hanging down. She shrieked, "Craig?" as she assumed control. With no time to think, she yanked up the collective and pulled over the cyclic to try to clear the precipice. "Shit, shit, shit!" she said as the aircraft passed a few inches over the ridge. Unfortunately, the rear rotor clipped the hill and disintegrated. With the aircraft out of control in a spin, she pleaded, "Craig, should I shut down the main rotor to stop us spinning and try an autorotation? Lieutenant?"

"He's out, Sam," Daniel informed her.

She vociferated, "Shit! What do I do?" Without waiting for an answer that no one had, she lowered the collective. "All the way down," she chanted as she harkened back to her training. "Right pedal—Careful! No tail rotor—enter autorotation;

engine disengaged, aft cyclic to make sure nose doesn't drop; watch RPMs and air speed; find good spot to land and keep it in sight." The spinning stopped, but the ground was coming at them at an alarming speed. Below them was a narrow valley with a small stream surrounded by precipitous, rocky gradients. Samantha struggled to lower the forward speed and descent speed of the aircraft while avoiding canyon walls and orienting her helicopter to the flat terrain.

*

Daniel was convinced they would plow into the hill with no need for further burial, but just when it seemed too late, Samantha flared the chopper to slow the descent and forward speed. They hit the ground hard and skidded forward ten meters to the base of the incline where the main rotor hit the rocks and spun the aircraft around. They all sat for a few dozen rapid heartbeats in the dust bowl initiated by the crashing helicopter before Talon said, "Let's get out. We're smoking bad."

Daniel unfastened his safety belt, but Talon was having difficulty because his left shoulder had been dislocated in the crash. Daniel noticed and helped him unbuckle. Samantha had turned her attention to Craig and was undoing his seatbelt, but Daniel said, "No, Sam! Let me check his neck before you move him." She and Talon left the Black Hawk as Daniel checked Craig. Discovering a piece of shrapnel sticking out of his helmet, Daniel cringed. If this went too far through, he would be in real peril. At least he was breathing.

Talon opened the pilot's door and yelled, "The bird's on fire. Get him out."

"I just need—"

"Now!" roared Talon as he used his good arm to pull the lieutenant out. Daniel jumped out the co-pilot's open door and ran around to help Talon drag their unconscious leader away from danger. Samantha, still in a daze, followed. Talon said, "Move it, Sam! Bird's going to blow." She trotted, and just as she caught them, the Black Hawk exploded. The shock wave knocked them all down, but none suffered further injury, although Talon shouted in pain when he fell on his injured shoulder.

Daniel returned his attention to Craig. Carefully removing the helmet, he found to his relief that although the object had penetrated the back of his skull it hadn't pierced his brain. He was bleeding enough to cause concern, however. Daniel pulled out a few basic medical supplies he kept in various pouches on his uniform and armor and got to work removing the shrapnel and staunching the bleeding.

"Is he all right?" asked Samantha in a shaky voice.

"I think so," replied Daniel. "The injury doesn't look that bad. It'll depend on what kind of shaking his brain took."

"We have to get away from here," advised Talon. "The fuckers who blew us out of the sky will be along any minute."

Daniel stood and said to Samantha, "Help me take off the Chief's armor."

"No!" said Talon. "We're sitting ducks here. We need to get to that clump of trees up there now. We can see what's coming from there and can defend ourselves."

Daniel picked up Lieutenant Ng and put him over his right shoulder, and the downed crew made their way up the steep slope toward the trees. After a few minutes, Daniel was puffing hard and slowing down. They were exposed on the hillside, still fifty sheer meters from the trees. Darkness was falling, but not fast enough for their current predicament.

"Let me carry him," offered Talon.

"With a useless arm?"

"I have two."

"Just give me a minute to rest."

"No time," said Talon. He knelt next to Craig and heaved him up with one arm to his shoulder. "Carry this," he said to Daniel as he kicked at his rifle. They resumed their upward trek.

After covering half the remaining distance to the trees, Daniel said he'd take the lieutenant from there. Breathing heavily, Talon needed no convincing. As Daniel lifted Craig onto his left shoulder, Samantha cried, "Look! Insurgents closing in on our chopper."

"Hurry," urged Talon.

The three chugged up the incline, with Talon staying behind Daniel to provide cover if needed. It was. The enemy spotted the three and began shooting. Bullets hit the ground all around them. They tried climbing faster, but the grade was too steep to make fast progress. "Come on, go," Daniel said aloud to himself as he battled stubborn gravity. Talon turned to return fire, but couldn't manage it with one shoulder out of commission. He pushed up the hill.

With ten meters to go to cover, Samantha took a bullet in her back that threw her forward onto the ground. She yelped in pain, the vest having stopped the bullet, but not all the energy. She struggled to get to her feet as a concerned Daniel reached her. "I'll help her. You keep going," said Talon. With the barrage from below continuing, Talon reached her and pulled her up to her feet, and the three covered the last few meters and dived into the trees with bullets still whizzing by.

The shooting from below stopped. Talon crawled forward to see what their situation was and saw two groups of insurgents commencing the climb toward them. "You need to fix my shoulder right now," he said to Daniel.

Daniel helped him off with his armor and examined his shoulder. He said, "It's dislocated. Is this your first?"

"Third time."

"That's actually good under this shitty circumstance. It means I can do a manual relocation. "Ready?" He nodded. Daniel popped his shoulder back in place. A grimace was the only indication of pain. Daniel produced a lollipop, which Talon put in his mouth as he crept forward to begin shooting down the declivity. They had a temporary advantage, but darkness, which was becoming their enemy, was closing fast.

As Daniel checked on the lieutenant, Samantha pulled out her pistol and crawled a few feet to assist Talon. "Hold your fire for now, Sam," counseled Talon. "From this distance you won't hit anything with that." Talon picked off two of the insurgents before they rethought their strategy and retreated. Talon stopped shooting, ammunition being in short supply. "They'll come up as soon as it gets dark enough," he said. "Don't worry, they don't have these." He pointed to his NVGs.

"This is all my fault," Samantha declared as her tears stirred.

Thinking a jest might make her feel better, Daniel looked up from Craig and said, "Yeah, Sam, it's Flying 101. Fly over the mountain, not into it."

Which was apparently a poor idea, since she replied, "Oh, sometimes, you make me so mad, I could just, just, jam my fist down your throat and haul out your spine. If you're ever going to take something seriously, you'd think it'd be this. We're in real trouble here. We stand a good chance of dying, and all you can do is joke. I crashed the fifteen million dollar chopper they entrusted to me, and I stranded us here, surrounded by people trying to kill us." She began weeping.

Taken aback, Daniel responded, "Here's what I know, Sam. You and Craig saved our lives. He dodged two missiles, and you took over when he was hit and somehow avoided splattering us all over the cliff, then brought us down in one piece. I thought for sure we were dead."

"Me too," seconded Talon. "Only a top-notch pilot could've saved us. It was amazing flying. So stop punishing yourself and start congratulating yourself."

Craig moaned. He was awake, but confused. After a few minutes, he'd recovered enough to ask, "What happened? Where the hell are we?"

Daniel smiled, concluding there'd been no serious brain damage. They explained their situation, to which Craig reacted, "Shit."

"Here they come again," called out Talon.

"Help me up," said Craig.

"Nothing doing," replied Daniel. "You need to take it easy."

"First of all, I'm in charge here. Second, we're in trouble, and I'm not going to be a burden; I'm going to help. So help me up!"

"Sir, please," begged Samantha. "You could make things worse for yourself."

He sat up slowly, then cursed about a splitting headache. Daniel dispensed Tylenol, and Craig crawled to Talon's position. Talon looked at him and opened his mouth to speak, but Craig said, "I'm staying!" as he pulled out his pistol. Samantha and Daniel joined them. They all put on their NVGs.

Talon suggested, "Sam, maybe you can keep an eye out behind us to make sure none of the bastards try to surround us."

"I'm not a frail female to be protected, Chief. I'm helping."

Craig said, "The Chief is right. We're vulnerable from behind. We have to keep watch in all directions. Sam and Dan, find two good vantage points back there and keep a lookout."

Samantha and Daniel crawled back to find good lookout spots. Daniel made sure he kept close enough to Samantha to help if needed. Frail or not, she would be protected.

Talon opened fire on the approaching enemy. He shot in short bursts for about two minutes and was running low on ammunition. The insurgents were getting close enough for Craig to join the battle when an Apache and two Kiowa Warriors came rocketing down the valley pouring fire onto enemy positions. An AC-130 gunship joined in, pounding both sides of the valley. The four cheered. The Apache took care of the insurgents encroaching on Craig and crew and a medevac came in. "Christ, is this what I do for a living?" Craig said as the Black Hawk hovered above them and took a few rounds from nearby Taliban. The Apache decimated the shooters. Tom winched the four up into his helicopter. They hugged Tom and Andrew when Daniel, the last on the ground, was pulled into the chopper and it headed back to base.

The mood was subdued at JAF because of the lost Apache crew. All medevac and Apache crews attended an observance for the two men at the chapel.

Given the loss, Craig's crew couldn't celebrate their rescue, but had a small barbeque to give thanks to the cavalry. Samantha cooked her now famous cheeseburgers for her crew.

"That's our Sam," bragged Daniel. "She might fly into more mountains than we'd like, but she sure can cook." She kicked his shin. He added, "The only thing more delicious than the cooking is the cook," which earned him a second boot. A final addendum, "Sam, you saved our lives. Stand up and take a bow, but face away from me and do it slowly," earned him a third kick.

They, of course, discussed the crash with other crews. Corporal Tamara Wheeler, the newest flight medic at JAF, asked what was going through their minds when they were in the spin.

"I had a premonition we were going to crash," answered Talon.

Samantha said, "I honestly can't remember what I was thinking; I don't think I was. Just reverted to my training. But I know what Beaton was thinking: "AAAHHHHH!"

"Yes, it'll probably end up as one of my top ten shits of 2009," confirmed Daniel.

Frowning at that odd statement, Tamara turned to Samantha and commented, "Good thing you weren't captured. I'd hate to think of what they might do to a woman."

"Don't worry, they only want virgins. They'd just kill us," said Samantha.

The crew was given the next week off to recuperate and await delivery of a new helicopter.

From: Samantha Hawkins
Date: Tuesday, May 12, 2009
To: Terry Hawkins
Subject: Big News!

I know you think that since I'm in a war I must have so much to tell you, but I'm not holding back. Believe me, I tell you everything that happens, except for most gory details of our missions that you don't want to know. And usually not much happens around here beside medevacs. But last week something did. Before I tell you, I have to preface it: everyone on our crew is just fine. So don't freak.

We crashed last week. We were trying to dodge some flak, and we managed to evade it, but in the process lost our rear rotor. I had to land in the mountains without it, and even though I ruined the army's fifteen million dollar chopper in the process, Craig has nominated me for the Distinguished Flying Cross for outstanding achievement in flying! I feel honored and embarrassed at the same time. We'll see if it comes through.

I think Paul is the real thing, sis. When I'm with him, I get so excited; when I'm not, he's all I think about. I'm pretty sure I'm in love with him, but I have no idea how deep his feelings go for me. The only thing I didn't like about him was he was pushing too hard and too fast for sex. I need him to know I'm no slut, that I want to be much more than a lover, and I was refusing to go all the way yet, but he gave me a friendly warning on our date last weekend where he implied if I didn't come across soon there were plenty of other willing women here. That upset me, but I'm not willing to give him up, so I knew I had to give him what he wanted faster than I would have liked. After the crash, he was such a comfort to me that I decided the time was right. So there you have it. I'm just as bad as Nurse Sweetland. A month and he's in. I guess I have to reassure myself that I'm twenty-four and he's only my second lover, so I'm not a huge slut.

I want to spend at least some of our next leave with him, and he's anxious for that, too, but he doesn't want to take me home with him. I know it's too soon, but I'm still disappointed. He's agreed to spend the last few days of our next leave together. Beaton's been saying how much fun the Gold Coast of Australia is, hoping to get me to go with him. Not a chance, of course, but from what he's told me, I would like to go there, and I'm probably closer here than I'll be any other time of my life. I asked Paul about it, and he likes the idea. I might tell Beaton I'll meet him there—he said he's going to see an old girlfriend there—then mention I'll be taking Paul along. That should at last get the message through to him that I want Paul, not him.

I hope I can make our weekend in the Gold Coast more romantic by buying a sexy negligee and making it the first time we do it au natural. I'm going to need birth control, and I'm not experienced with any of this, as you know. Neither are you, obviously. It's a little awkward talking to Paul about birth control, but I wanted a doctor's opinion. So, I told Beaton my roommate needed advice on the topic. Bugger said, "Tell her not to worry; her face is all the birth control she'll ever need." He's so damn exasperating. I'll have to rely on the Internet.

Love, Sam

CHAPTER NINE

Massacre – June, 2009

To help dispel the unrelenting boredom, Daniel dropped by Samantha's room. He saw that she was on her laptop and Susan was playing a video game. He said to Susan, "What the hell you playing *Call of Duty* for? Don't you get enough of the real thing?"

"Never enough. I'm pretending I'm blowing away dozens of little Daniel Beatoffs. It's good therapy."

"You need therapy. Entrusting an Apache to someone like you gives me nightmares."

"One day, if I'm lucky, you'll be a victim of my friendly fire."

Turning to Samantha, he said, "She-man has something to learn in the way of hospitality. She doesn't make me feel welcome in this war at all."

Samantha didn't look up from her computer.

Susan continued, "You're not a willing participant. You don't give a shit about the army or anything it stands for. You're only here to get some money to pay for college."

"So what? I benefit and so does everyone I help."

"You thumb your nose at all of us who've decided to make this a career. You don't respect the chain of command."

"I don't respect idiocy, so if someone who outranks me is an idiot, which is most often the case, then I don't respect him or her or both, as in your case."

"This is just what I'm talking about. As far as I'm concerned, you should be put in the stockade for insulting your superior like that."

"And this is just what I'm talking about. I save lives every day in this shit pit, but that doesn't matter to you. One insult to a superior is enough to cancel out, what? A hundred saved lives? All that matters to you is that I don't worship the Christly army and all its foolishness."

"Tell me, Beatoff, would you die for your country? Wait; you're Canadian, so who cares?"

"If either of my countries were truly at risk, as in World War 2, absolutely. Otherwise, not a chance. I'll die to save my fellow soldier or anyone who's at risk of dying, but I won't die because the politicians have gotten us into a war that ninety percent of Americans and Canadians put at or near the top of their who-gives-a-shit list. And I certainly won't die to advance some officer's or warrant officer's career."

"So, you want to cut and run?"

"No. That would leave the Taliban too much leeway to stir up trouble, especially in Pakistan. But we can't stay here forever, and I can't imagine the weak and corrupt covey of retards running this country being able to fend off the strong and corrupt retards trying to take back power. Sooner or later the Taliban will win unless something changes drastically."

"A bunch of Muslim fanatics won't beat us. God would never permit it."

"Amazing how neither side's zealots can see their idiocy reflected in the other side."

"Do you even believe in God?"

"You mean the creator of the universe, the giver of life, the source of everything good?"

She nodded.

"Not for an instant."

"You're pathetic," said Susan.

"You believe in Adam and Eve, Satan, Jonah and the goddamn whale, and all the rest of the nonsense?"

"It's in the bible, isn't it?"

"So, you don't believe that it's just supposed to be allegories?" She didn't appear to understand the question, so he clarified, "Parables, metaphors, symbols to get a message across, like Noah's Ark: respect my righteousness or I'll slaughter the entire planet."

"If it's in the bible, it's true."

"So evolution is crap?"

"Yes."

"The literal mind is a closed mind, a dull, lifeless mind, and this is what they put in charge of lethal weapons platforms."

"Enough, Beaton," asserted Samantha. "Show some respect for her rank and her beliefs."

"And if she believes in leprechauns, should I respect that, too? How about if she believes in the Koran?"

"You have no use for religion, but most people do, and you have to respect that."

"Respecting religion is what brought us here. How can you spend any time in this country and doubt that religion poisons people? Maybe it's okay when it subdues the unwashed masses by convincing them their life doesn't suck as much as it obviously does, but when it stirs them to mindless violence it becomes a real menace. And that's what this war is all about. It's not so much Islam versus Christianity and Judaism. It's religion against common sense."

"Get out of here, Beaton," yelled Samantha.

"Nice debating with you, Hawkins. I expected drivel from her, but not you. You disappoint me again. I've apparently overestimated you."

"Out!" screamed Susan.

He left.

*

In early June, a major from JAF came to the hooch to talk to the troops about volunteering some of their time to help the locals. "FOB Fenty outdid itself pitching in for World Environment Day last week," said Major Circelli. "But I noticed that our medevac and Apache crews didn't participate. I'm hoping to turn that around."

"Major, by definition, our first-up and second-up crews and our Apache escorts have to be here ready to leave at a moment's notice," explained Lieutenant Ng.

"I understand that, Lieutenant, but what about those who had the day off? No one from this unit showed up to help on June 5." He looked at his list. "Staff Sergeant Okeeweehow?"

"Here, sir."

"Did you do anything special to recognize World Environment Day?"

"No, sir. I didn't know anything about it."

"We put posters up all over the base. Specialist Beaton, what, if anything, did you do?"

As Craig held his breath, Daniel replied, "Well, sir, I flew to the Amazon to burn down a jungle, then to Africa to plug an elephant and saw off its tusks, then to Newfoundland to use the tusks to club adorable baby seals." Craig shook his head, but the major took it in stride; he was easy-going and liked by everyone.

"Most people in the medical corps like helping people," responded Major Circelli. "Don't you like helping people?"

"Helping people is overrated. I'm heartily sick of it. So sick of it that if a starving little African boy with big eyes and distended stomach tapped me on the knee and held out his hand for something, anything to extend his miserable existence, I'd tell him to go fuck a monkey. I've done enough for people."

Hearing Talon snirtle in trying to hold in a cackle, Daniel proceeded, "And if in desperation he persisted and tugged on my pant leg and pointed to a crumb clinging to my upper lip from a gigantic turkey dinner I just finished, I'd bend over to move my face close to his, fish the morsel from my lip with my tongue and curl my tongue into my mouth. I've done enough for people."

That burst the dam for Talon, who doubled over laughing, but Samantha was unmoved, so Daniel continued, "And if his big eyes overflowed and his shoulders slumped and he fell to his knees sobbing, I'd point and laugh at the little christer, and tell him to drop dead and rot. I've done enough for people!" That made Samantha snicker, which would have to do.

Chuckling, the major said, "Be that as it may, there are lots of children in this country who need our help, so I just volunteered you for vaccination duty at the primary school in Jalalabad on the twenty-sixth."

"Bad idea, sir. Perfect target for the Taliban," returned Daniel.

"Not even they would blow up kids getting vaccinations."

"Sir, these sons-a-bitches could've taught Hitler a thing or two about evil. They attack schools, teachers, and school kids all the time, especially if they dare to educate girls or dare to teach boys something beyond their Medieval theology."

"The school is just an open courtyard, and it's right next to a mosque. They're not going to blow up a mosque."

"No, they'll target the courtyard."

"Sorry, Specialist, this is not an option; it comes directly from the Major General in Bagram. Dispensing vaccinations is part of US policy. A lot of these children will die of preventable diseases if they don't get vaccinated. You're in charge of administering the vaccinations."

"Will you be joining me, sir?"

"I'd love to, but I'm not qualified for medical work."

"How terribly happy for you."

*

On June 26, a squad of marines, including a female engagement team of four, provided protection for the inoculation operation as Daniel and two nurses from JAF dispensed the MMR shots. They vaccinated hundreds of children during the morning and early afternoon, yet there remained a long queue at 2:33 in the afternoon when the marines suddenly scrambled. A female corporal shouted something, catching Daniel's attention. He looked up to see her lieutenant approaching someone wearing a burka. The marines had spotted something amiss: the woman—or was it a man?—was clearly agitated.

The lieutenant pointed his rifle at the person. One of the female marines hollered something in Pashto, and the children and their parents started screaming and running. A few seconds later, a flash and an enormous boom. Daniel and the two nurses were thrown backwards by the force of the explosion.

For a few moments he lay there stunned. He sat up, his head spinning, ears ringing, and eyes blurry. As the dust settled, and as he returned to his senses, he surveyed the massacre before him, not quite understanding or believing what he was seeing.

In front of him, about thirty feet off, was one of the female marines, at least it seemed like a female body. Most of the head was gone. Beside her was a young child, still moving its arms. The face below the forehead looked like it had exploded; it hung like bloody curtains from his eyes down. How the child was still alive Daniel could not fathom. Beyond them were bloody body pieces. How many human beings they came from, he could hazard no guess. He scanned from left to right; more dying and dead children. He got to his feet and threw up.

He staggered toward one little girl lying on her side. From her back he could see nothing wrong and thought maybe he could begin with her. He knelt and turned her gently onto her back. Her rib cage was in splinters; one had pierced the heart. She must have died quickly. Small mercy. Another girl nearby was twitching. Her abdomen was mince meat. No chance, he concluded. Farther on was a little girl, dead, half-open eyes seeing nothing, and a young boy, also dead, face without definition or expression. To his left, he spotted one of the male marines lying in an expanding pool of blood, pale, and slurring his words; he was in desperate shape. Daniel went to see if he could help, but the man stopped breathing.

Closer to where he and the nurses had been were at least a dozen children, several adult civilians, probably parents, six marines and the nurses. Most were injured, some were shrieking, some stumbled around, some lay writhing, some lay still. All were in a daze or unconscious.

Benumbed, he turned in place looking at the broken little bodies all around him. Overwhelmed and having no idea where to begin, he sat and began crying. A marine sergeant placed his hand on his shoulder and said, "You were giving the shots. Are you a doctor?"

"Uh, not yet. I mean, I'm a flight medic," he answered, wiping his eyes with his sleeve.

"I know this is tough, but you have to get going on helping these people."

"How?"

"Just start somewhere, anywhere!"

Daniel got to his feet and said, "Call for medevacs, from Jbad and Asadabad. All of them. I have to check on the nurses to see if we can get some triaging going. And whatever help your marines can give might save a few lives."

"There are only four of us left standing, and we need to provide security until reinforcements arrive, but we'll do what we can."

Daniel went to check the nurses. One was sitting up clutching her knees in her arms and sobbing. She didn't appear to be injured. He asked for her help, but she didn't seem to hear him. He asked again; same result. He found the other nurse unconscious. The back of her head was bleeding, but he couldn't see any further injuries. Checking her pupils and pulse, he concluded she'd been knocked out upon hitting the ground and should recover unless the brain was injured.

Returning to the other nurse, he tried appealing to her once more, but she kept weeping. He shook her and screamed, "Get to your feet and help me, for God's sake!" That snapped her out of her trance, and she looked at him. "Come on, we need to help these people." She swallowed hard and nodded. He handed her a Magic Marker. "Focus on the living only. Go to everyone, starting with those lying on the ground. They're probably hurt the worst. If someone can't get air, let me know right away. Otherwise, write on their forehead: u for urgent, p for priority, r for routine and, uh, I don't know, h for hopeless?" She nodded and commenced her appalling task.

Daniel recovered his medical rucksack and started with the child whose face was in shreds. The boy was breathing lightly, but survival was out of the question. He wanted to give the boy morphine in case he was feeling any pain, but he couldn't spare it. He had only three doses with him.

Next he went to a screaming child and determined her injury was not life-threatening. Not wanting to give her morphine, he offered her a fentanyl lollipop, but she screeched more. The disaster was such that he had to leave her as she was to see to more pressing cases.

He decided the best course was to follow in the tracks of the nurse to commence treating the urgent cases. Already she'd written a u on three foreheads. He began with the youngest, a girl crying softly. She was bleeding profusely from her left leg and left arm. Daniel extracted two tourniquets and called to the nurse, "When a patient is bleeding heavily, put on a tourniquet at once." He tossed over the two others he had left and called over to the sergeant, "We need any tourniquets your soldiers have." He went to collect them. Full reason finally restored after the shock began to recede, Daniel concluded the best use of their time until help arrived was to apply the ABCs of triage; airway before breathing before circulation. Keep them alive!

He put on the tourniquets and moved to the next patient. This was a woman who was conscious. She had a deep wound on her upper right torso and a collapsed lung. As he prepared to work on her, she flung her arms around. Daniel was ready to ignore her protests, but a female marine said, "She'd rather die than have a man touch her."

"You're shitting me!" he said.

"How can I help?" the marine asked.

He shook his head and said, "If she wants to let her goddamn religion kill her, so be it. I don't have the time to direct you."

"Will she die?"

"Yes," he replied as he knelt next to a young boy and started examining him.

"Then you have to help me to help her."

"Look around you, Corporal. Do you see all the u's on foreheads? They'll all die without immediate help. If I waste time supervising something I could do in a third of the time, three others will die." Glancing over at a little girl nearby writhing in pain and sobbing, he added, "As it is, every time I choose which child to help next, I wonder if I'm condemning another one to death because I didn't get to her on time."

The boy had a horrific wound covering most of his back and exposing muscle and even the spine in places. The youngster was moaning softly. This one should have had an h on his forehead. Daniel shook his head and gave the boy one of the morphine doses. That was all he could do for him. He went to the little girl.

Frantic parents began to pour into the courtyard, screeching and hollering, increasing the bedlam and making it more difficult to take care of the patients. Those who found their injured child screamed at Daniel to help theirs, but he had to ignore them to work on the gravest cases first. One came and pulled at his arm while he was trying to decompress the girl's lung. He shook the man off, but he kept at Daniel. He had no choice but to go to his son next. He had a p on his forehead and there were still u's to deal with, but he quickly put a bandage on the boy's back and gave him a Tylenol Bi-layer

Caplet. He got up to proceed to the next u, but the father appeared dissatisfied and grabbed him again. Out of patience, Daniel shoved him away hard and snarled, "Fuck off!" The female corporal stepped in to help, and the man returned to his son.

As if things weren't bad enough, Daniel was feeling sick. He'd been feeling this way for days now and was beginning to get worried. He was exhausted and had to pee so bad he was aching. With no time to do this, and drenched in sweat and blood and enveloped by the stench of mutilated bodies, he reasoned no one would notice, so he let go in his uniform. He had no time to get humiliated.

Next was another child with a penetrating chest wound. Daniel applied an Asherman Chest Shield, and dispensed the second dose of morphine and started an IV of Ringer's solution. The boy clutched his hand and didn't want to let go. "Corporal? You want to help?"

"Anything," she answered.

"Hold this boy's hand and keep this elevated," he said as he handed her the bag of Ringer's solution.

She sat next to him, took his hand, and held up the bag.

The first two medevacs arrived from JAF. With help here, Daniel proceeded to the person shrieking the loudest, checked his wounds, and gave him the last dose he had of morphine to shut him up. The wound was not that severe; his forehead read r.

Andrew and Tamara gasped as they beheld the gruesome scene. Daniel waved them over. "Fuck me," was all Andrew could say. Tamara vomited.

Daniel said, "Start with anyone with a u on the forehead, then the p's, then r's. The h means hopeless, but we may want to double-check our triaging as we go." They nodded. Daniel took Tamara to the woman who had refused his help, but she had died. Tamara focused on other wounded women.

Not long after, his medevac crew arrived on their day off. Paul was with them. Ten minutes later, the medevac from Asadabad arrived. Its flight medic, Sergeant Rene Willows, also winced at the slaughter. Overwhelmed, she nevertheless got right to work.

Daniel took a breather to look over at his chopper. He needed to see Samantha, if only for a moment, to avoid utter despair. Samantha's hand was over her mouth, and he knew she, too, was weeping, but the sight of her was enough to re-energize him and give him the will to proceed.

Paul identified the six most serious cases, and the medics packaged them. They were transported on Craig's chopper, with Daniel remaining behind in the dust, so much dust that nothing could ever grow.

Two long, horrible hours later, the medics and doctors had done all they could and had transferred the living to hospitals. Marines were in force at the school yard, providing protection and investigating.

Daniel took a last look at the awful scene. Some parents still walked around shouting and crying. Their children were probably in pieces, Daniel knew. Others wept over small bodies. At these sights Daniel would have shed more tears had he had any left. He saw that the female marine was still holding the boy's hand. She was rocking back and forth and stroking his hair. He walked over to her. "He's dead," was all she said.

"You can't do anything more here. You should go."

"No! I can't leave him all alone." His parents were probably among the dead. The corporal had been the one who had first noticed the suicide bomber, enabling the soldiers to yell a warning, thereby saving many children from death or grievous injury. Perhaps that would be consolation for her someday, but not here, not now.

The sergeant who had tapped him on the shoulder sat in the middle of the carnage holding a dead girl in his arms. He was devastated. Daniel looked at him to convey his empathy and walked in a daze to the Humvee for the drive back to JAF. This bloodbath would haunt him, and all the people who dealt with it, for the rest of their lives.

Arriving at JAF, he made straight for Major Circelli's office, intending to beat him blue. He barged into his office about to wail and punch, but was completely disarmed to see the major sitting at his desk, head on his arms, which were propped on his desk, crying. The major had gone to see the schoolyard and had broken down. Daniel had been too busy to accost him then. Major Circelli looked up to see who came in, then lowered his red eyes. "I can't believe they did this. I know you warned me. I'm sorry. It's my fault. Oh, God!" He wept for a few moments before taking a deep breath and saying in a subdued voice, "I know you want to kill me now, and I don't blame you. Do your worst. I won't try to stop you."

Daniel turned and left the office.

Samantha dropped by his room that evening. Only that morning, before all this, she'd told him, "You're always a poor specimen, Beaton, but lately you've looked like a walking cadaver." Now, his red, puffy eyes made him look more sickly.

"I think you need this," she said; she stepped forward and embraced him.

He latched on, pulled her close, felt her body against his, and breathed in her scent. So emotional over the events of the day and so overtaken with her compassionate gesture, he started trembling. He wanted to hold her and float far away to a place where they could be safe together. Samantha represented much more than sex to him; she was hope, she was life, she was love. Afghanistan was dust; Samantha was DUSTOFF. He didn't want to let her go, ever, but she was being a friend, he knew, not a lover.

*

He was becoming more than a friend to her, though what she could hardly tell. She knew he was an exceptional man, but lately she'd considered him more aggravating than anything. So, when she heard of the explosion in the schoolyard, that many were dead and terribly injured, she was taken aback at the potency of the dread that surged within her. The thought that Daniel might be dead was terrifying.

In a frenzy she'd rushed to get her helicopter ready. It took more time than usual because this was their day off and they weren't prepared. The entire time she was pleading with her crewmates to hurry. They'd had to wait a few minutes for Paul because he had to collect the supplies he might need, and she was shuddering by the time they took off. When she landed, she left the helicopter to find him, praying he was safe. When she saw him bending over a little girl, petting her hair and giving her a fentanyl lollipop, she fell to her knees in relief.

Only then did she take notice of the scope of the catastrophe. She ran back to her cockpit and wept.

So, Samantha was reveling in the hug as well because he was safe; how sound was another issue. She worried about his state of mind and hoped she could help by showing him she cared.

Finally, she ended the hug because he could no longer suppress a hard impression of his sexual desire for her. She kissed his cheek and left.

*

The medical personnel who'd dealt with the tragedy were ordered to undergo psychological counseling. Daniel went and began the session by dismissing the captain, saying she had to be there to understand.

"I was there," she said. "I knew my services would be needed, so I sucked it up and went to the schoolyard. No words can describe the horror. So, I might not have gone through what you did, but I do understand."

Daniel apologized and took her seriously from then on. The sessions helped, but the wound would stay raw for some time.

All medevac crews went to the chapel on base for a special gathering organized to pray for the dead and injured. Even Daniel, who hated anything to do with religion, went to pay his respects. But when the chaplain focused on one child who had been dug up alive from under the rubble of the mosque wall a day after the blast and slapped the miracle label on it, Daniel couldn't hold his tongue.

The brigade chaplain cited the mystery of God's way and how it is not for man to know why such disasters occur, but

He shows He cares through miracles like this one. "Thank merciful God for saving that tiny child," he declared.

"And curse merciless God for the butchery that overwhelmed it," said Daniel.

Turning to him, the chaplain said, "And what makes you think God caused the carnage, my son?"

"Well, pops, if He stepped in to save one person and let the other twenty die, He as good as caused it. The miracle would've been preventing it in the first place."

"For all you know, He does that all the time."

"Not all the time, obviously. If He can stop it, why doesn't He every time? If He can and doesn't, He's complicit."

"We cannot know the reasons God chooses to intervene at some times, but not others."

"So, then, how can you know that He in fact intervenes, that He in fact exists?"

"We are blessed with faith."

"You are cursed with naivety and gullibility."

"Enough, Specialist."

"There we have it. When you meet a heretic, you have to get rid of him lest he infect the flock. A few hundred years ago you'd have simply killed me. Now it's not so easy, but you'll still use whatever authority you have to silence the lonely voice of reason."

"Most of these men and women here believe in our Lord, and it's not your right to call them stupid or to question their beliefs."

"But it's your right to foist your foolishness on me?"

"No one's forcing you to believe."

"Only because you can't get away with it anymore. Radical Islam can and does, though. The Taliban blew up those children to force the local population to believe as they do, or else. Religion caused this whole Christly mess, yet here you are trying to give it credit for not wiping out quite everyone in that courtyard."

"Get the hell out of here!" screamed a corporal.

Daniel walked up to him intending to smash him in the face, but Samantha stepped between them. Unwilling to risk hurting her, he backed down. She grabbed his arm and dragged him out of the chapel. Outside, she said, "You have to learn when enough is enough, Beaton."

"The irony in there was killing me. Here we have this idiot preaching nonsense about God and everyone eats it up, clueless that that very nonsense killed those children and landed us here."

"If people find comfort in believing in God, where's the harm?"

"Where's the harm? Where's the fucking harm?"

"Calm down."

"The harm is all over that school yard. The harm is it's all bullshit, bullshit that costs millions of lives."

"At its worst, that's true; at its best, religion helps a lot of people. My belief in God helped me get past my parents' deaths and still gives me hope that I'll see them again."

"False hope."

"Says you. How can you be so sure?"

"Same way I know there's no Santa Clause or Easter Bunny. I thought about it and came to the obvious conclusion."

"Let's say you're right, and it's false hope. If it makes me happy, who are you to take it away?"

"False hope is the enabler. It's what gives the holy men power over us. False hope makes it possible to get idiotic zealots to blow up children. Who the hell are you to subject children to that so you can fool yourself that you'll see your parents again?"

And with that he walked away.

CHAPTER TEN

Sick – July 2009

"What's that?" asked Samantha. She had gone to her helicopter to ready her equipment for their second-up shift beginning in two hours. Daniel hadn't seen her coming, and she spotted him placing a needle against his finger.

He looked at her in shock and struggled for an answer. "Uh, nothing."

"Let me see that, Beaton," she demanded.

"It doesn't concern you," he replied.

"The hell it doesn't," she rejoined, grabbing for the needle. He withdrew it. "Dammit, Beaton, if our flight medic is an addict I need to know."

"An addict doesn't shoot himself up in the finger."

"Give that to me, or I'll go straight to Craig."

"Don't."

"Then tell me what you were doing."

"I'm testing my blood."

"Why?"

"Just a precaution."

"Bullshit. The look on your face when I caught you told me something is up. And you've looked awful for the past couple of weeks. What is it?"

"It's something that sneaks up on you and takes you by surprise. It comes on so quickly you don't even begin to suspect you have it until you've lost thirty pounds. Nothing leads you to think it could ever happen to you. It doesn't typically run in families.

"A person can explain away any symptom of it, even when he's a four-fifths doctor. Weight loss is nothing for a medic. Hell, we can drop fifteen pounds in sweat alone in a single afternoon, toiling in the 120-degree heat. And constant thirst? Well, a man who's just sweated out fifteen pounds needs to drink it back, doesn't he? Pissing every hour? To be expected when one is drinking so much. Voracious appetite? I'm working so hard I need a lot of calories. Extreme fatigue? Isn't that natural when a man works long, arduous hours in a sweatbox? And blurry vision? This place is a permanent dust bowl. But after the tenth person tells you you look like a zombie and you weigh yourself and discover you're down thirty pounds and—"

"Stop. What do you suspect?" She was getting scared for him.

"I finally put the clues together last week, and I said to myself, Oh, shit! No way! Fuck, Sophia, you wouldn't do that to me, would you? What am I saying? Of course you would, and you'd wait till the worst possible time in my life to smite me with it."

"With what?"

"When we were at Bagram, I bought this little number." He handed her a glucometer. "It measures blood sugar."

"Diabetes?"

He looked at her solemnly and said, "Probably. I was just about to confirm it."

"Well?"

"This is really personal."

"I'm not leaving you now."

He trembled as he opened the box and took the glucometer out. Samantha noticed the trembling as it began to sink in what this meant for him. He dropped the insert and removed a test strip.

"Shouldn't you read the directions?"

"God dammit, Sam, believe it or not, I'm a doctor. I've done this plenty of times, just not on myself." He positioned the needle at the tip of his middle finger on his left hand, held his breath, and pushed the trigger. Shaking more, he squeezed his finger to force out a drop of blood. "Shit! Didn't work." She, too, started quivering. Another piercing. Another squeeze. A drop of blood. He dabbed it with a strip and slid it into the glucometer. They held their breath for the reading. "Oh, Jesus!" He began crying.

"Dan?" His crying launched hers. She could see this was devastating for him.

"It's twenty-eight."

"What does that mean?"

"When blood glucose is twenty-eight millimoles per liter, it's sludge." Tears streamed down his face. "That high and ketoacidosis will damage my organs in no time."

She took his hand and said, "So you have diabetes?"

"Type 1, I'm guessing." He wasn't being clear, but it's hard to communicate when inundated in a swirl of emotions, none of them good. "My body has betrayed me; it's attacking itself. I'll die without insulin. What the hell am I going to do? What am I going to do?"

She hugged him and said, "We need to check you into the hospital right away."

"No!"

"But you just said your organs will be damaged."

Quavering and weeping, he exited the helicopter and vomited. "God help me, a lifetime of sticking myself with needles and watching what I eat and worrying that I'm going to black out at a critical time and wondering about my eyes and kidneys and ... God help me."

She embraced him again. "Come on. I'll go with you to the hospital."

"No! No one can know. The army will boot me out. I'll be considered a liability to myself and anyone near me in a combat zone."

Her initial impulse was to reject the notion that the army would eject him, but on second thought she knew that was a real possibility, especially with all the reprimands on his record. She returned, "They might just reassign you; maybe active duty here in the hospital or back home in a hospital."

"If I were a full-fledged doctor, maybe, but I'm just a flunky to them. From what I've been able to gather from the Internet, they'll probably discharge me, which means I can't fulfill the terms of my contract, which means they don't pay for my medical school, which means I can't finish medical school, which leaves me nowhere, which means I've gone through fifteen months of hell here for nothing!"

"If they kick you out, shouldn't they have to pay as promised?"

"I doubt it. I can't risk asking. You have to keep this quiet. My whole future rests on completing my stint; only six more months. I can do this. I have to do this. Shit. Shit. Shit!"

"And if you pass out on a mission?"

"I won't. I'll control it. The last thing in the world I'd want is to lose a patient because I started shaking or blacked out, but I'm sure I can handle this."

"And if you screw up, it'll be my fault, too, if I say nothing. The army could conceivably charge you and me."

"How many lives have I saved here, Sam? Five hundred? Maybe more? All I ask in return for risking my life every day to save those lives is for the goddamn army to pay for my last year of medical school. I just need to serve six more months. Just look the other way, and I'll handle this."

"I'll be watching you closely. Do you have insulin?"

"I bought some in Bagram just in case." He got back in the chopper, took out the insulin pen, dialed it up, lifted his shirt, pinched the slight bit of fat he had on the side of his belly, and injected the insulin.

"Did it hurt?" she asked.

"Not too bad. The prick on the finger was worse."

"Give me some back-up supplies, just in case."

"She-man might find them, then I'm done. The only potentially disastrous situation is an extreme sugar low. For that I'd need glucagon. If you can keep a dose of that buried in a pouch, I'd be grateful." She took it and put it in a pouch. He thanked her and walked to his room crestfallen. Samantha watched him with his hands in his pockets, head and shoulders low, clipped steps, and she went to her room depressed.

*

After some consideration, Daniel felt he had to confide in his best friend. Talon, too, promised to keep quiet, but to keep a close eye on him.

*

A man in civilian dress strolled across the flight line and stepped onto the porch called Club Medic. Andrew, Tom, Talon, and Craig were sitting in wooden chairs smoking cigars. The man went inside the hooch and spotted Daniel talking to Samantha. Daniel was holding a tube and saying, "Do you know how many women would kill to massage my feet with fungicide? Is there no romance in you? Why are you so damn hard to please? Why must you always spew black ice onto the expressway to your heart? Sam? Sam?"

She lifted her eyes from the magazine in her hands and said, "Oh, I see; you thought I was listening to you." Two weeks after he started taking insulin, he was looking so much better that her worry seemed to have receded and she was again rejecting his advances, but not in a callous way. Daniel thought maybe she had feelings for him, although she never gave him any encouragement to love.

Daniel turned and recognized the Special Forces soldier he'd saved a few weeks earlier. "Hey, look who's here. A fellow Canadian. Looks like you've made a complete recovery."

"Thanks to you," said Jason.

"What brings you to the sphincter of the universe?"

"Passing through on my next assignment. Figured I could spend a few minutes thanking the man who saved my life."

"It was a team effort. This is Samantha Hawkins. She flew you to Bagram that day."

He held out his hand to Samantha and said, "Jason Carter. Thank you, ma'am." She shook his hand with a nod. "A lot of us can only do what we do because we know DUSTOFF has our backs, so I speak for all of us when I say, thank God for you gutsy motherfuckers."

"Poetic," pronounced Samantha.

Jason turned back to Daniel and said, "The surgeon who operated on me told me he couldn't believe a flight medic did what you did. He said I should have died on the front lines with the wound I had. How the hell did you do it?"

"Dan's our four-fifths doctor," replied Samantha, then she explained what she meant.

"So I just happened to get the one medic in the army who had a prayer of saving me."

"The real hero is that dog," said Samantha. "If we hadn't been called out to rescue him, you'd have traveled home as cargo."

"You might want to consider signing up for JTF2, Dan," said Jason. "They could use a man of your capabilities."

"They?" Jason smiled, and Daniel continued, "Thanks, but when I finish my contract, I'm going back to finish my degree."

"If there's anything I can do for you, just ask."

"Can you make Sam rub this ointment into my feet?"

"I believe that's contrary to the Geneva Conventions."

Daniel got up to get himself a coffee and asked Jason if he wanted one. Jason accepted. As they stood by the pot, Jason said, "You're into Sam, I see."

"I spend too much time wishing I was into her. She's incredible."

"But she's a warrant officer and can't fraternize you."

"If that's all it was, I'd be laughing since I'm out of the army in a few months, then I could spend the rest of my days fraternizing her. But one Captain Paul Telfer stands in my way. He's a flight surgeon here. Sometime when you're bored and you're looking for something to do, can you maybe stroll by Telfer and fling out your pinky to break his neck?"

"Sorry, but he's on our side."

"All I ask in return for saving your life is one measly murder and you say no?"

"Afraid so, but what I can do for you is check into him. Find his skeletons."

"He leaves plenty of those all over the place."

"I know this guy who's a whiz on computers. I'll have him check Telfer out and get back to you."

"That sounds underhanded and desperate. Do it!"

*

Later that day, Daniel joined Talon and Craig as they finished their meal in the mess hall and handed Talon his phone, saying, "It rang three times in ten minutes, so I answered the third time in case it was important. It was, uh, I think you got a call from yourself."

"What do you mean?"

"Well, it sure sounded like you, and he said his name, which sounded like yours, but it could have been another Talon Okeeweehow; you bastards are everywhere."

"Must've been my brother."

"Don't tell me he's another Talon."

"No. His first name is Eagle, but he uses his middle name."

"Don't tell me: Penguin," said Daniel as he put something resembling rice into his mouth.

"Nope."

"Bob?" guessed Craig.

"Sun," said Talon.

"I like Eagle better," returned Daniel. "Did it bother you that your brother got a whole bird and you only got a claw?"

"No."

"I guess it could've been worse; your parents might have chosen another bird part like Fluffy Down Okeeweehow," said Daniel.

"Or Left Eyeball Okeeweehow," put in Craig.

"Or Anus Okeeweehow," said Talon as he left to return his brother's call.

"Anus would be a unique name," said Daniel to Craig. "I mean, you don't bump into too many of those—if you do, you're not the man I thought you were—but just think, he could say things like, 'Please, my buddies call me Asshole.'"

192

Craig tittered and shook his head at this inane discussion. Swallowing his last bite, he left.

Ten minutes later, as Daniel ate his dessert, Samantha and Paul were picking up their trays to leave. Daniel watched her as she slid the tray onto the tray holder. Suddenly a 107-millimeter rocket exploded about twenty-five meters outside the entrance to the mess hall. The siren started, and Paul ducked under the nearest table, but Samantha stood still. Seeing Daniel dart toward her, she ran to him as the eerie whistle of another missile grew to a scream. He thought she was seeking his protection, but as the bomb exploded right at the entrance, she dragged him under a table and tried to cover him. Having none of this, he tried to shield her. "Me on top first, Sam," he said.

"Medic!" shrieked someone.

"Shit. Got to go," said Daniel. He ran to an injured soldier. Samantha ran behind him.

A woman was on the ground writhing in pain and screeching. Daniel gasped when he first saw her. Part of her head was gone. There was nothing he could do for her, he knew. Samantha also gasped. "Sam, go to the shelter." Looking at the stricken woman, she vomited. "Please go, Sam. You can't help."

Paul arrived and ordered Daniel to "Move aside, Specialist."

"Sir, there's nothing we can do."

"I said, move!"

Daniel obeyed the command, and Paul made his assessment. With the hapless soldier continuing to howl and thrash about, Samantha begged, "Give her something for the pain at least."

"I have no medicine," answered Paul, as he struggled to contain the woman's flailing limbs. She was now reduced to gurgling as Samantha looked on, horrified. The woman's flailing and gurgling stopped.

Another explosion in the distance rocked the base. "That's near our barracks," cried Samantha. She and Daniel left the dead soldier to Paul.

"Jesus Christ, it knocked down a wall of my unit. I think the Chief is in there!" Daniel exclaimed. He sprinted to see about Talon. Samantha followed.

"Chief? Chief?" called Daniel as he scurried through the gap in the wall. He found Talon sitting amidst rubble, bewildered. He ran to him and knelt beside him. Daniel quickly checked his friend with his eyes and hands. Talon was bleeding from his scalp and upper chest. To test his alertness, Daniel said, "Shit, Chief, I ran all the way here worried about my Listerine. Is it all right?"

Talon broke out in laughter, which brought a smile to Daniel's face. Samantha came running up with a frightened expression, but relaxed as she witnessed Talon sitting up laughing. "Your Listerine is fucked, dude."

"Goddamn Taliban bum bangers!" bayed Daniel, shaking his fist at the sky. Talon laughed more as Samantha furrowed her brow.

"Listerine?" she said.

"Shush! The Chief doesn't know my Listerine is gin; he might disapprove. And I don't know his Listerine is vodka, so don't tell me, or I'll drink it," explained Daniel.

Daniel dug his backup medical kit from under his collapsed bed, shook off the debris and dust, and took out what he needed. He put on rubber gloves, cut off Talon's shirt, and wiped the blood off his lacerations. "I'll need to stitch the cut on your chest. Here, have a sucker," he said, handing Talon a fentanyl lollipop. "I need to get this out," he informed Talon. A small shard of Plexiglas was sticking out of the wound in his chest. Talon nodded. He took in a breath through gritted teeth as Daniel extracted the spear.

While Daniel disinfected the area, Lieutenant Ng trotted up, yelling, "You guys all right?"

"The Chief has a few cuts," replied Daniel. "He should be fine, once I get him stitched up."

"Good. Let's get him to the hospital once you're done."

"I'm fine, sir," assured Talon as he winced in response to Daniel's stitching. "Make sure it's a sexy scar." Daniel smiled and nodded.

"You'll get a thorough check at the hospital, Chief," ordered Craig.

"Yes, sir."

"Everything okay at home?" asked Craig.

"Oh, yeah. I'm an uncle."

"Congrats," said Craig. "It's not many days you become an uncle and get blown up."

Samantha knelt next to Talon and hugged him. "Don't you dare scare me like that again, you thoughtless man."

"Lucky bugger," said Daniel. "Next time I get to be bombed to get a hug from Sam."

"Dan! Are you there? I need a medic in here now!" screamed Tom, who had just arrived.

"I'll get back to you," said Daniel to Talon as he ran next door. Dashing past several other soldiers who were wandering about asking if any help was needed, Daniel saw Tom bending over his roommate, who was on the floor, his legs buried under debris. "Prophet Andy!" said Daniel, dashing to the supine man. Andrew feebly gave his religion's holy sign, which was a fist going up and down in front of his crotch. Samantha walked in and knelt next to Andrew. She wiped off his face, held his hand, and stroked his cheek to comfort him as much as she could.

Daniel turned to the gathering crowd and said, "Can I get some help getting this shit off him?" Tom and three other G.Is. came in and helped. As soon as they lifted a large piece of wood off him, Andrew's leg began to spurt blood, the main stream of which went right into Daniel's eyes. "Shit!" shouted Daniel as he wiped his face on his sleeve and tried to blink the blood out of his eyes. He managed to clear his eyes enough to push his knee into Andrew's thigh to pinch off the artery. "Tommy, I can hardly see. I need you to pour some water on my eyes right away." Tom pushed some debris away from his mini fridge and took out a bottle of water. He opened it and poured it onto Daniel's face. "Thundering Christ, it's freezing!" he groused as he shook his head and blinked continuously until he regained his vision enough to tend to Andrew.

He pulled a tourniquet out of his medical bag, took pressure off his knee, slipped the tourniquet onto Andrew's leg, and tightened it to stop the bleeding. "He's too pale; he needs AB positive blood ASAP. Sam, can you—"

While Samantha ran off to get the supplies, Daniel started an IV to replenish fluids and took Andrew's blood pressure.

"Fuck, it hurts," muttered Andrew.

"It's good that pain is registering."

"Not from where I sit."

"I'll give you some morphine." Injecting the medicine, Daniel went on, "Those Taliban bastards destroyed our holy shrine."

Andrew managed a weak, "Bushless heathens," and closed his eyes.

"Is he going to be okay?" said Tom, plainly alarmed about his good friend.

"Let's just think happy thoughts. Be hopeful and gay. I mean gay as in happy face, not gay as in sore ass," said Daniel with a smile. Tom was evidently too disturbed to return it. Daniel continued, "Sarge, I wouldn't be joking if I thought he was in peril. He should be fine once we replace his blood. Legs don't look too bad."

"Can I do anything to help?"

"We're going to need a litter."

Tommy sprinted to get one.

Samantha returned with the blood supplies, which Daniel immediately got going. When Tom got back with the stretcher, he and Daniel carefully lifted the unconscious man onto it, secured him, and rushed him to the operating theatre with the help of the other soldiers.

Afterward, Daniel stopped by to check on Samantha. "Anything in the way of Sam in here, She-man?" he enquired as Susan answered his knock on her door.

"Go to hell, Beatoff," greeted Susan.

"Already here," he answered. She scowled at him. "Funny how you can look discomposed and decomposed at the same time." Her frown told him she had no idea what that meant.

He turned to Samantha, who was sitting on her bed, and asked, "Are you okay?" He could see she'd been weeping.

"Not really." Seeing Daniel and Susan glare at each other, Samantha got up and walked outside. Daniel followed. "I can't get that woman's screams out of my head."

"It was pretty bad," said Daniel.

"God, I honestly don't know how you handle this shit all the time. I can just keep my head forward when I fly and try to tune out any screams. But when I see the blood and the brains, and see a person in such agony … That gurgling sound she made was torture. All I could think of was, please, please die. We're in a world where we regularly long for someone's death. God, it's horrible."

Daniel nodded and talked with her until she felt a little better.

The next day, Daniel visited Andrew in the hospital. An alert Andrew grinned and gushed, "My apostle! I owe you my life; I'd have bled out for sure."

"Least I could do for my prophet," he answered as he took a chair next to the bed.

"True enough, apostle. I'm sure you feel honored."

Nodding, Daniel responded, "I'd have thought Sophia would've protected you from all this."

"For shame, apostle! Know not you that I live only because of the blessed babe? Two minutes before the explosion I was lying on my bed, which was right against the wall that exploded. I had gone over to the altar to pay her my respects when the missile landed. And the wondrous bitch is getting me home. I was injured just enough to secure me a ticket out of this shit pit. I would say this is definitely a miracle, except I'm not a religious retard."

"Will you rebuild your chapel at home?"

"Might be a little hard to explain to my fiancée. You must rebuild here, apostle. I'll leave Sophia to your capable hands."

"But, Prophet, does that mean you'll be married in front of a false god?"

"Charlene is Catholic, and they have silly pagan rituals I'll have to pretend to accept. I'll say a few Hail Sophias and make believe Charlene is Sophia."

As Daniel stood to leave, Andrew took his hand and said, "Dan, I'll never forget what you did for me. Thank you."

Daniel smiled and said, "I'll miss you. Take care of yourself." He left.

Talon, Tom, and Daniel had to move into a tent while their plywood shack was rebuilt.

*

A deafening explosion briefly illuminated the entire valley as a Hellfire missile launched from a drone landed on an enemy position 300 meters to the northwest of a platoon of American infantrymen who had been attacked by RPGs. The medevac chopper sat on the ground in a fog of dust seventy meters to the south with rotors whirling. "All right, we need to fuck off right now," ordered the lieutenant as Daniel finished packaging his patient for evacuation. "The drone spotted at least three dozen of the fuckers in the process of surrounding us. Get him on the chopper now." Four G.I.s hustled their wounded comrade to the helicopter. Daniel trotted by his side.

"Lieutenant, can you lift us the hell out of here?" continued the officer.

"How many?" asked Craig.

"Twelve. We had ten ANA with us, but all but two of the pricks turned tail and ran as soon as the first bomb exploded."

"You'll have to squeeze in," answered Craig.

"Move it!" commanded the lieutenant to his men. While they piled into the helicopter, a soldier yelped and went down. He'd been shot in the foot. His sergeant picked him up and shoved him into the helicopter. As they slid the door closed, Samantha throttled up and, with a loud roar, the helicopter took off and strained skyward. The stomach-dropping acceleration jammed the soldiers to the floor in a jumble as Samantha pushed her aircraft to its limit to climb away from danger.

Unable to communicate with the medevac crew over the racket made by the engines, the sergeant had to push through his men to get to Daniel to alert him to another man down. Pointing to his foot and toward the back of the chopper, he got the message through.

"Craig, it looks like we've got another man injured back here," Daniel said over the radio. "I'm going to check on him. We better not detour to their base yet. We should get these men to the operating theatre immediately."

"You read my thoughts, Dan," said Craig. "Sam, head back to JAF."

"Chief, can you finish securing him while I help this other one?" said Daniel. Talon did as bidden while Daniel crawled back, squeezing past soldiers to get to the casualty. He examined the wound and gave the writhing man a shot of morphine. His pain turned to bliss within a few seconds. Working in dim blue light to avoid affecting the night-vision goggles used by the pilots, Daniel undid the boot laces and carefully removed the boot. He then extracted a tourniquet, put it in place, tightened it, and fastened it with Velcro. Daniel used hand gestures to get the men to move aside while he and the sergeant carried the man to a litter on the carousel. Talon secured him.

The first casualty had in the meantime begun stirring uncomfortably. Daniel hooked him up to the heart rate monitor and checked his vitals. On the man's face, he wrote his blood pressure, 115 over 95, and his pulse, 87, with a black Magic Marker. He sedated him with midazolam and wrote that information on the man's chest.

Back to the second casualty, he unbuttoned his shirt and wrote with Magic Marker on his chest, "20 mg morphine 0414; 2 FFP; 2 PRBC."

The helicopter raced to the field hospital at JAF, and Daniel handed his patients off to the Forward Surgical Team.

There, in the long, narrow operating room, Captain Telfer and his team operated to remove the bullet and shrapnel, repair the damage to the extent possible, and close the wounds.

A medevac team from Bagram picked them up later that morning for further medical care before their removal to the military hospital in Landstuhl, Germany the next day. A Chinook helicopter took the uninjured soldiers back to their forward operating base.

CHAPTER ELEVEN

Australia – August 2009

She was in Daniel's year in Monash University medicine, the girl all the guys wanted. Her Thai mother and white father made a delightful combination, which they labeled Kelly. She earned a good dollar doing local TV commercials featuring her long raven hair flowing across the screen as she tossed her head in slow motion and melted the camera lens with a sultry gaze. The medical school curriculum strained the limits of her frontal lobe, but she had no trouble getting all the help she needed from the male students.

The accomplished cock tease had her choice of men, and she chose the handsome medical students, focusing on fifth-year students because they would be gone at year's end. They tutored her and she tortured them, holding her juicy meat just beyond their dripping canines until she ejected them, hungry. By the end of her third year the twenty-one-year-old had rejected three marriage proposals. Her female classmates, none of whom would ever need a man, but who nevertheless wanted one, despised her.

At the outset of year four, she cast about for the next sucker. This time, none of the fifth-year students met her standards for looks, so she had to settle for a fourth-year man. Daniel caught her eye and ear. His Canadian accent was a turn-on. She'd never had to work to get a man's attention before, but this one was proving a challenge, returning her inviting smile with a shy one, but not following through. This both intrigued and confused her.

Kelly liked conquering men, then tossing them aside, but these marriage proposals were uncomfortable. A brilliant, good-looking guy with a Canadian accent and reputed to have no interest in marriage—well, he sounded perfect for provisional exploitation. She sauntered up to him and opened, "I know we haven't had much to do with each other, but that doesn't mean I haven't noticed you."

"I haven't not noticed you, too," replied Daniel.

"Oh?"

"You're well known in these here parts."

"And what do you know about me?"

"You get everything you can from a man, then jilt him with cruel joy."

"I hope I'm not too cruel. What else?"

"That you're the biggest producer of blue balls down under."

"Cute and funny, too. So, Dan Beaton, are you up for a challenge?"

"The trouble is I'll be up for the challenge until I'm blue down under, too, and you walk away."

"I hear you're not interested in anything long-term. So what if I walk away?"

"In the meantime what does it cost me?"

"You help me study, that's all."

"So, what's in it for me? I don't have the time for you, and I have no money; I mean none."

"So you're saying no?" He nodded and turned to walk away, but she grabbed his elbow and tried, "I have money. We can go out once in a while on me."

"What else do I get to do on you?"

"So, are you saying your price for this, uh, arrangement is sex?"

"I wouldn't be that crass, but yes."

"I like you, Dan, but your price is too high."

A few days later, having rejected the other two possibilities as boring, she walked up to him in the hospital and said, "You win. Let's fuck." He didn't believe her until she was madly thrusting up and down on him in her apartment twenty minutes afterward. After bleeding him of every last sperm in his body, she admitted to liking sex.

"When I heard about blue balls, I didn't think they meant black and blue."

"Ah, did I hurt you?" she said with a kiss. "I like the rumors. I'm no hussy, and I won't have sex unless I'm really captivated by a guy. You're only the third."

"And the first two?"

"They stopped captivating me. You will, too. You'll be lucky to last the year. Are you up for it?" she said while grabbing his penis.

"Getting there."

Their arrangement lasted for the first term, but then she broke it off because his core clinical rotations and part-time paramedic work were leaving too little time for him to tutor her. He accepted her decision too readily for her liking; she'd grown close to him, but he'd stayed aloof. She hadn't wanted another proposal, but the least he could be was heartbroken. Worse, and unexpected, she soon came to miss not only his tutoring—he had a knack for making hard subjects easy for her—but him. Even though they seldom did anything together outside of their apartments, he was so much fun to be around.

When she brought down her decree, she warned him not to call or email her. "I like a clean break," she explained. He nodded and followed her command, much to her annoyance. The others had called or emailed for weeks, but from Daniel, nothing. She'd see him in the hospital and smile; he'd return it, but made no attempt to talk to her. Nervy bugger. Good thing she cut it off after first term, she concluded. This guy might have ruined her plans for her future.

After the end of their fourth year, upon hearing that his mother had died and that he more than likely would have to take two years off to pay for the final year, Kelly came up to him, hugged him, and expressed her sorrow. She came close to admitting she made a mistake ending their relationship, but managed to bite her tongue. She did insist that he write to her.

So, when Daniel Beaton emailed her out of nowhere, well, Afghanistan, a year and a half later, she was pleasantly surprised. She'd heard nothing from him since that last day. Daniel said he'd be returning to Monash to finish his education the coming year and would be visiting Melbourne in August to make the necessary arrangements.

*

She wrote back saying she'd love to see him, which surprised him, but said she was now in the Gold Coast doing her internship.

The thought of Samantha and Paul on a romantic getaway together was killing him. Daniel's thinking in getting in touch with Kelly was to do his utmost to keep them apart and to show Samantha what kind of women he dated; she didn't need to know Kelly was the outlier. He arranged for a date in mid-August.

On the appointed date, Daniel met Samantha at the Gold Coast Airport and escorted her to her hotel. Later that afternoon, after Samantha had a nap to refresh herself, she met Daniel in the lobby of her hotel, where they sat awaiting Kelly. "Oh, here she is," said Daniel. He stepped forward to meet her.

A gorgeous, petite woman opened her eyes wide, hailed, "Danny!" and ran to him. She embraced him and fired, "I thought I'd never see you again. Why didn't you write all that time? You've really joined the American army? You're Canadian, aren't you? You've lost weight, but you look *really* good. I've missed you so much!" Then she planted an open-mouthed kiss on him.

Daniel looked for Samantha's reaction, hoping to see distress, but her expression conveyed something closer to incredulity.

*

Samantha was thinking, *Why would such a beautiful and successful woman be interested in him?* Then she dismissed the possibility, thinking maybe Australians French kiss just to say hi.

Kelly continued, "It's been what, coming up on two years since we've seen each other? Did you miss me?"

"There isn't a year that goes by that I don't think of you," he replied.

"That's not very nice."

"Kelly, this is Sam."

Kelly held out her hand and said, "Hi." As they shook hands, Kelly gave Samantha the once over, and Samantha perceived a latent sneer behind the forced smile.

Addressing Daniel, she said, "Your email didn't mention you'd be bringing a girlfriend."

Samantha and Daniel responded together, "He's/She's not my boyfriend/girlfriend," only Samantha's was a yawp and Daniel's a moan.

Kelly's sneer became more evident. "Excuse us a minute," she said to Samantha while pulling Daniel away by the elbow.

Samantha stood there and witnessed their animated discussion. Daniel ended it with a peremptory wave of his hand and turned to walk back to Samantha. She heard the last few words he said to her. "… not if you're going to be like this. Pardon me all to hell for bothering you. Let's go, Sam."

"No, Danny, don't go," Kelly said as she grabbed his wrist.

In witnessing this, Samantha reassessed her second thought. Her third was that this woman really was smitten with Daniel, which came as a surprise. Samantha still hadn't worked out her feelings for Daniel. Why bother when she was forbidden to date him and when she had someone better on the hook? She was well aware that Daniel had his attractions, yet she devalued his feelings for her, and not only for the disrespect it showed; it was more fundamental. Because her self-esteem was wanting—she had never thought of herself as pretty—she underrated a man who had been so simple to conquer, a kind of Groucho Marx logic: I'd never love a man who could fall so easily for the likes of me. But if this spectacular woman wanted him …

Kelly said, "I made a reservation for two at a nice restaurant, but I'll call them and double it. Till then, Danny's all mine." Samantha returned an unconcerned nod. Kelly told Samantha where and when to meet, then took Daniel's hand and led him away.

Samantha met Paul at the airport early that evening and accompanied him to the restaurant. They met Kelly and Daniel at the entrance, and Samantha introduced Paul.

Kelly wore a low-cut, body-hugging burgundy mini-dress that extended one millimeter below her butt. Her silken black hair, parted on the left, tumbled over her shoulders and bounced off her ample bosom. Her lipstick matched her dress, but otherwise she wore only eye-liner and light blush. When she adopted a sultry aspect, her striking black eyes made her look almost diabolical, the kind of woman who could emasculate a man with great pleasure, while the man enthused, "She's holding my bag!" But then she'd flash her glowing smile and she looked the part of an angel.

No woman could look upon this breathtaking creature without envy and without a blow to her self-esteem. Even the typical consolation that she was likely a clueless bimbo wasn't credible for Kelly; she was a physician. Samantha's reaction

THANK SOPHIA FOR SAM

combined envy and agitation as she observed Paul's wide-eyed awe upon being introduced to Kelly. She glowered at Daniel.

*

But Daniel was gazing at Kelly. He'd never seen Kelly look this ravishing and for the moment couldn't stop gazing at her. He, like Samantha and Paul, found it difficult to believe he'd ever dated a woman so clearly above him. It was one of the main reasons he made no argument when she cut him loose; he couldn't hope to hold onto her for the long term. The other was her insufferable ego. The five months with her had been thrilling, but he never regretted losing her; until this moment.

But it was a fleeting moment, for he soon switched his gaze to Samantha. His eyes lit up as they lighted upon her luscious figure. She wore a white mini-dress. It showed no cleavage, but did reveal most of her legs. He'd never seen her legs shaved. Despite the heat, she'd worn pants all summer to hide them, except from her man, he supposed. They were spectacular! Her mousy hair, which she'd been growing since she began pursuing Paul, was by this time about four inches long. It was unruly. Not that Daniel minded. It suited her personality.

For the first time since he met her, she wore makeup. When he remarked on it, she mentioned that she'd had to purchase the makeup because she hadn't owned any, adding the lady at the makeup counter had applied it for her after she'd told her she didn't know how to do it well. The dark brown eyeliner and mascara perfectly complemented her supernal dark brown eyes; a hint of pink blush accentuated her high cheek bones. Light pink lipstick completed the pretty picture. Here was

Daniel with stunning Kelly, and he couldn't take his eyes off cute Samantha, alternating between her eyes and her legs.

They entered the restaurant and were seated in the cocktail lounge at a small round table while they waited for a dinner table. Daniel sat next to Kelly and across from Samantha. Both women crossed their legs, and both men stared at the thighs across from them. Samantha watched Paul staring at Kelly's legs. Kelly watched Samantha watching Paul watching her, and smiled.

*

Samantha looked over at Daniel to convey her displeasure, but found she couldn't do it with her thighs, which his eyes were lapping. She glanced at his lap and, noticing a bulge, clicked her tongue and said, "God, Beaton!"

He blushed, covered up with his arms and said, "I erected it just for you, Sam."

"Oh? Then I guess you must think very little of me," she shot back.

Paul howled. Kelly sniggered. Daniel admired the wit, but frowned upon the message.

Kelly remarked to Daniel, "I like getting men excited. I guess Sam gets angry about it."

Samantha returned, "I get angry when it's the wrong man."

Kelly returned a look of genuine surprise, and said, "Wrong man?"

"Yes."

"Let me get this straight. *You* look down on *him*?"

"Kelly," said Daniel. She retracted her claws and returned her gaze to Paul.

The waiter came, and they ordered drinks. As they waited for their drinks, Paul initiated the conversation with, "So, how did you two meet?"

Kelly answered, "We were in the same class in medicine. Danny was my tutor for half of fourth year."

Daniel explained, "Kelly chose a different tutor every year. Usually a fifth-year male."

"Why?" asked Paul to keep her talking, so he could keep his gaze on her, guessed Samantha.

"Having tutors made med school much easier."

"Why a fifth-year male?" said Paul, as Samantha observed his fascination with this woman.

"Male, because I like men. Fifth year because they know the most and they'll be gone at the end of the year."

"She wanted an easy out," explicated Daniel, "but it didn't work very well. She got three marriage proposals."

"And two since," added Kelly.

"Did Dan propose?" Samantha asked Kelly, hoping he'd been spurned.

"No, thank God. I might've accepted, and that would've ruined my plans for marrying a millionaire, then divorcing him and getting half his money." She went on to explain, "I didn't really need money—I had done some modeling and made plenty of money—but I used to tell my tutors I was holding out for a millionaire, so they wouldn't get too attached. Danny was my favorite. In those five months I learned so much and had so much fun. I've never laughed so much. I kicked Danny out after first term because I felt myself falling for him."

"I thought it was because I had no time for tutoring you second term." She frowned at him. Turning to the others, he bragged, "I'm her favorite reject."

The waiter brought their drinks. While the drinks were served, Kelly slowly scratched her left thigh with Paul closely examining the maneuver. Samantha took the longest sip.

Paul said, "So, why did you chose Beaton? You say he was in fourth year with you."

"Simple. He was probably the smartest, and definitely the cutest, upper year male; the cutest in the whole school. I mean, just look at those dazzling green eyes and those kissable lips." Here she leaned over and kissed him. "And he has wavy, glossy hair most girls would kill for, though you can't tell with that crew cut.

"And, I liked his sense of humor. On the first day of fourth year, when I was choosing my next victim, I overheard his answers to two stupid questions from some idiotic doctor. I forget the exact questions, but the first was something like, 'Can you tell me what the nature of the problem is with this patient, and how you propose to go about treating him?' Without missing a beat, Danny said, 'Yes. I've seen this problem before; it's called death, and I guess I would treat him with embalming fluid.' The guy had died a while earlier, and the doctor hadn't noticed. I burst out laughing and stayed to hear what happened next. The doctor looked at the patient and realized, and said with a stern face, 'Okay, wise ass, what was the *cause* of death?' And right away Danny answered, 'Cause of death was a chronic case of obesity aggravated by an acute case of Toyota.' The guy was fat and had been hit by a car. I laughed so hard, I had to run down the hall before I got into trouble, too."

Samantha laughed at the story, but kept her eyes on Paul. Daniel kept his eyes on Samantha. Kelly and Paul were staring at each other. Paul's eyes darted from her legs to her breasts to her eyes and back to her breasts. Paul said, "If Beaton was the best looking man in your school, it must've been one ugly crop."

Samantha and Kelly chuckled. Kelly said, "Yeah, most of them were pretty bad, but that doesn't make Danny any less attractive. What do you think, Sam?"

"His chin gives out a smidgeon too soon," teased Samantha. "It gives him a boyish jaw line, rather than a manly, handsome jaw." Here she smiled at her strong-jawed boyfriend.

"Too bad for me," Daniel responded. "I read that women want to have sex with strong-jawed men, but want to marry soft-jawed men. Round chins apparently signal good parenting material. It was a dirty trick of Sophia's to make me a man girls want to wed instead of one they want to bed."

"Sophia?" asked Kelly.

"Don't ask," recommended Samantha.

"You would make a great dad, Danny," said Kelly. "When I'm ready, I'll look you up. You like children?"

"Of course I do. That's what my shitty round chin indicates, doesn't it?"

"Well, all I know," rejoined Kelly, "is regardless of your chin, I love fucking you."

Samantha gawked at Kelly, then looked at her date, who was practically panting with his gaze fixed on Kelly, and again cast an accusatory glare at Daniel. Daniel's eyes were focused on the table; he seemed embarrassed. She then looked back at Kelly, who was smiling salaciously at Paul.

Kelly proceeded, "Danny had all sorts of women flinging themselves at him at Monash. He never had to ask them out."

Daniel said, "Yeah, there were a few self-flung women, but I did ask Karen Balderston out."

"What'd she say?" asked Kelly.

"You know the look a girl gives a rat climbing up her leg? That's what she hurled at me, followed by a curt 'No!' before scurrying away." Kelly scowled at him. He went on, "I think she really just objected to the caravan of debt collectors circling my place. Anyway, to make a long story short—"

"Allow me," interrupted Samantha. "Shut up."

The waiter led them to their dinner table and gave them menus.

Evidently wanting to return his focus to Kelly, Paul said, "So, you paid your way through medicine by modeling? That certainly isn't hard to believe."

Kelly smiled and confirmed, "I did some TV commercials."

"I'd like to see them," said Paul.

Kelly leaned toward Paul so that her cleavage became more salient; she murmured, "We'd have to go to my place." Samantha observed as Paul's eyes jumped out to meet Kelly's breasts.

Samantha jumped in with, "Maybe some other time." She shot another censorious scowl at Daniel, which he seemed to understand since he lowered his eyes at once.

Paul asked, "So you ditched all your tutors?"

"Every last one."

"Once you got what you needed from them," noted Samantha.

"Precisely," Kelly boasted.

The waiter having returned, they ordered their meals. After he walked off, the discussion took a different turn. The two physicians exchanged medical stories, leaving Daniel to make comments here and there, and Samantha out of it altogether. Kelly mentioned a current case that was baffling the doctors at her hospital. A woman showed up with excruciating pain in her calf muscle but with no obvious injury. Paul tossed out possibilities, all of which had been tested for and rejected. Kelly mentioned two more possibilities, which she discussed with Paul. Daniel said, "Have you tested for necrotizing fasciitis?" He turned to Samantha and said, "Flesh-eating disease."

"No. That doesn't sound plausible," answered Kelly.

"Of course it's fucking plausible."

"Maybe I know a little more than you do now since I finished my degree." He sneered at her. "Calm down, Danny. I know you're smarter than I am. I just meant I have a bit more education than you now," she said in placation. She squeezed his arm and smiled sweetly. Samantha noted Kelly's distress in displeasing Daniel and concluded Kelly really did have feelings for him. Why then was she so obviously flirting with Paul? To make Daniel jealous?

"Leave the diagnosing to the doctors, Beaton. We're the experts," said Paul.

Daniel spit out, "Yes, army doctors have a tough job diagnosing patients. My diagnosis for the guy with a hole in his forehead: uh, bullet! And this set of intestines and charred severed foot: bomb! This one is a bit more unusual, but I'm guessing from the Humvee bumper up his arse that he got hit by a Humvee."

"So, are you saying I'm incapable of diagnosis?"

"I'm saying the army can neither attract nor produce good diagnosticians because of the nature of the work."

The meals arrived shortly after that, and the four made small talk. Kelly asked about the war, but the three soldiers said they didn't want to talk about it. After dinner, Kelly told them she had a plan to take them to the leading nightspot in town, but that it didn't get hopping until later, so suggested they pass a couple of hours drinking and dancing at a nearby nightclub. Samantha would have rather returned to the hotel with Paul, but he seemed so eager to follow Kelly's plan, she kept her mouth shut.

At the dance club they sat at a small table and drank. After a few minutes, Paul asked Kelly to dance. Samantha was upset at this and couldn't hide it. Seeing this, Paul added, "But first, I want to dance with Sam." He took her hand and led her to the dance floor.

*

Kelly said, "Sam isn't very smart when it comes to men, is she?" Daniel shook his head as he watched them dance. Kelly proceeded, "I mean, he's really handsome, too handsome for her, but he's obviously not trustworthy. He hasn't taken his eyes off me all night."

Paul and Samantha returned after two dances. He held his hand out to Kelly, who took it and stood. "Why don't you two dance?" suggested Kelly.

"I'm going to need another drink first; he's still too ugly," replied Samantha.

Daniel laughed, but Kelly challenged, "You don't actually think Dan is ugly, do you?" Daniel was about to say she was only kidding, but he decided he wanted to hear her response. Samantha said nothing. "Well?" pressed Kelly.

"Obviously he's not ugly," she answered.

"Sam, that's the nicest thing you've ever said to me," returned Daniel. "I think you're not ugly, too."

She chuckled and said, "Can you dance?"

"Picture an epileptic white guy with a lame leg and a club foot. Compared to me, he's Fred Astaire."

"Okay, but no touching."

The four went to the dance floor. When they began dancing, Samantha commented, "You're not as good as you led me to believe."

He grinned and said, "You're not good yourself."

A slow song commenced. Kelly and Paul immediately settled into each other's arms and drifted away. Samantha looked on with angst as her dance partner clutched her hand to draw her near. She withdrew her hand and asserted, "Not a chance."

His smile withered as did something lower that had been rising in eager anticipation of squishing against his charmer. "Come on, Sam; they're still dancing."

"I can see that," she yowled while stampeding back to their table.

Daniel followed her. Seeing her leaden eyes made him remorseful. "Sam, I have to conf—"

"Shut up!"

After three more songs, Paul and Kelly returned. Samantha looked at Paul with big, sad eyes, then narrowed them to scowl at Kelly and Daniel. After another drink, Paul asked Samantha to dance again. She smiled, and they went to dance. Kelly made Daniel dance, too.

Next, they took a cab to what Kelly promised was the most exclusive club in town. "You have to be famous or beautiful to get in," she said as they exited the taxi. Then she looked at Samantha and said, "Don't worry, I'll get you in."

Samantha replied, "I didn't know you were famous."

Kelly flashed a cold smile and went up to the door man. As she talked, the man looked at Samantha, Paul, and Daniel. Kelly returned a moment later and said, "Sorry, Danny, I couldn't get you in."

"Screw them then. Let's go somewhere else."

"Uh, Paul really wants to see the place."

Samantha grinned and said, "Guess you're out, *Danny*. Catch you back at JAF."

"So, you're just going to leave me alone?" he said with a gloomy and embarrassed expression.

"You could use a little humility," opined Samantha.

"Uh, I guess I wasn't clear enough," said Kelly. "You can't get in either, Sam."

Her face fell. She said, "Come on, Paul, let's go to our room."

He hesitated. She looked at him with an admixture of surprise, fear, and supplication. Daniel saw her tears well and could see her tremble while she struggled for emotional control. This was so far out of character that it jolted him.

Paul still hadn't answered, when Daniel, overcome with guilt and shame, said, "No, Kelly! That's enough."

"I thought this was what you wanted," Kelly responded.

"Not like this."

"What's she talking about, Beaton?" said Samantha with gathering ire.

"It's a tough world, Danny, and you have to be willing to play hardball to get what you want," said Kelly.

"Don't lecture me about what a tough world this is. You have no idea what tough is."

"You told her to come between us!" bawled Samantha. "You son of a bitch!" she continued as she punctuated her rage with a solid sock to Daniel's jaw. He staggered back. She tried to hit him again, but he blocked the second attempt.

Paul interceded and said, "Come on, Sam, let's go to our room. You can get aggressive as you want with me." Turning to Daniel, he said, "I'll deal with you back at JAF."

Daniel looked glumly at Samantha and said, "I'm sorry, Sam."

"Let's go," she said. She took Paul's arm and walked away with him.

Kelly shook her head at Daniel and remarked, "I had him. I'd have had him back to my place tonight. That would've ended things between them and left you with her."

"She was practically in tears. I couldn't. I just couldn't." He shifted his jaw back and forth to work out the kink.

"You're a nice guy, Danny, but you know what they say about nice guys."

"You can't possibly imagine how annoying clichés like that are to me after Afghanistan, so shut your frigging mouth."

"Why are you mad at me? You asked me to do this."

"You made it obvious what you were doing. Sam's not stupid; she glared at me all night. She would've hated me if I let it play out, but now she's with him, and she hates me anyway, so my defeat is complete."

"You must really love her," she said. He started walking. "Danny!" He stopped, but didn't turn back to her. "Any woman in her right mind would prefer you to him."

He turned to her and said, "Then every woman, including Sam and you, is out of her right mind."

"You're not jealous, are you?" she said with a coy smile.

"Not over you." He turned away again and resumed walking.

Her smile waned, and she jogged to catch him and walk by his side. "I want you to keep something in mind while you scourge yourself with your conscience tonight. He came halfway around the world to be with her, but he'd have left her tonight for a woman he just met. Ask yourself what kind of person can do that. If she's not stupid, she must be asking herself that now. We did her a favor and planted seeds of doubt in her mind. He'll cheat on any woman he ends up with. On the other hand, you were so upset that she was heartbroken, you gave her up to him, which I can tell is killing you. Stupid, but noble. That's why any woman, including me, would prefer you. If you were a millionaire, Danny Beaton, I'd propose right now."

He laughed and kissed her. She smiled and cooed, "You win; let's fuck." They grabbed a cab and went to her place.

*

After working up the courage on their way back to the hotel, Samantha confronted Paul upon entering their room with the question, "Would you have gone into that club with her and left me standing outside?"

"Of course not," he claimed.

"Why did you just stand there speechless when I asked you to come with me?"

"Come on, Sam, it was only a couple of seconds. She made it seem like it would be a great experience at that club, and I didn't want to give up so easily. I was trying to think of a way to get you in. I was just about to palm the bouncer a hundred bucks."

"Oh," she said, trying to believe him. "You paid her an awful lot of attention tonight."

"You're cute when you're jealous," he said, taking her hand with a smile. "Come on, Sam, stop pouting. I'm here with you; I'm not with her."

"But you stared at her all night."

"It was hard not to look at her when she was in my face flirting all night. I do admit she's a striking woman, but I prefer you."

"Paul, she's gorgeous, she's vivacious, she's a doctor, she's everything a man could want. How could any man prefer me to her?"

"That loser does."

"Is that supposed to make me feel better? Oh, I'm so mad at that son of a bitch! I'd have been rid of him a month ago if I'd done what I should have and told the army he has diabetes."

"He what? He has diabetes? How the hell did he even get in as a medic?"

"He just found out about it last month."

"So, why doesn't he want to get out of the army? He hates it."

"He joined on the condition the army pay for his last year of medicine. He's worried they'll kick him out and the army will use it as an excuse not to pay his scholarship."

"Perfect! I'll drum the little fucker right out."

Now second-guessing her impulsive decision to tell Paul, she said, "No, Paul, we can't do that to him."

"Why the hell not? We both want rid of him. You've handed me his head on a platter."

"He only has about four and a half months to go. I'll just make it clear that he leave me alone, or else."

"We both hate him. Let's get rid of him now."

"He's put his life on the line for a year and a half to save lives. The army can't just forget that."

"I save the lives; he merely preserves them."

"He preserves them with people trying to kill him."

"I've been out there, too, you know. It's a pretty straightforward job. Stop the bleeding, make sure they can get air, and take them to a doctor who can actually save them."

"He's maybe the best medic we have."

"I've seen better. Anyway, it doesn't matter. It's irresponsible leaving him out there. If he goes into a sugar low, people might die."

"You just said what he does is simple. Let him keep doing it for a few more months. I'll watch him closely."

"I have to report this."

"Paul, please. Please don't ruin him. Don't say anything. For me. Please?"

"I'll stay quiet for now, but if I see anything at all that makes me uncomfortable about the work he's done, about bothering you, or me, anything at all, he's out. Now let's forget he exists and get to each other." He embraced her and kissed her.

She had planned to tell him she loved him tonight, but she was too unsure of his reaction to admit her feelings at that point. "I have to change," she whispered into his ear. She ambled to her suitcase and removed a bag containing a sexy negligee. She went into the bathroom.

*

The next morning, as Daniel strolled the topless beach near Samantha's hotel, he told himself, *I fit right in here among all these bare boobs; I feel like it's my natural habitat.* Yet despite the sea of tits, his eyes were drawn to barely covered derrieres. One in particular caught his attention. Seldom does nature craft the perfect buttocks, and then only temporarily, but nothing on earth other than a pair of fine feminine eyes was better to behold, and nothing whatsoever was better to hold, he thought.

He meandered toward her as his eyes glided down the exquisite slopes of her lower back and up the flawless curves of her backsides. Then the maiden pushed her upper body up to put on her sunglasses. Her small but perfectly shaped breasts hung down, until she turned over to lie on her back, and they formed soft mounds surmounted by delightful brown nipples.

His entire being declaimed, *Oh, my God, that's Sam! Topless!* He took off his sunglasses for an unimpeded view. His eyes popped out of his head, his tongue unfurled, his heart raced, his breath panted, and blood rushed to where it was needed to do what every fiber of his animal being was urging him to do. Procreate! *My God, she's perfect!* he exclaimed to himself. His exclamation point was so enthusiastic it was underscored by two dots.

He wanted to freeze this scene in his mind for future reference. This would be the vision he'd draw to mind in the distant future when trying to get excited about making love to his wife of twenty-five years for the two thousandth time. He longed to go for a dip into her, beginning with a full-bodied belly flop. His eyes reluctantly yet eagerly left her breasts and traveled down. They drank in her long, smooth, edible legs. Delectable! Starting with her toes, he ran his mind's tongue over her soft skin, up her legs to her bikini bottom. Then his imagination kissed between her legs and pushed his tongue across her narrow waist and stomach, up her ribcage and stopped at her pert breasts. There his imagination bit and sucked playfully until Samantha opened her eyes.

*

Samantha had run the gamut of emotions the night before. After the upheaval with Kelly and Daniel was her much anticipated assignation with Paul, but the night hadn't been the heavenly event she had fantasized. She'd enjoyed the feeling of Paul without a rubber, but it was over in minutes. When he pleasured her orally, she did approach heaven, but then he wanted the favor returned, which she found harder to enjoy while gagging and choking on the ugly, smelly thing. When he attempted to enter her rear, she gasped and recoiled. It hurt too much, and she had to say no. Seeing he was disappointed, she apologized for being so "boring." Her love was undiminished, but what of his? After her first climax she had declared, "I love you so much!" but he merely smiled.

This was what was going through her mind when she noted through closed eyes a shadow hovering over her. She opened her eyes to see Daniel standing there with bulging eyes and pursed mouth as if sucking; he looked ready to eat her whole. She immediately sat up, and her breasts settled into place. His eyes grew even wider. She covered her breasts with her arms and glanced down to see, ill concealed by his bathing suit, his exclamation point. "Stop staring, pervert!" she insisted, getting to her feet and glaring at him.

"Why?" he challenged. "It's obviously okay for everyone else to."

"No one else was staring; this is normal here. But you're standing there with a hard-on practically drowning in saliva. You're disgusting."

"You're magnificent!"

That disarmed her for the moment. She'd been self-conscious about her body since puberty, especially her chest. Paul had never said anything about her breasts or paid them much attention. Last night he said "wow" when she stepped out of the bathroom in her red negligee, but when she slowly lowered the lingerie to reveal her breasts he said nothing, and when she turned, dropped the negligee on the floor and bent over, he again made no comment. She couldn't help feeling that Paul must have been disappointed by her body.

And this morning sitting on the beach, when she timidly removed her bikini bra, she furtively glanced around her to see if any man took notice. If any had, she'd have been so abashed, she'd have without delay lain down on her stomach. Since none had, she had become more certain of her inadequacies and promptly lay down on her stomach. But now, with Daniel standing here gazing upon her with heartfelt adoration, she could not but feel good about herself. Then she called to mind the previous evening and outrage eclipsed pride.

She knelt, picked up her t-shirt, turned around and pulled it on. Turning back to him, she said, "You have some nerve even coming near me after last night. You're the last person on earth I want to see, so leave now!" she commanded.

"Where's Telfer anyway? I'd have thought if things went well you couldn't be torn apart for the whole weekend. Argue about his behavior last night?"

This perceptive observation served to stoke her fury. She had intended to spend all day in bed with Paul, but he just wanted to sleep. "Jet lag," he explained. She'd suggested he accompany her to the topless beach down the street as a means of waking him up and maybe convincing him she wasn't boring. He told her to go by herself. More disappointment. She snarled to Daniel, "After what you pulled last night, you criticize his behavior?"

"Before I stopped her, he was just about to dump you for her, you know."

"You're wrong, asshole! He loves me, and I love him."

With everyone around them now staring, Daniel said, "Shush."

"All right." She stepped close to him and whispered, "We made love all night. I let him do whatever he wanted with me. We did everything a man and woman can do together in bed. *Everything!* It was heaven. He's so big and thick and hard, and he felt so good inside me; *deep* inside me. Without a rubber. He made me come again and again."

Daniel's shoulders slumped and his head dropped. His exclamation point shrunk to a sad little double-dotted semicolon. Samantha's anger died in the face of his devastation. She felt sorry for him, and bad about what she had told him.

But he was apparently feeling more than devastation, for he muttered, "That what you did with the colonel to become a pilot?"

Her dark eyes flashed lightning, she bared her teeth, the tendons in her neck jumped out, and she unleashed a roar in the vein of a bear at the moment the trap snaps shut, while launching a punch that landed in his right eye. Again caught by surprise, he fell to his rump as those around him laughed and applauded. He covered his watery and sore eye, got to his feet, and slunk away.

Upset, she gathered her things and returned to the hotel room.

CHAPTER TWELVE

Denouement, Late August 2009

The next morning, Daniel looked in the mirror. His right eye was red, the area around it puffy and the color of grape juice. His lip was a tad swollen from the clout to his jaw. To the airport he withdrew, sunglasses on, to see if he could get an earlier flight. He flew out of the Gold Coast a few hours later.

*

Talon noticed something amiss right away when he returned from leave and saw his roommate's face. He opened, "The two weeks away from the war have been less than peaceful, I see."

Daniel, who was reading a medical text, explained that Samantha had struck him "in the mandible and then administered a periorbital contusion."

"Black eye?"

"Aye."

"Looks nasty."

"Yeah, it still hurts. It's taking too long to fade, too. Diabetics take longer to heal."

"Did you deserve it?"

"Oh, yes."

"You didn't hit her back, did you?"

"Never."

"So all in all the trip didn't go according to plan."

"Perceptive, Chief. The outcome was highly unsatisfactory."

Talon asked for and got details. Daniel finished, "On the way back I was more depressed than I've ever been. I was kind of hoping the plane would crash, but then I thought of all the other people on board and how they probably wouldn't want to die because I was sad. Selfish pricks."

He patted Daniel on the shoulder and said, "Well, for what it's worth, I think you and Sam make a perfect match."

"Thanks, Chief, but she couldn't disagree more. But enough about me. How was your leave? You're in entirely too good a shape to have had a good time."

"Spent it all with my wife. Lots of sex. It was hard to come back here."

"Okay, enough about you. You never stop. A good measure of what a loser I am is I came back early. I have nowhere else to go. Fuck, I hate my life! If Sam ever needs a desperate loser, I'm in business."

"Let's have a Listerine. We're not on duty until tomorrow morning."

*

Samantha arrived that afternoon and asked Talon if the biggest asshole in the world was back. Somehow he knew to whom she was referring, so he simply nodded. "Tell him to keep his distance."

Talon returned to his room and mentioned to his roommate, "Sam just got back. She asks if she might stop by later to make your eyes match."

"She's still pissed?"

"Stay away from her for now. It'll pass."

*

The reuniting of the crew was awkward. Tension between the co-pilot and flight medic was palpable, though neither said a word to the other. Samantha played her silent role with hostility; he played his with melancholy.

This went on for several days before the lieutenant interceded. The whole crew was becoming infected by Daniel's glum demeanor. Craig got the details from Talon. He went to Samantha and said, "I want you to make up with Dan."

"It was all his doing."

"You bear some responsibility, too. In the first place, this business of dating a superior in the same command is questionable since it's now causing morale problems, but I've looked the other way on that till now, and I can't very well change your mind now. Second, this business of striking a crew member has to stop."

"He deserved it."

"Do I get to hit you when you deserve it?" She lowered her eyes. "We have the best medic in the army, and you've made him desperately unhappy, which has affected my crew and has made our working conditions much less enjoyable than they were. You're the superior, in rank anyway. You need to show better leadership judgment. Now make up with him. Understood?"

"Yes, sir. I'm sorry."

Talon, too, whom Samantha revered, said to her, "Hasn't he been in the dog house long enough? I gotta tell you, Sam, as special as you are, I don't see that you're any better than he is."

"I never said I was."

"Your sneers say it. Talk to him. Give him a break. Give us all a break."

She nodded and went to find Daniel. She found him walking back from the MWR and began, "Dan, we need to talk." He stood there waiting for her to resume. "We can't be crewmates and continue like this; it's just too uncomfortable. We have to at least talk to each other." He said nothing, so she went on, "I forgive you. For Australia. Let's put it behind us and be friends."

"No."

"No? Why not?"

"I can't be friends with you."

"Why?" He was looking at the ground. "Look at me. Why can't we be friends?"

He gazed into her eyes and proclaimed, "Because I love you!"

She looked at him with kind eyes. She suspected his feelings for her, so his proclamation didn't come as a surprise. What did surprise her was how good it made her feel. No man had ever said this to her, and it was thrilling to have moved a man so much, without even trying. He'd seen her at her worst, physically and emotionally; he'd seen her livid, mean and scared; he'd seen her hairy legs and armpits, her scrunched up sobbing face, her practically bald head; he'd taken her abuse; he'd seen her fists beating his face. Yet he loved her. That was the highest compliment she could think of, especially from a man with such manifold attractions. If only Paul would say it and mean it the way Daniel did.

She took both his hands and replied, "Dan, the last thing I want to do is hurt you," words that earned her a smirk from the bruised man. She read his expression and gave him a penitent smile. "But I can't return your love."

"But I'm out of the army in less than five months. Maybe then?"

"No, Dan, not then either. I'm in love with him. I'm sorry."

He withdrew his hands. "Which is why we can't be friends. I have to deal with you the same way I deal with my patients: wall off my emotions and feel nothing, otherwise I'll lose my mind."

"I'm really sorry to hear that. You know how much I enjoy your company. I miss laughing with you. Please don't shut me out."

He shook his head and walked off.

Two days after that, an upset Lieutenant Ng told Samantha, "I just got a request from my flight medic for a transfer."

"Shit."

"That about sums it up."

"Can't you just turn his request down?"

"I can, but then I still don't have my contented old crew back, do I? We had the best crew in the business, and you messed it up."

"Sir, I did as you asked. I went to him and said we should put our fight behind us. I asked him to be friends. He said he couldn't be just friends with me. I'm miserable about this, but I don't see what else I can do."

"You've become a great pilot. I trust you with my life without hesitation, but I question your leadership skills. You've got yourself into a questionable relationship with an officer."

"Craig, I'm in love with him."

"A large part of the reason I'm questioning your judgment."

"You don't like him?"

"What I think about Captain Telfer is not the issue. There's a reason the army frowns on these relationships; they cause shit like this. You went down this road without a thought about what it might mean for my crew."

"I didn't plan on Dan falling in love with me. That's the main problem."

"That is a problem, yes. So is your love affair. So is the situation we find ourselves in here with so many young, bored, horny men and so few women. It's unnatural, and it leads to shit like this, but we can't do anything about that. We can control our own behavior, though, something you've done a poor job of. Talk to him again."

Samantha was disconcerted at the news Daniel was pressuring to leave because of her. She went to his room and knocked. When he answered, she said, "Dan, I don't want you to go."

"If they approve my transfer I'm leaving."

"Dammit, Dan, I miss you. I miss *us*. I miss the laughter. I miss the camaraderie our crew had. You were always in the middle of everything. You actually made this place fun. Please stay. Please be my friend again."

"We were never friends, Sam."

"How can you say that? When we met, I was wary of all men, you know that, so I kept my distance. When I got to know you, I came to like you, but I had to keep things cool between us because relationships with enlisted men are forbidden."

"Don't you dare quote military policy to justify ignoring me, when you ignore it to justify your relationship with an officer."

"The fraternization rules don't forbid relationships between officers unless there's an adverse effect on fairness or authority—"

"Cut the shit, Sam. You fell in love with him, and if the army doesn't like it, fuck the army."

She took a breath and cast about for the right thing to say. "Poor leadership skills" rang in her ears, and she couldn't gainsay the assertion. She tried, "Okay, yes, I met someone I fell for, but all along I considered you a friend." He shook his head at that tepid declaration and started to close his door. She put her hand out to stop it and said, "Dan! Please hear me out. I fell in love with another man, but surely you must know I didn't do that to hurt you."

He narrowed his eyes and repeated what she'd said on the beach: "We did everything a man and woman can do. He felt so good inside me. He made me come again and again."

She blushed and dropped her head. It was a terrible thing to say to him, and it was obviously eating at him.

"It was a kneejerk reaction to the things you'd said and done to me there, but I'm really sorry I said it. It was hurtful and thoughtless." It was also a perfect example of the poor judgment the lieutenant was talking about, she mused. "I ask you; I'm pleading with you to forgive and forget."

"I will never forget that. Never. I can and will put it, put you, behind me, but I can't do it spending every waking moment near you. I certainly can never go back to the way it was."

He closed his door, and she went back to her room depressed.

That evening Craig let Daniel know there were no flight medic positions available for the time being, so he'd have to stay on his crew. Daniel shrugged and took a walk.

*

Late August, and the crew was speeding toward a tiny village nestled on a canyon wall that had been leveled by American firepower after insurgents had taken refuge there and pinned down American troops. Hellfire missiles had been fired at several dwellings and thirty mm rounds had been shot at men who had escaped the explosions.

Black smoke and thick dust rose from the ruins. As Samantha circled her aircraft above the destruction, she said,

"Christ, they might have said something to warn us, like, 'Oh, by the way, when you get there, you'll find it's no longer there.' I hope the hell no kids got killed or hurt." Samantha landed in a field beside a stream where Daniel and Talon jumped out and trotted to the former village.

As inured as Daniel was to grisly sights, he winced at the scene; at least seven dead that he could see, two of them children, and probably many more under the rubble. Two children were injured, one gravely. One woman and one man were also critically injured. Specialist Jack Rizzo, Andrew's replacement, was seeing to the man.

Several villagers surrounded the dead and injured, some crying, some glowering at the American soldiers. An interpreter was talking to the elders, trying to explain the American position.

"These people were hit by Apaches?" Daniel asked the lieutenant. The lieutenant nodded. Those hit by the thirty mm rounds didn't look human anymore. They were annihilated. He saw a severed head without a face, a body with no head and half a leg, bodies with half or more of the torso blown away and internal organs hanging out, and various other bloody chucks that he couldn't even identify. These noisome lumps of flesh were scattered everywhere as were bits of clothing. One body had been blown out of its clothes and was splattered against a rock wall. All would soon add to the pervasive dust that Afghanistan must live and die with. So much death, so much dust.

In a subdued tone, the lieutenant said, "We were taking fire. We could see the children; they made sure of it. We withheld fire for as long as we could without risking the lives of my men. After my sergeant took a bullet in the thigh, I gave the order." Overcome with emotion, he turned and walked down the slope.

Daniel checked the injured soldier who'd been treated by the company medic. He asked Talon to package him as he proceeded to the children. A man stood over a gravely injured girl, weeping. Daniel quickly determined there was nothing he could do; she'd be dead within a few minutes. She was unconscious, but Daniel gave her a shot of morphine in case she felt any pain and to be seen doing something for her by the villagers, not that anything he could do would make a dent in the hatred they felt for all Americans after this calamity.

Turning his attention to a young girl he could help, he knelt beside her and got to work. She had a stomach wound caused by a large splinter driven into her from a demolished house and was crying and shrieking. He gave her pain killer, checked to ensure the splinter wasn't occluding an artery, and removed it, but as he did, she screeched so loudly every person in the village looked. Jack came over; his patient had died. "Fuck, man, this is awful," he said. Daniel nodded as he continued his work. The medics did their best to stop the bleeding, but the little girl needed immediate evac if her life was to be saved. They strapped her to a litter and jogged her to the first up helicopter.

As Jack secured the patient in his chopper next to the injured sergeant, Daniel said, "What about that woman?"

"They wouldn't let me touch her," replied Jack.

"What?" he shouted.

Jack shrugged as he closed the door. Daniel backed away and watched the helicopter lift off. He turned to run back to the injured woman. Her left leg was in shreds, and she would bleed to death in minutes without help. As Daniel knelt next to her, a man grabbed his arm and yanked him away, screaming at him in Pashto. Daniel pushed him away and tried to get at his patient. The interpreter interceded and said, "This man will not let you touch his wife."

"Explain to this asshole, his wife will die without immediate medical help."

"I have, but it is not their way to allow any man but the husband to touch their women."

"Not their way? Does this jeezly moron understand his wife will die?"

"I have told him so," said the interpreter.

"Then he's a goddamn murderer!"

"He cannot abandon a lifetime of beliefs."

"Bullshit! He can't bother to look after a crippled wife in this prehistoric shithole, so he'll let her die."

"We cannot do anything about it."

The husband and two other men from the village stood in the way now. Daniel called over the lieutenant and left him to argue the case while he went back to check on the other injured girl. She had died. He looked at the father and shook his head with sad eyes to communicate she was gone. Daniel closed the girl's eyelids. Without saying a word, the father picked up his dead child and walked past Daniel. Though it was one of the most heartbreaking sights he'd ever witnessed, he couldn't stop staring at the bereaved father walking down the rocky hill carrying his dead girl.

He returned to check on the progress with the injured woman. The lieutenant told Daniel that unless they wanted to risk another firefight, they had no choice but to follow the wishes of the husband. Daniel shook his head and watched the woman die. He said to Talon, "This is what this religion does to its women; this is what a devout Muslim man does to his wife. This country, these people are beyond hope. Islam has brainwashed them; ruined them. This war won't change any of that. It's a useless waste of life."

*

Covered in blood and dust, Daniel trudged back to his helicopter. Samantha could tell he was crying and knew whatever caused it must have been horrific if it drove Daniel to tears. She longed to comfort him, but what could she say? What could anyone say? Talon boarded the helicopter and gave his roommate a knowing nod. "Let's go," said Craig, and they left as much of the devastation behind them as they could.

After they got back to JAF, Daniel secluded himself in his room for the rest of the day. He skipped dinner, which concerned his crewmates. After dinner, Samantha went to his room and knocked. When he answered, she smiled and held out a barbequed cheeseburger.

He took it with thanks and was about to close the door when Samantha said, "Dan, I know nothing I can say will make the hurt go away, but I think you need this." As she had after the catastrophe in the schoolyard, she took him in her arms. At first he attempted to pull away, but she squeezed harder.

He surrendered to the blissful sensation, put his arms around her, closed his eyes, rested his head on her shoulder, and breathed deeply. The world disappeared during their long embrace. There was nothing sexual about it, just two friends offering needed comfort to each other.

After two minutes, she finally let go before it did become sexual. "Thank you," he said. She kissed his cheek and left.

The next day he went to the hooch to pass some time. When he walked in, Susan was bragging about lighting up the village. Daniel fixed on her with an irate expression.

"Dan, walk away. Walk away now!" urged Samantha.

He stayed put, scowling at the co-pilot gunner. When Susan laughed, he stormed up to her and said, "I wish the Christ you had to deal with the slaughter you caused, you fucking heartless She-man proto-human bitch!"

"Dan! Get out of here now!" bellowed Samantha.

Susan was so taken aback at this affront, all she could do at first was gape at him, but soon she rallied, and with a look of outrage, she exploded, "No motherfucking insolent Specialist Beatoff talks to me like that!" Five-foot-ten of solid muscle and but eight pounds lighter than Daniel, Susan could pummel Daniel into red pulp, thought Samantha. Susan smiled, probably thinking the same thing. She reared back to sock him in the face, but he blocked it. Her next thrust at his stomach made her wince when she connected as if she'd punched steel.

Samantha warned, "Beaton, leave now. Remember, she's a boxer, and she's your superior. Sue, please stop. He's a lot stronger than he looks."

But neither listened. Susan's third attempt to smash him was the least successful. He caught her fist in his hand and squeezed so hard he brought her down to her knees in pain.

Tamara charged full tilt at Daniel, but buckled when she ran into his shoulder, which he'd lowered to repel her.

"Craig!" hollered Samantha. "Hurry, I need your help!"

Daniel knelt, brought his furious face close to Susan's, and through gritted teeth growled, "Little kids blown to pieces, women burnt to charcoal, men blown right out of their clothes and smeared over the walls, and you stand here bragging about it?"

"Dan. Let go now!" commanded Craig as he trotted in from the porch.

"I'll see you pay for this, Beatoff!" said Susan as tears of ire and pain came to her eyes.

"Specialist Beaton, I order you to let go of her hand!" screamed Craig.

Daniel obeyed and released Susan's hand. She then launched forward and landed a heavy fist on his cheek. Daniel fell back on his rear, but immediately jumped to his feet, grabbed her by the collar, and violently wrenched her off the floor with a look so seething that Susan's confident expression was displaced by one that betrayed her fear. Samantha clutched his arm. Perhaps thinking it was Tamara launching another assault, he turned with a vicious look that frightened Samantha. The moment he realized it was her, all signs of hatred and anger vanished. He let go of Susan and flashed Samantha a remorseful smile.

Talon entered and pushed Daniel back to the wall. He offered no resistance.

"Did you hit either of these women?" Craig asked. Susan was standing in shock in the middle of the room. Tamara was just getting to her feet.

"No, sir; they attacked me. I just defended myself."

"He came in here insulting me," said a reanimated Susan. "I want him charged!"

Craig turned to his medic and ordered, "Get out to the porch. I'll see you in a few minutes." Daniel and Talon left.

*

Craig joined Talon and Daniel on the porch nine minutes later. They talked about the incident and started joking about Susan. "She's the last word in brick house," said Talon.

"But she has a regrettable face," opined Daniel.

"She's just the wrong species. She'd be gorgeous if she was a gargoyle," stated Talon.

This got Daniel laughing.

"You feel better now?" asked Craig.

"Yes. I guess I shouldn't let mass murder get to me."

"You have to remember this is war, and she was ordered to fire."

"But she was standing there laughing about it. These frigging Apache hotshots should be made to accompany us once in a while to cope with the fallout."

"Might make them hesitate next time," said Craig.

"Good," replied Daniel.

"Not good if it costs you or us or other American soldiers their lives. Maybe her bluster is her version of your joking. Maybe it's how she deals with all the shit here. She has a tough job, and she does it well, so cut her some slack."

"I think she really enjoys it, and I think she's dangerous, but I'll keep my distance and won't cause her any more trouble."

"You'll do one thing before you stay away. You'll go to her and apologize."

"She attacked me!" protested Daniel.

"I don't care. I spent ten minutes talking her out of charging you."

"For what? Getting hit?" His cheek was throbbing, swelling and turning color.

"For disrespect, for crushing her hand, for … Never mind. You know I don't like to pull rank, but I'm doing it here. I order you to apologize to her, and don't antagonize her while you do it. If you do, I can't help you; you'll be in the stockade, maybe for years. Do you understand that?"

"Yes, sir," he said bitterly, and he left to carry out the order.

*

Two days later, as Daniel was strolling along the flight line in the scorching 120 degree heat, taking litters for cleaning after a mission, Jason Carter called out, "Hey, doc!" Daniel stopped and waited for him to catch up. "I've got news for you that should settle my debt to you." Daniel looked at him expectantly, and Jason went on, "Doc Telfer is married."

"You're shitting me!"

"Wife's name is Stacy. I emailed you the proof."

"This could alter things in my favor. Having a wife is definitely a drawback to getting engaged. Many women consider it a deal breaker. Thanks. I'm happy to release both of us from the burden of your debt to me."

"Happy I could help, doc."

Daniel ran to drop off the litters, so he could go tell Samantha straight away. On his way to her room, though, he stopped. How to break this to her? She was bound to get emotional and likely wouldn't believe him. If things worked out well, this could eventually deliver her right into his waiting arms, but he had to play it right. He detoured to his room to get his computer and look at the email. There were pictures of the Telfers getting married, and one of Paul, his gorgeous wife, and their baby girl.

With his computer in hand, he went to Samantha's room and knocked. She answered. Struggling for the best way to approach the issue, he stood dumb for a minute.

"Well?" she said.

"Uh, how much do you know about Telfer?"

"Oh, don't start with me."

"Please, Sam, just answer the question."

"I know he's everything I ever wanted in a man."

"You wanted a wife?"

She smirked and tried to close the door, but he stopped it.

The oblique approach wasn't working. "Sam, Telfer's married."

She blanched, and her eyes and mouth gaped. "Liar! He is not married."

"Have it your way, but you'll have to live in Utah, and that's a hell of a price to pay."

"You're just so desperate to get him out of the picture, you'll say anything. This time, I won't forgive you, Beaton. This is so underhanded, so mean—"

"Sam."

She shoved him out of anger. "What the hell are you doing checking up on him? How low will you go? I swear—"

"Sam!" he said. "Telfer has a frigging wife." He held out his computer, but she pushed it away.

"I don't believe you!" But it was apparent she did. Tears flooded her eyes and overflowed. "Just yesterday, I brought up the subject of marriage to see how he would react. He seemed open to it. I was overjoyed. He can't be married; he can't be."

Again he held out his computer, which was displaying the pictures. She took the computer, looked with grief at the undeniable evidence, and dropped to her knees sobbing. "I'm sorry, Sam," said Daniel.

"Go. Just go," she moaned.

He left. *Leave her to grieve*, he told himself. *And over the next four months, without Telfer in the way, I'll draw her closer, then propose the day I get released.*

Sitting on the porch with Talon, whom he had regaled with the latest news, Daniel saw Samantha march toward the operating theater. Daniel got up to follow. Talon said, "Make sure she gets there okay, but stay out of it or there could be real trouble."

He took Talon's advice, at first. He watched her go into the small facility and walked up to a window, hoping to overhear the overthrow of Telfer. He heard Samantha yelling and crying, but heard nothing from Paul. Curious, he went to the door, sneaked in, and found a spot to better spy on them. He saw them hugging, and his jaw dropped. Samantha said to Paul, "I'm so sorry I believed that son of a bitch. Can you forgive me?"

"Of course."

"I should've thought that pictures are so easy to doctor nowadays. I'll get that fucking Beaton."

This was all that Daniel could take. He stepped out with a vile glare at the couple and said, "For Christ's sake, Hawkins, you really are hopeless. Why the hell did I ever put you on a pedestal? You're obviously a moron."

"You bastard!" she cried as she ran at him. He put a straight arm out to intercept her and keep her from hitting him. "I hate you! I hate you!" she yawped.

"You tried to ruin a good thing, Beaton, and you're going to pay," admonished Paul.

"I merely told the truth, you cheating scuzzbag."

Paul charged at Daniel. Daniel pushed Samantha back so she wouldn't get hurt and turned to intercept Paul. He lowered his head and shoulders and tackled his attacker. Ending up on top, he smashed Paul in the face with two punishing punches.

Samantha tried to pull Daniel off, screaming, "This is the end, Beaton. You'll go to jail now, and we'll celebrate it. I'm going to call for the MPs."

As Samantha ran off, Daniel got off the officer and stood hovering over him.

Paul had been stunned, but recovered and started laughing. He got to his feet. "You're fucked now. Jail time and everything."

"I hope you don't love your wife and daughter," Daniel returned.

The smile left Paul's face, and he said, "What the hell does that mean? What did you do?"

"It means if you charge me and if you don't tell Sam the truth, I'll email Stacy and tell her all about Nurse Sweetland and Sam. With pictures and everything."

Paul laughed and said, "Then I'll simply tell her this Beaton idiot hit me and is trying to blackmail me into withholding charges by sending doctored pictures. You saw how easily Sam fell for it."

"Maybe your wife isn't as stupid."

"I'm sure I can handle her with no problem. And, let's say I told Sam about Stacy. What do you think would happen next with her? You think you win and get the girl?" He chuckled. "She told me about your crush on her; we laugh about it. She calls you a loser."

The two heard crying. They saw Samantha crouched at the door. She hadn't left to call the MPs.

She stood up trembling and said to Paul, "If you charge him with assault, I'll email your wife to tell her all about us."

He looked at her in shock and replied, "So you think you can blackmail me?"

"Absolutely," she answered.

"Here's what's going to happen," declared the captain. "Sam, you go back to flying and forget me and my wife. In return, I won't charge Beaton." Her silence betokened her acceptance. Paul went on, "But I can't allow Beaton to get away scot free after assaulting an officer. So, I will inform the army that this man is a diabetic and make sure he's drummed out without a cent for medical school."

Daniel exclaimed, "You told him?"

Samantha looked down at the floor and admitted, "In Australia. I was really mad at you, and it just came out."

"You stupid goddamn big-mouthed bitch!"

She looked sorrowfully at him and said, "I'm sorry, I thought I could trust him." She walked to him and reached out to take his hand, but he withdrew it and maintained his infuriated scowl. Turning to Paul, she threatened, "You do this to him, I swear I'll cost you your family!"

"Believe me, nothing you can do will cause that; she idolizes me. But I don't want the headache. I'll tell you what. I'm reasonable. I'll give him a choice." He turned to Daniel and said, "I won't tell the army, but I want you out of my life. You can finish your last four months as a field medic."

"No!" shouted Samantha.

"His choice. What'll it be, Beaton?"

"Field medic," he growled.

"You'll make a request to the CO for reassignment and tell him whatever you want to get it approved. Just make it happen."

Daniel stomped out and Samantha followed. "Dan, I'm so sorry."

"For once in your life, Hawkins, shut the fuck up. Just stay away from me." He walked toward his room with furious gait.

She trotted to stay with him and said, "He can't get away with this."

"It's done." He stopped to face her. "I never want to see you again. The spell is finally broken. God, I fucking hate you!"

His fierce and livid eyes and his bared teeth not only convinced her this was true, it made her apprehensive for her safety. He looked ready to rip her apart. And that's what he did, with words: "If I die out there, it's on you." He walked on as her heart stopped and her tears resumed.

Daniel told the commanding officer that he was nervous about flying after the crash and felt he could make a better contribution as a field medic for his final four months in the army. The colonel said fine as long as Lieutenant Ng approved. Craig didn't believe his story about fearing flying, so Daniel admitted he punched the captain and this was their agreed-upon settlement. Sighing, Craig gave his consent.

CHAPTER THIRTEEN

Valley of Death – September 2009

Specialist Daniel Beaton waved his hands before his face to try to make his way through the dust and away from the Chinook helicopter, which took off immediately and enveloped him in another cloud of dust. Hauling his heavy gear up a steep hill behind a private sent to meet him, he arrived at the Korengal Outpost exhausted, sweaty, and filthy; no escaping the dust in Afghanistan.

As the dust settled, he looked around at his new neighborhood. The small base was perched on a precipitous hillside along a ridgeline above the Korengal Valley. He noticed monkeys playing outside the wire on some gnarled trees. Looking farther out at the forested hills and high mountains, he realized how isolated they were from—everything.

The outpost itself consisted of perhaps a dozen structures of stone, wood, and canvas, including a brick and mortar headquarters, a medical tent, a mess tent serving a single hot meal a day, a few small huts and tents for sleeping and lying around, a water tank and sandbag bunkers for protection from constant harassing fire, all encompassed by concertina wire that stretched close to half a mile up a steep hill. An Internet linkup and a few phones were the only contact with the outside world, other than resupply helicopters.

Trudging upwards, Daniel saw a soldier urinating into a length of PVC pipe sticking out of the ground. He smiled thinking of the piss he'd let loose on his first visit here seventeen months earlier, a lifetime ago. Four brick stalls with shower curtains sufficed for the other bodily function. Up the hill a bit was an Afghan National Army bunker and a thousand feet up the steep hill was Outpost 1, a small redoubt set up to protect KOP against attack from above.

"You'll be in here," said the private as he led Daniel into one of the plywood huts. Daniel noted the magazine pictures of women decorating the walls and a few cots. Three of the cots were occupied by languid soldiers passing the time doing nothing. The cots were so close, the soldiers could reach out and touch the next man.

"Cripes, I hope none of you is a fag," mentioned Daniel.

"No, but you'd be surprised how nice a hairy ass looks after you ain't been with a woman for months," answered one of the men lying on his cot with his hands under his head.

"Just a friendly notice that if any of you gets any ideas about invading my ass, next time you need medical help, I'll chop off your shitty dick."

"Noted," answered one, and the others nodded.

"Would you take it hard if I told you I don't like what you've done with the place? It looks like you haven't dusted for ages."

They were too apathetic to continue the meaningless conversation, so Daniel put his gear down, unpacked what he needed to, and went to report to the commanding officer.

When Captain Stan Holman asked Specialist Beaton who he murdered to get transferred from a helicopter to "the shithole of the universe," he answered, "Apparently the army frowns upon pointing out what a pile of shit one of its officers is."

"That's not enough. What else? Spill it."

"A certain flight surgeon was dating the woman I loved, and I found out he was married and told her. She left him, which didn't impress him. We had words and there was the little matter of a punch or two."

"Got it. You punch me, I won't press charges or transfer you. I'll simply skullfuck you."

"Just make sure you use a rubber. I wouldn't want some hideous disease in my eyehole."

"Don't worry. You'll be dead."

"Can't be worse than being here."

"This a low point for you?" said Stan with a chuckle.

"My whole life has been a series of ever lower points; this is just a continuation."

"I took the liberty of speaking to Lieutenant Ng. He sang your praises and made it clear he was pissed he's losing you. He says your skills as a medic are second to none, so if you want an upside, you can do more good here than maybe anywhere else on the planet. He also said you're smart, but that you have a really smart mouth, which tends to get you in trouble. So, another upside here is there's practically nothing you can say to anyone that will make an eye bat. You're as far here from generals and colonels as you'll ever get in the army. We're informal. You don't need to salute or make your bed without a wrinkle or shine your boots." He took a sip of his coffee and frowned at its bitter taste.

Stan proceeded, "You have a weakness for pointing out what piles of shit officers are, fine. Go to it. But you're expected to obey your superiors; that's especially important for a new guy if you want to live. We don't give a shit about personal weaknesses here. What we do care about is each other. We're surrounded by hostiles here, and all we have for protection is each other. We'll gladly put our lives on the line to defend the platoon and every one of the men in it. As long as you have no hesitation to do that, then you'll fit right in."

Daniel nodded.

"I understand you're almost through med school."

"One more year."

"Don't try to come on cerebral with the men here. They're terrific soldiers, but they aren't big picture guys. They have no idea why they're doing what they're doing, and they've stopped questioning it. They can't worry about any of that. They know it's all futile. Just stay alive. The kooks we're fighting aren't exactly cerebral either. They're incapable of thinking beyond what they see before them. They don't give a shit what they can do for their god; they're interested in what their god can do for them, you know, heaven, virgins, on and on. They're in it for themselves, regardless of what they tell themselves. So, when we kill them, we're doing them a favor, getting them up to their virgins fast. That's what they're fighting for, right?"

"Are they mostly locals, or Taliban, or what?"

"We figure somewhere around half are local or Taliban from other provinces here. The rest are Muslim zealots from Pakistan, Saudi Arabia, Yemen, Chechnya, Uzbek, and other shitholes."

"Where do they get the arms?" asked Daniel.

"Pakistan mostly. We give those fuckers billions of dollars in aid, and they use part of it to help the Taliban. We're at war with Pakistan, but we refuse to admit it, and because we refuse to admit it, we'll never get any closer to winning."

"So what the hell are we doing here? If we were to win this part of the war, win this valley, what would we do with it?"

"Excellent questions, and I'd wager no one in the White House or Congress has a damn clue what the answers are. My best guess is the people in the Pentagon want to keep pressure off the Pech River Valley, which does have strategic importance, or maybe to tie up some of the worst zealots and keep their focus away from the cities. Doesn't matter to us anyway; we're here and we have to make the best of it.

"Our specific aim is to massacre the fuckers without losing any of our guys, but it's not as easy as the generals think. We have better guns and better equipment, but these mountains are their turf, and they know how to hide and how to find us, so that's a draw. We're much better shots, and we can kill them ten to one, but they have a never-ending supply of jihadists after their virgins, so again it's a draw. If they mass for an attack, the motherfuckers can overrun us. Sometimes only the Apaches keep us alive." Stan took another sip of coffee, cursed, poured the rest of it into the garbage, and said, "I've assigned Corporal Hunt to watch your back until you catch on to the tricks of staying alive on patrol. Your first trip outside the wire will be next week, unless something crops up before then. Now leave and find something to occupy your time. Good luck."

Early the first evening, Daniel was walking toward the mess tent when a brawl broke out. While he stood gawking, another man walked past paying the affray no heed. "Isn't anybody going to stop this?" asked Daniel.

"Go ahead," the private invited as he continued on his way.

Daniel looked on as eleven soldiers beat hell out of each other for almost ten minutes before three of them broke away and tottered laughing in Daniel's direction. Reaching him, they attacked, catching Daniel by surprise. He took a hard fist to his cheek and another to his stomach. Before he could react, one of the men got him in a chokehold. Daniel couldn't breathe and was just beginning to panic when he lost consciousness, a forearm and biceps constricting his carotid arteries.

Daniel came to, after a few moments, with several men surrounding him and laughing. "Welcome to Korengal, doc," said one of the men who had punched him. Still dazed, Daniel sat up and tried to collect his wits. Most of the men walked off, leaving the three who had assaulted him.

A private grabbed his hand and pulled him to his feet. "No hard feelings," said the private as he and the two other assailants chortled. As Daniel's ire built up inside, his face turned red. The men's laughter got louder. Daniel put on a phony smile to catch them off-guard. Once they turned to walk away, Daniel launched his right foot between the legs of the largest man, reducing him to a writhing moaner on the dirt. Upon turning to redress this manoeuvre, the second man absorbed a punishing punch to his Adam's apple. He, too, collapsed to the ground, holding his neck. The third man tackled Daniel, but an enraged Daniel had little trouble overcoming him.

While Daniel repeatedly punched the private and kicked the other two men still on the ground, a sergeant ran up and ordered him to stop. He turned and screamed, "Where the hell were you when these bastards attacked me and choked me out?"

"Calm down, doc. They were just welcoming you to Korengal Outpost."

"And I was returning the favor."

"You were beating the shit out of men who couldn't defend themselves."

"Fucker kicked me from behind in the nuts," yelled the corporal, who was just getting to his feet.

"Cheap shot, doc," noted the sergeant.

"What the hell set of rules you go by here? It's okay for three men to launch a surprise attack on one man and choke him out, but you can't kick a man in the nuts?"

"Nuts and eyes are off limits."

"I'll get you back, fuck head," warned the miffed man.

"You going to gang up on me again, pussy?"

The man ran at Daniel and knocked him flying. Daniel got to his knees and drove his fist into the man's crotch, which finished him.

"What the hell did I just say?" said the sergeant.

"You just barked out a set of arbitrary rules, which I choose to ignore."

"Keep ignoring orders, and I'll have you charged," admonished the sergeant.

"If we're now pulling rank, then I want these privates charged for attacking me!" said Daniel.

"Listen, Specialist. We do have a set of rules that have evolved after a year in this dump. The men go through hell and need ways to alleviate constant stress and boredom. The fights are one way of blowing off steam. They fight each other and don't get angry or hold grudges. This really was their way of welcoming you aboard, but you've managed to fuck that up so bad, I don't know if they'll ever accept you now."

The sergeant walked away, and Daniel cursed, skipped dinner, and went to his bunk.

The next several days were uneventful. Daniel found himself shunned by the men, but that was fine with him; better than suffering their love punches. On the other hand, not being a part of the group could have deleterious consequences during a battle. Would these men abandon him if he fell behind or got wounded?

One of his roommates, he learned, was Scott Humphrey, the wife of one Susan Humphrey of Apache fame. He was six feet five inches of muscle. He greeted Daniel with the news, "The wife asked me to kick the shit out of you."

"I hope you don't let her boss you around."

"She said you two had a fight that wasn't a boxing match. Did you hit her?"

"No, never even tried. We had an argument, and she tried to punch me. I got hold of her fist and squeezed hard to try to make her stop her attack. Then she punched me in the cheek, and I grabbed her by her collar and lifted her off the floor, but I didn't hurt her."

"If you had, I'd have fucked you up your descending colon, then broken your neck." He punched Daniel in the chest so hard he was thrown back to the wall and collapsed onto the floor trying to get air. "There. I'll tell her I beat you up. You got off easy." He walked out with Daniel still on the floor struggling to breathe.

On his seventh morning at KOP, Daniel finished brushing his teeth and felt a momentary regret that he'd accomplished the only task he had in mind until lunch. He moseyed along by bales of unused concertina wire thinking that he was setting the new world record for tedium. Out of nowhere incoming rounds started zinging by. He instinctively crouched. Distant pops confirmed that bullets were coming his way. He fell to the ground and looked around for better cover, but he had no idea where the shots were coming from, so he froze where he was, trying to get swallowed up in the earth.

He saw tracers coming in, but it didn't help; they were impossible to dodge. Bullets passed over his head with a distinctive snap. He couldn't believe what was happening. He'd been in the war for seventeen months, but this was the first time he'd been a target when he had the leisure to panic. And because he wasn't trained for front-line duty, he felt this situation was out of his control. When he tended to the wounded, a job he was highly trained for, he was in control and there was no time nor reason to panic.

But here there was no semblance of control; it was sheer chaos. He wasn't so much afraid of dying, he was terrified of getting horribly maimed and surviving, like too many of his patients. Mortars began to fall. For some reason he thought of sitting in Melbourne in a classroom writing the medical licensing exams. What could be more opposite to this? He looked up the slope. Grunts were crouched behind a set of earthen barriers, their rifles pointing at the ridgelines above. He looked at the entrance to the closest bunker, barely visible through the dust and smoke; too far.

The explosions got closer, blasts so loud and bright they disoriented him. The dust stirred up by the explosions choked him. He had to get to the barriers, but he couldn't coax his body to move. The men were now returning fire. Time seemed to slow, and he noticed minute details. Many of the soldiers were dressed in gym shorts. Their boots were unlaced. They'd torn the arms off their shirts, and he could see three had "DTV" tattoos on their upper arms—Damn the Valley, he'd learned earlier—but had their body armor on. The dust clogged their rifles, and they had to use their spit to keep them working. Time sped up. The blinding and deafening explosions, the bullets rocketing by, the dust, the screaming; pandemonium.

A mortar landed close to the men. "Doc!" bellowed one of them. "Charlie's hurt. Get over here now." Daniel pushed his arms against the ground to get to his feet, but the earth seemed to suck him down. He tried again. Nothing. "Medic!" shrieked the sergeant again. His strength insufficient to overcome his fear, he had to use his will. Daniel mustered all his courage, pulled himself up, and sprinted in a crouch to the injured soldier. It was exhausting, terrifying, stupefying and, once he'd made it to cover, thrilling. "It's about fucking time," yelped his sergeant.

But Daniel paid no attention. All his concentration was on the injured man. The concussion from the explosion had thrown him into a wooden shed, dislocating his right shoulder and breaking his arm. He was grimacing and grunting in pain. Daniel had only basic supplies with him in pouches and pockets. He extracted a needle and gave the man a shot of morphine. Once that took effect, he popped the shoulder back into place. Then he grabbed a piece of wood that had been blown off the shed in the explosion and used it to immobilize the broken arm by taping it to the arm and putting the arm in a sling.

"Okay, doc, get over here and help us," ordered Sergeant Chenkin. "Where's your rifle?" Daniel looked over at the spot where he first threw himself to the ground.

"Fuck me, Beatoff, you gotta use your head here or you'll lose it. Here, take Charlie's. He won't be needing his anytime soon."

Daniel crawled over against the barrier. He'd never shot a weapon against a live target. But as horrible as that prospect was, another problem dwarfed it. He found it impossible to jut his head above the cover to shoot at the enemy. Thinking about the many head wounds he'd seen, like the child whose face had been peeled back from the eyes down and others who'd had half their brain blown away, he couldn't do it.

He looked with awe at the private next to him, head and shoulders above the barrier, firing away with a cigarette stuck to his lips. Daniel felt ashamed of his cowardice. Sergeant Chenkin had just begun baying at him again when, "Medic!

Medic!" wafted through the dust from another set of barriers about fifty meters across the compound. Without a thought for his own safety, Daniel darted through the shooting gallery to his next patient. He left the rifle behind.

Private Bell had taken a bullet in the stomach and was screeching in pain. He and his buddy had evidently been asleep when the attack commenced. They had only boxers and unlaced boots on. "For fuck sake, give him some morphine," said his friend who was shooting his rifle at the distant muzzle flashes. Lacking his medical rucksack—he made a mental note never to leave it behind again—Daniel had no more morphine on him. For now the best he could do was stop the bleeding. He pulled a tampon out of a pouch and gingerly pushed it into the wound.

"Oh, sweet fucking Jesus! Fuck!" screeched the wounded soldier in obvious agony. "Ahhh!"

Daniel gave the man a fentanyl lollipop and examined the wound to assess the damage. The man was having difficulty with the sucker because he started coughing up blood. The man screamed again. Daniel took back the lollipop and tossed it aside. "I'll be right back," he promised. Then chanting, "Fuck, fuck, fuck," he sprinted down the hill to his cot where he'd left his rucksack. On the way back, bullets raked the ground just behind him as he sped uphill as fast as his legs would carry him. He dived behind the barrier with his heart pounding so hard his ears pulsated. Inhaling deeply, he extracted a morphine injector and gave the wretched man a shot. As the medicine deadened the pain, Daniel opened an Israeli field pack dressing and placed the pad against the wound. He then wrapped an elastic bandage around the man's abdomen.

By this time, American artillery was pounding enemy positions, and the insurgents quickly withdrew. Daniel sat for a while to slow his heart and tried to figure out what the hell just happened to him. He felt a strange sense of exhilaration.

His rifle landed next to him, and he looked up to see Sergeant Chenkin smirking at him. "Beatoff, you're a lousy fucking soldier, but you put everything on the line more than once to help my men, so we'll keep you, but for your sake and ours, try to remember the following. This is your fucking gun. It's part of you. It has a trigger, which comes in handy when you want to stop the motherfuckers on the other side from killing us. Next time, use it; and don't leave it behind again. Got it?"

"Got it, sarge."

Daniel looked at his watch and couldn't believe the firefight had lasted twenty-three minutes. He'd have said two or three minutes. He went back to his patients. A half hour later, he handed them off to Jim's medevac crew.

Daniel soon learned the routine. Nothing to do over ninety percent of the time. Guard duty, helping troops with medical complaints, the occasional sniper attack on the camp and treks outside the camp rounded out the experience. Playing a video game or two in the command centre and surfing the net constituted the available leisure activities. And once a week or so, Daniel would email a letter describing what was happening in his life. Samantha had asked Talon to make this request of Daniel, since he wouldn't talk or write to her. Talon let her read the letters.

From: Dan Beaton
Date: Thursday, September 10, 2009
To: Talon Okeeweehow
Subject: In the shit in the Stan

Did you know that, compared to KOP, JAF is Las Vegas? I struggle to think of an adjective to describe the place. Cozy doesn't quite capture it. Horrid is closer to the mark, but still too kind. A poet might describe KOP as a tumbledown prospect, but we soldiers refer to it as a shithole. This morning I was just about to put on my boots when one of my roommates warned me to check them. I'm glad he did because a scorpion was snoozing in my left boot, and I wouldn't have wanted to disturb his sleep, so I killed him. This place could use a bit of napalm to spruce it up.

And boring; oh, sweet Sophia, is it boring! Yesterday I spent ten hours accumulating dust while the local fauna got fat off me. Clouds of fleas eat you alive here, and the only defense is to wear a flea collar around your ankles, but still we sit here scratching ourselves all day. That's the only pastime, unless, of course, the bad guys start firing at us. That, let me tell you, is not boring. Amazing how the same spot can be the most exhilarating and most boring on the planet, depending on the whims of our enemy.

I was in my first firefight this morning. I know we sometimes ran through bullets to get to casualties, but this was different, I think because I had time to pay attention to it. The sounds, the explosions, the terrifying violence, the adrenalin surging; it's awful, but it's exciting as hell, too. Multiply the best video action game by a million, and that's combat. There's more excitement squeezed into a twenty-minute firefight than in a businessman's lifetime. Assuming one comes out of it in one piece, that is. I've seen so many more cases who came out in smithereens than any of these guys that I'm at a disadvantage. I'm scared! A couple of the new guys were whooping it up when a bullet zoomed by, and I'm thinking, uh, you do know this isn't a video game, right? Do you know what a real bullet does to a real human being?

To answer your question, Humphrey caressed my chest with his fist and left me in a heap on the floor, but he let it go at that. But tell She-man he did pound hell out of me or her husband will rape my colon and break my neck, apparently. I don't really blame the shithead; he was just standing up for his gargoyle.

There is one positive about this place: not one Telfer to blacken my day. If you have to come to KOP, don't let him tag along. I swear, Chief, if I see him, I'll kill him.

Be safe,
Dan

A few days later, the sergeant poked his head into the hut where four men were lying around passing the time. Daniel was reading about the digestive system; the others were snoozing or looking at the ceiling. Sergeant Chenkin opened his mouth to say something, but Corporal Hunt cut him short with, "Wait, I know what you're going to say."

The sergeant smirked and said, "Is there room in here for a dead malamute?" The stray dog the company had adopted had died that morning.

"Oh. Guess I was wrong," conceded Hunt.

"Beatoff, come with me," said the sergeant.

"That's pretty fucking gross, sarge," pointed out Hunt.

"Now, doc."

"Suck my sweaty, salty, swinging sack, sarge," said Beaton.

"What was that?"

"I said, of course, Sergeant."

Daniel put his notes on his cot, exited the hut, and walked with his sergeant, who said, "Ramon is real sick again. He's all puffed up on his neck, and he has a bad headache. Another nose bleed, too."

"Probably mono, possibly mumps. Either way, there's no treatment except pain killers, rest, and time. I'll give him some Tylenol."

"Take his guard duty tonight at midnight."

"I'll try to fit it in."

The first few times on guard duty, Daniel was nervous and thorough, checking out every sound or movement, but after hearing and seeing monkeys, birds, goats, and various other animals for a few days he got used to them and dismissed them.

This night he noticed movement inside the camp and radioed to his colleague, "Look just beside the mess tent. What the hell is that?"

"A mountain lion."

"Did you say *lion*?"

"Yup. They're good climbers and jumpers. They can get past the wire. They roam around looking for food."

"Christ, you're calm about it considering you qualify as food. Aren't lions bad for us?"

"Don't bother it and it won't bother you."

"What if someone gets up to take a shit and runs into it?"

"Should make the shit come faster. If it's endangering someone, then shoot it."

"When I think of how many years I've been taking it for granted that when I got up to take a shit I wasn't going to get eaten by a jeezly lion."

"We've all been there."

"What's next in this shithole?"

From: Dan Beaton
Date: Wednesday, September 16, 2009
To: Talon Okeeweehow
Subject: Prophetic

The other night while I was on guard duty I saw a goddamn mountain lion in the camp, and I thought, man, if somebody meets up with it while going for a shit, it would be a real stinker. Well, last night someone was up to take a piss and, wouldn't you know it, he ran across the lion. He immediately started screeching at the top of his lungs, and it was not a very masculine falsetto, let me tell you. This woke up a good portion of the camp, who came running out to see what the fuss was, and they saw the lion take off and this man with wet pants still screaming.

He simply could not stop himself until finally someone slapped me.
Dan

CHAPTER FOURTEEN

Patrol – September – October 2009

Corporal Ken Hunt called Daniel to wake him for a midnight patrol to check out a concentration of a dozen or so figures spotted by a Predator drone two and a half kilometers south of the KOP. "I'm supposed to keep you alive so you can keep us alive," he informed Daniel. "So do what I say if you want to live. If you don't, stay the fuck away from the rest of us."

"That's touching, thank you. You should be one of those up-with-people assholes."

"Grab your gear, put on your NVGs, and be outside in five mikes."

Daniel had to wait until his bunkmates left and quickly grabbed his kit, which contained a glucometer, testing strips, needles, insulin, glucagon, and Life Savers. He checked his blood sugar, popped a few Life Savers and exited. Weighed down under eighty pounds of body armor, equipment, and supplies, Daniel stood uncomfortably with about twenty other men waiting for the signal to leave.

"Just to let you know, they don't take prisoners," said Ken as he walked up to Daniel.

"Shit, I was looking forward to Taliban hospitality," retorted Daniel.

"We can't walk too close together on patrol, or we'll be targeted. I can't yell you instructions, or I'll be targeted, so listen. Out there, always be on the lookout for potential cover. The attacks come without warning, and if you just stand holding your cock, you'll be dead, then what good are you to us? How much water you got?" Daniel showed him. "Not enough; get more."

"I'm already carrying—"

"Listen, it's hard slogging through these fucking mountains. If you get too dehydrated, you're not ready to do your job if someone gets hurt. Get more water."

Daniel dashed to get another full canteen of water and returned.

While waiting for Lieutenant Torrez, a private shouted over to Daniel, "Doc, if my dick gets shot off, I want you to sew it back on."

Daniel answered, "If that happens, Murphy already asked me to shove it up his ass." That got the troops laughing as the lieutenant showed up.

"Ready to die today, boys?" said Lieutenant Torrez. "We're searching for some bad guys about two point five clicks out. We need to locate them and identify them as hostiles or civilians, or whichever one they are at the present time. If they're insurgents, some hellfire missiles will fuck them up. Sarge."

Sergeant Chenkin said, "Remember, whichever of you dies, I'll go and tell your mother in person. I'll break it gently while I'm clutching her waist and ramming her from behind. Let's go."

"One more thing," said Hunt to Beaton as they filed out of the KOP. "When we're under fire, sometimes we're pinned down, but if we stay there the mortars or grenades will start. They'll correct a couple of times, then we're dead. We have to move, so we do something called bounding. Heard of it?" Beaton shook his head. "One group runs, another covers, then opposite. This way we can overcome tactical disadvantages, and it can make the difference between living and dying." Beaton nodded. "You're in my group. Follow me every step of the way, but not too close!"

Struggling up steep crags and through narrow gorges, slipping on sharp rocks and wading through frigid brooks, the soldiers proceeded along mountain trails. With the moon a one-eighth sliver, it was impossible to see without NVGs. How the enemy managed was anybody's guess.

It was such hard work, after two kilometers Beaton collapsed to his knees, exhausted. He had thought he was in good shape, but carrying this load on this terrain proved too much for a diabetic who hadn't reckoned on this amount of strain when determining how to balance his blood sugar.

"Sarge," said Hunt in a loud whisper. "Hold. Doc's down."

Sergeant Chenkin gave hand signals, and the troops stopped to rest.

"Breathe deeply and drink some water," advised Hunt.

Beaton was trembling, his skin was clammy, he was sweating, anxious, and hungry. His sudden realization that he was experiencing hypoglycemia almost made him panic. He didn't need water, he needed sugar, right away before he fainted. Fainting out here would put him and his entire platoon at risk and could lead to the discovery of his diabetes. A glucagon shot might be best, but how to dissolve the powder into the diluting fluid and inject it with the men looking at him? He took out his Life Savers and put the rest of them into his mouth. Then he tore open an MRE, discarded the main course, and ate the Pop-Tarts. He washed it down with water.

"You okay?" asked Hunt.

Beaton nodded, though he was in no shape for more of this drudgery.

After another few minutes respite, the platoon continued toward their objective. Beaton steadied himself and walked carefully, willing himself to continue. The sugar helped, but the resumption of the toil did not. Fortunately, they soon reached their objective. The latest intelligence from the drone was that the congregation of men was ahead two hundred meters, but dispersing. Several were heading toward the platoon. They needed to get a look at them before they got away.

The lieutenant used a night vision scope and scanned the coordinates provided. Speaking into his radio, he said, "I can only see one of them. He's wearing a BDU. Do we have a go for the Hellfires?"

"BDU?" queried Beaton of Hunt.

"Camouflage jacket," explained Hunt.

"You can shoot someone for wearing a jacket?"

"No civilians wear them."

"Wait, I see three more," said Lieutenant Torrez. "They have A.K.s. Copy that." He turned to his men and said, "Fireworks in a minute."

Within seconds the drone unleashed three Hellfire missiles. It got most of the insurgents, but not all, as the Americans found out when shots echoed out and strafed the trail all around them. The Americans scrambled to find cover, but not knowing where the shooters were, they had to keep moving.

Hunt grasped Beaton's arm and pulled him behind a boulder. "There! Muzzle flashes." Hunt began returning fire, as did the rest of the platoon. "Come on," insisted Hunt, "help out."

Beaton, who'd never yet shot at anyone, and who maintained his aversion to getting his head splattered, sucked in some air and popped up. He fired continuously toward the muzzle flashes until Hunt hollered, "Stop! Shoot too much and your gun jams and, worse, you draw fire."

Sure enough, most of the bullets came their way. Bullets ricocheted off the boulder and cracked against the tree trunks behind their position.

Crouching behind the boulder, Hunt said, "You have to learn to focus and manage the adrenalin. Take your time, find the target, shoot in quick bursts, and get down."

An RPG exploded up the trail, and a few seconds later someone shouted, "Doc, get over here!"

Happy to be relieved of shooting duty, he sprinted to the wounded soldier. It turned out to be a flesh wound. While the private kept up the assault, Beaton cleaned and patched the laceration. Another explosion lit up the mountainside. The drone's last missile silenced two of the shooters, leaving three more. With a couple of minutes at his disposal, Beaton checked his blood sugar. "Eighteen. Shit," he read and concluded. He had taken too much sugar, but he decided not to take any insulin because he had a long march back to camp in front of him.

Another RPG exploded near Hunt, but the boulder protected him. Sergeant Chenkin ran through the heavy dust to the lieutenant and recommended they move away from the area since the enemy had grenades and the high ground, and there was little point risking lives trying to pick off the remaining two or three insurgents. The signal was given to the platoon, and the Americans bounded down the trail toward KOP.

Beaton followed Hunt. Once away from the fire, the Americans slowed their pace. "How did you get so good at fleeing for your life?" asked Beaton, breathing hard.

"Practice," answered Hunt.

Over two hours later, the weary troops marched into the KOP, mission accomplished, with no serious casualties. Beaton had managed by eating an MRE along the way. He collapsed onto his cot and woke up eleven hours afterward.

*

From: Dan Beaton
Date: Tuesday, October 13, 2009
To: Talon Okeeweehow
Subject: KOP

Yesterday, we went pottering around the mountains again to see if we could get shot or blown up, and one of the ANA soldiers succeeded. RPG. Poor bugger will lose both legs, I'm sure; maybe his nuts, too. As I was working on him, he's asking me if his balls were still there. They were pretty much a bloody mess, but maybe they can save one, if he's lucky. Lucky. That has to be the most relative word in the language. So, he keeps asking about his nuts. I mean, what do you say to a man who's maybe lost his nuts? "Too bad about your nuts. Maybe you can join a boys choir."

You know what he gave his legs/balls for? To give people in a nearby village some food. Their harvest failed after they neglected to protect their farm against a flying pest: a 500-pound laser-guided bomb dropped by an F16. Makes one wonder what the laser was pointing at. I can only hope that feeding a few insurgents and their families will be some solace for the loss of his balls.

A bullet whizzed by my head yesterday. It was shot by our ally, an ANA soldier. They often do that, I'm told, mostly by accident, but sometimes on purpose. Had I been a bit to the left, you wouldn't be reading this now. The arbitrariness gets to you. But for a step, a half-inch, a quarter of a second, you'd be dead or horribly injured. If you dwell on it, you can't make a move because you start second-guessing everything, the very steps you take, for Sophia's sake. So you don't dwell on it; you simply refuse to think about it. Same as we do dealing with a man in pieces.

I've discovered that details that don't matter anywhere else can get you killed here. Sophia help you if you carelessly kick a rock down a hill and it makes a racket, and the lieutenant lets you know you just put the entire platoon at risk, and they look at you as if you were Benedict Arnold, and you want to run home to get a hug from your mommy.

But major failings that matter everywhere else either don't matter a bit here, or they actually help. This one corporal here shoots anything that moves with a gusto awesome to behold. Anywhere else his penchant for murder would be considered a fault noteworthy enough to make him the number one draft choice of Attica State Pen, but here it is at worst a minor character flaw; at best it'll earn him medals after he saves all our lives. He lives for the excitement of combat. Most of the guys here do; it's why they joined. It's a real rush. When they see a buddy go down, or they go down themselves, it dawns on them that combat has a downside, yet most of them still relish a good firefight. I often wonder how these men will get along in society after this. How do they relate to people without a bullet as a go-between? What could ever excite them after the intensity of combat? I read that booze and drugs replace the adrenalin rush of the firefights when they get home, and many end up divorced,

```
unemployed, bankrupt, or dead if they
decide living is too painful.
    All in all, I don't think war is all
it's cracked up to be.
Dan
```

From mid to late October there was a lull in the fighting, which paradoxically caused problems in the KOP. The accumulation of stress from months of battle and sorrow from seeing so many friends hurt or die, and the overwhelming boredom that pervaded the interim between firefights, combined to create a kind of insanity. The men began wishing for combat, anything to break the unrelenting tedium. They slept as much as possible to pass the time. Many took sleeping pills; some took antidepressants. It would have been many more, but Daniel controlled the supply and tried to prevent addiction. When awake, they mostly sat silent. There was nothing to be said that hadn't been said a thousand times. Occasionally they'd have sporadic maunderings.

Lying on his bunk looking at the stained ceiling, Daniel tried to think of something original to say to his three bunkmates who were lying on their bunks with their minds elsewhere. He hadn't been here that long and often tried to end the long silences. "Fuck me, Hunt, you must be past due for your weekly shower. The flies drop dead when they get near you." There was no response. A few minutes later, he tried, "By the way, I can report that 'May I compliment you on your extraordinary tits?' is not an effective opening line." No response. So, he tried, "What do you think those moronic cock lickers we're fighting say before going into battle?" Finally a response.

"They must pray to Allah," said Hunt. "Please assist me, most perfect Allah, to crush the spine of my enemies and lop off their infidel heads."

Daniel continued, "And Allah, good buddy, grant me a nuclear bomb or two so that I may spread your love to Israel and America. I can scarcely wait to gaze upon your sacred face so you can personally thank me for my campaign against Western evil and vice. And please make my virgins prettier than the sows in my village. What do you think, Davies?"

"Doubt it," answered Davies.

"It's in the Koran, arsepipe. Look it up."

No further remarks. Daniel gave up.

A half hour later, Humphrey said, "The wife called me one big ugly fuck last week."

Daniel responded, "I hope that didn't come as a surprise. Did you not believe the evidence in the mirror?"

"How would you like a cracked skull?" said Humphrey.

"Nice of you to ask, but I think I'll pass."

"Because it's no problem for me. One pop with my fist."

"I think he's threatening you, Beatoff," observed Hunt.

"Nothing half-veiled about it," Beaton responded.

"My wife never called me an ugly fuck to my face at least," said Davies.

"No, she just left you for that collision shop dude," pointed out Hunt.

"You should have spotted the signs, Davies," commented Beaton. "Getting in fender benders every week and getting all dolled up to go to the collision shop."

"Giving you a Chevy bumper for Christmas," added Hunt.

"Hard to spot the signs from this dump," returned Davies. "I'll give the sonabitch more business when I get home, repairing the bumper that caved in his fucking skull."

Humphrey said, "Hope the wife don't leave me."

"I guess you just gotta tell the bitch I love you and all that shit," advised Davies.

"But don't put it like that," counseled Beaton.

After another spell of silence, Beaton peeled a banana and sang, "Come, Mr. Taliban, fuckie this banana."

Hunt and Humphrey responded, "Daylight come, and we wan' go home."

Davies said, "What's at home? Might as well stay here. Or just die. Don't really care if I die."

"Be less boring," said Hunt.

"There are positives to dying," contributed Beaton. "Just think of how much you'll save on groceries." He turned to glance at Davies and noticed tears rolling down his cheek.

*

From: Dan Beaton
Date: Thursday, October 29, 2009
To: Talon Okeeweehow
Subject: KOP

By the calendar we have about two months before our Afghan tour is done, but in KOP time, that's two ice ages from now. Can't wait till we get together to paint some American town red. I hope we survive till then, because otherwise it means that we can't drink as much as we want, and also that we're dead.

The army has mined a brand new rich vein of stupidity by turning out a West Point lieutenant who is a Fobbit through and through, and sending him here while one of our lieutenants gets a well-deserved break from this hellhole. You can imagine how well he's going over with the men here who are less formal than apes.

Picture this. Men are walking around in ratty sweatshirts that double as napkins and pants in shreds. They haven't showered in days, so they're caked in mud, every crease on their body is black with filth. They smell like scrambled intestines. They're unshaven. Their hair is too long and out of control. Their boots are beyond redemption. Every third word is profanity. They pass the time burping and farting and scratching their nutsacks. And along comes Lieutenant Gray with mouth agape in shock at these animals, who happen to be the best soldiers in the regular army. He starts screaming silly orders and threats, and the men look at him as if he were upchucking all over them and proceed to ignore him, which spawns more yelling and the cycle continues, until the other officers step in to set him straight about life at KOP. Next day he's back to screaming at everyone he outranks. He's stupid enough to go far in the army, but he'll get himself involved in a friendly fire incident here if he doesn't learn soon.

Yesterday he marched us out to a nearby village during daylight hours. The Taliban were probably watching us the whole time.

We walked into the village where we know
they live or hide. Why, you ask? So that
Lieutenant Gray can get his combat badge,
so he can become a captain faster. That's
why he requested a transfer from Bagram,
where he no doubt served the cause by
making sure boots were shiny.

So there we are in this little
settlement of rock and mud jutting out of
a stony hillside. Everything about the
place shouts hopelessness and despair,
though the villagers seem deaf to it. They
sympathize with the Taliban and hate us,
predictable since they have the same Dark
Ages belief system as the Taliban. Girls
don't get educated; women don't circulate;
men adhere to strict religious doctrine.
Yet here we are in a powwow with the
elders, trying to persuade them that
Western ways are best. Futile and we all
know it. We also know the villagers have
their signals to let the Taliban know
where we are, and they're busy signaling.
We regularly walk into villages where the
insurgents hang around, hoping to draw
them out into an open firefight. We're
bait. Our aim is to get ambushed. All to
maintain the stalemate. Talk about insane.

So, of course, the enemy attacks the
minute we start for KOP, and the seasoned
soldiers here do what they're supposed to
do, but Gray is kneeling behind a rock
barking out ridiculous commands that
everyone ignores because they're not eager
to die. It's clear this arsewipe has no
idea what he's doing, which goes way

beyond irritating in a life or death situation.

Rumor has it that the Army is getting set to pull out of the Korengal Valley, a tacit acknowledgement of a failed strategy. Some in the company see it as a slap in the face, an abandonment of a mission without success; an admission that all those men died or suffered for no reason. Others, me among them, are all for a pullout. Why put more men at risk in a bootless effort to root out the Taliban because others had died? We can't put all the blame on the brain-dead Taliban for this intractable mess we're in; we have to give a lot of credit to their brain-dead counterparts in the Pentagon.

In the meantime, more folly is afoot. We're off to another village tomorrow. Lieutenant Gray will get his badge if it costs every man in his platoon his life.
Dan

*

October 30th. The Americans went on a foot patrol along the impossible terrain and made their way to a village on a rocky hill on another hopeless mission to get the elders on their side. The elders received them with handshakes. They didn't speak English and, of course, the army sent someone who spoke a dialect of Pashto different from that of the villagers, so the powwow was mostly hand signs and smiling. Hopeless. The Americans brought some food as a good will gesture. The Taliban would eat well tonight. Meanwhile, villagers lit fires and sent dense puffs of smoke out their chimneys to let the Taliban know where their targets were.

The soldiers assembled at the edge of town. While they waited for the Taliban militia to set up their ambush, they sat and ate their MREs.

"Jesus!" said Humphrey as he sat on a stone wall eating. "What do they put in these goddamn MREs? It tastes like horse come."

"Okay, sarge," responded Beaton while looking at Chenkin, "you're away from home, your wife is half a world away, there are no decent women around, so you tear a slit in your MRE and fuck a pound cake. It's understandable, but did you have to serve it to Humphrey?"

The men roared. Hunt said to his sergeant, "Tell me when you go to confession. I gotta hear you tell the priest you fucked an MRE."

"That'll be two Our Fathers and a blowjob," said Beaton.

Pretending to read the MRE label, Hunt said, "A product of Juniper Stables."

The Americans commenced their arduous trek back to camp. They descended the slope toward the stream. "Eyes and ears open," said Lieutenant Torrez.

After Hunt and Humphrey crossed the stream, a bomb exploded, killing one American and injuring another. Then the insurgents began shooting and launching grenades. With bullets zipping by all around them, the divided Americans scrambled to find cover, but it was a challenge since they had no idea where the shooters were. They finally located the enemy, some of them anyway. They returned fire and called in air support and medevac.

Beaton got to the casualties. One private had no more head. Another private's legs were pitted with shrapnel from toes to thighs. The largest wound, on the back of what used to be his right calf, was bleeding profusely. He was writhing in pain and grunting. Beaton dragged him into a bombed-out house, and removed his boots. His filthy feet were grey and bloody. It was hard to know where to begin.

*

Hunt and Humphrey were trapped across the stream and had no choice but to move closer to the enemy to find protection. While their lieutenants conferred to find a way to force the Taliban off and allow the ensnared Americans to escape, a spotter, a child of twelve years, helped the enemy home in on the trapped troops, who were by this time huddled against rocks at the base of a hill. Mortars began raining down. "Kill the little fucker now!" voted Gray, but Torrez wanted to reserve this as a last resort.

Hunt and Humphrey looked terrified and were on the verge of making a suicidal rush back across the river. When the mortars got dangerously close, Lieutenant Torrez reluctantly ordered the child shot. A sniper took him out. The mortars continued, forcing the trapped soldiers to make a run for it, back across the stream. Humphrey fell, shot in the leg. Hunt turned to help and got shot in the chest for his trouble. The bullet didn't penetrate the body armor, but the impact knocked him down.

Lieutenant Torrez cursed and looked askance at Lieutenant Gray. He ordered his soldiers to lay down suppressing fire and throw smoke grenades to cover the withdrawal.

Straining to breathe, Hunt lifted Humphrey to carry him across the stream. A mortar landed close enough to throw both men fifteen feet. Both were knocked cold and ended up lying in the stream, Humphrey face down. Their cohorts rushed in to carry them to the comparative safety of the ruined house.

*

Beaton, who had wrapped large battle dressings on his patient's most serious wounds, looked up from his patient to see two of his roommates being carried into the house. Examining the new casualties, he discovered that Humphrey wasn't breathing. He couldn't find any penetrating wound beyond the one in his leg, which was not life-threatening; it wasn't bleeding because the heart wasn't beating. Beaton asked what happened. "He was lying face down in the water," said one of the men who had brought him in.

Beaton began mouth-to-mouth resuscitation. He then started chest compressions. Chenkin hustled in to check on his men. He observed Beaton pound on Humphrey's chest with his fist and count thirty more chest compressions before trying mouth-to-mouth once more. Humphrey started breathing, but it'd been at least two minutes since he last breathed. Shaking his head as he placed a breathing bag over the man's mouth, Beaton commenced squeezing. He looked at a corporal standing by and said, "Take over here." As the corporal complied, Beaton put a tourniquet on Humphrey's leg and wrapped a bandage around it.

*

A livid Lieutenant Gray got on the radio to urge command to approve a bombardment of the village. Torrez protested that they were mostly unarmed civilians. Grey pointed out, "At the very least they provided intelligence to our enemy to assist with their attack. And more than likely, most of the fuckers shooting at us are from the village." He provided this rationale to command, which determined it was insufficient to destroy a village. Gray kept arguing.

The Apache helicopters arrived. Enemy fire stopped. The Taliban slipped away to blend in with the population or hide in the hills. Maybe two or three of the insurgents were dead; the Americans never knew for sure because the insurgents carried away their dead. The enemy left the dead child for the villagers to see. Good advertising for the Taliban.

*

Beaton next turned to Hunt, who had come to. He had a broken leg. Tossing him a lollipop, he said, "You need to be patient while I deal with this." Hunt nodded and sucked as Beaton returned to his original patient. He'd staunched the bleeding, but the man had gone into shock. He got another breathing bag going and asked the sergeant to squeeze it while he applied dressings and bandages to the smaller leg wounds.

Beaton looked up as he heard the medevacs cycle in. Samantha landed next to the stream as Talon and their new flight medic, Sergeant David Mueller, debarked and scurried into the bombed-out house. Beaton nodded at Talon and, while writing on the man's chest what drugs he'd given, said to Mueller, "This man is in shock, more than likely from loss of blood. He needs oxygen, PRBC, and a bolus of Hextend right now. Both legs are in tough shape, as you can see. This man drowned; he wasn't breathing when they brought him in. No oxygen for at least two minutes by the time I brought him back, and he has a bullet wound in the left calf; no drugs yet. This man has a broken femur. I haven't had time to check him further, but he was unconscious when he came in. He's only gotten a sucker." Beaton and Mueller continued to work on the casualties.

The second medevac arrived. Wheeler packaged Humphrey and Hunt and took them back to JAF. Mueller packaged and took the private in shock. Beaton helped carry the litter to the chopper. Samantha waved, but he ignored her. After grabbing three more morphine injectors, Beaton shook hands with Talon, stepped back and watched his old crew leave for JAF.

The shell-shocked grunts re-assembled and started the three-hour trek back to KOP, but the fireworks were not yet over. A drone had spotted several men with rifles slip into the village mosque. The camera also showed women and children milling about the mosque. The decimated platoon was ordered to turn around, with Lieutenant Gray now more insistent on leveling the village.

As the platoon approached the village, more gunfire greeted them. They scrambled for cover, but one private didn't reach it before taking a bullet in the knee. He screeched in pain as Beaton grabbed him and dragged him behind a large pine tree. Lieutenant Gray was squatting behind the same tree. While Beaton got to work on the hapless private, the sergeant shot and killed the sniper. Lieutenant Torrez came to check on his injured man and took his medic aside to tell him to slip Gray something to put him out of commission. "He's putting my soldiers and innocent villagers at risk. Oh, and I never ordered you to do this." Beaton nodded.

Beaton extracted a morphine injector from his rucksack. He removed the red safety plug and asked Gray for help holding his patient steady while he gave him a shot of morphine. Gray did as asked, but careless Beaton knelt on something that threw him sideways. As he fell, the injector went astray against Gray's arm, and Beaton depressed the plunger to fire the injector. "Oh, shit, I'm really sorry, sir," said Beaton.

"You careless goddamn moron," declared Lieutenant Gray as he sat, then lay down with a smile. Torrez clicked his tongue and told Beaton to be more careful. He ran off toward the village.

*

As commanders deliberated about what to do, Susan had just learned that her husband was among the casualties below. Devastated and furious, she turned her gunship toward the village.

*

287

While Lieutenant Torrez focused on the mosque through binoculars and conferred with Sergeant Chenkin, a bright flash and explosion made him gasp.

*

Beaton had given his patient a shot of morphine, and he was resting. Feeling weak and worried about his blood sugar, he'd torn open an MRE and began eating. He heard the explosion and looked toward the village. Then he heard an anguished cry from the nearby hills above him. Reaching for his rifle, he looked through the scope and spotted a man with an SA-18 rocket. The man was pointing it up.

Beaton aimed for his chest, but hesitated. He'd shot wildly at muzzle flashes, but had never looked at a human being directly and pulled the trigger. The idea of killing horrified him, but what choice did he have? As he made his decision to shoot and squeezed the trigger, the man launched the rocket. Beaton saw the man fall, then saw a fiery explosion in the sky. The Apache plummeted to the earth in a ball of flames. He dropped his gun and fell to his knees, having utterly failed as a front-line soldier. His vacillation, a mere second or two, had just cost two American lives. And he'd shot and killed a human being. The grief, stress, and toil took their toll, his vision started to blur, and he started to tremble. Hypoglycemia! He quickly mixed a glucagon shot. As he injected himself, he blacked out.

A few moments later, maybe more, he couldn't tell, he opened his eyes. Feeling dizzy, he sat up slowly and looked around. His patient was sleeping, and Grey was placidly gazing at the sky. There was no one else around. Black smoke was billowing from the village to the south and from the Apache wreckage to the east. Still in a daze, he pocketed the needle.

Chenkin came running up to his position and asked how the private was and what happened to the lieutenant, but Beaton was murmuring, "I had him in my sights, but I shot too late. It's my fault."

"What the hell are you talking about?"

"The guy who shot the rocket. I heard him scream, and I spotted him through the scope, but I pulled the trigger too late. He got the missile off. The Apache pilots are dead because of me. I know all of them. I served with most of them for over a year." He lowered his head and wept.

Patting the young medic on his back, Chenkin said, "The pilots are dead because of the fucker who shot the missile. Is he dead, by the way?"

"Yes."

"Good." Seeing the torment in Beaton's eyes, the sergeant went on, "Most of us here have shot too late one time or another, or shot and missed, or shot one of our own. Bury it, or it'll bury you."

"A good soldier would have cut him down before—"

"We both know you're not a good soldier. You shouldn't be here, but you are, and thank God for that. You saved two of my guys and helped two others today alone. You're the best medic I've ever seen. So, keep doing what you're good at, and we're all happy. Is Malone all right to move?"

"Uh, yeah, he's stable."

"What happened to Gray?" said Chenkin.

"I accidently gave him a shot of morphine."

"Accidently?" Beaton nodded. Chenkin chuckled and said, "You need to get to the mosque, or what's left of it. Everyone who was inside is gone, I'm sure, but a few outside are hurt bad. Get going."

The scene in the village was reminiscent of the one in another village months before when the Apache let loose on it. An unknown number of villagers and insurgents were dead in the rubble of the mosque, and there was carnage outside of it: two children and one woman dead; one child and three adults injured. A layer of dust covered everything. While Beaton triaged the patients and dealt with the most severe injuries, a medevac from Asadabad arrived.

Rene brought better equipment and more supplies, and both worked feverishly on the four wounded, Rene focusing on the females. One died as Beaton was working on him, but the other three were stabilized and packaged for evacuation. G.I.s ran the litters to the waiting chopper, but as Beaton walked beside the wounded child, her mother ran up and began beating him about his shoulders and screaming at him. Though no one spoke her language, she made it clear she was unwilling to let the Americans take away her child. They couldn't leave the little girl behind or she would certainly die, so Rene, via sign language, invited the mother onto the helicopter to accompany her child. She spoke to a man, presumably her husband, who got on board.

The medevac departed with the three wounded villagers, the father, Gray, and the wounded grunt, and the platoon set off for KOP. Three hours later, Beaton managed to hobble into camp and collapse onto his bed, his knees and lower back throbbing, his blood sugar in disarray.

When he awoke, Daniel got in touch with Talon and learned Susan Humphrey and Colin Stedman were the Apache pilots. Though he hated Susan and had no liking for Colin, he felt terrible since he'd let it happen. He had told no one else after his sergeant.

The guilt of this, along with the guilt of killing a man, ate at him and began to affect his mental and physical health. His blood sugar spiked up and down for several days as he tried to contend with the stress of that awful day. He recognized symptoms of post-traumatic stress disorder, reliving the events awake and asleep in vivid detail, seeing in slow motion the man he shot collapse after a mist of blood exploded from his body, and seeing the Apache explode and plunge to the ground. In his nightmares, he'd sometimes witness Susan and Colin burning to death and shrieking in agony while he stood there helpless. Other times, he was the one who shot the missile.

With this critical breach in his defensive wall, it began to crack, and he started reliving other horrors—the mutilated children, civilians splattered on walls, people being swept over the cliff in the avalanche, and so many dying soldiers. The cracks spread, and the wall began to crumble. He had no family, and his dreams of making a new one with Samantha were dust. Dwelling on the emptiness of his life, he became depressed. He kept to himself and stopped joking. He often wept. In his worst moments he considered suicide.

CHAPTER FIFTEEN

Back at Jalalabad – Autumn, 2009

Once Samantha's dreamy notion of an idyllic life with Paul came crashing down upon learning of his unscrupulousness, her life was a shambles. In her imagination, they were to have made their careers in the army, never posted apart, with her taking time off to have two darling children, a boy who looked like his father and a girl the image of her mother; a comfortable, secure, prosperous life growing old with her loving, faithful husband by her side.

Now, as she lay on her bed, she shook her head at her naivety. Thus far, her overwhelming emotion concerning Paul was anger, but as it ebbed, sorrow was beginning to overtake it. Not sorrow over the loss of this dreadful man, for she felt nothing but hatred for him, but sorrow over the loss of her cherished future. Her dreams, too, were dust.

And this wasn't half the disquietude besetting her. The loss of the good man who had loved her was devastating. Feeling responsible for putting his life in jeopardy in the valley of death, she spent every waking minute and many a nightmare panicking that he would get killed or maimed, knowing she'd never forgive herself. Every time a nine-line call squawked over her radio, she cringed until she could confirm Daniel wasn't a casualty. And if he survived that awful place, would the experience end up ruining him anyway?

She mourned the loss of Daniel, but not Paul. She spent weeks trying to work out her anger, disappointment, guilt, and sorrow to determine why. Was it because the loss of Paul was his fault, but the loss of Daniel her fault? Was it because she realized too late that Paul was a scoundrel and Daniel was a fine man? Both, probably, but there was more to it than that, she sensed. She felt an enormous void in her life, and it wasn't in the shape of Paul.

As if these personal woes weren't enough, she found it hard to face Talon and Craig. Talon and Daniel had grown close, and Craig was forever boasting that he had the army's number one flight medic and reveled in Daniel's offbeat humor. They missed him, and she picked up a few fleeting scowls in her direction. Daniel had been the heart and soul of their crew, and she'd been to blame for ripping them out.

The new flight medic, David Mueller, was personable and competent, a fine complement to any medevac crew, but he could never replace Daniel in their minds. There was little laughter on their missions now, and with the misery undiminished, the laughter was sorely missed.

Samantha withdrew and spent most of her time in her room. Her roommate was of little help. She wasn't the sympathetic type and hated Daniel. She kept saying they were all better off with Beaton gone and once said she hoped he would die there, which prompted Samantha to scream, "Shut the fuck up, you heartless bitch!" Susan grew red with anger, but controlled it before she hurt her roommate. When it came out that Susan got her husband to beat up Daniel, Samantha was fit to be tied and bawled at her for ten minutes. The roommates, never the best of friends, came to abominate each other.

Evidently worried about his depressed crewmate, Talon tried to help by talking or joking with her. In discovering her weeping in the cockpit one October morning, Talon invited her to talk about what was bothering her.

"God, Chief, I hate that smug asshole. I see him strutting around smiling, and I want to strangle him. What he did to me; what he did to Dan. And he couldn't care less. God, I'm an idiot. Why was I the last one in the world to know he was married?"

"You weren't," Talon assured her. "I'm sure nobody in China knew before you, and I'd be surprised if the peasants in Bangladesh know even now, though the upper crust is probably snickering."

She tittered and said, "Thanks, Chief." Then she took his hand and said, "Talon, I'm so sorry for taking away your friend and ruining our crew."

"First of all, you didn't ruin our crew; we're still the best in the army. Second, he's still my friend. Third, don't hang yourself with this. You know I think the world of Dan, but he had no business saying this was your fault. This was Telfer's doing."

"If I wasn't so stupid to fall for that son of a bitch and to tell him about Dan's diabetes—"

"You fell in love with the wrong person. You're human. And if Telfer didn't use his diabetes against him, he would have likely sent him to the stockade for attacking him. Dan made a big mistake attacking an officer, and he'd have to pay for it one way or another. Korengal is dangerous, but the great majority of men come out of there in one piece, so stop worrying about something you have no control over and stop crucifying yourself before we lose the best co-pilot in the business."

Samantha stepped out of her cockpit and hugged her crew chief.

Samantha read Daniel's letters to Talon over and over, her way of keeping him in her life. She laughed and cried at the same time. She prayed for his safety. Never had she worried so much about anyone in her life.

On October 30, their medevac was called out for an urgent evac from a village near the KOP. Samantha's heart fell to her stomach as she lifted her Black Hawk into the sky and sped northwards. By the time she landed next to the stream near the village, she was so upset, she began to tremble. She sat panicking as Talon and David jogged to the bombed-out house. An eternity later, she breathed again when she saw Daniel helping to carry the litter. She waved at him. He saw but returned only a blank stare. He backed away, and she took off. Looking down at him standing there alone while turning her ship south, she reflected, *he's supposed to be here with us, with me.*

When Samantha learned later that day that her roommate was killed in action, she wept. She didn't like Susan, but the thought of her dying in a fiery explosion was shocking and distressing. Just hours ago, Samantha lay on her bed cursing her roommate for snoring, but now she was gone forever. It was hard to believe and harder to accept; and she felt guilty for the way things were left between the two of them.

Six days after that, Samantha read Daniel's latest missive to Talon:

```
From: Dan Beaton
Date: Thursday, November 5, 2009
To: Talon Okeeweehow
Subject: Going downhill
    It's getting harder, Chief. Being here.
Being  anywhere.  So  much  death  and
destruction,  some  of  which  I  caused.  It
builds  up,  and  you  try  to  hold  it  down,
but  you  can't  forever.  Sooner  or  later  the
lid  blows  off.
    It  isn't  the  ever-present  fear  of  death
that  gets  to  you,  as  a  medic  anyway.  It
isn't  the  blood  and  gore.  It  isn't  blaming
yourself  for  losing  still  another  patient,
though  you  always  do  to  some  extent.  It's
taking  all  the  hurt  to  heart.  It's  losing
your  ability  to  wall  off  your  emotions
when  a  young  soldier  looks  into  your  eyes
and  squeezes  your  hand,  begging  you  to
save  his  life,  and  you  know  there's
nothing  you  can  do.  It's  thinking  about
his  parents'  devastation  at  burying  their
young  son.  It's  thinking  about  everything
that  young  man  will  miss  dying  so  young.
It's  thinking  about  what  you  could  have
done  to  save  someone's  life,  but  didn't
because  you  were  too  weak  or  slow  or
stupid.  It's  thinking  about  what  a
```

```
horrible, useless waste of human life war
is, and how it never seems to end. When
you can no longer ignore these things,
that's when you're in trouble. I'm in
trouble.
```

Samantha sat at the screen terrified over what this implied. She begged Talon to write back right away, imploring Daniel to seek help. Talon did as she asked.

CHAPTER SIXTEEN

The End at Korengal, November, 2009

"**B**eatoff, wake up," ordered Sergeant Chenkin at 0347. "I'm awake."

"You need to get up to OP1. Two of our guys were wounded on a recon outside the wire. Another is missing."

"How bad are the wounds?"

"One's in the foot, another in the arm. They've got tourniquets on."

"They're going to need a medevac anyway, and it'd be quicker."

"Ceiling's too low apparently. They'll come as soon as they can fly, but you need to help them until then. You need to get there ASAP, so leave most of the weight behind. Take your NVGs, medical bag, rifle, IBA, and Kevlar only."

Daniel quickly dressed, grabbed his medical kit and some plasma, and set off with two other soldiers, a corporal who had been in the KOP for almost a year and a private who had arrived two days prior. The hill was so steep, it took the men forty-five minutes to wend their way through the KOP and past the ANA bunker, then climb a thousand feet to the tiny outpost. The private, unused to this degree of toil, slowed them down as he struggled for breath.

Approaching the entrance, Daniel asked Corporal Hernandez, "Why in the name of God does this base even exist?"

"To try to stop the plunging fire onto the KOP from this hill."

"Plunging fire?"

"Shooting down from above; gives them a huge advantage."

"But isn't it even more vulnerable to attack than the KOP?"

"You looking for sense from the fucking army? We shouldn't be in this valley at all."

"Hey," said the nervous private, "if I shit myself in my first firefight, keep it to yourself."

"What do I want with your shit?" said Hernandez.

"I mean don't tell anyone."

"No shit, Gerhard."

As the three soldiers walked through the gate, the guard lifted his M-4 and shouted, "Get down!" The three complied and turned their heads to see someone behind them walking around in a daze. "Jesus Christ! Is that you, White?" hollered the guard.

The man didn't answer, but continued to meander toward the gate.

"That's Private White. He went missing after we got hit," said the guard. He yelled, "White! Get the fuck in here! You're lucky I didn't plug you."

Daniel got up to check the disoriented man, who was missing his rifle, gear, and helmet. "You all right?" he asked.

The man replied, "I can't find the damn remote anywhere. I'm missing *Family Guy*. Shit!"

"It's in here," said Daniel, leading him inside the wire. The man walked in, with Daniel checking for something obvious that might explain his behavior. Finding no head trauma, Daniel concluded the man was either shell-shocked or exhausted or both. He gave him some sleeping pills, left him with a bunkmate, and went to check the wounded soldiers.

Daniel was surprised to find one of the soldiers in bad shape when he got to them, with eyes sunken, face blanched, and body shivering. The bullet had hit an artery in the arm, and the man had lost enough blood that his life was in danger. He was conscious, but chanting, "Fuck, I'm cold."

Daniel turned to a private and said, "Get him more blankets fast." He called for an update on the medevac, informing command that the private would be dead within the hour if he wasn't evaced. He got Ringer's solution and plasma flowing, put a pressure bandage on the wound and gave the man a sucker. When the extra blankets were brought, he wrapped him in them.

He then inspected and dressed the foot wound and gave the man midazolam for sedation.

Returning to the serious case, he found the man had slipped into shock. He cursed, squeezed the plasma bag, elevated his legs, and got the private to put on and squeeze an air bag. While he started a second plasma pack, gunfire erupted from the surrounding hills, and a man nearby shrieked. A bullet had taken off Private Gerhard's left ear. As he stumbled around in a state of bewilderment, another soldier tackled him to get him out of the line of fire. He screamed for the medic.

With the G.I.s returning fire, Daniel sprinted over to help. Gerhard was writhing, kicking, and screeching so violently, Daniel gave him a shot of morphine to calm him down before examining and cleaning the wound and applying a bandage.

The firefight ceased as suddenly as it began. The insurgents appeared to be probing for weaknesses.

Making his way back to the patient in shock, Daniel heard over his radio, "DUSTOFF Three Seven inbound." His old crew. Flying in this fog. Into a hot zone. At night. Samantha managed to land the large aircraft on a grade in a confined space. She had to be among the best in the army at this point, he thought.

David and Talon debarked and ran to his position with two litters. "We'll need two more of those," Daniel said. The men hastily packaged the three casualties, along with Private White, and ran them to the waiting helicopter.

Daniel backed away from the chopper; Samantha waved, but he scowled at her. As his mental state deteriorated over the past week, he'd come to loathe her.

Beaton and Hernandez were ordered to stay at the Outpost for the time being; Beaton because timely medical help might be critical, Hernandez because the complement at the outpost was dangerously low. With the injuries and with some soldiers at KOP for a break from what had been a long, boring stretch of inactivity at OP1, there remained only eight soldiers at OP1.

Daniel figured his blood sugar should be low after the toil and stress of the last two hours, but he had had to urinate twice in that time, one indication of high blood sugar. He tested it and got a reading of twelve. He'd wrestled now for over a week to get it under control, and he wasn't having any success. Starved after the exertion, he decided to eat two MREs. Typically he would inject himself with insulin after eating, but he decided to do it then because no one else was around, and he might not have a chance to do it unobserved afterward. He injected a liberal dose of insulin and was bringing the first forkful to his mouth when the first explosion occurred.

*

Although the number of attacks on American encampments had declined in recent months, the insurgents were honing their skills. Wary of eyes in the sky, they were careful about massing for attacks. They communicated by radio to orchestrate an offensive. The Americans were monitoring their communications and knew something was imminent, but couldn't decode what it might be. Good night for it, they knew, because the clouds and fog would keep the Apaches and Warriors grounded.

At 0500 the insurgents paused to pray to Allah for help to crush the infidel, then converged on Outpost 1. About a hundred fighters launched the assault with heavy gunfire and RPGs, attacking from three sides, pinning down the American troops. Hundreds of flashes from the hills looked like the flashing of cameras at the stadium.

*

In OP1 it was chaos, like being in a towering black cloud discharging blinding lightning and deafening thunder with each passing second. The sense the urgency was manifest in the chilling pleas for reinforcements. Coughing with all the dust and smoke in the air, the sergeant radioed to KOP, "Fire from everywhere. RPGs and mortars are blowing us apart. Dozens, maybe hundreds of insurgents are attacking. We need help right now!" A few minutes later, "We're taking casualties. We're hopelessly outnumbered. Help us!"

Hernandez grimaced in pain and grabbed Beaton's arm. His eyes conveyed panic; he couldn't get his breath. He'd taken shrapnel in his upper right side. Beaton pulled out the shrapnel, removed the body armor, and cut away the shirt. In checking the wound, he was relieved to discover that the body armor prevented the projectile from penetrating more than an inch, although it had collapsed a lung. "I'm not going anywhere," he reassured his patient. He had to yell that into his ear to be heard. The corporal maintained his tight grip.

Mortars rained from the sky, and bullets streaked in from every direction. While Beaton applied an Asherman seal, he started to feel light-headed. He shook his head to clear it. Another man yelped, "Doc!" from across the compound. He'd probably been screaming this for a while, but couldn't be heard above the pandemonium. Beaton looked over and spotted the man waving to him. Hernandez's grip loosened as his breathing eased, and he passed out.

As Beaton got set to sprint, an explosion knocked him on his backside. He couldn't see for a moment, but before he could panic, his vision returned. He poured water onto his eyes to clear the grit. Coughing and sneezing as his body tried to eject the raging dust, he got back to his feet and dashed through the hail of metal toward his patient. When he neared the stricken man, a bullet slammed into his back, sending him sprawling. The body armor stopped the bullet, but he was having trouble breathing. He dragged himself to the cover of a demolished wall where his next patient lay bleeding. A bullet through the back of the knee; not life-threatening, but painful. "Morphine, doc, morphine!" Corporal Goddard pleaded.

"You need to stay alert to defend yourself," said Beaton after recovering his breath.

"What?" he said, coughing.

"You have to stay awake!" he yelled into his ear. He dug out Mobic and a Tylenol Bi-layer Caplet. His arm was shaking as he held them out to the corporal.

"It fucking kills! I want morphine!" Beaton put his hand next to his ear to indicate he hadn't heard. "Morphine!"

"No way—" he replied before being cut off with a pistol at his head. "Christ, Corporal, take it easy. Lower your frigging weapon." It was hopeless trying to communicate with the tumult.

"Morphine!"

Beaton had a massive headache of his own, which made an impossible situation painful. It was easiest to comply, so he gave the corporal morphine. The man lowered the gun and settled back, head against the wall.

The explosions ceased, and the shooting slowed. "They're coming!" screamed the sergeant. "Hold your fire!" he commanded. Beaton peeped through a hole in the wall and saw about twenty men hurtling toward the camp. Shouting "Allah Akbar!" they scuttled toward the wire. With the closest man within thirty feet of the outer perimeter, and Beaton wondering why no one was doing anything to stop them, the sergeant detonated the Claymore mines. All but two of the attackers were dead within a second. Those two were screeching in agony on the ground. When the dust cleared, Beaton gaped at the carnage and lowered his eyes in horror.

A severe hunger pang suddenly surged through Beaton. Looking at the spot where the makeshift barracks had stood, he saw black smoke climbing out of the ruins. He never got to eat his lunch, but he'd taken a generous dose of insulin in anticipation of it. Sweat poured off him, and his tongue began to tingle. "Fuck! Hypoglycemia," he concluded. He looked back at the smoldering hut and put his hand in his pouch to get his glucagon. It wasn't there. "Shit," he exclaimed, recalling he had never replaced it after he took a dose at the village. Nervous, he checked his pockets for candy, a snack, anything with sugar in it. Nothing. "God dammit!"

Working on Goddard's wound, he said, "You got anything to eat? Goddard?" The corporal's eyes were open, but he didn't respond. Beaton checked the man's pockets, but found only cigarettes.

"Hey, give me one of those, doc," suggested Goddard.

"Another wave!" yowled the sergeant.

Another two dozen men came rushing toward the camp. "Allah Akbar!"

This time the sergeant detonated the inner ring of Claymores with the closest insurgent within feet of the C-wire. This left a few of the attackers standing. American fire cut the rest down.

The shooting and mortar bombardment of the camp resumed.

"Jesus H Christ!" said Beaton as he held his aching head in his hands, wanting to dig a thousand feet down to get out of this hell. A small structure nearby exploded and splinters rocketed everywhere. One struck Beaton in the upper arm, and he screamed out in pain. Grunting and gasping, he pulled out the spear. Shaking hard, he managed to wrap a bandage around his arm and swallowed the Tylenol he'd removed for Goddard. His headache was now debilitating, and he was feeling bewildered.

"Where the fuck is my artillery?" bleated the sergeant into the radio. A minute later, American artillery from the KOP began to hit enemy positions around the camp. He was told that two drones were on the way, armed with Hellfire missiles.

"Medic!" hailed someone to Beaton's left. "Medic! Medic!" Beaton finally heard the screaming between explosions.

Lowering his head, he sprinted toward the injured man. Suddenly the very air shuddered as an explosion close by sent him flying twenty feet. He lay there confused for a time, then sat up. Something hit his head, and his helmet flew off to his left. Every hair on his body stood on end. Blood trickled down his face and into his left eye. His head was aching, but no worse than before. This wasn't too reassuring since he knew the pain often came subsequently, unless death precluded it. Nervously, he ran his hand over his head to assess the damage, but it seemed to be nothing more than a laceration. The bombardment slowed. He got up and tottered toward his next patient.

"Here they come again," said the sergeant. "Must be fifty of the fuckers this time." There were only five soldiers left standing at OP1. "Wait till they get close, then cut the fuckers down! Make sure of your ammo!"

Beaton got to the next casualty. The sergeant ran over to the same position. The private had been shot through the neck; blood everywhere, choking man with panicked eyes. Beaton struggled to remain focused. "Help him, for Christ's sake!" ordered the sergeant as he opened fire. Confused, Beaton put his fingers on the gusher to slow the bleeding, but he couldn't figure out what to do next. "Doc?" said the sergeant.

It took a few moments for Beaton to understand and to reply, which he did, slurring his words. "He'ss bleeding out, ssarge."

"Can't you stop it? Specialist?"

"Uh, I, I don't think sso."

"Fuck!" the sergeant said as he continued to fire on the enemy encroaching on the camp.

The Americans cut down many of the fifty before a mortar landed right on top of two Americans. Seconds later, another was shot through the head.

As the first insurgents penetrated the wire, Hellfire missiles exploded at eight locations surrounding the base. The sergeant, the only man left fighting, was shooting at the enemy now in the camp.

"Where the fu—"

The sergeant was cut off by a bullet through his temple. Beaton gasped and opened and shut his eyes, trying desperately to wish it all away. His heart beat violently while he wiped some of the sergeant's brain off his face. He looked down at the dying private and up to the sky. "Where are the stars?" he whispered. By the time he lowered his eyes back to his patient, the man was dead.

He looked around and realized he was the only one in the camp uninjured. The shooting continued as the enemy rushed into the base. Sitting between the two dead men, scared out of his mind, Beaton closed his eyes. He felt himself losing consciousness as hypoglycemia took its toll. "Oh, God, this is it, this is it," he murmured, as his consciousness ebbed away.

The dust continued to descend, smothering the life out of everything.

CHAPTER SEVENTEEN

The End at Jalalabad – Late 2009 to Early 2011

"The nine-line call came in at 0509. When the crew gathered at their Black Hawk, Craig looked somberly at Samantha and said, "Outpost 1 is being overrun by Taliban."

Her eyes betrayed her terror. "Is Dan still there?" Her greatest fear since Daniel was sent to the front was that he'd be killed or seriously wounded. His final words to her—"It's on you"—were by now a depressing echo that reverberated in her head every waking moment.

"I don't know. Maybe."

She began to cry and pleaded, "Let's go, let's go!"

"We can't fly in this, Sam."

"We have to! I can do it, Craig."

"I'm sorry, Sam, but the CO has made his decision. We can't see more than a hundred feet."

"Oh, God, this can't be happening. What if he's up there dying?"

"Forecast has this lifting over the next hour or so."

"Dan might be dead by then!" Samantha's tears dripped off her cheeks as she paced in quick steps near the aircraft.

"Try not to panic, Sam," said Talon. "We don't even know he's there."

"If he wasn't when it started, he'll be there soon, and he'll do everything he can to save everyone who needs help, even if it means his life."

"Yes, he will, but he won't be alone. KOP will send reinforcements. Dan's a survivor, Sam."

But his calming words had little effect, for Samantha's pacing, crying, and panicking didn't let up for the forty-four eternal minutes until Craig called the CO at her behest, begging for permission to fly the mission. The ceiling having lifted somewhat, he gave his permission, and at 0554 Samantha spooled up the engine.

The second the tower gave them the green light, Samantha applied full throttle, pushing the crew down into their seats as the helicopter roared up and turned north toward the Korengal Valley. Craig had to insist twice that she slacken her speed given the poor conditions. Twenty-two minutes later, approaching the small outpost with dawn breaking, she gasped at the panorama of gore beneath her. There were dozens of bodies and pieces of bodies surrounding the camp, and at least a dozen bodies within the camp. As she touched down and scanned the grisly scene petrified of spotting Daniel, her tears resumed. She undid her seat belt and jumped out of the helicopter.

She looked around and her heart fell. She thought one of three lifeless bodies to her left might be Daniel. Her hand to her mouth, weeping and praying it wasn't him, she jogged to the three, and upon recognizing Daniel's face, collapsed to her knees shrieking, "No! Oh, please, God, no!"

Talon, seeing Samantha's reaction, ran over.

There was Daniel lying on his back, his head and shoulders propped up on another body, hopeless surrender etched on his bloody, filthy face, mouth half open in a grimace that conveyed anguish, eyes crescents drawn down at the both edges, his cramped left hand clutching his pants, the other hand lying limply on the ground, his sweaty, soiled, tattered uniform sticking to his body. With Samantha sobbing, Talon went to his knees beside his friend and shook him. "Dan? Dan, are you still with us?"

Craig called over the radio, "I see Sam crying. I guess that means the worst?"

"Dan is down, but we don't know if he's alive." Talon called David over. "This is Dan. Please tell me he's not dead." David checked for a pulse and shook his head.

Samantha shrieked again. "It's my fault," she wailed.

"He's still warm," noted David as he put his ear to Daniel's chest. "I've got a heartbeat," he said. Samantha cried out. David poured water on Daniel's face and wiped it. "He's very pale. A scratch on the head and wound on the arm is all I can see so far." He undid the bandage wrapped around the arm. "Not too serious. Nothing to account for his physical state. Let me turn him over—"

"He's diabetic!" shouted Samantha.

"Diabetic?" said David.

"Yes. It's a long story. Maybe he's in a sugar low?"

"It does look like it could be hypoglycemia." Samantha handed David something from one of her pouches. David looked at her as if to ask, *What the hell is going on here?* but said nothing and mixed the glucagon shot Samantha had provided. He gave it to Daniel. A few moments after that, Daniel opened his eyes.

Samantha fell against him and embraced him, weeping tears of joy. Talon clutched Daniel's shoulder and relayed the good news to Craig.

*

Daniel lay there confused for a few minutes, having no idea what was going on. Samantha sat up and said, "Dan? Are you okay?"

He sat up slowly and looked around. The battle, not yet an hour over, recurred to him as he surveyed the decimated outpost. When he spotted Hernandez and Goddard, his mouth dropped open. Each had a bullet hole in his forehead. He began to weep. "I had them stabilized, but they were helpless. Those bastards murdered them!" Samantha cried with him. He then looked at the soldier shot though the neck and went cold. His immediate verdict: he was guilty of his death because hypoglycemia had clouded his judgment. He shouted, "Why the hell didn't they shoot me?" Samantha looked at him with a frightened expression.

"You looked dead already," answered David. "You're covered in blood, your breathing was shallow, and the bits of skin showing through the blood and mud are pale as a ghost. It was only when I listened to your heart beating a mile a minute that I knew you were still with us. When Sam informed me you were diabetic, I gave you a glucagon shot, which she just happened to have with her. What are you doing on the front lines?" Daniel shrugged. Turning to another soldier he said, "He's okay to transport."

Just as the soldiers were about to lift him, he said, "Stop!"

"What is it?" said Samantha. "We need to get you to the hospital right away."

"I seem to remember some Taliban asshole was moving me around. Move back."

"Lieutenant!" hollered Talon. Lieutenant Torrez jogged over. "He thinks he might be booby trapped."

"Hobson!" yelled Torrez. The explosive ordnance disposal expert dashed up. "Check him for a booby trap." He turned to call out a general command to his soldiers: "Don't move any of these bodies!"

"Don't move a muscle," Hobson told Daniel. He gingerly moved Daniel to and fro, and ran his hand underneath him. "He's sitting on an IED," he informed his lieutenant. Turning back to Daniel he said, "If you move one inch, the last thing that goes through your mind will be your ass."

Samantha resumed crying and moved toward him.

"Stay back," said the lieutenant. "That's an order," he stressed. Samantha, still crying, stepped away.

Continuing to probe the ground underneath Daniel, Hobson said, "It could be something as crude as a mouse trap contraption that trips a switch when you get up, it could be a wire attached to you that'll detonate the bomb as soon as you pull away enough, or it could be triggered remotely with a cell phone or garage door opener. I'm hoping that since we're all still alive it's not remote control."

"Sir," Daniel said, "I don't want anyone killed trying to get me out of this jam. Just leave and—"

"I'll be damned if I lose another man in this godforsaken place."

"Really, sir. I honestly don't give a shit if I die."

That prompted simultaneous exclamations from Samantha and Torrez. "Don't say that!" exclaimed Samantha.

"Shut up, Specialist," ordered the lieutenant.

Hobson looked Daniel in the eyes and said, "Just don't fart." That prompted a sad smile. Hobson was good at his treacherous job. He didn't even wear protective armor. Daniel asked why. "It would make me a target for the assholes." After examining the device with his fingertips, Hobson said, "Oh, I see. Trip wire attached to your pants." He severed the wire. "Should be okay to get up."

"Move away from me first," Daniel suggested.

He pulled Daniel to his feet. "I know what I'm doing," he said.

"Yes, you do. Thank you, Sergeant," he said as he shook his hand, but part of him was disappointed he got out of it alive.

"We'll put you on a stretcher, Dan," said Talon while he hugged his friend.

"No, Chief, I can make it to the chopper," answered Daniel.

It was fifteen more minutes before they checked the other American bodies and loaded them onto the medevac. With Samantha still overcome with emotion, Craig said he would fly home. "I'm okay, Craig. I think it'll help if I have to concentrate on flying." He nodded, and she took off.

As they banked south over the valley, Daniel said, "I'm going to kill him as soon as we get back."

Talon replied, "Lucky for both of you, then, he shipped out last week."

"No!" said Daniel. It was ejaculated with a growl of such anger, Samantha turned to look at him. His filthy face and teary eyes conveyed pure rage. She appeared apprehensive and listened for his next utterance. It came a few minutes later. Calmly he stated, "I understand now; I know why he jumped. It makes perfect sense."

Samantha turned her head immediately and screamed to Talon, "Grab him! He's going to jump!" just as Daniel slid the door open. "No, Dan, don't!" Samantha yelled, but out he leaped.

She bawled in horror until Talon declared, "I've got him by his foot!" David tried to get hold of his other foot, but Daniel kept it away from him.

At this point, his foot was the only part of him inside the chopper as they sped over the valley. Daniel looked down at the ground three hundred feet below. Even in his hazy, confused state, he was afraid, but he was so tired of being scared, so tired of all the gore, so tired of seeing young lives snuffed out or forever ruined, so tired of feeling guilty, so tired of being helpless to halt any of it; tired of everything. All he had to do was kick Talon with his other foot, and he'd be free of all this wretchedness, all this depraved, depressing misery. He had nothing and no one to live for anyway. And he deserved to die after letting his last patient die because he hadn't controlled his diabetes. His selfish decision to hide his condition so the army would pay his scholarship had just cost a young soldier his life, he told himself. Daniel looked up at Talon, who was struggling to pull him back in.

Talon saw his intention as he tensed his leg to kick. "Don't do it!" he said, but Daniel's boot caught him in the side of the head, and he let go.

"Fuck you, Sophia, I'm …" He was about to say, *free*, but at that instant he hit the ground. Samantha had managed to land just as he freed himself from Talon's grip. The five-foot fall was insufficient to produce the intended effect, but it was ample to produce two broken ribs. He rolled over into a fetal position and blacked out again.

Daniel woke up on the helicopter only to see David administer midazolam. He was secured to a litter and soon fell asleep.

The next time he opened his eyes he was in the small medical facility at JAF. Craig, Talon, and Samantha were there looking at him with concern.

"How do you feel?" asked Craig.

"I want her out of here," he said.

She looked forlornly at him and withdrew, but stood at the open door.

Daniel tried to scratch an itchy cheek, but discovered his arms were restrained.

"You tried to kill yourself," resumed Craig. "We have to know you're not going to try again before we set you free." He waited for Daniel to respond, but he said nothing.

"Well, you'll have to talk to the psychiatrist in any case. Just let me say, Dan, that we all care very much about you, and we'll help you through this."

Talon stepped forward and grasped Daniel's arm. "Don't try anything like that again, dude. I don't want to lose my best friend." Daniel gave him a half-smile. "Can Sam come in? She really wants to see you."

"No."

"She said something that I wasn't supposed to repeat, but I think you might enjoy it. She said, 'You know what he'd say to one of us if we did that? I know how you feel; I've felt like killing you, too.'" His smile grew a tad. "She's beside herself with worry over you. Dude, you have to know she's spent the last two months panicking over you."

"Good."

"Come on, Dan, you're being unreasonable. It was Telfer's doing, not hers," put in Craig.

"I don't want to think about either of them ever again."

Samantha walked away crying.

Talon said, "Tell me, Dan, do you intend to kill yourself?"

"I'm on the fence on that one."

"We were hoping you weren't in your right mind because you were in a severe sugar low."

"Might have had something to do with it; not sure."

At this point, the battalion psychiatrist came in and shooed Craig and Talon out.

She spoke with Daniel for an hour and left him in restraints.

*

The psychiatrist subsequently spoke to Craig and said she considered Daniel to be a risk to himself, and she'd be recommending he be returned stateside immediately.

Overhearing this, Samantha went to Daniel's room. She stopped at the open door when she saw him weeping. With his hands affixed to the bed rails, he had his head turned into the pillow as best he could to try and muffle the sobs. This affected her so profoundly, she immediately began crying, too. She was about to back away to let the storm pass, but he opened his eyes and saw her.

He said, "Great. An audience. A touch of humiliation was just what I needed to reach rock bottom." He rubbed his eyes against the pillow to wipe away the tears.

"Dan, I—"

"Quite the spectacle, eh? A grown man balling like a little baby. Not sure why you're crying, though. This was what you wanted, wasn't it?"

"No! How can you think—"

"You did such a good job getting rid of me, I've even lost myself."

"Oh, Dan, please don't say that," she said, walking to him.

She stroked his hair, but he pulled his head away, and screamed, "Don't!" with such vehemence she stepped back in fear.

After a nervous moment, she said, "I pray, I mean I hope, with time, you can forgive me. You must know I never wanted—"

"Christ, Hawkins, go away, will you? Here I am trying to wallow in self-pity and you're spoiling the mood." He took a punctuated breath and added, "I'm so goddamn depressed, I'm having trouble taking the next breath and hoping somehow it won't come—"

Her hand shot to her mouth as an anguished cry burst from deep within her. Its forcefulness surprised both of them; he started and she put both hands over her face. She turned to leave, but stayed still for a moment. Then she wiped her tears, took a deep breath, turned back to him, and said, "They're taking you out of my life tomorrow, and you're going to hear what I have to say." He turned his eyes to the ceiling and said nothing. "Please, *please* don't kill yourself! You're an amazing person. You have a brilliant future as a doctor. Just one more year and—"

"I'm not going back to Monash."

"What? Why not?"

"I'm through dealing with broken bodies."

"You can't just give up, Dan. You must know that the work you've done here saving lives has made a world of difference, not only to the people you saved, but to their families. Multiply your grief by a thousand and that's how much pain you've spared other human beings. You'll save so many more lives in the future. You can't give up!"

"Do you know what the last flickering thought I had was before I blacked out? I'm about to die, and no one, not one soul in the whole fucking world, will care."

"You know that's wrong. You know I care; you know Talon and Craig care."

"No family to grieve. One good friend: Talon. A couple of acquaintances: you and Craig. No one who wouldn't get over my death in a couple of days."

"That's not true. You're just down right now, and it's making everything look worse than it is. After what we've been through together, you have to know I'm much more than just an acquaintance."

He looked at her and said, "You spent seventeen months pushing me away, including a final shove all the way to KOP, and you have the nerve to claim friendship with me? Get out."

"I realize now I never loved him. I loved the person I thought he was, but he was never that person. You tried to tell me, but I was fooled by his lies."

"Get out!"

"Because of the army and because of him, I never let myself get close to you, but that doesn't mean I didn't see how special you are. I really do consider us good friends, and I'm sure we can be more. You're out of the army in two months and—"

"Get the hell out!"

Samantha lowered her eyes and head. She turned and walked out.

*

The chaplain dropped by a while later, and before he opened his mouth, Daniel said, "Chaplain, I've found God! I tried to take my own life by jumping out of our chopper, but I was saved—when three tiny school children broke my fall. It's a Christly miracle, father! And I'm told that one of the children might even survive, so it's a double miracle. Hallelujah!"

"I know you've gone through hell, and you're lashing out at God; it's understandable."

"No, that's not your line. You're supposed to threaten me with eternal damnation."

"I've never once done that. I'll pray for your soul."

"Don't bother. Pray for your own. It's your kind that have caused this unholy mess in this country, and in so many others."

"I'm sorry you think so. I sincerely hope you're no longer considering taking your own life. I'm sure you don't want to hear the typical spiel about how blessed you are and how much you have to live for; I know how hollow that sounds to a person who's been through hell. I will say that you've done so much good here, and if you choose to live, you'll do much more in the future. Never mind God. Live to continue helping other people. Whether or not you believe in Him, He couldn't ask for more from any human being." The chaplain patted his hand and left.

Craig and Talon came in to say goodbye. Daniel and Talon hugged. They promised to keep in touch.

Early the next morning, Daniel left Afghanistan in the dust. He was flown to the military hospital at Landstuhl, Germany and later that week to Walter Reed Army Medical Center outside Washington, D.C. He spent his last two months in the army at Walter Reed.

The psychologist he saw every workday before his discharge helped him through the crisis, then to sort out the many painful memories besetting him. They made good progress and were just starting to consider his future as the date for his release approached. Daniel was worried that he wouldn't be able reconcile his future with his past. "How can I go back to something that I can't even see the point of anymore?" he asked his counselor. And more generally, how was he to handle on his own all the hurt he still had bottled within him? "It makes you panic, because you don't know what'll happen if you can't manage the misery anymore. It could well kill me. If I let my guard down, will I lose my mind? It's too scary to even contemplate."

There were no pat answers for such loaded questions, but the two spoke about the issues at length. On his own, because he hadn't told anyone about his last patient, Daniel finally subdued his debilitating guilt, reasoning he couldn't have saved the man even with a clear head; the wound was too deep, the bleeding too heavy. He needed immediate surgery and IV fluids and probably a blood transfusion. And the Taliban would have shot him anyway. The case was hopeless. Still, he'd been irresponsible and selfish, and he could have cost people their lives.

The psychiatrists at Walter Reed were satisfied he was no longer at risk for suicide when he was released. The U.S. Army gave him an honorable discharge and kept its commitment to pay for his final year at Monash University. But when the first rotation commenced in late January, he was still in the United States undecided what to do with his future. His life before the army seemed like it happened to someone else. What he was, what he wanted to become, were no more.

His psychologist invited him to see him after his discharge, and Daniel took advantage of the offer. The psychologist argued that he should return to medical school to finish his degree. It was already paid for, would give him something to do, and would give him the possibility of a good future. He met Daniel's objections by pointing out that everyday medical work couldn't possibly be as gory as what he'd had to face as an army medic, and that if he hated it, he could always quit, but that he'd never know if he gave up now. He remained to be convinced.

Daniel rented a small apartment near the hospital. He faced the typical challenges war veterans face when trying to make the transition back to civilian life. It took a concerted effort to lose the military lingo, reduce the profanity, and operate without the acute sense of purpose that defined his job in the army. February came and went.

His combat experience made the adjustment that much harder. Everything about ordinary life seemed dull and frivolous. He'd snicker at people getting exercised about something trivial, yet he got easily frustrated over minor issues such as people getting frustrated over minor issues. "Look at that asshole foaming at the mouth over missing a green light," he'd tell himself. "Don't you know how stupid it is getting upset about that? I should shove that red light up your arse, you stupid prick!" March passed.

A feeling of listlessness continued to overwhelm him. Every morning he woke up with a knot in his stomach. He had little to do and didn't even want to do that. Everything seemed pointless, the future hopeless. He had no one, he had less than nothing, and he honestly didn't care what happened to him. He felt angst over nothing and struggled to find a purpose, a reason to get up in the morning.

The psychologist used this to convince Daniel that medicine would give him a reason to get up, and eventually the logic sunk in. There was also the matter of his huge debt and no means to pay it off. Daniel chose to return to Monash, arriving in late April 2010. By then, the first two rotations of fifth year were done, but he was permitted to begin with rotation three and would end with rotation two a year later.

In the hospital environment, he found his war experience made him a worse doctor in some respects. It left him with no patience for the trivial complaints of most of his patients. How was he to take acne seriously when he had dealt with bloody curtains that had been a face? Few people in the world were better at bringing people back from the brink of death after a violent trauma, but these kinds of patients were comparatively rare in the civilian world. It was like being a star in the majors and coming back to the minors only to be perceived as ordinary.

Moreover, the typical Aussie med student, who was a little to the left of Trotsky in Daniel's opinion, had gone from annoying before he went to war to infuriating afterward. He was often tempted to stop a blabbing mouth with his fist, but forbore it. Once word got around that he'd been in the war, most gave him the same welcome they would've normally reserved for a man with Ebola.

When one female student originally from Pakistan called him a murderer, he suggested she turn in her hijab for a burka "to spare us all a little suffering." She reacted with fists, which he easily parried, until a doctor intervened. School administrators either thought that implying a person was ugly was worse than calling a person a murderer and striking him, or thought that chastising a Muslim was impolitic, for they called Daniel on the carpet and demanded he apologize to her. He refused, which put the administrators in a bind. Expulsion was too severe a penalty for an insult. Or was it? It was, after all, illegal under the Racial Discrimination Act to insult someone based on race. But was his insult a racial slur?

They checked and learned he got along well with the Muslims in the school. Asked whether Daniel showed any hatred toward Muslims, his friend Hafiz said, "Beaton hates Islam, but not Muslims. He also hates Judaism but not Jews and Christianity but not Christians. His hatred is purely non-sectarian, and you have to admire that." Told what Daniel said to the woman, he laughed, and said it was ridiculous to construe this as some sort of hate crime.

The administrators might have left it at that but another incident overtook it. Three men assaulted Daniel from behind as he was unlocking his bicycle next to the hospital. One hit him over the back of his head with a rock, knocking him down. "That's for insulting our sister, infidel pig," said the attacker as Daniel sat on the ground rubbing his sore head. "Get up and fight like a man."

Daniel accepted the invitation with enough alacrity to catch the man off guard, which resulted in a dislocated jaw and the loss of two teeth. The second assailant socked Daniel in his face, and Daniel returned the favor, busting his nose and knocking the man out. Seeing his brothers down and at the mercy of a madman, the third man ran off, with Daniel screaming, "Yeah, there's a job for you in the ANA, you chicken shit!"

Daniel rode home, took some aspirin, and went to bed. A couple of hours later, he woke up as someone pounded on his apartment door. "Who is it?" he called through the door.

"Police. Open the door."

Daniel did as instructed and was given a lift to the police station, under arrest for assault. Some busybody newspaper reporter got hold of the story and decried the plight of the poor Muslim brothers at the hands of a man who "apparently thought he was still at war." This steeled the resolve of the school to expel him.

Daniel threatened to bring suit, but no lawyer would touch the case; might attract unwelcome attention from the zealots. With the television stations poised to join in on the calumny, Daniel caught a break. A security guard produced a video of the incident captured by a security camera, which showed the dastardly nature of the attack on Daniel. The police immediately dropped the charges. Daniel asked about charges against his assailants. "Don't push it," he was warned; no sense riling up the zealots. The TV reporters abandoned plans for the story; stating the facts of the case might insult a Muslim somewhere and garner unwanted attention from the Australian Human Rights Commission. The newspaper dropped the story, deciding against setting the facts straight; might put the paper on the bad side of the zealots.

The med school apologized and told him he could come back. Probably still worried about his threatened lawsuit, they also promised him excellent references.

So he carried on and completed his medical training in April 2011. He left Melbourne for Halifax to await his residency.

CHAPTER EIGHTEEN

Ms. Samantha Hawkins – Autumn 2010

"Samantha Hawkins, newly unemployed, having received her separation from the army a week prior, grabbed her heavy duffle bag and suitcase and shuffled to the arrivals area in LaGuardia Airport to meet her sister. "Sam!" called Terry, waving excitedly. Terry ran to Samantha, and Samantha dropped her bags. They melted into each other's arms crying.

Terry was overpowered with happiness, but it was tinged with worry. Her big sister was the strongest person she'd ever met, yet it was clear she was having trouble adjusting to a normal life after the war. From their many phone calls and emails, Terry knew Samantha had been doing a lot of crying and not much sleeping since returning stateside nine months ago.

*

Feeling indebted to the army for saving her and Terry, Samantha had intended to make a career in the army, but the accumulation of hurt over three years of war, in particular the last half year in Afghanistan, had been too much. The beginning of the end was the crash. It had been a challenge for her to get back in the cockpit, and she was afraid of missiles every time out after that. Then the tragedy in the schoolyard, the denouement with Paul, her responsibility for Daniel's banishment to KOP, the stress of worrying about Daniel there, and his brush with death and subsequent suicide attempt overwhelmed her. Rotated back to the States, she was separated from her crew, Craig having been promoted to captain and no longer flying medevac, and Talon assigned to Hunter Army Airfield. She knew no one. Her new role was training rookie pilots at Fort Rucker, which couldn't compare on any level to what she'd done in Afghanistan. Not that she wanted to return to war.

Maybe if the army had decided to award her the Distinguished Flying Cross she might have felt compelled to re-enlist, but she got a nicely worded letter stating that the incident didn't quite meet the stringent criteria for the medal. She was commended for her performance during a crisis. The army offered her a $30,000 bonus to re-enlist, but she declined, at least for now.

Samantha had no qualifications beyond helicopter pilot and approximately two years of college credits through the University of California online extension system, and had no idea what to do or where to go next. She agreed to her sister's suggestion she come live with her for the time being.

Except for two years when Terry lived with Samantha during her training for the army, Terry had never drifted far from their childhood neighborhood in Hamden, CT. She'd attended New Haven University and, after graduating, got a job in the employment office of the Yale-New Haven Hospital. She lived in an apartment in New Haven.

Terry led Samantha to her car, and they drove ninety minutes northeast to New Haven. After a quick stop at Terry's apartment to drop off Samantha's suitcases, the sisters went out to get lunch. Terry took her sister to Applebee's in neighboring Hamden. Upon arriving at their old stomping ground, Samantha said, "I can't believe I'm here. Most of me thinks I'm dreaming." It had been six years since she'd been here, and over four years since the sisters parted, with Terry heading back to Connecticut for university and Samantha off to Iraq. They'd spent two or three weeks together every year, but they got together in vacation spots, usually on a cut-rate cruise at Samantha's expense.

After lunch, they drove into their old neighborhood. Samantha commented, "It feels so strange being here. Nothing seems different from how I remember it, yet it's hard to believe it's the same place. I'm trembling just looking at it." She had found her way home, but it wasn't home anymore.

As they drove past their high school, Terry said, "You'll never guess who I ran into last summer. Jeff Michener." Jeff was the high school heartthrob who'd never paid any attention to Samantha, except to nickname her "flatso," which had mortified her so utterly, she wore baggy clothes for the rest of grade twelve.

"Oh? What's he up to?"

"He's an electrician; probably makes a bundle. He's got the start of a beer belly, but he's still handsome. Not sure if you want to hear this, but I noticed a wedding ring." Samantha shrugged. "Didn't stop him from hitting on me, though. Men are such pigs."

"Have you heard anything about Jessica, Ashley, or Amanda?"

"I'm surprised you ask. I thought you hated them when they did nothing to help after Mom … I'm sorry, Sam. You don't need to think about that."

"My so-called friends abandoned me, but then so did Mom." Samantha turned her head away as her tears began.

"Sam—"

"Let's not make excuses for her anymore, Terry. I'm still paying for what she did to us." Terry reached over and clutched her sister's hand. Samantha wiped her tears and continued, "I don't really care what's become of my old friends. I'm just a little curious, hoping maybe they married assholes or got run over or something."

"I haven't heard anything about Jessica. I think maybe she moved out west somewhere. Amanda's married. Don't know about her husband. She works at the Honda dealer doing accounts or some god-awful thing. I hear Ashley's at Yale taking law."

"Figures; she's brilliant."

"I can't imagine how big her head is now."

"Can't be too big with what's fronting it."

"There's my favorite sense of humor."

They approached their old street. Terry drove past. Samantha said, "Hey, you missed it."

"Do you really want to see it again?" Samantha returned a slow nod. "You look exhausted. Maybe it's better if we go back to my place."

"No, I want to see it. Turn around."

Terry took her sister down their old street and stopped in front of their childhood home. Samantha gazed at the simple bungalow atop a knoll, facing Sleeping Giant Mountain in the distance. Her tears began anew, and Terry again took her hand. Samantha squeezed her sister's hand as she struggled with powerful emotions that alternated between a yearning for the halcyon past and a repulsion over how it all came crashing down. Thinking about the circumstances that sent her to war was too painful, and she tried to block it out, but going back further was too remote. So much had happened since, so many calamities, that she had lost touch with her happy childhood and couldn't bring it back to mind with equanimity. The upheavals she'd faced during the past seven years had rendered everything further back foreign to her. Maybe it was best to forget it for good, but how was she to build a future without any foundation in the past?

She took one last look at her childhood home and spotted the stained glass she and her mother had fashioned. She recalled the day she and her father mounted it in the middle slot in her bedroom window. He was hopeless at anything that required hand skills. He cursed amply and almost gave up several times, but would look at his daughter's big eyes and go back to it. Finally they finished, and she hugged her dad. Thinking of this, her love for him came rushing back and sent her over the edge. She broke down sobbing. It reached such a pitch that she began convulsing and found it hard to get her breath.

Terry undid her seatbelt and slid over to embrace her sister. "Everything's going to be okay, Sam. We'll get through this together."

"I miss him so much."

"Daddy?"

"Yes. Mom too."

"Me too. Cry as much as you need to. I'm here for you."

"I know. I love you, sis."

"Me too."

After settling down for a few moments, Samantha said, "Oh, to go back to a time when my biggest worry was that Jeff wouldn't pay attention to me. Just think, if none of this happened, maybe I could be his wife now, and he'd be trying to cheat on me with my sister." Terry laughed. "Let's go home."

Terry invited Samantha to talk about her issues, but Samantha would never say much, worried about bringing it all back, worried that a small crack would end in an earthquake that would destroy her. She needed to control her memories, which for now meant stowing them beneath consciousness. It was too much misery to shoulder without support, and proper support required knowledge and experience of the misery she had gone through. Samantha had had no idea the wars were affecting her so deeply when she was in the midst of them. She had controlled it there, but it seemed there had to be a time of reckoning. Often she thought of Daniel, how he had gone through so much more than she. How had he dealt with it, especially without any family to help? Had it changed him? Had it ruined him?

*

Samantha spent most of her time in the apartment doing nothing and too often drinking. Terry tried to interest her in getting out once in a while. Samantha would accompany Terry shopping or to lunch, but showed little interest in socializing with other people, especially men. At first, Terry thought it was because Paul had annihilated her self-esteem and her willingness to trust a man, but it became clear that he wasn't the main issue. It was Daniel; what she could have had with him if she'd met him under any other circumstance, or if she had handled their relationship with more skill. The more Samantha said, the more Terry became convinced that what her sister needed was Daniel. But that was impossible, wasn't it?

Terry suggested several times that Samantha get together with her best friends from high school, but Samantha demurred, so Terry took matters into her hands by calling Ashley Baker and asking her to call Samantha. Ashley called, and Samantha agreed to meet her and Amanda Hudson at a coffee shop in New Haven the coming Friday.

*

On Friday, Samantha arrived and saw Ashley sitting at a table studying a textbook. She got a cup of hot chocolate, which was what she used to drink when she got together with her high school friends, and went to Ashley's table. "Hi, Ash."

Ashley looked up and opened her eyes wide at Samantha. She stood and hugged Samantha, saying, "God, I hardly recognize you. It's so nice to see you again after all this time. Sit."

The ladies sat. Samantha opened with, "I hear you're a Yale law student. Impressive."

"Yeah, it's incredibly competitive to get in. I spent four years doing nothing but studying to get in. Now I do nothing but study in law school. Seems to never end. So, what brings you back to us?"

"Terry. I'm staying with her till I figure out what to do next with my life."

"Amanda should be here any minute. She's turned into a dowdy housewife at the ripe old age of twenty-four." Samantha hadn't forgotten Ashley's tendency to talk behind everyone's back. She'd be Ashley's target with Amanda when she left, she knew. Ashley went on. "Her husband is awful."

"What, does he beat her?" said Samantha.

"No, not that I know of. He's just a nitwit and ugly as a bulldog. Oh, here she is."

A chubby woman in a dark blue pantsuit shambled to their table and said, "Oh! Look at you!" Samantha stood and they hugged. "Have you ever changed. You're so pretty now, though you could still use a few pounds. I wish I could give you some of mine." Amanda laughed at her witticism. "So, how are you, Sam?" she said as the women sat.

"All right. And you?"

"Frazzled. Same as always."

"I hear you're married."

"Yup," she said, holding out her hand to display her rings. Samantha tried to look impressed. "His name is Gary Chisholm—I kept my last name—and he's originally from Hartford. He's a fire fighter, and he's hot. Bet you thought I'd never get a hotty." Samantha looked at Ashley, who lifted her eyes. Amanda asked, "How're you doing, Ash?"

"Working my butt off. It's nuts what they expect of you here, but I guess they're preparing us for the real world, which is even tougher. The epitome of the dog-eat-dog world is top lawyers duking it out for a partnership. May neither of you ever experience that kind of pressure."

Samantha lifted the cup, looked through the steam at her former friends, then sipped her hot chocolate. It was so hot, it scalded her tongue. She cursed to herself.

"Oh, I don't know," returned Amanda. "You don't have my boss. Everything has to be done yesterday. Somehow I get everything done, but do I get the credit? No. He takes credit with the owners for all my work. He's completely useless, but they love him because of me."

"Junior lawyers get all the shit and none of the credit," noted Ashley.

"Look at us monopolizing the conversation," said Amanda. "Sam, I heard you were in, was it I-raq?"

"Iraq and Afghanistan," said Samantha.

"You were in a helicopter?" said Amanda.

"I flew them."

"*You?*" said Ashley. Samantha nodded. "Our little Samantha a helicopter pilot in the army. Who would've thunk it? Those he-men in the army must've loved that."

"They were fine with it."

"Did you see any real action, like dead people and stuff?" asked Amanda. Samantha nodded. "Must've been scary." Another nod. "Were you ever shot at and stuff?" A third nod. "Well, tell us all about it."

"I don't like talking about it. I'm trying to put it all behind me." She blew on her hot chocolate.

"Oh, okay. What about men? Have anyone on the string?"

"Not really, no," answered Samantha.

"With all the men in the army, a pretty girl like you couldn't bag one?" said Amanda.

Samantha shook her head with her eyes cast down. She tried another sip; it seemed to be getting hotter. It made her eyes water and her nose run.

"Probably none worthwhile in the army," responded Ashley. "Bunch of big dumb, violent thugs, way beneath her. What about a Yale law student, Sam? Talk about cream of the crop. They'll make oodles of money and be at work all the time, leaving you with the gorgeous pool boy. That's win-win. All the handsome ones are taken, but I can introduce you to a couple of passable ones."

"No thanks. What about you? You have a man?"

"Not interested in any of them," claimed Ashley.

Samantha glanced at Amanda, who raised her eyes. Samantha suspected that Ashley retained her considerable aptitude for turning off men. She said, "But they're good enough for me?"

"No, I mean, I just mean that I'm far too busy to have a boyfriend. As it is, I'm all stressed out with exams coming up and two papers due. It's hell; you wouldn't believe it."

Samantha focused on the steam rising from her drink.

"Try my life," said Amanda. "Super hectic. And I get pressure from home, too, that you two don't have. Gary wants a kid, but how am I supposed to make accounts manager with a kid? It's easy for him to say; all he has to do is bonk me, then it's my problem. Even now he won't do his fair share of the housework. It'll just get worse with a kid. Yesterday was a perfect example. We called a plumber to fix our leaking shower before it ruins the basement ceiling. I asked Gary to stay home for it, but do you think he would? No. So, I stay home and guess who never showed up? The plumber. God, I just wanted to scream. It's like I'm being pulled in so many different directions, I can't stand it. I'd take stress leave at work, but that would guarantee I'd never get promoted."

Samantha took another sip. Still too hot.

Ashley said, "I have a therapist who helps me cope with all the stress. Want her name? She can really help."

"Sure. Maybe that's what I need to deal with my life." Ashley wrote the name and number of the therapist on a piece of paper and gave it to Amanda. She also gave her a Valium. "Thanks," said Amanda. "So, Sam, what are you doing with your life nowadays? You left the army?"

"Well, I'm in the reserves for two years, which is a weekend a month plus two weeks a year. Otherwise, I'm doing nothing."

"Sounds wonderful!" enthused Ashley. "How I'd love to have nothing to do for a change. Leave behind all the deadlines, all the work, all the pressure. You're lucky, Sam. It must be so nice to have nothing to worry about."

"Yes, nothing," said Samantha. Disgusted with her hot chocolate, she pushed it away. "Well, I feel guilty taking up so much of your valuable time. I'll let you get back to your busy lives while I have a nap."

"What I wouldn't give to have your life," said Ashley. Amanda seconded it. The three ladies hugged and went their separate ways. As they parted, Samantha overheard Ashley say to Amanda, "She's pretty, but so what? She's a failure."

When Terry got home, she asked how it went. Samantha answered, "I sat there longing for the normality of their life, but loathing the pettiness of it. They went on and on about what hectic, stressful lives they have and how lucky I am to be out of the rat race. They have no fucking idea, Terry. None! They can't possibly understand what true stress is in their pampered existence. What would these people do if they had to face a real problem? Seeing therapists and taking drugs to deal with their trivial complaints. It was all I could do to prevent myself from screaming and tearing them apart."

"You're right, they haven't a clue, but that's how everyone is here. If you write them off, you write off everyone."

"Fine by me."

"You can't separate yourself from our entire society. Sorry to say, Sam, you're going to have to come to an accommodation on this. Americans aren't changing because of what you went through."

"Then I'll lock myself away."

"No, you won't; I won't let you. You've only been out of the army a couple of months. Don't panic. You'll find your rhythm here."

*

Samantha kept in touch with Talon, who was still in the army, stationed in Georgia training crew chiefs. She learned through him that Daniel had returned to Monash. She wondered out loud to Terry, "Wouldn't it be great if Dan got a residency at Yale? I guess there's not much chance of that, though."

Terry shrugged. She thought there might be a reasonable chance, but didn't want to raise Samantha's hopes. Terry's closest friend, Jenna Boyd, was the medical staff office manager at the Yale-New Haven Hospital. Terry wrote to Talon, explaining the situation with her sister and asking him to get in touch with Daniel to determine whether he might be interested in coming to Yale, and if so, whether he could get his records to her as soon as possible. Two weeks later, she had Daniel's file in hand when she went to Jenna's office.

"Monash? Where the hell is Monash?" responded Jenna to Terry's query about pulling strings to get Daniel a residency at Yale.

"Australia. I checked, and they have the same standards as here."

"Technically, Albany has the same standards as Yale, but I know where I'm looking for residents."

"Here are his records."

She thumbed through it. "Five-year undergraduate medical program; he doesn't have a separate bachelor's degree. No MCATs. Not needed for Australian schools, I guess. USMLE Step 1 score of 230. Pretty good, but our residents are typically 240 and up."

"For God's sake, Jenna, he saved hundreds of lives under fire in Afghanistan. Surely that's worth ten points on some standardized test. Just think of the experience he could bring here. How many of your 240 USMLE students have that?"

"Could conceivably work against him with some of the pacifists here."

"Serving your country in a war works against you at Yale?"

"I'm just saying, some of the decision-makers might worry about how violent he is, or whether any post-traumatic stress might cause the hospital trouble."

"You've got to be joking. This is outrageous!"

"Calm down, Terry. I'm just stating the facts. Being a veteran may or may not help, but it's the Monash business that's the real problem. I mean, when we get almost all our residents out of the Harvards, Yales, and Stanfords of the world, how does a Monash grad compete?"

"Sam's lost her hope for the future; that's what concerns me most. I have to give her a reason to hope again. Please, Jenna, please do this for Sam; for me."

"I'll see what I can do."

"Thank you!" She hugged her friend.

"Set up an interview time with him."

Terry wrote directly to Daniel to set up the interview.

Daniel did it by phone, with Terry listening in. He had some clear weaknesses, but with Jenna pushing hard, he was accepted for an internship—one year. He would have to show he was up to Yale's standards and not adversely affected by the war to qualify for the full three-year residency.

Terry wrote with the offer.

He accepted.

On a day when Samantha was particularly down, Terry unveiled the surprise. Samantha threw her arms around her sister and cried for joy.

CHAPTER NINETEEN

Summer – 2011

Had the internship offer come from a lesser university than Yale, Daniel would have declined, wanting nothing to do with Samantha, but how could he decline an opportunity to come to Yale? The top places weren't exactly lining up to offer him a residency. Neither were the middling or lowly places for that matter.

He figured this was Samantha's way of apologizing for what she'd done to him in Afghanistan, so in accepting the offer, he was accepting an olive branch from Samantha. Despite the lure of Yale, he took a few days to consider the offer and the string attached to Samantha before concluding he had no choice. He would meet her and try to help her through the problems Terry said she was experiencing, but nothing further. Not that he thought this would be a problem for Samantha. She'd never had any use for him in the past, so she wouldn't now.

Still, the thought of seeing her again was unnerving. Daniel was determined not to put Samantha on a pedestal again. He would take no more notice of her hypnotizing eyes, her radiant smile, her soft, perfect curves. He would pay no attention to her one-of-a-kind personality, her indomitable spirit, her wonderful wit, and he already forgot what a fine pilot she is and how brave she is. Yes, sir, he was officially over her.

Terry picked Daniel up at the bus station and brought him to her apartment. She let Daniel know she hadn't told Samantha when he was coming, wanting to make the reunion a happy surprise. When Terry knocked on the door, his heart jumped out of his chest.

"Who is it?" said Samantha behind the closed door.

"It's Terry. Open up."

Samantha opened the door.

Their expressions were similar for the split second they gazed upon each other before she shrieked and slammed the door in his face.

As the door eclipsed Samantha, he was still processing what he saw. Her face was pale and drawn; her eyes were red and puffy as if she'd been crying and black underneath as if she hadn't had any sleep for a month; her nose was red and runny, either from a cold or from crying; her mousy hair was frizzy, and much like her personality, every strand went its own, unpredictable way, but whereas that made for a bewitching personality, it made for a witchy hairdo; her body—he couldn't tell since it was shrouded in her shabby terrycloth white robe, which made her look frumpy. Marshal all this into a horrible grimace upon seeing him, and Daniel's grimace was a natural reaction.

"I guess this wasn't a very good idea," said Terry. "You better go."

She went into her apartment, and Daniel left.

The next day, he went to the hospital for initial meetings with administrators, Terry among them. After completing the necessary forms and making arrangements to start the next day, he was on his way out of the hospital, and he looked up to see a truly feminine Samantha strolling his way.

She was decked out in a smart white pleated skirt suit. The skirt fell just below her knees; the jacket with curved hemline hugged her svelte figure. Her black high heels showed her sleek calves to great advantage. Her shoulder-length chestnut brown hair was silken and lustrous; obviously she had dyed and straightened it. Samantha's naturally lovely face would have been the perfect complement, but it was masked behind heavy makeup that looked like it had been applied with a mop. His face must have communicated this last observation because Samantha yelped, "What?"

"Nothing. You spruced up for an appointment or something?"

"Nothing? You were frowning at me."

"No I—"

"Yes, you were. Why?"

"Cripes, Sam, who did your makeup? Stevie Wonder? You look like a reject from Clown School."

She responded with her hand. Rubbing his cheek, he said, "Dammit, Sam. Here we go again. I'm not putting up with your shitty treatment anymore."

Then something out of character: she put her hand to her mouth, started crying, and ran to the washroom. For the moment he was too shocked to respond. Her sister, who had been watching the proceedings, came up behind him, shoved him, and commented, "Jerk!"

Daniel said, "Does battering men run in your family?"

"Sam was horrified the way you saw her yesterday. She screamed at me for twenty minutes for taking you to her without warning."

"Why would she care?"

"She's been looking forward to seeing you again since you left Afghanistan."

"Why? No man to push around?"

"She decided she needed to overcome the impression she left yesterday before it became indelible, so she borrowed my nicest suit, spent the morning getting her hair done, and worked on her makeup for almost an hour."

"Oh."

"Then you tell her she's ugly."

"I never said that."

"Believe me, that's what she heard."

"It's just her makeup is awful."

"Yes, it is. She just needs more practice at it."

"She needs no makeup at all. Nature took care of everything for her."

"Why the hell didn't you say that, then, instead of cracking a crappy joke about her makeup?"

"Since when is Samantha Hawkins sensitive, anyway? She's the toughest woman I ever met."

"This isn't Afghanistan. Here she doesn't have her guard up, and she can be herself."

"She might not have her guard up, but she still has a hell of a right cross." He rubbed his cheek again.

"Sam is a passionate person. It sometimes gets the better of her."

"Which makes it the worse for me. She's not exactly a model of self-restraint."

"You know she had to be tough to protect herself in Jalalabad. She needs to learn to adjust back to the normal world, but she's having a hard time. Since getting out of the army, she's been lost. I don't need to tell you what three years of war does to a person. She might be tough, but she still has human frailties. She's bored, lonely, and depressed. You saw her yesterday. She'd been crying. She cries a lot. I pushed hard to get you a residency here because she needed a good friend who understands what she went through."

"I hate to tell you this, Terry, but we never were good friends. I admired, even worshipped her, but the feeling definitely wasn't mutual. She treated me like shit. The slap she just handed me was standard treatment, and I'll tell you what I told her. I refuse to put up with it anymore. Afghanistan ended up a disaster for me, and she played no small role in that. She messed me up so bad that she actually felt guilty about it. So she gets you to get me a choice internship at Yale to assuage her guilt. Even though it was my best option by far, I thought long and hard about taking it because I didn't want anything to do with Sam."

"Don't say that."

"I said it, and I meant it. If this position comes with dealing with Sam, I'll leave."

"Yes, you will leave. We have an agreement that I get you a position here and you help Sam. If you don't follow through, I'll see that you're kicked out."

He glowered at her, but she held firm, giving him no choice but to relent. "She can cry on my shoulder from time to time. That's it." With that he walked away, and Terry went to comfort her sister.

Two days later, Terry walked up to Daniel in the ER, grabbed his arm, and said, "Come in here with me. I need to speak to you." She led him into one of the emergency rooms and closed the door behind him. "Sam's been crying almost non-stop for two days." Terry's tears started. "I'm really worried about her, worried she might kill herself. I think she placed all her hope in you, and when you brushed her off, something inside snapped."

"I'm sorry to—"

"I'm not interested in your apologies! I want your help. If you won't help, I'll have no choice but to commit her, and I can't do that to my sister, so I'm not taking no for an answer. Get your coat."

"I'm on duty here for another half hour."

"I took the liberty of speaking to Dr. Rosenbloom. He's given his okay. Come on."

She drove him to their apartment and walked with him to her door to make sure she got the two together. Terry knocked once and used her key to open the door. Samantha, in her pajamas and looking dreadful, dropped her jaw in shock upon seeing Daniel. She cried, "Oh!" and ran to her bedroom and closed the door.

Terry warned Daniel, "Don't you dare move a muscle!" and went into Samantha's room. He heard Samantha yelling and Terry yelling in turn. A few minutes afterward, Terry emerged with the news, "Sam's getting dressed and is coming out in a couple of minutes. When she comes out, you won't insult her, you won't dismiss her, you'll talk with her for as long as she needs. Like an adult."

"Not like you're talking to me, then."

"If you act like a child, I'll treat you like one."

Raising his voice, he retorted, "And what makes you think I'll put up with it? I buried my mother three and a half years ago, and I'm not looking for another one."

"Please help her. *Please!*"

"On one condition." Terry awaited his terms. "Leave." She walked to the door, cast him another pleading look, and left.

Four minutes later, Samantha opened her door and stood before him. She was dressed in black jeans and pink shirt. Her hair was drawn back into a ponytail. She wore no makeup; her eyes were red.

"I'm sorry for what I said the other day, Sam. What I should've said was heavy makeup is never a good idea for such a pretty face."

Samantha smirked. "Yeah, look at my face. I look awful."

"No, you don't."

"The truth, Dan. Nothing but the truth today, okay?"

"Okay. This is the worst I've seen you look since Thursday." She tittered. "But even then you were still prettier than ninety-five percent of the planet."

She laughed. "This is the first time I've laughed since … I can't remember." She went to the couch and sat. "Sit," she said, patting the couch beside her. He sat a little farther away than the spot she patted.

"Terry tells me you're going through a rough time. Do you want to talk about it?"

Her tears resumed. "I don't want to bother you with this."

"Sure you do."

She smiled sadly. Looking at the floor and speaking at little more than a whisper, Samantha said, "I can't sleep for any more than an hour at a time; so many nightmares. On the odd occasion when I have a good sleep, I wake up feeling happy for a few seconds. Like I used to be. Then suddenly it all comes rushing back: Afghanistan. The death, the hurt, the heartbreak, the shrieks, the stench, the fear, the goddamn dust, how I went after the wrong guy, how I treated you." She glanced at him and returned her eyes to the floor. "I tense up, my stomach aches; I start crying. I'm completely lethargic. So I sit in my apartment all day and do nothing, or drink, while the life I should have had passes me by."

"I've been there, Sam. We all have."

"I know. I'm sorry. You had it so much worse than I did, and here I am whining to you. How did you get through it?"

"You think I'm through it? Most days the same sickening feeling hits me when I wake up, and it's a relief after the nightmares I just had." She smiled with a knowing nod. Daniel continued, "As you know, I was ready to end it all by the time I got out of there, so I was in a deeper hole than you're in now, and I climbed out, most of the way anyway. A good counselor helped me. Your sister says you've been talking to one?"

"Yes. I used to be temperamental, now I'm just mental."

"You lost your temper, eh?"

"Guess so. Counseling does help a little, even just to talk about it with someone. But he wasn't there; he doesn't know."

"I'm here; I know, and I'll listen."

She embraced him. Her vulnerable side continued to surprise him. She seemed like a different person; more human, more feminine. She felt so good against him, he struggled to repress his carnal desires. *Easy*, he told himself. *She wants your shoulder, not your dick, so don't be a pig. Just remember how she treated you and how she will again if you give her the chance.* That logic defeated his desire, and he held onto her until she was ready to let go.

"I'm really glad you decided to finish medical school."

"It was to save myself. I had to get back to work to stop obsessing about Afghanistan. You need to do that. It helps. Have you flown since the army?"

"One weekend a month I serve for the reserves; that's it. I'm not sure I want to go back to it full-time."

"You need the same pep talk you gave me. You're a fantastic pilot. Don't throw it away."

The couple talked for two and a half hours, and with Samantha yawning twice a minute from lack of sleep and Daniel picking up the habit, he said, "I should go. I need to be back at work at midnight."

"That's still almost eight hours away. Stay for dinner."

"I need to sleep. I'm already exhausted, and I start a thirty-six-hour shift at midnight."

"Stay just a little while longer, please, Danny." This was the first time she'd used that nickname, he noticed, except when she was making fun of him in the Gold Coast. She sat against him on the couch and took his hand in hers. "I'm afraid of going to sleep because of the nightmares." Leaning her head on his shoulder, she said, "Do you mind?" but before he could answer, she was asleep.

He sat there for ten minutes wondering what to do when she turned toward him in her sleep and draped her arm across his stomach and her leg across his crotch. This was an interesting situation. She felt so good and smelled so good that he immediately hardened. But he couldn't take advantage of her vulnerability and violate her trust, so he reminded himself how she treated him and how she would again if he gave her the chance, and thus drove down his desire, but then she twitched her leg and moved her head so she was breathing deeply into his ear, and his desire rebounded in an instant. After a few minutes in this heavenly torture, he tried to extricate himself, but she latched on more tightly. Uncomfortable after another fifteen minutes in the same position, he lifted himself and her a little, brought his legs up onto the couch and laid his head against the padded arm of the couch. He closed his eyes.

Some time later, the front door across the hall slammed, startling both war veterans enough that they jumped up together. Samantha sought and got the protection of his arms. He was sporting one stiff neck and one sore boner. "What time is it?" she asked, noting the dearth of light.

"Just what I was wondering. I can't see my watch." She reached over to turn on the lamp. "Oh, shit. It's twenty to twelve," he said. Over seven hours of uninterrupted sleep and not one nightmare between them. It was the best sleep either of them had enjoyed since Afghanistan. "I have to go," he said as he hurried toward the door.

"Will I see you again?"

"Uh, yeah," he replied as he opened her door.

"When?"

"I don't know. What day is it?"

"Sunday, I think."

"I'm on call till noon Tuesday. What about lunch on Tuesday?" She nodded with a smile. "I'll drop by then," he said.

"Danny, thank you."

He nodded and dashed to the hospital.

*

Tuesday at 12:15 he knocked on her door. *I'll tell her today,* he insisted to himself as he waited for Samantha to answer. *I'll help her through her crisis, but then I have to stay apart from her. I can't fall for her again. I can't go through that again. As it stands, I'm over her and ...*

Samantha opened the door, and his eyes popped open as he beheld her. She wore no makeup, and her hair was pulled off her face into a pony tail, displaying her natural beauty to full advantage. She wore a simple black dress with a floral pattern in white that dipped down to show off the top of her breasts and stopped in time to reveal plenty of leg. Cinched around her waist was a silver chain that served to emphasize her svelte figure. *And I'm in trouble,* said Daniel to himself.

"You look great, Sam, but if you're expecting a good restaurant, I have to tell you that I keep bankers in bonuses with what I pay in interest. McDonald's is beyond my budget."

"I don't care where we go as long as we're together," she responded.

What's her game, anyway? he asked himself. *She want to control me again?*

They drove around in Terry's car, trying to decide where to go. At one point, a truck blared its horn at another driver who had cut him off. Samantha jerked and lost control of the car. It fishtailed, and she jammed on the brakes, coming to a stop a few inches from a telephone pole. She and Daniel stared at each other with bulging eyes and hammering hearts. "I'm sorry," she said. He nodded. He understood.

They ended up at a mall north of Hamden. Walking toward the food court, he caught a whiff of an old friend. "Oh, Christ, that smells good."

"Cinnabons? We can't have that for lunch."

"Why not?"

"Because it's a dessert."

"Loosen your girdle, mommy. Lunch is whatever we eat at lunchtime. Surely after six years in the army you must know lunch doesn't have to be real food. At least this tastes good. I haven't had a cinnabon in years. I want one."

"As a diabetic, you stand a reasonable chance of dying of cinnabons," noted Samantha.

Answering, "Good way to go," he stepped up to the counter.

"That'll be a million carbs, won't it?"

"So, I'll take a bucketful of insulin. Want one?"

"I'll share yours."

"Watching your calories? Worried about reaching the 120-pound plateau?"

"I'm watching your carbs. Someone has to."

He ordered two, with extra icing, and they sat at one of the small plastic tables. Drowning in saliva, he pulled out his little kit and extracted a lancet device. He pricked his finger, dabbed a drop of blood on a test strip, and put the strip into his glucometer. Error. "Shit! These things don't work half the time. I'm shredding my fingers, and these damn strips cost half a buck each. I swear they fine-tune these glucometers so they return errors half the time so you have to use twice as many test strips. Pecker heads." He pricked another finger, squeezed a drop of blood out, and tested it. He took a forkful of the cinnamon bun, put it in his mouth, and went, "Mmmmmm!"

"You don't need insulin?"

"After I eat."

"I may need some, too, after I eat this."

Samantha couldn't or wouldn't eat all hers. She picked up the plate to throw it away, but he put his arm out and grabbed it. "Throwing away a cinnabon is a cardinal sin."

"God, Dan, isn't one enough?" He pronged a forkful with a grin.

"Screw it."

"Dan—"

"I can handle this, Sam. I've lived with this for two years now."

After finishing, Daniel extracted his insulin pen, dialed it up, lifted his shirt, pinched a bit of fat at his waist, and injected the insulin. A lady walking past scowled at him. "Oh, that's good heroin," he said to Samantha so the lady could hear. Samantha simpered as the lady quickened her step.

On the way home, she suggested they walk around the university. He agreed. As they wandered through campus, she showed that the sense of humor he prized was undiminished; he'd been wondering. A haughty Yale law student dressed in a Brioni cashmere V-neck sweater, Brioni pants, and Berluti shoes, accented by a Cartier watch, showing off in front of his similarly attired friend, came up to her and said, "Hey babe, what's your story?"

Samantha answered, "Once upon a time, fuck off. The end."

Daniel burst out laughing, and the future lawyer blushed.

The friend stepped forward and said, "I can't imagine you don't know who this is."

Samantha replied, "Then you have a shitty imagination."

Daniel guffawed again.

Now evidently intrigued with the quick-witted lass, the student changed tactics. He produced a dollar bill and said to Daniel, "Here. The Salvation Army is just over there. Go and dress up a little, while I get to know this fascinating woman."

Daniel took the money and responded, "Thanks." He reached into his pocket, took out a packet of Life Savers, removed a red one and said, "Here. Go fuck it."

With Samantha chuckling, the friend thrust forward and growled, "I'll teach you to make fun of Roger Tannenbaum."

Undaunted, Daniel answered, "Not necessary, my little toady. I'm pretty good at that already." Roger's friend curled his fingers into fists.

*

"Easy, boys," counseled Samantha, who knew and respected the Tannenbaum name. Roger was the son of wealthy Senator Harold Tannenbaum. "Let's not let this get out of hand. Let's go, Dan."

Seconding the motion, Roger said, "Let's take the lady's advice." Turning to address Samantha, he said, "I'm sorry for my classless opening line; I misjudged you. You're obviously much more than a beautiful woman. Please tell me who you are."

Now defanged, she answered, "Samantha Hawkins."

"Is this your boyfriend?"

She hesitated, but Daniel asserted a definitive, "No." When Roger asked for her phone number, the disappointed young lady gave it to him.

On the way back to Terry's car, Samantha worried about what Daniel's next remark would be. When he said, "So, you better rush home and camp out by your phone for his call," she told herself, *I knew it. Dammit!*

Covering her consternation, she returned, "You mean this one?" as she extracted her cell phone from her purse. Ball back in his court.

"You must be excited to have a millionaire on the hook."

"No way he'll call."

"Of course he'll call."

"You know damn well what he wants from me. Once he gets it, he'll be after the next girl who catches his eye."

"You sell yourself short, Sam. Like any man, when he first sees a pretty woman like you, his first thought is penetration. But your biting wit raised you to a new level in his eyes. He said it himself: he finds you fascinating."

"As I'm sure you recall, I tried once before for someone out of my league. It didn't turn out well." This time she couldn't hide her consternation at his reaction, which wouldn't be out of place in a toilet, something to be flushed in a hurry. She flushed and looked at him with an expression that combined contrition with alarm. "I mean—"

"I have another midnight start, and I have to get some sleep before then."

"I'm sorry. It was stupid of me to bring him up."

"Never mind. Telfer was not out of your league; you were far too good for him. Any man with any sense will be endlessly fascinated with you." Her eyes screamed, *Well?* but he ignored them and went on, "When he calls, don't turn him down. I have to go."

"Let me drive you home."

"It's only a few blocks. I want to walk."

"I had a great time with you today."

He nodded and walked down the road. Her sad eyes followed him until he turned the corner. She drove back to her lonely apartment.

After telling Terry of the meeting with Roger Tannenbaum and its aftermath, Samantha expected her sister to commiserate and agree with her sentiment that she tell Roger she wasn't interested and tell Daniel he never called. She gathered from Terry's response, "Are you out of your mind?" that she didn't agree.

"Come on, Terry, if my experience with Paul taught me anything, it was that reaching too high was a mistake. I make a good playmate for a rich or striking man, an interesting premarital or extra-marital diversion. They end up with women like Kelly, and Kelly can have them."

"Yet Kelly preferred Daniel. What does that tell you?"

"That she was smart."

"It tells you that rich or striking people demand more than looks in their mates to keep them interested. Daniel is right; you are a fascinating woman."

"Oh, that made me so mad, saying any man would find me fascinating while walking out of my life."

"He hasn't walked out. Never mind Dan for a minute. Roger Tannenbaum is fascinated by you already, and he has no idea yet how much more you are than pretty and witty. I guarantee you he's never met any woman who flew through missiles and bullets and foggy mountains for years to rescue dying people. You're courageous, strong, feisty, and exciting. You're bound to end up with a great man like Roger Tannenbaum."

"In the first place, neither of us has any idea whether or not he's great. Second, I don't care if he is. I want Dan."

"Another mistake you made with Paul was shutting yourself out to any other man who showed interest. You're single and allowed to shop around. Saying yes to Roger doesn't mean giving up on Dan. Roger might, as you say, drop you, or you might drop him. And, one more thing; you told me you had to admit that you might have underestimated Dan when you saw Kelly. Two can play that game. When Dan sees that Roger Tannenbaum has fallen for you, you can only improve in his eyes. Then make it clear to Dan that you'll willingly give up life as a millionaire for him."

That made the desired impression on Samantha and convinced her to accept a date with Roger, should he call.

CHAPTER TWENTY

Fall 2011

Terry answered Samantha's phone. She smiled at her sister and said, "Yes, she's right here."

Samantha took her phone with a smirk, went to her room, and closed the door. She emerged a few minutes later.

"Well?" said her sister.

"He invited me to Nantucket for the weekend."

"Wow!"

"I said no."

"What? Are you nuts?"

"I don't even know this man. He's taking everything for granted before we've said ten words to each other. As far as I'm concerned, it was an insulting invitation, and I told him so."

"So, is that it, then? You toss away the opportunity to date a handsome millionaire?"

"Jesus, Terry, if he weren't rich, you'd be saying something like, 'What does he think you are, a slut?' Give me a break, will you?"

"So, what now? You sit here and mope, waiting for Dan to call?"

"Do you think he will?"

"He's left it up to you every time so far, so I doubt it."

"Shit. Why is he being like this?" It was Terry's turn to smirk. "Okay, I treated him like shit before, and he's worried I will again, but I'm being so nice to him now. Why does he keep seeing CW2 Hawkins? He knew I couldn't have a relationship with him in the army. Why can't he accept that that wasn't the real me? I mean, JAF wasn't exactly a normal existence. This is, and I'm showing him who I really am. Why can't he see that?"

"Ask him."

Samantha called and asked to see him. He said he couldn't see her for the next three days because of work. On the fourth day, he came to her apartment. "You wanted to talk again?"

"Is that the only reason I can call you? Can't we get together because we like each other's company?"

"As what? Friends?"

"More, if you want."

"All right, Sam, let's stop this bullshit. What the hell do you want from me?"

"It's not bullshit. I just want to be with you."

"Just like old times?"

"No. Let's start over."

"Impossible."

"I know I wasn't very friendly to you there, but you know the army strictly forbade us to have a relationship."

"The rank business was just a handy excuse. You had no interest in me. You looked down on me because I was your underling."

"It wasn't an excuse, it was a hard-boiled fact. I never even considered a relationship with you because of our ranks, not because I looked down on you. Also, I fell for another man whom I misjudged. And I misjudged your intentions. Until right near the end, I thought you had never taken me seriously as a person."

"That still mystifies me. I adored you."

"Your continual passes and sexual innuendos despite my insistence that you stop made it clear you had no respect for me."

"You laughed at a lot of them."

"Because they were funny, but that didn't make them appropriate. I was your superior in the army—and no, I'm not saying I'm your superior outside of the army. I'm fully aware it's the opposite now. You wouldn't stop making passes, even though it was forbidden, and even though it could well have cost me my career if I let you seduce me. That told me you didn't respect me."

"So, whenever I made you laugh, I was actually making it worse for myself?"

"No. Sometimes. I don't know. It might not have made a difference because of our ranks and Paul, but you just went so overboard with me. We never once had a serious discussion like this there, except when we were discussing some catastrophe that we'd dealt with."

"Humor was all I had to get you to pay attention to me, my best chance to break you away from him. You were my hope for a better future, Sam; the hope for you was all that stood between me and despair in that hellhole. When you chose him and rejected me, I lost everything. It was only a matter of time until I disintegrated."

She took his hand and said, "I'm so sorry, but it's not too late. We can still be together."

"I'm the same man now as I was then, and if I wasn't serious enough or good enough for you then, I'm not now." He withdrew his hand.

"Dan, please be reasonable. The army forbade me to even consider you. You have to understand that."

"It forbade me, too, but it didn't stop me from falling in love with you."

"You know we had different perspectives on the army, and it's a much more serious offense for the officer involved."

"We're back to the rank business; we're going in circles, and it leaves us nowhere."

"We're not in the army anymore. I'm the same woman you fell in love with."

"The same woman who told me the complete asshole she fell for was better than me in every way?"

"No, I mean—"

"The same woman whose final betrayal all but destroyed me?"

Samantha crossed her arms and stepped back. Her eyes began to flood. "I've apologized again and again. What else can I do? Tell me how I can earn your trust back."

"You can't."

"I blurted it out in the heat of passion after you played a really dirty trick on me. I didn't tell him with the intention of hurting you. It was something I said in confidence to a person I trusted. Can't we please put it behind us?"

"Then what?"

"We start, maybe, seeing each other?"

"So now you're interested in me? Why? Because I'm a doctor?"

"You know me better than that!"

"I don't seem to know you at all, because I can't figure out how all of a sudden you seem to want me after so forcefully and consistently rejecting the same person for a year and a half. You said yourself, you never even considered me then, so why now?"

"Because we're not subject to the army's regs anymore."

"And again, we're back to the fraternization rules. Remember you told me that even if the army didn't stand in the way, you still wouldn't be interested in me and *never would be*?"

She closed her eyes and sighed. "Dan, I … you … We had just had a huge argument, and we both said things we didn't mean. You seem to remember only the worst moments between us there."

"There was no *us* there; you made sure of that. Here's what I think. You're comfortable with me because I can empathize with what you're going through, and that's fine. When you need someone to talk to about Afghanistan, call me. But you've never had any use for me as a man, and I don't believe you do now. I don't want to get close to you because I know you'll discard me as soon as you no longer need my shoulder to cry on."

"That's not true!" she said.

He went on, "Or as soon as a better-looking doctor comes along."

"You think I'm that shallow?"

"You went after Telfer, even after I demonstrated to you he was a phony, and even after Kelly showed you how untrustworthy he was. You chose to ignore all that because he was so handsome. If a man did that, women wouldn't hesitate to label him shallow."

"Here's what I think. We're no longer in a place where the men outnumber the pretty women a hundred to one. You have your choice, so, as you predicted, I've disappeared in your eyes."

"Or is it that there's so much female competition around now, you figure you have to settle for me?" She looked down. "You're no longer my hope for the future, Sam; you're a major part of a disastrous past. Goodbye." He left.

Her shoulders fell, her eyes overflowed, and she sat on the floor to cry.

*

The next morning Terry marched up to him in the hall and hollered, "Who the hell do you think you are?" Everyone in the hall looked.

His fierce scowl took her aback, and she stepped back when he yelled, "I know the Hawkins sisters think they're hot shit who can talk down to any man they please, but I won't put up with it. So, piss off!"

"Calm down. Let's talk in my office."

"Go to hell," he said as he walked down the hall.

She followed and said, "You will hear what I have to say."

He stopped short, looked down into her eyes, and said, "You think because you got me the internship you can talk down to me like Sam used to? Wrong. Stay the hell away from me."

"Unless you're going to hit me, you won't scare me off." He resumed walking. She followed, so he walked into the men's room. She followed. A man was just finishing at the urinal. He looked at her, but said nothing and left. Terry said, "Sam's no longer your bright future; she's your dark past? How could you say something so horrible to her? She cried all night." That disconcerted him and dispelled his anger. Perceiving this, an emboldened Terry proceeded, "She didn't make up the army rule that forbade you two to have a relationship."

"She never had any use for me regardless of what the army said. After I told her I loved her, I said I'd be out of the army in a few months, and maybe then we could be together. She rejected me then, too."

"Because she was in love with another man. He turned out to be the wrong man, but she didn't fall in love with him to mess up *your* future. The world does not revolve around you."

"Believe me, I know that."

"Put yourself in her place for just a minute. You're in love with this beautiful, successful woman. You think she's everything you ever wanted. But there's this other woman who's after you. She doesn't care that falling for her would cost you your job, which is galling enough."

"Tell me, Terry, if you fell in love with someone and the hospital told you you can't do that, would you snap your fingers and fall out of love?"

"If I knew that going in, I'd fight against falling in love in the first place."

"Well, aren't you just the obedient little company woman? I don't let anyone or anything dictate my feelings."

"In Sam's case, the army saved her and her sister's lives, so she would obey its edicts. Back to my argument, this woman who's after you doesn't care you're in love with someone else."

"Tell me, Terry, if the person you love was in love with someone else, would you just give up? Is your love that fainthearted?"

"Enough with the analogies. This is about your telling Samantha she's the main reason for a disastrous past because she obeyed the rules and loved someone else. That's so unfair."

"Okay, you're right; I went too far, but I'm in her former position now. I have a woman after me who I'm not interested in, so I'm trying to keep her at a distance."

"Keep her at a distance? You devastated her!"

"She's your sister, so I understand you see things from her perspective. Try mine for a minute. The time I spend with her may help her, but it hurts me because she reminds me of a past that I desperately want to forget."

"Forget for one minute her supposed betrayal, which is such bullshit anyway. You loved my sister there. You saw her at her worst, yet you loved her because you saw her for the wonderful person she was. She's still that person, and she's been nothing but nice and respectful to you here. So, what the hell is it with you? If she treats you like shit again, you'll start loving her again?"

"You got that backwards. If I start loving her, she'll treat me like shit again. I can't believe the person who spent seventeen months pushing me away really wants me now. Every time she opens her mouth I expect a putdown. She conditioned me to expect her to hurt me."

"Yet you fell in love with her?"

"She's an amazing woman. My attraction to her has never been the issue; hers to me always has. She's depressed and lost, and she's comfortable with me because I understand what she's going through, but I know she has no real feelings for me. Seventeen months of rejection convinced me of that. If I let her into my heart again she'll reject me again, and that would ruin me."

"You're wrong about her feelings for—"

"Enough! You've had your say, and I listened. I'll apologize to Sam for what I said and tell her again she's welcome to talk to me anytime she wants. But nothing more. And if you ever yell at me in public again, I'll have nothing to do with her. Got it?" He left. She looked around, spotted two feet under one of the stall doors, and rushed out.

*

That evening on his dinner break, he went to see Samantha. He apologized for what he said and reassured her she was welcome to talk to him whenever she felt down. They also decided to get together once a week for lunch and to talk, beginning the next Saturday. He said, "And don't worry, I'll be perfectly solemn."

"What?"

"You told me I was never serious enough for your taste. So for our little talks, I won't joke. I'll be the straight man."

"That's not what I meant, and it's not what I want. I love to laugh with you."

"That's not what I heard yesterday."

"What I said was you went overboard. You were *never* serious with me."

"Well, now I will be."

"Without any humor?"

"That's right."

"So, you hope to drive me away by being boring?"

"If I'm not funny, I'm boring?"

"No. Stop putting words in my mouth … You were about to say what you wanted to put in my mouth, weren't you?"

"I want to put nothing in there. I'm due back at work. I'll see you Saturday afternoon."

The two met weekly as planned and talked between meetings occasionally, but nothing developed. He was kind and understanding but turned aloof when she tried to get closer. True to his word, he always kept his part of the conversation sedate. He could be serious, he proved, yet interesting. Still, she missed his humor. She tried to prod him into some repartee. He would laugh at her witticisms, but wouldn't take the bait. By Christmas, which he spent with the Hawkins sisters, she had made no progress with him and was beginning to think her cause was hopeless.

CHAPTER TWENTY-ONE

Double Date Two – January, 2012

Samantha was leaving the hospital and stopped abruptly upon seeing Daniel talking to a pretty woman in scrubs. The woman was smiling warmly at him. Samantha turned to escape, but Daniel saw her, so she had no choice but to walk up to him. "I was having lunch with my sister," she explained.

"Samantha Hawkins, Brittany Delp," he said. The women shook hands and smiled. "Brittany's a med student here; Sam's a pilot."

Brittany said, "So, are you two, like, old friends or something?"

Daniel answered, "Two-three years ago I was in love with Sam, but she was in love with someone else. Sad story. History. Now we're just friends." Samantha lowered her eyes, and Brittany raised her eyebrows.

Brittany clutched Daniel's arm and said, "So, where are you taking me on Friday?"

Samantha said, "Nice to meet you, Brittany. I have to—"

"Sam!" called out Terry. She jogged up to her sister and said, "Hi, Dan." He returned the greeting. Turning back to Samantha, Terry said, "Your NFLer will pick you up Saturday at five. He's taking you to a restaurant named Thomas Henkelmann in Greenwich. Fancy." With Samantha glaring at her, Terry smiled and left.

"NFLer?" said the nosey Brittany.

"Yes. He plays for the Jets," answered Samantha, with a glance at Daniel.

"Not Jordan Moore?" Samantha nodded. "No way!" Samantha nodded. Brittany went on, "Jordan went to my old high school; he was in twelfth grade when I was in ninth, and all the girls, including me, wanted him. He's like the only famous person to ever have gone to West Haven High, so we all follow his career." She let go of Daniel's arm and said to Samantha, "You wouldn't possibly want to, uh, go on a double date, would you?"

"Why not?" replied Samantha. This was working out after all.

"Great!" said Brittany.

"Wait," said Daniel. "Don't I get a vote?"

"Wouldn't matter," pointed out Samantha. "We have the majority. I'll call and make sure it's okay with Jordan, and if so, we'll meet you at the restaurant at six." Addressing herself to Daniel, she added, "Dan, if you really don't want to."

"No, it's fine," he said, though he didn't seem too pleased.

Samantha excused herself and, while walking home, phoned Terry. "What possessed you to tell Dan I'm dating a football player?"

"I figured you'd only improve in his eyes if he knows you're dating an NFL player."

"Well, he didn't seem to care, but the woman he was with apparently admires Jordan and suggested a double date. It's all set for Saturday."

"Oh. My plan exactly."

"Uh-huh. Next time, mind your own business."

"It worked out perfectly, didn't it? You were nervous about the date, and you get to horn in on Daniel's date. You can thank me by cooking us a nice dinner tonight."

*

At the Greenwich restaurant on Saturday, the four exchanged names and handshakes. Afterward, Jordan talked to Brittany and Daniel to Samantha. Admiring Samantha—the contrast between her adorable, innocent face framed by a new pixie cut and her delectable body as displayed by her slinky red dress was most compelling—Daniel struggled to stave off ravaging her, merely observing, "My, you look natty."

She smiled and said, "And you look dapper." He was wearing black dress slacks and a burgundy button-down shirt that set off his eyes and dark brown locks.

"Jordan's one of those insecure types who tries to make a man feel like a wimp by crushing his hand when he shakes it," noted Daniel as he flexed his sore paw.

"Looks like he succeeded."

"So, how long have you been dating your behemoth?"

"About an hour."

"Oh. And what do you think of him so far?"

"He's attractive in a bonehead kind of way," answered Samantha. "And your American Kelly?"

"She's no Kelly, but she's attractive in a boner kind of way."

"Not funny."

"That's what Brittany kept saying to me on the way here. She doesn't appreciate my funny bone—er."

"Keep trying, Beaton. You're bound to hit on something funny just by chance one of these times."

"I'm not supposed to be funny near you anyway."

"I never said that, and you know it. I love laughing with you."

"Then you'll have to supply the wit. I've been trying and failing tonight so far."

"What are you two mumbling to each other back there?" said Brittany.

"What attractive dates we have," replied Daniel.

"Aren't you sweet?"

"Jones, party of four," called out the maître d'.

A ponderous woman said, "That's me."

Elbowing Daniel, Samantha said, "She's a party of four," which got him laughing.

A minute later, the maître d' showed them to their table. Jordan excused himself to go to the bathroom but not before saying to Daniel, "Order me A.H. Hirsch 16 Year bourbon; make sure it's 16 year."

Daniel saluted him and gave Samantha a *Yes sir!* expression. She smiled.

"So, you're a pilot?" said Brittany. Samantha nodded. "What do you fly?"

"Helicopters. I have a part-time job up in Yalesville flying sightseeing tours and doing flight training. And I fly for the army reserves one weekend a month."

"Sounds, uh, interesting."

"That's one word for it, yes."

"Were you in the war?"

"Two wars."

"What was that like?"

"Sorry, but it's not something I like to talk about."

The waiter came and the ladies ordered their drinks. Then Daniel said, "Bring me a beaker o' beer, lad."

The man frowned and started on his way, when Brittany said, "You forgot Jordan's drink."

He'd done that on purpose, but now that Brittany reminded him, he said, "Oh, yes, the other member of our party, who's currently draining his member—"

"Dan, that's not appropriate at a five-star restaurant," rebuked Brittany.

Samantha shook her head and said, "Tch, tch," with a half-smile.

"Oh, sorry, um, you told me your name, but somehow I've forgotten it," said Daniel.

"Jerry," said the waiter.

"Yes, Jerry. Forgive my remissness and my gaucheness. On occasion I betray a lofty disdain for good manners. Our absent friend would like, um, sixteen something."

"A.H. Hirsch 16 Year bourbon," inserted Brittany. The waiter gave an approving nod to Brittany and left.

Brittany turned to Samantha and said, "I heard you were dating Jim Buckthorn."

*

Which means you've been asking around about me, mused Samantha. Terry had set her up with Jim, but Samantha didn't like him. She replied, "We had dinner once, then I broke it off."

"Oh, Jim's a nice guy. What happened?"

"I believe Sam objected to his ugly face," budded in Daniel.

"Dan, at five-star restaurants we refer to him as horribly plain," corrected Samantha, anticipating Brittany's objection.

"He's not that bad," Brittany responded, "and he's intelligent. He'll be a great orthopedic surgeon."

"He sounds perfect for you," noted Samantha.

"Dan," said Brittany with a sneer at Samantha, "we're going to be covering the business of breaking bad news to families next week. Do you have any pointers?"

"It's never much fun. Just say you're sorry, but—"

"Oh, I couldn't just say it outright."

"Then focus on the silver lining: 'I have good news. You can now collect your mother's life insurance.' Or make it a parenthetical comment: 'The debt burden we face in this country is beyond belief. I really don't see (your mother's dead) a way around it."

Tittering, Samantha added, "Or ease your way into it. 'Rotten weather we're having, and your mother's dead.'"

Brittany smirked, Daniel chortled, and Jordan returned.

"What have I missed?" he said.

"Your date was a helicopter pilot in Iraq and Afghanistan," said Brittany.

"Huh," he replied as he studied the menu.

"But she doesn't like to talk about it," added Brittany.

"He doesn't seem overly enthralled about it anyway," noted Samantha.

The waiter came back with their drinks and took their orders. Brittany ordered a salad, Samantha salmon, Jordan prime sirloin, and Daniel veal.

Brittany said, "How can you do that to a precious little baby calf, for heaven's sake? If you could see one, you'd know they're so, they're such a … what's the word I'm looking for?"

"Delicacy?" guessed Samantha to Daniel's laughter.

"I'm a vegan," boasted Brittany, "and I'd hoped you would have respected me enough to at least forego meat when you're out on a date with me."

"I'm a carnivore, and I'd hoped you would have respected me enough to have a slab of baby cow when you're out on a date with me," retorted Daniel.

"That's not the least bit funny."

"Sam's laughing."

"Yes, she seems to be your little laugh track. Now, what were we talking about? Oh, yes, Sam's a helicopter pilot."

"Not sure how I'd feel about a female pilot," said Jordan.

"Well, why don't you ask Dan? He was in my crew," said Samantha.

"Having a female pilot was awful. There'd be a missile tracking us, and she'd just cry and scream, and our male pilot would have to take over and save the day. Or we'd need to rush out on an urgent call, and she'd be prattling on the phone and refuse to hurry. Or she'd be doing her hair in the chopper and fly us into a canyon wall. And God help anyone who got in the chopper when she was on her period."

"Dan; five star," interrupted Samantha.

"So, you were in the war, too?" asked Brittany. Daniel nodded. "Can you tell me what it was like?"

"Talk about old times? Sure. Remember that night we picked up pieces of Afghan villagers under the dusty moonlight, Sam?"

"You don't have to get ridiculous," Brittany reproached. "I don't like your sarcastic attitude with me. You're treating me like an idiot."

"And I'm tired of your constant criticism, so if you want to call it a night, that's fine with me."

After a short pause, Brittany said, "No, I'm sorry. I do tend to get overly critical sometimes. It's just that I'd like to know more about you."

"Fine. Here's some useful information. Never ask anyone who was on a medevac crew in Jalalabad what it was like."

"Fine."

"Back in a minute," said Jordan as he got to his feet.

"Bothered by incontinence?" said Daniel.

"Five star," said Samantha. Brittany glared at her.

"I left my wallet in my jacket," Jordan said.

"Oh, look there," said Brittany, gesturing with her head to a man two tables over. "They say famous people always eat here. Oh, no, now that I look more closely I don't think it's him, but he sure reminds me of … what's his name."

"Me too," said Samantha. Daniel grinned.

The conversation stalled for a moment. The three sipped on their drinks. Then, Brittany said, "So, Sam, where did you meet Jordan?"

"My sister is friends with his sister and set us up on this date. I was a little uncomfortable going on a first date with a football player, so I liked your idea of a double date."

"He seems like a perfect gentleman," she observed as Jordan returned. "You must be excited dating an NFLer." Jordan smiled at Brittany. She returned it. "So, Jordan, can you tell us what it's like to be a professional football player?"

"Fast, brutal, exciting, hard, dangerous."

"You must have to be very brave," opined Brittany.

"Name me one other profession where a man has to stand up to monsters who are doing their best to demolish him." Samantha's eyes met Daniel's. Jordan continued, "People think it's all so glamorous, but I put life and limb at risk every week. It's hard to imagine just how risky it is, and I wish people would give us more credit for the guts we have." Samantha's and Daniel's eyes continued to communicate.

"Yes, God knows NFL football players don't get the adulation they deserve," said Daniel. "They are the world's greatest unsung heroes in my book."

"Well, I don't know about that," said Jordan in all modesty. "Maybe not the world's greatest."

"I mean, after all, you're performing a vital service swatting away pesky linebackers," added Samantha.

"Pesky? They try to knock my head off."

"A bunch of 300-pound mutants knocking each other's heads off. No wonder you're all worshipped," rejoined Samantha.

"We should be for what we risk."

"Of course, you're well paid for the risk," noted Brittany.

"If you ask me, a million five per is a bargain for someone who puts that much on the line."

"What did you make as a flight medic, Dan?" said Samantha.

"About point-zero-two-five million per. Mind you, I never had to worry about being tackled."

"It's not only that," returned Jordan. "There are so few positions and so many thousands of men after them. It's a constant pressure-cooker to stay sharp, or else you're gone. That and injury mean the average career is only three years, so the pay reflects all that."

"A flight medic would have to work 180 years to make what you make in three years. Of course, there aren't that many people after the jobs and, if you don't stay sharp, someone else is gone, so it seems fair," said Daniel.

*

The food came, and the four ate and drank and engaged in small talk for another hour.

For Daniel, diabetes was no big deal anymore; just a manual external control of blood sugar level as opposed to an automatic internal one. Nothing more than an inconvenience. The main issue was how a woman might react. Does he come right out with it before she gets to know him and risk scaring her away? Does he try to hide it until he knows the relationship is going well? If he does, will she react poorly simply because he hid it? With Brittany, though, he didn't care. Just as well, for she frowned at him as he pulled out his insulin pen and pulled up his shirt a bit to inject the insulin into his side. "You're diabetic?" asked she with a tone that screamed, *Defective!*

"Yup."

"Oh," she said in the same tone.

What am I doing with this woman? he asked himself, looking at Brittany, *and not that one?* he continued as he switched his gaze to Samantha. She smiled at him. Then he answered himself. *Because, just like before, she's looking higher than me. Here she is with an NFLer, for Christ's sake.*

The check came, and Daniel waited for the one-point-five-million-dollar kid to claim it, but he sat silent. After five uncomfortable minutes Daniel picked it up, read $485.67, and pulled out his wallet. Finally, Jordan said, "Oh, I'll get mine and Sam's. What'll it be?" Daniel quickly toted it up in his head and said, "About $290." Jordan withdrew three hundreds from his wallet and tossed them on the table. Daniel took the cash and put his Visa card on the table. He'd have to cover the tip.

Daniel was ready to leave and said, "Well, this was fun and informative. Jordan's covered the waterfront from quarterbacks all the way to fullbacks, and I feel well informed about current events now. Shall we call it a night?"

"Come on back to my place," ordered Jordan as he seized Samantha's hand.

"You go," replied Samantha, taking back her hand.

Jordan frowned, apparently trying to comprehend the novel notion of rejection. "I don't think you understood me."

"Let me put it in terms you'll understand," said Samantha. "You're down by four, it's fourth and goal with two seconds left on the clock, and you're not getting laid tonight."

Daniel's gust of raucous laughter was evidently the final straw for Jordan. One minute Daniel's at the table in Connecticut with three other people, the next he's back in Afghanistan in a diabetic stupor dimly aware of the Taliban rifling his pockets, terrified he's dead or about to be.

"Dan? Danny? Are you okay?"

"That's Sam," Daniel deduced in his stupor. "What's she doing back in Afghanistan? What am *I* doing back in Afghanistan?"

"Danny?"

He opened his eyes. Her angelic face upside-down, he furrowed his brow. How did it get that way? Then he realized his head was on her legs.

She was crying. "God, Danny, I was so scared you were really hurt. Are you all right?"

"What happened?"

"Jordan smashed you in the face."

He lifted his head and quickly replaced it on her lap. Best place to be in the world, plus he couldn't do anything vertical for the time being. His head ached intensely, and he was embarrassed for succumbing so easily, so he did his best to make light of it. "Did I make a good showing?"

"Not bad; you were runner up. How do you feel?"

"I can't think of a good word to express how I feel, but if you want to know, simply charge full speed head-first into that wall."

"Poor baby. Can you stand up?"

"I like it here. Wake me up again in the morning."

"Come on. Get up." She helped him to his feet. He had to lean on her to stay upright.

"Fuck, my face is some frigging sore." He looked around and realized something. "I seem to be one Brittany short."

"She left with Jordan." He scowled. Samantha explained, "After he hit you, I told him to get lost. He grabbed Brittany's hand, and she left with him." He sighed. "I'm pretty sure you've been dumped, but you don't want somebody who would do that anyway."

"So you're left with me, lucky girl," he tried.

"Yeah, she gets the rich, handsome NFL guy. I get the bankrupt pansy he knocked out with one punch."

"You stayed to peck at the remains of my ego?"

"I'm only kidding. I'm glad I'm with you, but I'm worried about you."

*

Samantha helped him out to her sister's car, which he had borrowed for the evening. She drove them back to New Haven with Daniel sitting inert, head on a pillow against the passenger window. Concerned, she continually checked on him and suggested three times they go to the hospital, a notion he rejected twice, but the third time, as they approached New Haven, he didn't respond. "Dan? Are you sleeping? Dan? Dan!" Worried, she pulled over and checked on him. She shook him, and he roused briefly but closed his eyes again. She took him to the ER at his hospital. They had to put him on a wheelchair to get him into the hospital. He was diagnosed with a mild concussion and kept overnight for observation.

*

At the hospital the next day he got plenty of ribbing about his black eye and swollen nose, but he took it with good humor. When Brittany showed up, however, the story was different. Instead of being penitent for abandoning him the night before, she took the offensive. Cornering him in the locker room, she delivered a warning. "Jordan said to tell you that if you try pressing charges or try suing him, he'll bury you with his expensive lawyers, and I'll testify that you were teasing him all night."

Apparently expecting him to fold as easily as he had collapsed the night before, she was astounded at his non-verbal response, which consisted of smashing the locker an inch from her head with his palm, putting a large dent in the metal, and making a similar impression on her mettle. The speed, strength, and aggression with which he moved and the deafening crash it made elicited a screech from the petrified young lady, who teetered on the brink of a swoon for a moment, but caught herself and ran out crying.

This impulsive response, naturally, had negative repercussions. The next morning Daniel was summoned by the head of medicine to explain himself. Brittany was there, as was Terry.

"Ms. Delp says you frightened her out of her wits with that outrageous display of testosterone in the change room," began Dr. Sloan. "We can't put up with our male residents threatening our female medical students. So, before I decide what to do with you, please tell me what you were thinking."

"Before telling you that, let me set you straight, because you've swallowed her version without bothering to ask me for my side."

"I'm not used to my residents addressing me like that, Dr. Beaton."

"I was in the army for two years, and the army has no shortage of thoughtlessness, yet I can't recall one instance of anyone condemning me before hearing my side of the story."

"Maybe you'd like to go back to the army, then."

"Dr. Sloan," Terry interrupted. "Dr. Beaton spent two years fighting a war for our country. While Ms. Delp was turning the pages of textbooks, he was flying through missiles, bullets, and dust storms to rescue our injured soldiers. While she studied long hours and missed a few winks of sleep in a safe university, he was out in the hundred-degree heat desperately racing against the clock to save someone's life while people were shooting at him. While she got government loans and grants to fund her studies, he was earning the money to put himself through med school as he risked his life every day. You heard her side. Is it really asking too much to hear his?"

"Fine," she said. "Dr. Beaton, tell me what happened."

Daniel gave a nod of thanks to Terry and began with a brief recitation of the double date on Friday. He concluded, "So after dumping me for him when I was unconscious, she shows up yesterday morning, not with an apology for abandoning me, but with a warning not to press charges against Moore or else she'd testify on his behalf. She stood there with a 'What are you going to do about it?' smirk, so I smashed the locker next to her head to let her know she won't get away with treating me like a doormat. So from my perspective, she's not a sweet, innocent female med student, she's a double-crossing slut."

"How dare you call me that!" screamed Brittany.

"Settle down, Ms. Delp" said Dr. Sloan. "And name calling definitely doesn't help, Dr. Beaton."

Still exercised, Brittany said, "He teased Jordan all night. He got what he deserved."

"I made twenty-five grand a year facing bombs and bullets, and that pile of smegma sits there straight-faced telling Sam and me that he's working in the most risky profession on the planet and earns one point five million a year because it's so dangerous. Instead of smashing him, which he richly deserved, I merely got sarcastic. He had no cause to knock me out without warning. And she had no cause to go with him, except she wanted him." Turning to Brittany, he concluded, "Ergo, you are a slut."

"I'll sue you for slander, you bugger!"

He laughed and said, "I hope you win everything I have. You'll owe about a hundred and sixty grand."

"May I make a suggestion?" said Terry. Dr. Sloan nodded. "Ms. Delp and Dr. Beaton agree to steer clear of each other for the last few months of the term. This means no more threats or name calling by either of you. Dr. Sloan, if you would speak to your staff to ensure, to the extent possible, they don't have to deal with each other at the hospital. And if either of you decides to sue the other, leave the hospital out of it, because we're not taking either person's side."

"Sounds fair to me," said Dr. Sloan. Brittany and Daniel nodded. "And please act more professionally while you're here, both of you. Dr. Beaton, no more damaging hospital property. The cost of repairing the locker will be deducted from your next check." He nodded. "Leave."

Daniel clutched Terry's elbow in the hall and said, "She was ready to hang me until you came to the rescue. Thank you." She nodded and smiled. He smiled back. She was a fine-looking woman. And after she started treating him with respect, he began to see how smart and sensible she was. Similar enough to Samantha to be intriguing, but different enough to render the thought of having her agreeable.

CHAPTER TWENTY-TWO

All in a Day's Work – February, 2012

Sitting in Dr. Sloan's office at 7:45 AM awaiting his six-month evaluation, which, he noted, was taking place after his seventh month, typical hospital efficiency, Daniel noticed a fancy box and went over to examine it. She had excused herself for a moment, but returned while he was peering into the box. "Put that down!" she yelled.

"Ashes?"

"My husband. Put it down."

"He looks dehydrated," he quipped as he put down the box.

"Perfect segue into one of my major points: your inappropriate jokes."

"Wow, I'm back in the army."

"Meaning?"

"Meaning I spend my time saving lives, though no one is trying to kill me now, yet all the higher ups notice is a few jokes."

"I notice more than that, Dr. Beaton, and we'll get into that, but I'll let you know yet again that not everyone shares your sense of humor. Telling that woman she was lazy because she did nothing but sit around all day. I mean, honest to God, that was in poor taste."

"Since she's confined to a wheelchair, she must have known it was a joke. She chose to make an issue out of it because she wanted the attention."

"And Mr. Howe? You joked about his death?"

"Dr. Sung asked me how he was doing, and I said about as well as all the other corpses. No one heard it but Sung, who has no sense of humor at all if he has to come running to you bitching about it."

"Believe it or not, Dr. Beaton, most people don't think death is funny. I just ask you to keep that in mind. Now, in general, you have some weaknesses you'll have to work on for your final few months here."

"So, you've already decided that I won't be staying for the three years?"

"To be honest, that's the way I'm leaning. You're a competent physician, especially in the ER, but you do have two glaring weaknesses. You seem almost dismissive of many patients' complaints."

"I can't deny that. After seeing bloody stumps where feet were, I can't get serious about a hangnail, even if it is making the patient uncomfortable."

"You can't put everything into the context of war."

"I know. I'm working on it."

"Work harder. Second, your diagnostic skills are not where they should be, where they have to be to work at a hospital like this. I have several recommendations on how to improve."

As Daniel nodded, someone knocked, and Dr. Sloan said, "Yes?"

A third-year resident in charge of the ER at this hour opened the door and said, "A sniper in Harkness Tower is shooting at people."

"Oh, my God," exclaimed Dr. Sloan. "Any dead?"

"Only rumors. I've heard anywhere between one and five. We've been told to expect multiple casualties with gunshot wounds. Dan, we'll need your particular expertise on this. I want you in charge of triaging and initial treatment." Daniel looked at Dr. Sloan, who nodded. He left with the resident.

Daniel hadn't had to contend with gunshot wounds since leaving Afghanistan and had been worried about how he might react, but when the first victims were wheeled in, he went into automatic mode and, with great efficiency, applied the ABCs and directed other medical staff on how to deal with each kind of wound to keep the patients alive until they could be sent for surgery. Within thirty-five minutes he had triaged and treated or supervised treatment of all eight casualties, and six were in surgery with the other two stable in ER.

*

At 8:29 the SWAT team put a call into ER requesting a doctor at the site of the attack. The gunman was holed up in the tower still shooting at anything that moved with a rifle. He had barricaded himself on the roof, and the police were busy trying to get in without too much damage to the historic tower. A medical student who had been out for his morning jog had been shot in the leg and had taken shelter behind the Pierson statue near Harkness Tower. The student was on the phone to the police. "I've used my shirt for a tourniquet, but I'm still losing blood. If you don't get me out of here within the next fifteen or twenty minutes, I'm dead. You have to get help to me!"

Police had tried tear gas, but the sniper had brought a mask. They needed a doctor's opinion on the severity of the injury and advice on how to proceed with respect to the wounded man.

*

Dr. Sloan asked Daniel to go. Terry bade him good luck and grimaced while watching him leave with a police officer.

A police car sped Daniel the half mile to the SWAT sergeant in charge at the scene. He explained the situation and pointed out the student and gunman. Daniel asked to speak to the student. He was given the phone. After speaking to the student, Daniel concluded, "It sounds like he's in danger of going into shock. I have to get to him right away."

"Run out there into the line of fire? No dice," said the sergeant. "The sniper has booby trapped the barricade he set up, but we're working on it. We'll be through in about twenty minutes."

"I'm pretty sure he'll be through before then," said Daniel, gesturing to the injured man.

"I'm pretty sure you'll be through if you run out there. I can't allow it."

"Can't your sharpshooters cover me? It's what? Forty yards?"

"Doc, this ain't the ER, and this is no video game. I don't think you understand the risk."

"Sergeant, you see all the windows facing this plaza? Put a gunman in every one of them and throw in a grenade launcher or two and that's what I had to deal with as a medic for two years in Afghanistan. This is like a stroll on a sunny beach for me. I can do this."

"Where were you?"

"Jalalabad Airfield as a flight medic and at the front lines in the Korengal Valley as a field medic."

"Death Valley? Fuck me. I was in Kandahar and that was bad enough." Turning to look at the injured student who was now begging for help, he said, "That man will die before we can get the gunman? You're sure?" Daniel nodded. He turned to another officer and said, "Give him a shield and a vest." Turning back to Daniel, he said, "We think he's got an M77 Hawkeye .308 caliber. That can shoot armor piercing bullets, but so far he hasn't used them."

Daniel donned the vest, grabbed the most essential medical supplies, and got set to go.

"When we open up on the gunman, run your ass off. Ready?" Daniel nodded. "Fire!"

With the SWAT team pouring gunfire into the clock tower, Daniel held out the ballistic shield and sprinted toward the stricken student. Daniel reached the man and slid down beside him behind the statue. The sniper fired, but couldn't get a clear shot at either man.

"I recognize you," said the medical student. "You're a resident, aren't you?"

"Yup," answered Daniel as he cut off the man's pant leg and put a tourniquet in place. He removed the student's makeshift one and tightened the genuine one. The student grunted in pain. Daniel then took off the man's jacket to start an IV.

"Why the hell are you doing ..." The man trailed off as he began to lose consciousness.

"I'm just reliving old times," he returned while extracting a bag of plasma. The student started to go white. "Stay with me," said Daniel, but the man blacked out. "Shit. I should've brought another vest!" he said aloud. Daniel picked up the man's phone, which was still connected to the sergeant's phone, and informed him that the man had gone into shock and that he had to get him out right away. "Give me two minutes, then give me cover again."

"What's your plan?" asked the police sergeant in command.

"I throw him over my shoulder and run him out."

"It'll take too long to run that distance carrying a man, and you can't carry the shield while you're carrying a man. The sniper will pick both of you off. Can't you give him basic treatment there while we deal with the sniper?"

"He won't make it. He needs PRBC, plasma, oxygen, and surgery in short order. I need to get him to the hospital right away."

"I can have a bullet-proof vehicle to you in seven minutes."

"I hope it's a hearse, then, because he'll be dead. Keep the gunfire going for fifteen seconds, and I'll have him out. I'll let you know when I'm ready."

Daniel took off the vest and put it on the student. He put the man over his right shoulder, holding the man's legs across the back of his knees. He had to run diagonally away from the gunman, exposing his right side and back. Thinking about the man's head vulnerable back there, he put the man down and set the vest so that all of it hung down over the man's back and covered his head. He picked him up again and told the officer he was ready.

Police gunfire resumed, and Daniel ran as fast as he could to the safety of the building. Daniel made it to within fifteen yards of the police position by the time the sniper shot. A bullet hit between the shoulder blades of the injured student, throwing Daniel forward onto the ground. Police commenced shooting toward the muzzle flashes, forcing the sniper to desist, but the sergeant was convinced it was all over. "Jesus Christ," he said, but then he saw Daniel scrambling and realized the vest was on the student. As police pumped bullets into the tower, the sergeant and two of his men scampered out to drag the two men to safety.

Daniel was stunned; he'd scraped his face and right shoulder. The sergeant shook his hand and smiled at the fellow veteran. Paramedics put the student on a stretcher, and Daniel joined him in the back of the ambulance. The paramedic got plasma and oxygen going on the three-minute ride to the hospital.

While Daniel was being treated for his scrapes, Dr. Sloan came up to him and thanked him for his work and added, "I know I wasn't positive with you this morning, so let me add this: I've never seen any doctor so professional, calm, and efficient in dealing with a dire emergency. And I stand in awe at your intrepid rescue of our student. If this were the norm, you'd be our best doctor."

He thanked her and thought about what she implied. Since this kind of calamity is the rare exception, you're not valuable enough to keep on.

*

That evening as Terry and Samantha watched the local news, they smiled as the reporter said, "News Channel 8 has identified the doctor who performed the daring rescue as Daniel Beaton, a resident at the Yale-New Haven Hospital. He has refused our requests for an interview, but sources tell us he was a medic in the Afghanistan war and was used to this kind of boldness." Daniel also refused to talk to the other networks, which had made the sniper the lead story nationally. The networks reported that the gunman had shot himself as police broke through the barricade. Only one of the nine who made it to the hospital, a professor emeritus, died. Two others died at the scene.

Terry had asked him to come to her place to treat him to a homemade dinner. He'd initially refused, pleading fatigue and pain—the abrasions on his face and shoulder were smarting—but she insisted. "Is that pretty much what happened?" Terry asked after the news report concluded.

"Actually, I was walking through the plaza minding my own business when someone started shooting, so I grabbed this guy who was handy and used him as a shield. Luckily he absorbed the bullet."

Speaking to Daniel with a grin, Samantha said, "When I knew you at JAF, you'd run out in front a dozen gunmen. Now only one? God, Beaton, have some balls."

"No, thanks. It's all I can do to lug around the two I have."

"Uh-huh. I always thought a man couldn't get much uglier than you, but here you've gone and outdone yourself with that nasty scrape on your cheek."

"Are you suitably overawed?"

"You, Daniel Beaton, are an amazing human being." She kissed his uninjured cheek. "And I'm glad to hear your wit again. I've missed it." She gazed into his eyes and moved in for a kiss, this one intended for his lips. He turned his head. Seeing she'd gone too far, she sat back and offered him a drink.

"Sam, Terry, I'm sorry, but I'm really sore, and I just want to go home and sleep."

"You have to stay for dinner," responded Terry. "It'll be ready in half an hour."

"I'm not even hungry. I'm on pain killers, and I'm ready to fall asleep. I'll take a rain check," he said as he put on his coat.

After he left, Samantha groaned, "I drove him away. Why did I have to try a kiss? God dammit!"

"Tell him how you feel. Look him in the eyes, take his hands and scream if you have to, *I love you, you stupid bastard!* Cross your heart, pledge your first child, take off your clothes, make him believe it."

"God, Terry, he won't even let me kiss him. If I tell him I love him, he'll run for the hills."

"He loves you, Sam. I can see it when he looks at you. He even admitted to me his feelings for you are not the issue. He's afraid of you, afraid you'll hurt him again. Convince him you won't."

"I've been trying."

"Try harder. He's dated three women now that we know of. Lucky for you he hasn't hit it off with any of them yet."

"I have to take it slow, so I don't scare him off."

"You better not take it too slow. You can practically hear the wedding bells clang when the women ogle the Yale residents, even the ugly ones. The eye-catching ones like Dan are under constant siege. I overheard Julia Maloney—she's a beautiful med student—I heard her joke that she'd have to put her career on hold while she has his children."

Samantha's face fell. "How am I supposed to compete with a beautiful med student?"

"You did fine against what's her name in Australia."

"And right after that, my big mouth … Wait! I have an idea."

"What?"

"It might work to keep him away from other women while I worm my way back into his heart."

"What?"

"You won't like it, but you need to do it."

"What!"

"You go out with him."

"What? No way. And don't ask me why not. You know damn well why not."

"And when he marries Maloney and they cart me away to the booby hatch, how will you feel? How will you feel about your loving sister who sheltered, clothed, and fed you and helped put you through college? How would you feel about her in a horrible place like that?"

"Sam, please."

Samantha's tears started as she slumped onto the couch. "I love him, Terry. I *crave* him. I see him and I ache inside, I want him so much. I want to take him in my arms and never let go. If he marries someone else, I really think I would just fall down and die."

"Shit, Sam, how can I say no now?" The sisters hugged. "But how do you know he even wants to go out with me? We haven't exactly seen eye to eye."

"You're beautiful. Just flirt with him. He'll go out with you."

The next week, neither Daniel nor Samantha could manage a lunch date, so they met for coffee after his shift ended at 8 PM on Wednesday. Afterward, he walked her to her apartment and said goodbye, but she said, "Don't you want to come in for a drink or something?"

"No thanks. I have to be at work tomorrow at seven."

"Just a few more minutes. I just want to talk a little more."

He nodded, and they walked up to the second-floor apartment. She opened two beers and handed him one, and they sat on her couch.

"Dan, I just wanted to tell you how much our little get-togethers mean to me. You keep me sane."

Terry walked out from her room to the kitchen. She didn't appear to notice the two on her couch. She was clad in form-fitting pajamas, with blue silk shorts on the bottom and a low-necked blue top. Samantha observed his eyes pop out and trace the outline of her superb figure and continue down her shapely legs before bouncing off the floor for the return trip. When Terry opened the fridge and bent over to get the orange juice from the bottom shelf on the door, his eyes grew wider. She turned to get a glass and noticed the two. "Oh!" she said. "I'm sorry. I'll get out of your way in a second." She poured her orange juice, put the container back in the fridge, and strolled back to her room and shut the door.

"She's a beautiful girl, isn't she?" said Samantha. He shrugged. "Come on. Your eyes still haven't dragged their way back to their sockets. Why don't you ask her out?"

"Until a month ago or so we pretty much hated each other."

"She's never hated you. She's just over-protective of me, and she thought you were being mean to me, and she always speaks her mind."

"That she does."

"When she speaks her mind to me, she tells me you're handsome and funny. She was in awe of you after you rescued the shooting victim. She called you incredible. If you ask her out, she'll say yes."

"She's a bit overbearing with me."

"She's like that with all men. She's had them wrapped around her little finger since high school, but I'm sure you can handle her." She turned her head toward Terry's room and shouted, "Terry?"

"No!" yelped Daniel.

When Terry opened the door and jutted out her head, Samantha said, "Dan would like to take you out to dinner on Saturday." Terry looked at her sister as much to say, *What about you?* But Samantha went on, "I think you two would be great together."

"Okay. I'll be ready at six." She closed her door.

Daniel gave a *What just happened?* gawp at Samantha.

CHAPTER TWENTY-THREE

Winding Down – March to June 2012

The dinner date went well. The two discussed everything from the desperation the sisters felt after their mother died to the Yale shootings. On the way home, however, Terry got nervous. She was driving because he had no car, and she pulled up in front of his apartment building. She turned off the engine and said, "Uh, I'm not coming up with you."

"I hadn't counted on that for a first date."

"It's more than that. We didn't actually touch on this tonight, but this is really awkward for me, with my sister, I mean. She has real feelings for you, regardless of what you think."

"So, are you saying you don't want to date me again?"

"No. I just want you to know I'll step aside if you, uh, want her."

"I don't," said Daniel.

"Are you sure? She's such a special person."

"Is that what this is all about? You take me out to get me to relent on Sam?"

"No."

"It's clear you don't want to see me again. That's okay. Thanks for a nice evening," he said as he got out of the car.

"No!" she exclaimed as she, too, got out of the car. If she let it end like this, Samantha wouldn't be happy. To prevent that and to ward off sex, she had to admit something. "It's not that. I enjoyed myself tonight. I need to tell you something about myself. When I was fifteen … I was raped."

"Shit. I'm sorry."

"I was in eleventh grade, and I was dating the most popular guy in the school. He got me drunk and got my clothes off. I tried to stop him. I was screaming and crying, but he raped me. I haven't been with a man since."

"Did the bastard go to jail?"

"No, I didn't want everyone knowing. The boy's father was a colonel, and Sam went to him demanding he punish his son or she'd go to the police. I guess he screamed and threatened her, but she didn't back down. He ended up grounding his son for the rest of senior year and promising that he'd join the army and would be kept in line. That's also how Sam got to be …" She stopped and looked down.

Daniel said, "How Sam got to be what?" She didn't answer. Then Daniels's eyes opened wide and he said, "Pilot!"

She nodded.

"But how?"

"The dark cloud had a silver lining: I was a couple of weeks short of sixteen and Matt had just turned eighteen. When Sam told him my age, the colonel knew the charge would be statutory rape, so he started trying to bribe her by offering her whatever position she wanted. She hadn't gone to him for any personal gain, but she thought we would both benefit if she got to be a chief warrant officer and pilot. Please don't tell her I told you. She had top marks in all the tests to get in, and got top ratings all the way through training, so it's not like she cheated the system. She's a natural pilot."

"That she is. Listen, I can't pretend to understand what it's like for a woman when some animal rapes her. If you're too uncomfortable dating, I understand."

"I want to see you again, but I need you to understand I'll need to take things very slowly when it comes to sex."

"Okay."

"Really? You'll be patient?" He nodded. "You won't see other women while we're dating?"

"No."

She kissed his cheek and asked him for a date the next week. He said yes.

When she got home, Samantha was waiting up for her. "How'd it go?

"The dinner went fine. He's fun to be with, but it was awkward as I dropped him off. I know you know this, but men expect sex sooner or later when they date a woman."

"He didn't pressure you, did he?"

"No. He was a perfect gentleman. Anyway, to dampen his expectations for the foreseeable future, I told him."

"What? The rape?" Terry nodded. "I'm sorry to have put you in that position, sis. It was wrong of me. Let's stop this now."

"No. We have him where we want him now, in a holding pattern. He won't push me for sex, and he said he won't date other women. That gives you more time to change his mind about you."

*

Terry and Daniel saw each other weekly for March and April. They enjoyed each other's company, on an intellectual level at least. She wasn't as much fun as Samantha, lacking her wit and vivacity, but she was just as pretty and smart, and she didn't put him down as Samantha had done so often. As time passed, though, Daniel's impatience for the type of intercourse that didn't require conversing rose.

When she declined to accompany him into his apartment on their date at the end of April, he said, "You know, I really like your hands. Holding them is nice, but at this rate I'll only be to your elbows by Christmas. I mean, even if your hands would hold something else of mine." Her contrite smile served to stir his anger. "I've tried my best to be sensitive about your past, but this is getting ridiculous. I'm sorry, but this just isn't working out."

When he opened the door, Terry said, "Wait! Close the door." He did. She leaned over, unbuttoned and unzipped his pants. She took out his reproductive gear, and he could have sworn he heard, "Eeew," which he considered inauspicious. She began to yank on his penis and squeeze his testicles, too hard in both cases to make him hard. She'd never done this before, he concluded. Either that or she was punishing him for being a man. As she proceeded, he asked himself, *Should I get her to stop? Ouch! Tell her poor job well done. Ah shit, woman! Will that upset her? God, my balls are in a vice grip. Should I tell her she's not milking a cow? Ow! Will a little friendly instruction insult her?*

"What's the matter?" said Terry.

"As a kid you were really good at tug rope, weren't you?" He pushed her hands away.

She gawped at his eyes with a jumble of emotions that expressed themselves in an anguished wail and tears. Perturbed at upsetting her, Daniel apologized, did up his pants, and bid her good night.

*

She drove home and was still crying when she got there. Samantha was watching TV and noticed Terry's distress as she tried to slip past her to her bedroom. "What's wrong?" she asked. Terry slammed the door. "Terry?" Samantha knocked on her door. "Terry, what happened? Did Dan do something to hurt you?" She opened her door to see Terry face-down on her bed.

"I tried. I tried so hard," she said.

"Terry, calm down and tell me what happened."

"The time I bought by telling him I was raped caught up to me today. He said we were finished, and I was so afraid of letting you down, I, I …"

"You what?"

"I tried to give him a, a hand job." Samantha's eyes opened wide. "I didn't know what else to do. It was so disgusting, and

I was getting sick, and I was panicking about getting you angry doing this to him, and nothing was happening with him."

"You mean—"

"Yes! I don't know how to do that, and he was wincing. I was actually hurting him. Then he pushed my hands away and said something about tug rope, and I was so embarrassed and humiliated and worried, then he left, and I went through that for nothing, and we're done, and I failed you." With this she buried her head in her pillow and continued crying.

Samantha sat on the bed, hugged her sister, and said, "It's my fault. I should never have asked you to date him. It was a stupid idea. I'm sorry."

"But now he'll go after other women."

Samantha gave a resigned shrug.

In early May, Samantha got a call from Ashley asking her to a small party she was having for a few graduating law students. They had only seen one another twice since their reunion meeting a year and a half earlier. Out of sheer boredom, she decided to go.

At that party, Ashley introduced Samantha to the class's most eligible bachelor. Ashley's expression changed from pride to shock when Roger said, "Sam! It's so nice to see you. You were right: my invitation to Nantucket was tactless. I guess I'm not used to dealing with such a classy woman. Can I get you a drink to make it up to you?"

Samantha might not have said yes otherwise, but with a flabbergasted Ashley looking on, she couldn't resist. "That sounds great."

Samantha walked off with Roger and spent the evening with him. She found him charming and accepted the offer of a dinner date.

Samantha enjoyed the expensive date and agreed to another and another. But after he pushed for sex on the third date, she recognized the danger signal.

At home that evening, Terry asked how the date went.

"Roger's a player," Samantha answered.

"How do you know?"

"Just like Paul. The way he laughs with his mouth but not his eyes; the way he studies every good-looking woman; the way he pushes to get what he wants too fast and warns me that other women would be thrilled to please him. He tried undressing me in the car."

"That's too bad. I was hoping it would work out."

"Well, I was just about to break up with him when he invited me on his father's yacht. I was telling him no when he sweetened the pot. He said I could invite some friends. I thought, why not? Invite Jenna and her husband. We'll go after I get back." Samantha had set aside the first two weeks of June for her required annual service.

"I can do better than that. I can invite Dan."

"You broke up."

"Not officially. We're friendly when we see each other. He seems to be pretending that night never happened."

"Dating him was a bad idea, remember?"

"I saw Dan talking to Julia Maloney today. She was busy giving him every sign a woman has that she's interested."

"Shit."

"You have to make your move soon. This may be your last chance."

"How will that work? I tell Dan I love him on Roger's boat?"

"You wouldn't do it in front of Roger, but if you do it on his yacht, maybe it'll show Dan what you're willing to give up for him. I don't know, maybe it's a bad idea, but he needs strong evidence that you really do love him. It's the best I can come up with."

*

Daniel was surprised to get an invitation to go yachting with Terry. He had thought things were over and said as much to her.

Terry responded, "Oh. You never actually said that to me. Sam is going with Roger, and my friend Jenna and her husband are going. I don't want to be the odd one out, so maybe just this one more time?" She could see he was still reluctant, so she added an incentive. "You can teach me how to, um, how to do what you want me to do."

Daniel agreed.

On June 18, a sunny, warm Saturday, the Tannenbaum's motor yacht sailed out of the Noroton Yacht Club in Darien, CT into Long Island Sound. Daniel had shown up at the last minute, having rushed down in Terry's car after his shift at the hospital. Terry had come with Samantha earlier, and both were sitting on the deck in bikinis. Roger was piloting the ship. Daniel smiled broadly at the pretty ladies and took his duffle bag downstairs to a cabin to change, and on his way back upstairs he walked by another cabin as Jenna walked in. He glanced in but wished he hadn't.

Sitting between the sisters, he mentioned, "I think I just saw Ted as I walked past an open door. He was facing away from me and, uh, bending over to pull up his bathing suit."

Terry laughed and said, "Must've been Ted. What color was his hair?"

"All I noticed was that it had a disgusting part in the middle."

Samantha burst out laughing, spraying him with vodka and orange juice. Fidgeting as if she was nervous, she went to mix her fourth drink and Daniel's first. Daniel watched her walk to the bar, admiring her beauty. Terry smiled.

Samantha returned with the drinks and sat. Daniel took a sip and put his hand on Terry's leg. She flinched. He frowned at her and said, "Sorry to gross you out."

"You didn't. You just surprised me."

"When a woman reacts to me as if she was being French-kissed by a leper, she's not showing surprise; she's showing revulsion."

"You didn't gross me out. It's just that I'm still uncomfortable … It's hard to talk about. I keep everything inside of me."

"Got room for one more thing?" She blushed. He looked at her sister, and she looked distinctly uncomfortable. Turning back to Terry, he said, "When you invited me on our little cruise, I just assumed, you know, but you definitely have the air of a woman who's about to not pleasure me. I've breathed that stuffy air all too often in my life."

"Tell him, Terry," insisted Samantha.

"Tell me what?"

Looking at the deck, Terry said, "I'm in love with, with someone else."

She glanced up at his shocked visage and again focused on the deck. He looked at Samantha to see if maybe this was a practical joke, but her face showed sadness and something else. Maybe fear? "This isn't just a shitty joke or a way to get out of sleeping with me?"

"She's in love with Jenna, Dan. My sister is a lesbian."

Daniel looked back and forth at Terry and Samantha to see if there was a trace of a smile, a smoldering snicker, anything to indicate they were pulling his leg. "I don't believe you," he finally said, just in case they were fooling, but he was almost sure they weren't. It explained a lot about Terry.

"It's true, Dan. I'm sorry," said Terry.

"But why? Why did you date me at all?"

"I really enjoy your company, and I'm not ready, not in the position to, uh, come out of the closet yet. Jenna's married and … I'm really sorry."

With heated expression, he turned to Samantha and demanded to know, "Why did you set me up with her? Some sort of practical joke to make a fool out of me?"

"No—"

"A decoy to help your sister keep her secret?"

"You don't understand."

"I understand perfectly. You think so little of me that you think it's okay to play with my feelings, with my life. You've never been anything but a bitch to me, and I'm such a goddamn idiot I keep letting you get away with it. Well, this is it, Hawkins! Once I get off this fucking boat, I never want to see you, either of you, again."

"Listen to me! I'm in l—"

"Just shut the hell up. God help me, I hate you."

Samantha's face fell.

"Let her speak, Dan," implored Terry.

"Kiss my arse, both of you. You go screw Roger, and you do whatever lesbians do with each other. I'll be downstairs getting drunk. By my jeezly self!"

He put in his earphones and turned on his iPod to earsplitting level as he stomped to the bar, grabbed a forty of Crown Royal, and marched down the stairs in humiliation.

*

Samantha was too shocked to cry at first, but as the shock receded, her sorrow amplified, and she was soon weeping. Terry took her to an unoccupied room. Finding it impossible to settle Samantha down, she gave her a sedative and left her to sleep. She tried to get in to see Daniel to tell him Samantha loved him, but he had locked the door and wouldn't answer her knocks. She went upstairs to tell Roger Samantha was ill. He nodded and continued drinking.

*

A half hour later, out in the middle of Long Island Sound, a thoroughly inebriated Roger left the helm with the ship still moving and went downstairs to check on Samantha. Seeing her sleeping in her bikini, he nudged her. She opened her eyes but was still asleep. Roger removed her bikini bra and started sucking on her nipples. Samantha offered no resistance, so he put his hand down her bikini bottom. That woke her up, and she pushed him away.

Suddenly he heard screaming from above, and there was a deafening crash. Both Samantha and Roger were thrown off the bed onto the floor. Samantha sat up, mystified about what was going on. She was drunk and sedated and had banged her head when she hit the floor. Dazed, Roger left the room and went upstairs to find out what had happened.

*

"Holy jumping Jesus," Daniel muttered as he got up off the floor to which he'd been flung. He opened the door and saw the passageway filling with water! Dashing up the stairs, he saw a small ship just off port. They'd obviously hit it.

Roger was running back and forth in a panic. Terry and Jenna were holding each other and crying. Jenna was bleeding from her upper arm and neck. Ted was lowering the life boat.

"Where's Sam?" Daniel said.

No one answered. The boat listed. It was taking on water fast.

"Where's Sam?" he repeated. Still no answer. Terry and Jenna, neither seemingly aware of what was going on, were getting into the life boat. Roger was heading there as well. Halting Roger mid stride, Daniel said, "Where the hell is Sam?"

"Let me go! I need to get off before we sink."

Terry looked around and said, "Where's my sister? Sam? Sam!"

Holding fast onto Roger's arm, Daniel asked him, "Is she downstairs?"

"Uh, down in my cabin, I think."

"You *think*?"

"Sam!" screamed Terry.

"She hit her head hard. I think she's knocked out," said Roger.

"And you left her down there?" Daniel shrieked as he sprinted down the stairs. Water was pouring in a large gash in the hull. Opening the door to the cabin, he saw Samantha standing there. Blood had matted her hair to her head. The water was up to her waist.

She bawled, "Oh! What are you doing? Get out. Get out!"

"Come on, Sam, we need to get out of here right now. The boat is sinking!"

"No! Get away from me. You can't see me like this."

With no time to argue, he grabbed her. She screeched and scratched down his cheek and down his neck. "Cut the shit, Sam!" he said; he threw her over his shoulder. The yacht was now half submerged and going down fast. With Samantha flailing and screaming, he ran, then swam up the stairs.

As the boat disappeared under the surface, Samantha and Daniel were caught in the vortex and pulled under. The suction was strong enough that it dragged them down a good twenty feet before it ceased. Worse, his hold on Samantha was precarious. He had her by her hair, which was only about three inches long.

Getting short on air, Daniel looked around and saw light. Toward it he swam, tugging Samantha by her hair. By the time he broke the surface, he was desperate for air and took in a huge breath as he pulled Samantha's head above the water. She was unresponsive! Mouth-to-mouth resuscitation almost impossible in deep water, he tried mouth-to-nose ventilation.

"Over here!" called out Terry from the life boat, which was about thirty feet away from Samantha and Daniel. "Is she okay?" she asked.

"No! Help me get her on the boat; she needs help right away." While the boat maneuvered to them, he continued mouth-to-nose resuscitation. The four on the life boat pulled Samantha and Daniel into the boat. "Move aside," he shouted. He laid Samantha face up in the bottom of the boat and started chest compressions. Then he commenced mouth-to-mouth ventilation, followed by more chest compressions.

"Please, God. Please don't let her die," beseeched Terry.

Finally Samantha vomited. He turned her head sideways and removed the vomitus with his finger. Samantha began breathing again. She opened her eyes and looked around, apparently trying to figure out what was going on. Terry, balling her eyes out, stooped to hug her sister. Daniel's heart beat furiously. He hadn't had time to think about Samantha being dead while she was dead. Now, looking back on the incident, he reflected in horror at what had just happened. The thought of losing Samantha forever was petrifying, yet he was livid with her. Everything was too emotional and too recent to sort out his feelings.

"Dan, can you please check Jenna?" said Terry. Daniel turned to her and determined her wounds weren't serious. He couldn't do anything for her in any case until he got supplies. Turning his attention back to Samantha, he noticed for the first time her bare breasts when she sat up. Her nipples were hard from the cold water. It seemed indecorous to stare at her breasts under this circumstance, but to him they were so perfect, he couldn't avert his eyes, despite his anger, until Terry wrapped Samantha in a blanket. Then he realized he was shivering. That water was freezing, he remembered, though it hadn't registered at the time.

The small ship that had been hit was unable to move, but in no danger of sinking. The captain had sent a mayday and helped the six aboard. Obtaining first aid supplies from the skipper, Daniel saw to Jenna's wounds.

Roger had some explaining to do to the other skipper, who had been sunning himself on the deck with his mistress when they were interrupted by a thirty-foot yacht. Roger would also have to talk to the Coast Guard, whose nearest ship was on its way. He'd need daddy to get out of this scrape.

Since Samantha had been unresponsive for a short time, Daniel kept a close eye on her. She was beginning to understand what had occurred by the time the Coast Guard ship brought them aboard. Seeing the scratches on Daniel's face, she vaguely recalled what she did and wept her apology.

The six were taken to the hospital when they got back to land. Samantha was the only one admitted, needing treatment for a concussion. Terry stayed, but Daniel left. He refused to visit Samantha.

*

Terry learned the next week that Daniel's internship was not to be extended into a residency at the hospital. She protested, but there was nothing she could do. Daniel, it turned out, had been told weeks before.

Terry saw him in the ER that afternoon and said, "I found out they won't let you continue your residency. I think that's really unfair. You should have been given the entire residency on the basis of that one horrible day alone." He nodded and turned to walk away. "You're still mad at us?" He started walking. She walked with him. "Everything I did was because I love Sam. Everything she did was because she loves you." He smirked but said nothing, so she said, "I don't care if you won't forgive me, but I ask you to forgive Sam. Please, *please* go to see her!"

"And get the rest of my face scratched off?"

"You know she wasn't thinking straight when she did that."

"I'm pretty sure she never thinks straight when I'm around."

"And why is that?"

"She loves to torture me."

"No, she simply loves you."

"I know. She told me at JAF: she simply loves me like a brother."

"No! She sees you as … She just loves you, all right?"

"Has she told you this?" he said, with a sardonic smile that seemed to convey his absolute rejection of the notion.

"Yes. You're the only one she acts like herself around."

"Yes, it was just like her to set me up with her sister the lesbian."

"Ask yourself why she did that."

"Asked and answered. She lives to humiliate me."

"Wrong. She wanted to make sure nothing would happen."

"Like sex."

"And marriage."

"In the meantime she's after Tannenbaum. That's how much she loves me."

"You wouldn't ask her out. Anyway, that's over."

"Yeah, when a man leaves a girl to drown, she ought to get the hint. And the football player? She date him out of love for me, too?"

"Again, you wouldn't ask her out, and that, too, was over as soon as he hurt you."

"Seems every time I'm around her, I get hurt."

"Shut up, dammit! She loves you, moron. She lights up around you. She makes sure she looks her best every time you're around. Remember she nearly killed me that time I took you to her when she looked like shit? She laughs at everything you say, even though a lot of what you say isn't funny. She's forever telling me about what you said or did in the war. I think I have a hundred emails, a lot of them talking about what you did or said."

In the face of Daniel's doubtful scowl, she said, "It's true! You kept her sane there. It was after you left that she started falling apart. She's all nerves around you, so she overdoes it trying to hide that and gets devastated every time she messes things up with you. She's been crying about scratching you since she came to her senses because she thinks you hate her now."

"I do."

"That's not true, and you know it. You act the same way with her as she does with you. You light up, and you turn on the charm and show off. It's so obvious you love each other. You're both playing that stupid high school game of holding back all your feelings for each other for fear of getting hurt."

"Look at my face! These are tracks of nails, not tears. She hurts me every time she's near. You sit back and make observations from a safe distance, but I'm in the middle of the shit storm. I don't believe someone could be so incompetent at love that she manages to communicate the opposite. I'm leaving here, and I'm not looking back."

"What do you mean, you're leaving?"

"I found a residency where they'll give me credit for my first year here."

"Where?"

"Dalhousie University in Halifax."

"In Canada?"

"You see? Americans aren't hopeless at geography."

"You can't go that far away! She needs you. I'm really worried about her. I don't know what she'd do." Terry began to cry.

"She'll be fine, Terry. She's smart and funny and beautiful; and she's strong. Any man she sets her sites on, she can have. Surely she must know that, given how easy it was for her to get an NFLer and a millionaire in the last few months."

"She wants you."

"I'm sorry, but I don't want her anymore. It just hurts too much. Goodbye, Terry."

He left her in distress. The next week he left New Haven for Halifax.

CHAPTER TWENTY-FOUR

Caught Up – July 2012

Daniel had avoided Samantha for his last few days in New Haven. She had phoned, emailed, knocked on his door, and even came to the hospital, but he wouldn't communicate with her. He moved to Halifax in late June.

In early July, he received an email from Terry, which he decided to open. It read:

From: Terry Hawkins
Date: Monday, July 2, 2012
To: Dr. Daniel Beaton
Subject: Fw: Heartbreak

Dan, these two emails were sent to me by Sam from Afghanistan. They were meant for my eyes only, but I need you to read them. Please get back to her. Please!

From: Samantha Hawkins
Sent: Friday, August 28, 2009
To: Terry Hawkins
Subject: Heartbreak

The worst has happened. I found out that Paul is married. Two-timing lowlife! I hate him! As if that weren't devastating enough, he got Dan sent to Korengal Outpost as a field medic, and it's my fault! I had told that bastard that Dan is diabetic. That was the night with Kelly, and I was so angry with him, I just said it to Paul without thinking of the possible consequences for Dan.

I confronted Paul with Dan's charge that he was married. He denied it, said the pictures Dan showed me of his wife and daughter were doctored. I believed him and was ready to strangle Dan, but he had followed me and stepped forward furious that Paul had fooled me yet again. God, I'm stupid. Things got violent, and Dan hit Paul. I was so furious at Dan, I was going to get the MPs to arrest him, but something told me to stop and think. I remembered the night in Australia: he couldn't let Kelly take Paul from me despite his love for me. He loved me so much he couldn't bear to see me so unhappy. So, how could he do something as awful as faking pictures to ruin my relationship? And I remembered Paul's behavior that night. So I stayed at the door and listened and heard Paul threatening Dan to keep him from emailing his wife. I started crying, and Paul knew it was over.

But because Dan had punched him, Paul had him over a barrel. He could have gone to prison. I threatened to tell his wife about us, so he backed down on that. Instead, he gave Dan the option of going to KOP or being ejected from the army and losing his funding for medical school. How could he make any other choice but going to the front lines? Otherwise all the grief and pain he's suffered for the last year and a half would have been for nothing. But, God, Terry, how will he survive there? It's got to be the planet's most dangerous place. Dan blames me for my big mouth. He said if he dies out there, it's on me. Oh, Terry, I could just die. I haven't stopped crying since. I'd gladly give my life so that Dan would live, but I'm helpless here while he dodges bullets and bombs. And how will he control his diabetes there? What happens if he slips into a sugar low when he's under fire? How can

Shit, a medevac call.

From: Samantha Hawkins
Sent: Thursday, November 5, 2009
To: Terry Hawkins
Subject: Dan

Dan's been at KOP for over two months now. I've seen him a few times when we've gone to Korengal to pick up wounded soldiers or deliver medical supplies. He looks gaunt, and I worry so much about him. He won't look at me, he won't talk to me, he won't write to me, and I'm miserable.

I'm over Paul and thankful he's out of my life. He went stateside last week. With his dark shadow gone, I can see clearly once again, and I've started to ask myself if the man of my dreams was with me all along here.

At first I thought the terrible void in my heart I feel now that Dan is no longer with me was just guilt because I got him sent to KOP, but it's not that. I miss him so much. I know now he was the best friend I ever had, and he could have been so much more. Subconsciously I think I've known this for a lot longer. A few months ago missiles began to fall on our base, and one landed close to us. Paul and I were just finishing lunch in the cafeteria. When the first one exploded, Paul took cover right away, neglecting me, but I didn't even notice at the time because I'd spotted Dan, and he'd spotted me, and we ran to each other. He wanted to protect me, and I wanted to protect him. I had no idea why I dashed to him then, and I put it out of my mind because I thought I was in love with another man. But now I ask myself why, when the stakes were potentially at their highest, did I go for Dan and not Paul? And a month or so before that, when I thought Dan might be dead when the bomb exploded in the schoolyard, I shook and cried so much I threw up.

As I look back on it, the clues about my true feelings for Dan were obvious in Australia in August. I took great pleasure in Dan's admiration, which no woman would do from a man she didn't covet. When he

told me as I was standing on the beach practically naked that I was "magnificent" with such conviction, he made me feel beautiful for the first time in my life. When he told me he loved me, he made me feel wonderful and sad at the same time; wonderful that such a man could love me, sad that I couldn't return his love. He loved me at my worst; he loved me despite my faults, despite how I had treated him. That is true love, and it is truly thrilling. Most of us are lucky if it happens once. I can't believe I'll ever have a chance for a man like him again, but I don't deserve it after what I did to him. He hates me, and I don't blame him. I think I'm inconsolable, but I'd be grateful if you'd try. Sorry to bring you down, sis, but all this pain gets to a person after a while.
Love, Sam

Daniel decided to read Samantha's email note that he had deleted the week before without reading.

From: Samantha Hawkins
Date: Wednesday, June 27, 2012
To: Daniel Beaton
Subject: Please read!
    I love you. I've been afraid to say those three simple words to you since you first came to New Haven, because I was worried you'd flee. Now that you're leaving anyway, I have nothing to lose, but, I hope and pray, everything to gain by telling you I love you. I planned to

tell you this on that horrible day on the
yacht, but you reacted so strongly when we
told you about Terry. And I've tried to
tell you since then, but you hate me so
much you won't see or hear me. I'm sorry
for scratching you. I didn't know what I
was doing. I never seem to around you
because I'm so nervous I'll do something
stupid to make you run away that I do
something stupid to make you run away.

If Terry is right that your main problem
with me is that you don't trust me and you
think I'll hurt you, all I can do is
declare, proclaim, scream to the world
that I love you, Daniel Beaton, and I want
to be with you forever.
Love, Sam
P.S. Thank you for saving my life.

Daniel wiped the tears from his eyes and wondered what to do. Write to her? Go to her? Forget her? He was too tired to make such a weighty decision then, so he went to bed. Early the next morning he had to go to work.

*

Her heart pounding, Samantha walked into the emergency ward and looked for Daniel. She spotted him. He was hugging a woman; her head was on his shoulder. Samantha's shoulders drooped and tears rushed to her eyes. Her future was on the line with her planned overture, but seeing him in the embrace of another woman made it clear to her that her quest was hopeless. She had to let go. Somehow she would put him behind her and go on.

She ran out of the hospital. She saw and heard nothing.

*

As she ran out, Daniel saw her. "Sam?" he called as let go of the woman. "Sorry, I have to run," he told her as he took off in pursuit. By the time he got outside, she was near the avenue. "Sam!" he hailed. "Look out!" he shrieked as she ran in front of a bus. The bus driver swerved and slammed on the brakes. Samantha went down. "Sam!" Daniel bellowed. "Jesus Christ!" He sprinted to her and dropped to his knees by her side. "Sam? Where are you hurt?" She was lucid, lying on her back on the ground looking into his eyes.

The bus driver emerged, saying, "It wasn't my fault; she came out of nowhere." He looked down as Daniel checked her over. Her left arm was broken. Daniel looked up at the bus and saw the side mirror was broken. She'd put her arm up at the last minute to deflect the bus, but the bus had deflected her.

"Sam? Talk to me. Tell me you're all right."

"I'm all right, but my arm really hurts." Daniel took her gently in his arms and cradled her. "You're shaking," she said.

"I've never been so scared in my life."

"That can't be true after Afghanistan."

"I'm telling you, when the bus hit you, I've never in my life felt such pure terror."

"Who was that woman you were hugging?"

"Her father just died; she needed a hug."

"Oh. Now I'm really embarrassed." A group of gawkers had assembled.

"Why are you here?" he asked as he stood with her in his arms and headed through the crowd toward the hospital.

"Why do you think?" She winced in pain with each step he took. He softened his steps. "I love you, Danny." He stopped and looked at her, still not sure of her. She continued, "It's true. I'm here to tell you I love you and see what happens." He walked her into Emergency. "Danny?" Putting her on a bed, he remained silent. "Say something!"

He grasped her hand, looked into her eyes, and entreated, "Marry me, Samantha."

Her eyes and mouth popped open in shock. "You're serious?"

"Samantha Hawkins, you have enthralled me since the moment we met. I fell desperately in love with you not long after. I've wanted you for my wife for four years now. Please make my dreams come true and say you'll marry me and share your life with me."

With tears in her eyes, she answered, "Of course I'll marry you and share my life with you." She went to throw her arms around him, but remembered one of them was out of commission and grimaced.

He gave her something for the pain, then put his hand around the back of her head, gently pulled her head to his, and gave her a long, slow kiss. He pulled back and said, "I've been dying to do that for years." She smiled. "And no," he added, "I don't do that with all my patients—just the pretty ones."

*

While Daniel went to set up an x-ray and get supplies for her arm, Samantha made a phone call. "Hello?" answered Terry.

"It's me," Samantha said, masking her joy.

"What happened with him?" asked Terry.

"Well, first I got hit by a bus, and—"

"What?"

"I'm fine, except for a broken arm."

"You got hit by a bus?"

"Yes."

"A *bus*?"

"Just its mirror. Danny ran out and carried me into the hospital. I told him I love him, and he said something, I can't recall what. Wait, now I remember," she said phlegmatically, before exclaiming, "We're getting married!"

"Really?"

"Really!"

"Wooooooooo!" screamed Terry out of pure joy.

"He proposed in the ER. Not the most romantic setting, but who cares? He's mine forever, and I'm the happiest woman on the planet."

*

Three days later, Samantha and Daniel got married with only Terry and Talon present. Craig was posted in Korea and couldn't make it. He sent a congratulatory note that said, "Though I couldn't say this at JAF, I always thought you two would make the perfect couple."

After the ceremony, they went to her hotel room. She was nervous about their first time together. He'd been dreaming about this for years, she knew. How could she possibly live up to his fantasies?

She went into the bathroom and put on a negligee she'd bought just before the ceremony. She looked in the mirror and wondered if he would be disappointed. *I'm not exactly voluptuous*. And that damn unsightly cast on her arm didn't help.

Taking a deep breath, she opened the door. His lustful, adoring gaze reassured her. She flashed him a lascivious smile and strode out, turning just before him to display herself. He was naked under the sheet, and a significant part of him registered his robust appreciation. She bent over and pulled down her negligee until her breasts popped out. His eyes popped out to meet them. He reached out for them, but she playfully slapped his hands away, saying, "No touching the merchandize, naughty boy." He grinned.

She turned her back to him, bent over and slowly pulled down her negligee. His breathing quickened, and he said, "You're spectacular!"

She cherished the adulation in the eyes of the man she loved. It was so thrilling to be wanted so much that her entire body buzzed. She pulled the sheet off him, grabbed his penis, and said, "I'm all yours."

He pulled her onto the bed, rolled her onto her back, and knelt next to her. Gingerly clutching her left arm, he set it on the bed above her head. He then took her right arm and placed it next to her left arm; he gently pinned her wrists down with his left hand and used his right hand to explore her body. She relished the mock domination and lay there in ecstasy as he fingered her and playfully bit her breasts, neck, and ears. He let her wrists go and turned his attention lower. He started with her big toe on her right foot, biting just hard enough to elicit a squeal out of his bride. Then he licked up her leg; when he kissed her clitoris she gasped. Proceeding to her other foot, he bit and licked up her left leg and once more kissed her clitoris. She gasped again. Then he licked up her stomach and lavished attention on her breasts.

Unable to withstand his teasing any further, she took control. She grabbed his hair and pulled his head down between her legs. He licked and sucked her clitoris and slid two fingers inside her. That propelled her over the edge, and she gloried in the most passionate climax of her life.

She pulled him up and guided him inside, cooing, "Your turn." But being inside the woman of his dreams was a bit too exhilarating, for he lasted but seventeen seconds before he, too, reveled in the best climax of his life. They kissed and professed their love.

*

That evening, the four celebrated together at a Halifax hotel. Talon raised his glass to the exultant couple and said, "It's about time, you two."

"God help us, yes," said Terry as the four clinked glasses and drank.

"Credit where it's due," said Daniel. "I have to thank Sophia for giving me the best woman in the world, but I must say it was right in character to run her over with a bus to bring it about."

Samantha hugged her husband and said, "From now on no more Sophia. I'm your only goddess."

He smiled and kissed his goddess and wife.

END

ABOUT THE AUTHOR

Novelist ROBERT POWER was born in Canada, but raised and educated in the United States. He stayed in university so long, Berkeley eventually gave him a PhD to get rid of him. Working as a consultant from home, he drove his wife crazy until he took up writing fiction in his too-ample spare time. Neither he nor his wife know what they were thinking when they decided to have four children, but they're happy they do—most days. They live in southern Ontario. Visit his website: rdpower.ca.

ALSO BY R.D. POWER

2020

For Power or Love

For Power or Love 2

Forbidden

Taylor Made Owens